THE ROSEWOOD HUNT

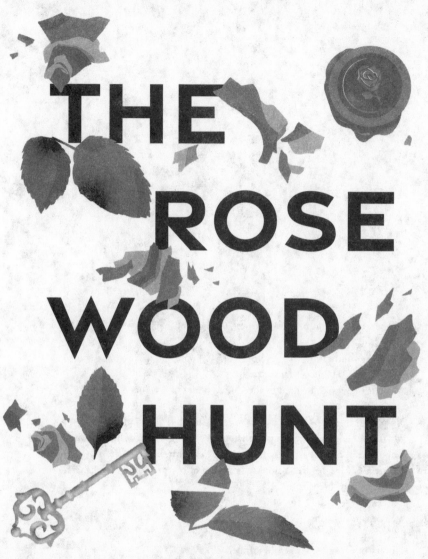

THE ROSE WOOD HUNT

MACKENZIE REED

HARPER TEEN
An Imprint of HarperCollinsPublishers

HB 08.10.2023 0428

To my parents
For believing in me and my stories
And for always reminding me
I'm never alone

I

If there's one thing that's true about my family, it's that we sure as hell know how to throw a good party.

A server in an all-black ensemble weaves through the horde of bodies stuffed into my grandmother's great room. I snag a flute of champagne from the fleeting tray, the pale liquid quaking thanks to the heavy bass thumping through the speakers mounted to the corners of the room. In the foyer, the DJ is set up, playing everything from ABBA to Harry Styles. We could have hired any band we wanted, of course, but Gram's not exactly big on dishing out more money than she has to.

I raise the glass to my lips, eyes darting over the crowd. I'm perched on the back of my favorite cognac leather love seat, the perfect place to oversee the many familiar faces mingling. Everyone in town showed up tonight. They always do.

Near the fondue fountain, the reporters for the *Rosetown Chronicle*, our newspaper that will likely provide party highlights tomorrow, laugh while dunking assorted fruits in the melted chocolate. Directly under the glimmering chandelier of Swarovski crystal is the committee for the Rosetown Museum of Fine Art, headed by Angeline Murphy and her fellow art fanatics, probably discussing the next exhibit to feature in the museum.

Even the police make an appearance at the infamous parties Gram throws. Chief Blaine Claremon hovers with two deputies around the charcuterie table piled high with Italian meats and aged cheeses, their uniforms and handcuffs replaced with sharp tuxes and gilded cuff links. It's as if a town-wide whisper scatters through the streets. *Don't mess around on June fifteenth,* it hisses. *You know what night that is.*

And everyone does. It's Gram's birthday, also known as the official kickoff for summer, a.k.a. the season of Rosewood parties.

Besides, it's not like Rosetown is exactly a crime magnet, save the few rebel teens who like to sneak into the abandoned factory at the edge of town once in a while. And anyone who'd ever do anything they shouldn't is here anyway. Because that's the beauty and the curse of parties at Rosewood Manor. A wax-sealed invitation gets dropped off at each and every house.

I take a swig of the champagne just because I can, downing nearly the entire flute in one gulp as the music mixes with the cacophony of chattering party guests, washing over me like one big, chaotic tidal wave. When I lower the glass, Chief Claremon eyes me, a slice of prosciutto almost falling off the cracker in his hand. He's not used to seventeen-year-old girls blatantly defying his authority, especially in a sea of people we both know.

I quirk a brow, holding the glass up defiantly. My ruby lipstick is stained on the edge. *What are you gonna do about it?*

He turns away, stuffing the cracker into his mouth. *Absolutely nothing.*

For a moment, I let a smirk ghost across my face. Of course he isn't. He *can't*. Because I'm—

"Lily Rosewood!"

My name is tinged with a faint English accent, the voice unmistakable. I had hoped I wouldn't hear it tonight. No wonder Chief Claremon was eyeing me. His daughter was coming up on my six.

"Ell, hi!" I spin around once my most dazzling smile is stapled to my face—only to drop it as I take in Ell Claremon, barely recognizing her, except for the beauty mark by her lip. She's dressed to the nines in a stunning black cocktail dress and bright scarlet heels, freshly dyed platinum hair cascading over her right shoulder. She's only four years older than me, but her time at the London College of Fashion has transformed her into something of a model, complete with plump pouty lips and teeth so white she could be the poster girl for a Colgate commercial. She looks nothing like the demure brunette teen I grew up following around like a puppy.

"I'm so glad you could make it." The lie is bitter on my lips as she presses twin kisses to my cheeks. The thing is, I *want* to be happy that Ell is home. Back when we both used to bond over our love of fashion and she treated me like a little sister, I was distraught at the thought of her leaving for college. But every time she's home, she's always chatting Gram up about Rosewood Inc., our luxury-coat business that was started over a hundred years ago by my great-great grandmother. When Ell expressed interest in going to college in London, she struck a deal with Gram that if she worked at our London headquarters while studying fashion, she could have a permanent place with Rosewood Inc. after graduating.

Since then, Gram's been obsessed with teaching her the ins and outs of the company via Zoom calls. Especially in the past year, since she's gotten closer to graduation. And that's fine and all, but Gram was supposed to be spending this year teaching *me* about her role as chair of the Rosewood Inc. board.

"I missed you, Lily," Ell says, moving closer to me as a tipsy couple staggers across the polished marble floor of the great room. Her eyes shine with concern. "Have you been okay? I know it's been tough for you since . . . everything happened."

Understatement of the year right there. My throat threatens to close, and the feelings I've been shoving down all day bubble up. When I was carefully applying my makeup earlier, I promised myself I would keep my emotions reined in tonight. It's just another party. I can make it through one night. I have to.

"I'm fine," I force out, irrationally mad at her for saying anything. "Besides, living with Gram has been great."

The last part thankfully isn't a lie.

Ell brightens, glancing around. "Speaking of Iris, have you seen her?"

"Uh—"

It's a good question. Gram made a spectacular appearance at the beginning of the party over an hour ago, descending the grand staircase in the foyer in a chic floor-length emerald dress and her signature necklace—a twenty-five-carat teardrop-shaped ruby the size of my thumbnail hanging from a delicate gold chain at the base of her throat. I have yet to see her since, although with nearly the entire town packed onto the property, it's easy to disappear. Desired, even. Because when you're the matriarch of the richest family in southern Massachusetts, everybody wants a piece of you.

A quick scan leaves me helpless, although a server catches my eye and thinks I'm looking for hors d'oeuvres.

"Shrimp cocktail, ladies?"

"No, thank you," Ell says quickly, backing up a couple of steps. "I have a shellfish allergy."

I've already had more than enough appetizers, but I grab a shrimp from the tray anyway and pop it into my mouth. Anything to help rush this conversation along. Suddenly, everything feels too much. The music too loud, Ell's expression too knowing, people too close. I need some air.

Ell warily watches me chew and swallow. I plaster on a smile, the kind that I've worn all night. Easy, breezy, *I feel like I'm dying inside, but I can't let anyone know.*

"I'm sure Gram is around here somewhere," I say. "I'm more than happy to pass along a message."

"Oh, no worries. We have business things to discuss."

"Right." I keep smiling, but annoyance churns in me at her evasiveness, as if I can't be privy to *business things*. "You'll have to excuse me. I have to check on things in the kitchen."

"Absolutely. Nice to see you, Lily."

I make it two steps when her voice stops me. "And, by the way, your dress is absolutely *beautiful.*"

I bristle but muster one last smile.

I quickly move through the warm bodies standing between

me and the two-way doors leading to the kitchen, thankful the lights are dimmed so no one can see my flaming red cheeks. If the comment had come from anyone else, I'd be elated. The dress *is* beautiful, a rich shade of crushed teal velvet. I thrifted it from my favorite vintage shop three towns over, chopping the gorgeous gown at the knees and stitching the hem into a flirty swing skirt. The bust was a little snug, but nothing I couldn't fix by attaching a cream corset to the back to disguise the half-up zipper. By the time I finished, it looked nothing like the original gown I bought.

But Ell lives and breathes high fashion. I bet she recognized the dress as a vintage design that, in her eyes, I butchered by making it my own.

Well, she can mind her own business.

I'd love to tell her so, but there's far too many prying ears around. Besides, then I'd have to explain *why* I had to thrift a dress and make it my own. Why couldn't I just tap into the enormous Rosewood fortune and buy a brand-new number for myself?

It's a question I've been trying to answer for the past year.

With a sigh of relief, I burst through the doors to the kitchen, nearly taking out a server carrying bite-size caprese sandwiches in my haste. "Sorry," I mumble, my rigid posture slouching now that I'm away from the eyes of the guests. I love being a Rosewood, but sometimes having to be *on* all the time in front of townspeople gets exhausting.

"You look like a girl on a mission," a familiar voice says, entering the kitchen behind me.

"A mission to get away from Ell Claremon." I turn, taking in my friend Miles, whose cheeks are tinged pink with exertion. "You look like *you're* on a mission."

"Yeah, to find *you*," he pants. "I've been looking for you for ten minutes. Finally spotted you and was yelling your name across the great room while you blitzed over here."

"Sorry, just needed some air." My heels click across the spotless white tile floor toward the sliding glass door leading to the pool patio. It's open so only the screen stands between us and outside, but between the stuffy heat of the kitchen and the muggy summer weather, it's not much of a reprieve.

Miles follows me, smoothing the wrinkles from his khaki dress pants and navy button-down. His blond waves dip into his blue eyes, the color complementing the robin's egg shade of paint on the wall behind him. He peers through the screen at the packed backyard of the manor, quirking a brow. "Lily, what looks strange about this scene?"

I take in the guests in the pool and lounging on chairs. "There're too many people on the flamingo pool floatie?"

His laugh is bright. "Okay, *two* things." He points to a boy about our age sitting to the side in an Adirondack chair.

"Who is that?" I ask.

"I was hoping you would know."

"I *should* know," I say.

The boy's dark brown skin glows teal from the reflection of the chlorinated water. He nurses a bottle of water, wearing khakis and a sweater. Overdressed compared to everyone else on the patio in only swimsuits.

"I know every face here and addressed every invitation. I got hand cramps for these people."

"Thank you for your brave sacrifice," Miles says solemnly.

I elbow him in the side, glancing back at the boy. His eyes behind his square black glasses are the tell-all kind. It looks like he'd rather be anywhere than here.

"He does look familiar," I say, trying to place him but coming up short.

"He's kind of cute, don't you think?" Miles asks.

I hum in agreement, just happy for a couple of moments of peace with Miles, who's taken up the role as my sole best friend for the past year.

He's all carefree optimism and easy distractions, and now's no different as he gives me a conspiratorial grin. "Dare me to go talk to him?"

"You'll do it even if I don't," I point out.

"No fun."

"Fine, I dare you to sweep mystery guy off his feet. Bonus points if he falls in love with you by the end of the night."

"And how many points if I fall in love with him?"

"I will let you sleep in tomorrow and open the deli by myself," I swear, a risky gamble because DiVincenzi's Deli is hopping on Sundays with people visiting after church. It usually takes both of us to handle the rush.

That said, I don't think too many townies will be going to church tomorrow, given they're getting wasted here.

"Deal." Miles opens the door, then stops, pulling something from his pocket. "Oh, I almost forgot. The entire reason I was looking for you. Your gram told me to give you this. She said something weird." He pauses, puzzling over it. "'Not all in one bite,' I think? And also, 'to eat it ASAP so it doesn't melt.'"

He drops a marble-size orb wrapped in green foil into my palm. I frown at it. "'Not all in one—'"

He's already striding across the patio, tossing one last bright smile over his shoulder at me with a thumbs-up. I glance behind me at the chefs still busy at the enormous range passing new plates off to servers. Delicious aromas waft around me, sweet and savory and everything in between as full and empty trays are traded left and right, the vast kitchen feeling tiny from the number of workers crammed in to keep up with the flow of food. I don't recognize any of them. Gram must have given the usual crew the night off.

I roll the orb between my fingers, looking for anything that would make this one special. There's an entire tray of chocolates by the fireplace—Gram knows I could have just gotten one myself. Peeling off the green foil reveals a dark chocolate truffle. I check the inside of the foil because it'd be on brand for Gram to put a message in there. But it's just shiny silver. Nothing unusual.

I dig my teeth through the exterior. Pieces spill into my mouth, melting as they hit my tongue. Sweetness explodes, followed by the usual delightful bitter tinge of dark chocolate. But then something else falls onto my tongue, rough and—

"Ack!" I spit it out into my hand. A piece of paper was hidden in the chocolate. Because of course it was. *Classic Gram.* I snag a napkin to wipe my saliva off it, unfolding it as Gram's familiar cursive script slowly appears.

Disappearing ink, an old staple that Gram has always used when writing notes. It used to be how she secretly communicated potential business deals back in the day before email, but now it's become a special thing between the two of us when leaving silly notes around the manor, like, *Saved this last eclair for you* and *Pizza and* Project Runway *tonight?* There's always a bit of a smudge on the paper, which signifies the special ink has been used. It reappears when wet, and in this case, my spit did the trick.

I should have known the note wouldn't have been on the foil. That would have been too easy.

Dear Lilylove, it reads. *Meet me at our spot at eight.*

I glance at the clock above the sink. Two minutes. I was almost late.

The party in the backyard is no less raucous than in the manor as I step outside. If anything, it's worse because this is where the *youth* congregate. I descend the grand stone steps leading to the patio, passing the pool to get to my destination. Nearly my entire class is stuffed in the turquoise water, my younger cousin Daisy precariously balancing barefoot on the end of the diving board. With only three months separating us, we could be twins thanks to our fair skin and matching dark red hair, a staple Rosewood gene. But that's the end of our similarities, since she inherited her mom's brown eyes and slight frame. Meanwhile, I got Gram's ivy-green eyes and curves.

We're different in other ways besides our looks, too. While I'm held in high esteem throughout the town as the firstborn for our generation of Rosewoods, Daisy's kingdom is high school. To our classmates, she might as well be an A-list celebrity. It doesn't help that she's a TikTok star with nearly half a million followers.

She throws her hands into the air, her short silver bodycon dress dangerously riding up, and cheers rise from the water. Someone hands her a flute of champagne. Half sloshes over the side and onto the head of Gram's yard boy as she pretends to use it as a mic.

"'Sweeeeeeeet Caroline!'" she belts off tune.

"BUM! BUM! BUM!" they scream back.

"Jeez," I mutter, hurrying away. Only second-borns can get away with being publicly ridiculous like that. If it were me, I'd be eaten alive by the *Rosetown Chronicle*.

A pang of jealousy thrums through me. Unlike me, Daisy doesn't have to worry about being perfect for anyone, not Gram and certainly not the town. It must be nice not carrying that pressure around and always being surrounded by friends who would do anything for you.

The music and laughter fade as I curve around the side of the manor. Everything is meticulously manicured, roses lining every inch of the exterior, red blooms vivid against the pristine white brick walls that tower three stories up. Their scent is sweet, and I pause for a moment to take it in and shake the envious thoughts away. Streaks of sunset paint the sky gold, navy infringing. For this one moment, I'm alone, something I've been longing for all night.

The peace is broken by the velvet timbre of a voice I'd know anywhere.

"Hell of a party, isn't it?"

2

"Always is," I reply to Gram, pushing past a wrought iron gate with honeysuckle twisting through it and stepping into my favorite place in the world.

The Anything but Roses garden is barely big enough to hold ten people, but that's not why I like it. Enclosed by towering white stone walls and complete with a life-size marble statue of Saint Anthony smack-dab in the middle, it's something of a hidden sanctuary among the sprawling grounds. Flowers bloom around us, lilies and daisies and daffodils and peonies. Hydrangeas are budding, and ivy crawls up the walls. A magnolia tree takes over the left corner, a cherry blossom in the right.

Across the back wall is a map of Rosetown carved into the surface. It shows every monumental stop in town—the manor near the southern tip, the museum to the northwest, Saint Theresa Church in the center, the harbor to the southeast. Toward the left-hand bottom, there's even the old factory, which never appears on recent maps because it's on the edge of town. It closed when I was seven, but I still remember standing on the mezzanine, watching workers hand-stitch coats, the supple feel of faux leather and furs gliding past my fingertips.

Gram stands beside Saint Anthony, stately as ever and boasting the same red curls as mine, though hers are streaked with white and held back with a tortoiseshell clip. Her green eyes shine fondly as she holds a plate out to me piled high with meats and cheeses. "Try the salami. It's my favorite."

I make a show of lifting the salami to inspect it for anything hidden. "Can never be too careful with you," I muse, taking it and a piece of Gouda. "Thank you for my note, by the way. It lost a bit of its charm after nearly giving me a papercut on my uvula."

"I need to keep you on your toes, Lilylove." Her forever nickname for me draws a genuine smile, my first of the night. She cups one of the lilies, weathered finger tracing the petal. "Beautiful, aren't they? Leo does a fine job tending to the gardens. And he's an even better chess mate."

I barely refrain from rolling my eyes. Gram's fondness toward her yard boy is a little much at times. Leo DiVincenzi is a hockey jock extraordinaire, king of parties, and Daisy's right-hand man. Besides, I have skeletons with him buried too deep to dig up.

"He's not supposed to be playing chess with you, he's paid to trim the shrubs."

"He's excellent company. Have you seen him yet?"

"Last I saw he was wasted in the pool while my dear cousin splashed champagne over his head. By now, he might have even drowned. Shame."

Gram laughs, the tail end breaking into a cough. She pats her chest. "Oh, to be young. I hope you're having a good evening, at least."

"It's been . . . okay," I settle on. Tonight was never destined to be a good evening. One year ago, at this same party, everything was different. Dad was spinning me around the great room. Mom was laughing. I had no idea the horrible summer that was ahead of me. No idea that everything I ever knew would change.

Well, not everything. Gram stayed the same, inviting Mom and me to move into the manor with her after Dad died and the awful truth was revealed that he had dug half the town into debt—himself included—thanks to his financial advisement business going south. The big house I grew up in was taken as collateral, leaving Mom and me no choice but to take Gram up on her offer. Most of our things were confiscated, too: Dad's flashy sailboat and Mom's designer bags. But none of it mattered to Mom. His death in July broke her, and she was gone by August, disappearing like she was never here at all. I haven't seen or heard from her since.

Gram clears her throat. Despite putting on a perfect front, the first Rosewood party without Dad can't be easy for her, either. "Tomorrow, will you be joining me on the patio for lovecakes?"

It's our tradition. Before I lived here, I'd always sleep over after parties so the next morning we could eat fluffy pancakes drenched in syrup while going over new designs for Rosewood Inc. My heart pangs that she's trying to keep some level of normalcy this summer.

"I picked up an extra shift to open the deli tomorrow," I remember, unable to keep the sadness from my voice. That was the one condition Gram had for me to stay with her at the manor. She'd pay for any necessities, but I had to get a part-time job to pay for everything else. Which was fine with me. It's the least I can do since she's taken me in.

"Saving up for business school?" Gram poses it like a question, but I know it's a suggestion.

I break eye contact with her. With senior year approaching, she's been trying to broach the subject more and more with me, leaving pamphlets on the counter or my dresser. But the Fashion Institute of Technology is my dream school. Last summer, that was the plan. Go on the Milan study abroad trip for my first semester of senior year this fall, which would make me a shoo-in for FIT, and then graduate with my degree in fashion design and join Gram at the helm of Rosewood Inc. My entire life laid out before me.

But that was before I found out Dad blew my college fund.

"Yeah," I finally say, turning to pluck a bud of honeysuckle from the gate so she can't see the lie on my face. I have zero desire to go to business school, but at this rate, I'll never afford FIT. And if Gram's not-so-subtle prodding toward institutions with prestigious business programs is any indication, she'd never approve of fashion school. She's expressed that a comprehensive business education is essential when leading a team and business, despite never having gone to college herself.

"You're going to do wonders at Rosewood Inc. someday," Gram told me one night last summer, pride shining in her eyes. It was right after Dad died, the day Mom and I moved into the manor. Mom was spending nearly every hour in her room, so I distracted myself by sketching new designs to transform my old clothes into. I had spent all day making a sundress out of a too-tight jumpsuit.

"Is that something you'd want?" Gram asked me after I showed her my sketchbook of dress ideas. "To take my place as chair of the board of directors when I'm ready to retire?"

I nearly keeled over then and there. "It's all I've *ever* wanted," I gushed. I thought after that, she'd start teaching me more about the company and being the chair, especially after Mom left. But it's been nearly a full year now, and she's given Ell way more attention in that department than me. I want to ask why, but every time I try, I can never find the right words without sounding ungrateful or pushy.

I can't be mad at her, though. Giving me a place to live is enough without anything else. What matters most is proving I can be who she wants me to be so that Rosewood Inc. is still in my future, even if it sucks that FIT isn't.

"I'm glad you like working at the deli," Gram says. "It's so important for you to learn this independence early on. And I like that friend of yours, Miles. You should invite friends over more often."

I don't correct her that he's my *only* friend. The truth makes a pit of loneliness yawn open inside of me. Instead of tumbling into it, I bring the honeysuckle to my nose, inhaling its sweet scent. It calms me down. I let the flower drop, turning back to Gram with a forced smile on my face. "He's not a bad secret-note messenger, either, right?"

For a second, a concerned crease forms between her penciled brows. I know she can see right through my act. She's the only person who always can.

"Not bad at all." Gram finally breaks the silence, her concern gone in a blink and replaced with a beaming smile. While I know she cares, I also know how highly she values keeping up appearances. Gram's never been one to show weakness.

She raises a piece of salami in cheers. "We'll rain check our breakfast date. I'm proud of you, Lily."

Pride fills my chest at her statement, the enormous pressure lifting for a moment. I bop my salami against hers. "Happy birthday, Gram. I hope you're having a good time tonight."

She pulls me into a hug, pressing a kiss to my temple. "Marvelous."

I pull away with a grin. "And in two weeks, we get to do it all over again for my birthday."

Her smile withers slightly. "Actually, Lily, there's something I—"

"How are two of my favorite ladies doing tonight?"

Gram and I look to the gate, and my breath catches. Dad stands there, the dying rays of the sun silhouetting him and turning his thinning auburn hair gold. He wears a crisp navy tux, a signature red rose pinned to the lapel.

But it's not Dad, of course. It's his twin—Uncle Arbor.

I swallow down the disappointment, wishing the wound didn't feel so fresh even after an entire year. Glancing at Gram, I wonder if she feels the same throbbing in her chest. Like looking at Dad's ghost that will never quite stop haunting us.

"I thought I'd find you two here." He gives me a small smile and opens his arms. I fit into his hug, and even though it's not Dad's arms, it's close enough to pretend. "It's almost quarter after."

I pull away. "And?"

Gram sighs. "I suppose it's time for the true party to start."

Realization dawns. "Of course."

It's universally acknowledged that Rosewood parties don't turn truly unforgettable until *after* cake, when the wine starts flowing and the furniture in the great room gets pushed toward the walls to make a massive dance floor. Even the most conservative townspeople let loose.

We strut through the gate, a wild twine of honeysuckle nearly tripping me before Uncle Arbor grasps my arm.

"Thanks," I mumble, wishing he'd waited just a few more moments before interrupting Gram and me in the garden. What was she about to tell me?

My heart races. Maybe something about my eighteenth birthday coming up on the twenty-eighth. A thread of hope stitches through my chest that she was going to talk to me about Rosewood Inc., maybe start showing me the ropes like I've been waiting for. After cake I'll bring it up again.

We pass the pool, now empty. Two servers stand by the back double door, opening them for us. I nod in thanks, stepping into the air-conditioned great room of the manor and feeling like my short time in the Anything but Roses garden was a mirage.

Someone must tell the DJ to shut it, because the current song tapers to an end. Everybody turns toward us, Gram's presence magnetic as they step closer. Some people are dressed in extravagant ball gowns, and others barely pulled together a button-down and matching pair of slacks. These are the people of Rosetown. All together at one magnificent party.

"Oh, please, don't stop for me."

Gram's breezy words are met with laughter. It's easy to pick out the people sucking up to her. Liz Zhao, the owner of the most popular wedding venue in town, the Ivy, chuckles a second too long. It's no surprise, given that last week she asked if Gram would be interested in investing in the restoration of the second ballroom. I'm sure Gram declined. She usually does.

Gram's been the sole keeper of the Rosewood fortune since it was passed down from her mother, Petunia. Rumor has it my grandfather, who took Gram's last name to keep up the tradition and died before I was born, never even had a say in it. And neither did Dad or Uncle Arbor, although I know she used to dole out occasional allowances until they made their own money.

It's a rare occasion for her to part with anything sizable, which I can tell bugs some townspeople. But Dad was different. He invested in everything town-related, sometimes with Uncle Arbor, too. It's why he started his advisement business to try to help local businesses and families.

Funny how everyone forgot about that part when he died.

"I want to thank you all for celebrating with me this evening." Gram's voice is that of a leader, easily heard throughout the cavernous room despite the barely noticeable breathy undertones. Probably just due to our brisk walk from the garden. "Winters are long in Rosetown, but I always look forward to this party. Not just for my own sake, of course. Summer is the time when our slice of the world thrives. Just like the roses blooming, I watch the rest of you do the same. If my grandmother could only see how magnificent the little plot of dirt we all now call our home has become, she'd be thrilled."

People clap. Whoops and hollers come from my classmates,

who have dried off since the pool and now crowd around an antique circular table overflowing with food. Daisy stands with them, tugging out one of the ornate dining chairs and stepping onto it. Even with the height bonus, she's still barely a head taller than most guests.

I grin from behind Gram, watching Daisy try to get the room's attention and fail as everyone breaks out in singing a terribly off-pitch version of "Happy Birthday." I join in extra loud just to add to the din. My cousin rolls her eyes.

But I underestimate the lengths she'll go to to have every eye on her. She takes one of the sushi platters from the table and plops it into the arms of Leo, who looks as if he's minutes away from either passing out or sprinting outside to throw up all over the shrubs he *so carefully* tends to. *Gram sure knows how to pick 'em.*

"Ahem!" Daisy clears her throat, standing atop the table and brushing her chin-length waves away from her eyes. She sways to one side, and a slew of people reach out just in case she falls, but she laughs and swats their hands away. I glance at Uncle Arbor, his grip white around his glass of merlot.

"I have something I'd like to say," Daisy continues, tugging her dress down to mid-thigh. She flashes a glittering smile around the room before focusing on Gram. "We all, of course, owe the grandest of thank-yous to our stunning matriarch for hosting such a lavish bash, but it'd be wrong of me not to express my own gratitude."

I'm going to puke. Why does she start talking like she's from a different century whenever she's tipsy? It's gaudy. I shove down the impulse to disappear into the kitchen to skip the rest of her spiel, wanting to know what this *urge* to thank Gram is about.

"I'm excited to announce that I'll be spending the first half of my senior year abroad in Milan studying fashion."

The room erupts in cheers for my cousin, and my throat constricts. Daisy's eyes skip to me for a moment and flash with victory before settling back on Gram.

"Thank you, Gram, for making this incredible opportunity possible. After all, the trip filled up last fall, so it really was Gram's magic touch that secured me an extra spot."

Magic touch? It's not that at all. It's Gram's *money*. Money I desperately needed last year. Money I *begged* Dad for, not knowing he had none. I knew a study abroad trip to Milan would skyrocket my application to FIT. That and the Rosewood name would carry me straight to an acceptance letter.

But when Dad refused without explanation, I turned to Gram. It was the one time I asked her for anything. And she turned me down.

Then Dad died, and none of it mattered anyway. But now to find out Gram did all this for *Daisy*? My cousin has never shown a scrap of interest toward the family business. *I'm* supposed to be the one setting my future up for Rosewood Inc.

I finally look at Gram, only to find her already staring at me. Chatter blooms in the room, the party resuming around us, but time is paused. *How could you?* I want to lash out. But all I get out is a broken, "*Why?*"

"Lily, I—" She reaches for me, but I stumble out of her grasp. Except, I don't notice the server emerging from the kitchen wheeling out a cart with a towering five-tier cake on it. Not until it's too late.

I try to change direction but lose my balance, tripping in my heels and smashing into the cart. I topple over it, and the cake goes with me, both of us crashing onto the ornate Persian rug. Pink frosting smears across my face, coating my lashes like mascara as bits of cake litter my dress.

Hands immediately are on me, lots of them, pulling me to my feet as if that could reverse the absolute humiliation I just caused myself. The room is dead silent, and I don't need to wipe the frosting from my eyes to know that every single gaze is on me.

Someone nudges a napkin into my hand, and I use it to clear my sight. The cake is in ruins on the ground, literally not a single piece salvageable. I look up, taking in the first expression I see. Liz Zhao isn't laughing anymore, and her daughter, Quinn, a girl in my class whose resting bitch face is usually stapled on, stares at me with her jaw unhinged. Antony DiVincenzi, Leo's dad who owns the failing Ice Plex rink across town, looks like he's smothering a laugh. A quick sweep of the room shows that's pretty average for everyone.

Tears burn behind my eyes. I turn to Gram. "I'm so—"

"I think it's best if you go get cleaned up, all right?" she says quickly, gesturing for the DJ to start back up.

Music blares through the speakers, the beginning notes to Aerosmith's "I Don't Want to Miss a Thing." I want to strangle them for the song choice.

Apologies brim on my lips, but Gram takes my elbow—also sticky with frosting—and leads me to the foyer. Her voice is careful, the same tone she uses when on business calls with the Rosewood Inc. board. I recognize it immediately as damage control.

"Party's nearly over. Why don't you sleep at your uncle's tonight? I think a night away from the manor could be good for you."

I stare at her. "But this is my home."

"What the hell?" Daisy stomps over. Her brown eyes are bright with fury as she gets up in my face. "You couldn't let me have ten seconds of attention? All eyes always have to be on you, huh?"

"Enough," Uncle Arbor snaps, grabbing her arm before she can start throwing fists at me; I wouldn't put it past her, especially in her tipsy state. He turns to Gram. "Mom, are you—"

"Daisy, you go, too," Gram says.

Daisy's gawks. "*What?* Why do I need to leave just because of *her*?"

"Because you're being an embarrassment," I hiss, gaze flicking to the entryway of the great room where guests are gathering to watch our show.

She scoffs. "I'm not the one looking like the Pillsbury Doughboy after a sugar rush."

My cheeks burn, a retort hot on my tongue. "You—"

"Stop it," Gram commands, shuffling us outside and away from the guests' stares.

"I can take them," Uncle Arbor offers, glancing uneasily at my dress. He's probably not keen on vanilla cake smeared across the back seat of his red Mercedes.

"Frank will," Gram says, pressing a hand to her chest, shutting her eyes, and taking a deep breath. When she opens them, the disappointment they hold makes me shrink.

"Frank?" Daisy asks as our family's lawyer steps through the doors to join us outside, summoned by Gram. "Where's Stewie?"

Nobody answers about the whereabouts of our usual driver. Frank already has keys, unlocking a black SUV parked in the giant looped driveway flooded with cars. I turn back to the door to plead with Gram, or at least apologize, but she's already stepping back inside with Uncle Arbor on her heels. The door slams behind them.

"I think we best get going," Frank says in his ancient, gravelly voice. Gram's lawyer is more like a great-uncle to me after growing up with him always around, so I slide inside, leaving a frosting skid mark in my wake. The tears I barely choked back now flow down my cheeks as mortification hits me like a train, the shock wearing off and leaving me burning with shame.

"This is bullshit," Daisy fumes, slamming the car door closed behind her.

"Since when do you care about Milan?" I choke out before she can tell me off again. "That was *my* dream. I've spent hours picking and cutting and sewing fabrics. Sketching designs. I study Fashion Week like a textbook. I'm committed to working for this."

Her gaze hardens, any brief sparks of sympathy flickering out. She opens her mouth, but a banging on her window makes us jump. Quinn glares from the other side.

"You said we would talk!" she yells through the glass at Daisy, annoyance bright in her dark eyes. Her short black hair is pulled back into her usual bun to show off her undercut. I've heard a rumor that she hides a knife among the strands.

"I'm a little busy!" Daisy screams back.

Quinn angrily bangs on the glass again and steps aside as Frank pulls away. We watch through the back windshield as she sticks double middle fingers up until she disappears around the bend of the driveway.

"What the hell was *that* about?" I ask Daisy, my meltdown momentarily forgotten.

"Mind your business," she huffs, folding her arms across her chest and glaring out the window as the boom of the party fades behind us.

Frank catches my eye in the rearview mirror, wrinkles embedded in his warm brown skin. He looks tired, more than I've ever seen him before. We pass through the open gates of the manor, black wrought iron that twists into the sky. They're barely ever shut, and even when they are, I know there's a spot in the hedge on the western edge of the property that's sparse enough to slink through.

"Frank—"

"Miss Rosewood, I have no more answers than you," he sighs. His expression is as stoic as always, but his brown eyes soften. "This is a big, stressful evening for your grandmother. And you, as well. I assume she realized perhaps it was a little much for you."

"I can handle it," I snap.

"Clearly," Daisy mutters.

"Give your grandmother grace," Frank continues as Rosetown

bleeds by in a blur of sunset colors. "After all, she's never let you down before, has she?"

It's not meant to be a question. I force a smile to my face to keep another round of tears at bay, biting back the hurt burning a hole through my already-singed heart. "Never," I lie.

3

SUNDAY, JUNE 16, 10:03 A.M.

"'All in all, Lily Rosewood, perhaps the last person one might expect, was an unlikely and unfortunate ruination to an otherwise perfect evening.'"

Miles's blond brows shoot up as he sets today's copy of the *Rosetown Chronicle* down on the counter. We both wear the same grubby white apron with the words *DiVincenzi's Deli* embroidered in red script across the front. Mine also sports drying tearstains thanks to opening the deli this morning to see the paper on the front stoop, an image of me plastered on the cover with chunks of cake in my hair and my expression frozen with horror.

"Damn, they didn't pull any punches, huh?" Miles says.

"It was a disaster," I groan. For a few blissful seconds when I first woke this morning, I forgot all about it. But then I realized *where* I woke up, in one of the spare bedrooms at my uncle's house. And then, all it took was opening Instagram, and Snapchat, and TikTok to see myself everywhere. One video even went viral. I had to turn my phone off just to escape the notifications.

Despite wanting to hide under my covers all day, I had to wake Uncle Arbor to get a ride to work, where so far every customer has either given me a pity smile or saucer eyes. If one more gaze burns into me while slicing provolone, I'm gonna lose it.

"It'll blow over," Miles assures me in an easy way that's his trademark. Things rarely bother him, even the fact that he just graduated and has to take a gap year before college to work and save up. "You know how this town is. People just want things to talk about."

"I hope your night ended better than mine. How was the mystery guy?"

He reaches over me to grab a fresh-baked loaf from the rack, looking down at me coyly. "Mystery guy has a name—Caleb Johnson."

He slices the loaf. I already know he's making himself his usual turkey on sourdough with Swiss, which I'll eat half of even though it's barely ten. It's slow today thanks to the party, just like I expected.

"He's cute. Smart as hell," he continues. "We bailed before the cake thing and talked literally all night. I know he seemed nervous at the manor, but once we left, he opened up more. We just drove around town for a while before I took him home. He's from Creekson."

"Creekson?" I ask, picturing the town on the other side of the train tracks that separate it from Rosetown. "People from there hate us and think we're snobby. What was he doing at a Rosetown party?"

He shrugs. "He got an invitation."

"Gram must have sent that one. Will you see him again?"

"Tonight. I'm meeting him at the movies in Creekson."

I pass a few slices of Swiss to him. "Romance king. I'm glad

28

you and Caleb from Creekson had a good night."

He grins, a smile full of slightly crooked bottom teeth and front ones that jut over them. "How 'bout you? Meet anyone nice last night before cake gate?"

"As if. I was busy." *Getting frosting in my eyes.*

He gives me a slightly exasperated look. "Too busy for what? Flirting? Friends?"

"Both." I straighten the cannoli in the case so he doesn't see my face. Friends are a sore subject for me. My sophomore year, I rivaled Daisy as the "it girl." While she was surrounded by every athlete in school, I had my own crew of people, the AP elites. At least, I thought they were my friends.

And then Dad died, and I had to leave my big-ass house. My "friends" skipped the funeral. A lot of their parents had made investments advised by Dad and lost money. I got booted from our group chat. Junior year started, and my golden spot in the booth closest to the drinking fountain in the cafeteria was taken. Gram insisted on still inviting them to the party yesterday, but thankfully, only their parents came.

It doesn't hurt as much since I started this job and got to know Miles last fall. He invited me to eat in the art room with him, and it became our regular thing. He'd work on yearbook stuff and draw since he was trying to build a portfolio to get into animation school, and I'd use the time to create new dress designs in my sketchbook and bring thrift finds to school to work on alterations. Sometimes, he'd even drive me to the nearest thrift store in Creekson. And he never once asked me why I was thrifting in the first place.

"It's just—" He's suddenly so focused on the turkey sandwich you'd think it was a flashy art piece in the museum. I know what he's going to say because we've already had this talk. "Since I graduated, you should try to open yourself up more."

So you're not alone for your senior year.

He doesn't say the last part, but it's in the silence. It's not like I want to be alone, because I don't, and it hurts seeing everyone else have friends stop by their lockers to laugh over memes or cry in the bathroom together over shitty relationship drama. But what he doesn't understand is I'd rather be alone than *feel* alone with friends who only care about my last name and how much money is in my bank account. Which is currently, like, none.

The bell above the door chimes, saving me from more of *that* conversation. Miles sighs, slipping into the back as I step up to the counter to greet our next customer. From the large sun hat blocking her face, I know exactly who it is and start pulling ingredients.

"Hi, Mrs. Capolli," I greet my third-grade teacher. She's a regular. "Here for your usual pastrami on rye?"

"Yes, dear," she says, eyes on her phone. "Don't forget the . . ."

A few seconds pass as I add the pastrami and slather on some mustard. When she doesn't go on, I look up.

"Don't forget the what?" I ask.

She stares at her screen, lips parted.

"Mrs. Capolli?" Her head jerks up, brown eyes wide. "Everything okay?"

Her lips move, but no sound comes out. That's when I realize there's no sound *at all*.

The chatter from the few patrons having their morning coffee at the mismatched tables in the corner has ceased, their shocked gazes turned to me. A chill sweeps up my spine, and I glance helplessly behind me for Miles, but he's still in the back.

"Are you okay?" I ask Mrs. Capolli again, because she's just staring at me, and it's getting weird. "Mrs. Capolli?"

"Oh, Lily—"

The bell rings again, stealing her words. "Miss Rosewood!" Mr. Hayworth exclaims, the lead reporter for the *Rosetown Chronicle* and likely the culprit who snapped me covered in cake last night. "If I could have a brief word—"

"You leave her alone!" Angeline Murphy jumps up from where she was sipping her latte that Miles always makes extra sweet.

Mrs. Capolli is still in front of me, but Angeline nudges her out of the way. She grabs my hand with both of hers, always overly touchy and eccentric, pulling me close so we're inches apart. The door chimes again, but she holds me fast so I can't even pull away to look.

"You don't need to say a *word*, Lily. In fact, you should go to your uncle's. I can drive you, if you'd like."

"I can drive her," a voice says from behind. I nearly do a double take as Liz Zhao, the owner of the Ivy, steps beside Angeline. I didn't think I'd ever catch her dead here, where the scent of sub sandwich oil is stronger than the cologne blasted throughout Abercrombie & Fitch.

But her eyes are bright, the liner rimming them smudged, tipping me off that she likely didn't wash off her makeup after returning home last night. Angeline opens her mouth to protest, but Liz cuts her off.

"I will take her. She's my daughter's friend, after all."

That spurs a shocked laugh. If Quinn's middle-fingered salutation is anything to go by, I don't think she holds me in much higher esteem than Daisy. "I'm sorry—what?"

The other patrons crowd the counter. Mr. Hayworth is holding his iPhone up like he's *filming*.

"Lily," he repeats. "I understand this is a highly emotional time. But please, give me a few words about your grandmother. Did she say anything to you before you left last night?"

Now *that* royally pisses me off. As if last night's humiliation wasn't enough, he's looking for scraps of gossip?

"No." I guard my tone so it doesn't come out as frigid as I wish.

Mrs. Capolli has her eyes closed and is slowly shaking her head. My stomach drops.

I gesture to the back. "Um, I have to check on—"

Despite the glares the other patrons throw him, he plows on.

"She told you nothing?" he asks. "No last words or legacy? Nothing specific she wanted you to carry on?"

I blink at him. "Wanted?"

"Hey!" Miles shouts, suddenly beside me. "One at a time!"

But he sounds far away as Mrs. Capolli hands me her phone with a choked apology. I take it, our local news pulled up in her browser with a breaking article. As Miles argues with Mr. Hayworth, I scan the post, words jumping out at me like grenades. *Fortune. Family. Iris. Rosewood.*

Dead.

I drop the phone, barely aware of the screen shattering into pieces all over the tile floor. I lean over the counter, locking eyes with Mrs. Capolli. "What's going on?" I rush out, a single frayed thread keeping my heart together, threatening to snap. "What's happening?"

Mrs. Capolli's gaze is horrified. "I'm so sorry," she cries. "Your grandmother was found dead this morning at the manor."

She says something else, but there's a ringing in my ears. Or is it the door? Are more people coming? I can't turn my head to look. Someone tugs me. My feet listen even though my brain can barely keep up. What does she mean, *dead*? Gram can't be dead. She was completely fine yesterday. She can't be dead. She just *can't*.

The door to the kitchen shuts behind me. I look up to see the fingers pulling me aren't Miles's at all, but a weathered olive-toned hand. "Nonna?" I breathe.

The owner of the deli, Maria DiVincenzi, who insists the entire world calls her Nonna, stares at me with an expression that cracks my heart. It's pity; it's anger; it's fear. It confirms that whatever's going on out there, all the ludicrous things people are saying, aren't a trick.

"She can't be," I gasp, stumbling against the oven. The heat coming from it is scalding, but I barely register it against my palms. "Tell me that's not true. It can't be true."

Nonna gently pulls me away from the oven, guiding me toward the back door. "I just heard myself," she grits out, her Italian accent thicker than usual due to the emotion in her voice. "Your uncle called. Said he couldn't get ahold of you. He's coming."

My phone. I scrabble for it in the pocket of my apron but can't bring myself to power it on. "I had it off," I say, my voice small. "I never have it off."

I can hear Miles trying to talk over everyone in the deli, a feeble attempt at crowd control. Nonna shoves the back door open, the warm summer air hitting us. I step outside, shaking despite the beating sun. Had Gram called me? Did she need help and I didn't answer because I couldn't bear to see a couple of dumb social media posts about myself?

"I don't get it." My voice wobbles. "Gram was fine. She *is* fine."

Nonna grabs my hands, staring into my eyes. Hers are stone gray and sharp despite her age. She looks like she wants to say something but swallows thickly. I've never seen her speechless, always jokingly yelling in Italian over our subpar salami-slicing techniques or wistfully talking about her childhood growing up in Sicily and the ache to return.

There is nothing joking or wistful about right now, this moment that will surely be branded in my brain forever.

Tires scream against asphalt as a red Mercedes pulls into the lot. Nonna gives my hands one last squeeze, then nods toward Uncle Arbor's car. I wrench open the car door and throw myself into the passenger seat, barely closing it before we take off. An awful, terrible silence hangs.

I turn to my uncle, trying to speak around the lump in my throat. My words come out strangled. "Those people said—"

"I know," Uncle Arbor cuts me off. His grip tightens around the steering wheel, a muscle in his jaw popping out from how hard he's clenching it.

When he turns to look at me, I recognize his expression. I saw it a year ago on myself, after coming home to find Dad unresponsive on the bathroom floor. I stared at the mirror, waiting for the paramedics to come, for my mom to pick up, for somebody to save him even though I knew it was too late.

I stared for so long, I memorized what my eyes looked like, blood vessels etched like spiderwebs. The tracks the tears made on my cheeks. The ruby sheen of my lips.

Now, my uncle wears the same face—that of someone who's discovered a dead person.

4

Everyone wants to see the body.

All day, townies have filtered through the doors of the manor, kneeling at Gram's casket. Flowers cover it, roses of course. Uncle Arbor picked them, but I wish he hadn't. Gram would have been rolling her eyes.

I can't believe—

Stop. I can't keep slipping into denial. The past week has felt like a dream. I've cried. Screamed. Lain staring at the ceiling. I skipped every shift and ignored Miles's texts because I could barely summon the energy to pick up my phone. Despite the police inspecting the manor and finding no signs of foul play, Frank urged me to stay with Uncle Arbor for the week so further investigations could take place. As of this morning, they came up with nothing.

It's been a week since I've been back, but it could have been thirty for how foreign everything feels. The manor feels different without Gram. Like someone else's home and not the one I've lived in for nearly a year.

I plop into Gram's studded leather desk chair, my shoulders slumping in the solitude of her office. I had to escape the unending stream of people who have been handing us bouquets and chocolates and gifts. Like it's fucking Valentine's Day and not the visiting hours of my grandmother's wake.

I guess I shouldn't complain, though. It's more than we ever got for Dad.

After five spins in the highbacked-chair, the tightness in my chest releases enough to gulp down the stale air. Behind me is a bay window taking up the entire back wall, the late-day sun streaking through and shining directly on the crystalline vase full of wilted roses sitting on the end of Gram's desk. Technicolor light splashes across the smooth wooden surface. It's massive, more like a dining room table, made of antique rosewood from before it was illegal to cut down the rare trees. The coloring is beautiful, alternating between rich dark hues and reddish lighter ones. The family lore is that my great-great-grandmother Hyacinth herself went to Madagascar to cut down the very trees that made it.

There are still papers on it, requests from businesses in town for investments and Rosewood Inc. documents. There's also one pen. I run my finger over the custom silver barrel, Gram's initials *IHR* carved into it. A tiny smile edges at my lips. No one but me would know that the ink within it disappears only minutes after writing.

"How're you doing, Calla?"

I jump at Uncle Arbor's voice, my bare knee smacking the underside of the desk painfully. It rattles the vase, and a few dried red petals fall, like drops of blood against the white papers strewn over the desk.

"Not my name," I say, although it does draw a teeny smile.

"Used to call you that all the time when you were little." He chuckles, holding out a chocolate-dipped strawberry someone sent; I shake my head at the offer. He pops it in his mouth, his gaze roaming the large room. In front of the desk are two forest-green wingback chairs. I wonder if he recalls sitting in the left one while Dad always took the right during meetings with Gram. When we were little and would sleep over, Daisy and I used to eavesdrop in the hall until our not-so-subtle giggles were heard and we'd get scooped up and tucked back into bed in our rooms across the hall from each other upstairs.

He passes the chairs, stepping up to one of the floor-to-ceiling bookcases built into the walls adjacent to the door and window. They're mostly packed with editions of Rosewood Inc. catalogs, prior to everything being fully digital. Before I learned how to read, I used to point to issues and Gram would hand them to me, letting me gaze longingly at the pictures. It's one of my first memories of the office—me upon her knee, a fall edition from years before I was born open on the desk, my finger trailing over a dark red coat that came to the model's ankles.

Some days, that's all I remember from my childhood. Coats and fabrics and days running through the winding halls of the manor, sometimes with Daisy, sometimes without. But always Gram just around the corner, whether in the office, or the great room, or soaking in sun on the patio. Never far.

Tears prick my eyes.

"How are *you* doing?" I ask my uncle before I can sink into a grief spiral. He's spent the past week getting arrangements in order, speaking to the police and funeral director and Frank so often I've barely seen him. I can tell it weighs on him, especially since he was the one who found Gram unresponsive on the floor of the great room last Sunday morning when he went to help clean up from the party after dropping me off at work. His green eyes are strained and bloodshot, a look I'm mirroring. While I wear a simple black dress with a lace hem, he's donned a fitted suit, an outfit I've seen him in more often than not since he's one of the advisers for the Rosetown Council. On it sits some of the town's most influential individuals, all of whom have passed through today to give their condolences.

"As good as can be," Uncle Arbor replies, giving me a weak smile. "You taking cover in here?"

A week ago, I would have never admitted needing to "take cover." But now, I nod. I'm certain opening my mouth will also open my tear ducts.

"Me too," he sighs, sitting on the corner of the desk.

"I should have known."

The words come out fast and harsh, a wave of tears rising like I knew they would. He pauses mid eye rub, frowning.

"Known what?"

"That Gram was sick!" I burst. "That something was wrong. I've been with her *every* day. And I didn't notice anything. Just like—"

I break off, unable to finish. But from the way his eyes soften, Uncle Arbor knows. *Just like Dad.*

"It's not your fault," he tells me. "You heard what the coroner said. Coronary artery disease is common, especially in women her age. Many people live with it for years. We couldn't have anticipated Mom's heart attack. It's unfortunate and terrible that she never told us, but that's how she was." He places a hand on my shoulder, forcing me to meet his gaze. "Knowing her, she probably didn't want us to worry. Especially you. She has been under a lot of stress with the company. I just wish she would have asked me for help. Unfortunately, it's never been her strong suit."

"She could have told me." I wipe my eyes. Maybe if I knew, I wouldn't have let things end the way they did between us at her party. My last words to her weren't anything special. Not an *I love you* or even a full apology. Just me, embarrassed and confused, wasting my last moments with one of the people I love most.

It's a nasty habit I have.

A throat clears across the room. Daisy stands in the doorway, the setting sun turning her hair bright orange. Her eyes burn into me, smoky with shadow, her lips pressed in a thin, tight line. "Frank wants us all in the great room," she clips. "Now."

She turns without a second glance, stomping down the hall. From beside me, Uncle Arbor scrubs a hand down his face. I don't remember the exact time the problems started between them, but it only got worse after Daisy's mom—Aunt Janelle—up and left four years ago. Mom following suit just confirms more Rosewood lore: We're not lucky in love. Everyone either dies or ditches.

I remember that summer vividly. We were about to be freshmen, and Daisy and I went from hanging out nearly every day to a few times a week, and then hardly at all. I'd find out she was making plans without me. I stopped getting invited over.

I'd come to the manor to swim and be with Gram, and she'd say she was coming but never show up. Her mom leaving changed her. And I understand it now. Because Mom leaving after Dad died changed me, too. It brought me closer to Uncle Arbor and pushed Daisy further away than she already was.

"Let's see what's going on," he says now, leading the way out of Gram's study.

I go to follow, but my shin bangs into something. A muffled curse escapes, and I glare at the bottom left drawer of the desk that's slightly open and empty. I rub the sore spot on my leg, nudging it shut with my foot.

We walk down the hallway to the great room, portraits of all the Rosewood women who went before me on the walls, the first two painted by a famous French artist who also has a big piece in the Rosetown Museum of Fine Art. The portraits start with Gram's grandmother Hyacinth Rosewood. She married and refused to take her husband's name, which was a big deal back in the day. He died young and left her a bunch of money, so she quit her seamstress clothing-factory job and spent it on founding Rosewood Inc. Built her own factory on a plot of land where nothing else existed before. Because of the jobs the factory created, people moved nearby and more houses were built. She saw an opportunity and seized it, founding Rosetown, a place that prospered as more people invested in the idea of a sparkling town on the edge of Massachusetts overlooking the Atlantic.

I stride past the next oil portrait, Gram's mom, Petunia Rosewood. The beginning of a tradition of flower names and Hyacinth's only heir. From the icy remarks Gram made about her, I don't think they had the best relationship. Petunia married young, kept the Rosewood last name, had Gram, and then divorced her husband three years later. Gram's never outwardly said it, but Petunia almost tanked Rosewood Inc. Apparently, money management wasn't her specialty. Gram started working when she was sixteen, taking over the business in every facet except legally. As her own connections were fostered, she slowly built it back up into the thriving empire it is today. Petunia had more interest in the bottom of a bottle. She paid for it, too, dying of liver disease by the time she was sixty.

In one last stride, I'm at Gram, an amused smile on her painted lips. By the time she married my grandfather, she didn't need money or support. She had been the sole proprietor of the business for years. She kept the Rosewood name, made international deals that eventually brought our factory to London, and juggled raising twin boys the entire time. I've never known a woman as powerful and accomplished. She was perfect. She had to be.

So do I, if I ever want to follow in her footsteps.

"What's going on?" Uncle Arbor asks Frank as we enter the room.

The huge grandfather clock in the corner shows calling hours ended ten minutes ago. Frank must have shuffled any lingering townspeople out immediately, because it's just us, Daisy, and two other women I haven't seen around town before.

My stomach twists as I take in the scene. A briefcase lies on one of the round tables, which just a little over a week ago was laden with charcuterie for the party. The women stand stoically, waiting for what's to come.

"We were able to rush the process of reading the will," Frank says.

A heavy silence descends over us, tension coating the air like humidity. I glance to where Gram's casket was, but it's gone, already taken to the church.

Frank clears his throat, gesturing to one of the large mahogany tufted leather couches. "If you'd like to take a seat, we can begin."

Daisy perches on the edge of a velvet emerald chaise, and Uncle Arbor sits in the center of the couch, so I lower myself to sit on the arm. My entire body coils, so much that my abs physically hurt.

One of the women opens the briefcase. She pulls out a large envelope, then three letters stamped with red wax seals. The Rosewood crest—a circle with a rose in full bloom and a single thorn on its stem.

Frank takes the envelope from her, pulling a letter opener from his dress shirt pocket. I recognize it as Gram's favorite, gilded in gold with the handle twisting into a small rosebud. He must have snagged it from her desk earlier.

Using the sharp tip, he neatly slices open the envelope, extracting a piece of paper and clearing his throat to read it.

"'Last will and testament of Iris Hyacinth Rosewood. I, Iris Hyacinth Rosewood, residing at One Rosewood Lane, Rosetown, Massachusetts, being of sound mind, declare this to be my last will and testament. I revoke all wills and codicils previously made by me. Article one . . .'"

I can hardly breathe. I've been through all of this before, after

Dad died. I remember sitting in this very room, listening to the reveal that every crumb of his money had gone into his financial business and he'd put our house as collateral. When it went under, our family and half the town who'd listened to him lost everything. It put us in massive debt. Mom was devastated. He'd never even told her.

I can't help the sting of anger that rises at this memory. And I hate it, because he's dead and I miss him so much that sometimes it knocks the breath from my lungs. But he kept everything from us, every secret and lie. When he said he couldn't pay for the Milan program, I thought it was because *I* had done something wrong. If he had just said something then, not tried to carry it all on his own—

I focus back on Frank. Gram assigned Frank as her personal representative to administer the will. No one argues. He's the only one we would trust.

He pauses, and I know what comes next. "'Article two.'"

The room falls silent, electrified. I might as well be hovering over the couch, that's how lightly I'm sitting on it. My hands are clammy, the dying rays leaking through the windows no match against the AC.

"To Daisy Rosewood, my granddaughter and daughter of Arbor Rosewood, I devise, bequeath, and give my white Mercedes-Benz and the letter addressed accordingly."

My jaw hangs. Gram barely even drove her own car, let alone let any of us drive it. To pass the beautiful custom ride off to Daisy is guaranteeing a future of curb hitting and mailbox plowing.

"The White Rose," Daisy gasps, our nickname for the vehicle hanging in the air. But her expression shifts as Frank clears his throat, ready to move on. "That's it?"

Uncle Arbor's gaze is stern. "That's a wonderful inheritance," he says curtly, although really, when dealing with a fortune that equals close to a quarter of a billion dollars, I'm not sure it is. From the muscle that jumps in his jaw, he knows it. "Frank, please continue."

I swallow, my gaze darting to my uncle before I can help it. I always wondered what would happen to the fortune. It makes sense that Gram would split it between her sons. With Dad gone, I can't help but hope I might get his portion.

"'To Arbor Rosewood, my son, I devise, bequeath, and—'"

My breath feels stuck in my chest. If Uncle Arbor gets all of it, I can't be mad. I know he'll use it to take care of me. Maybe he'd even pay for me to go to FIT. But still, there's a feeling in my chest, uncomfortable and too close to the entitled girl I was last summer. Wanting everything. *Expecting* everything.

She died with Dad. I made sure of it. And yet, that poison still lurks deep inside me. The hunger of never having enough.

Greed.

Frank continues. "'Give the key in my bedroom safe and the letter addressed accordingly.'"

I don't have time to cover my gasp. Daisy's jaw is on the floor. My uncle stammers, something I've never seen him do before. "Certainly, there must be—"

"That's all, Mr. Rosewood," Frank smoothly cuts him off. "Shall we move on?"

All eyes rotate to me. But the only gaze I care about is Uncle Arbor's. His eyes bleed with hurt.

"Of course." He flashes a tight smile that might as well be plastic.

I don't know what the key might lead to, but I hope it's something good. He doesn't need the money anyway, not like I do. Gram probably figured that.

"Just one left." Frank glances at me.

Holy shit. That means Gram left me everything.

I can't help the thrill that shoots through me.

"'To Lily Rosewood,'" Frank begins.

My nails dig into the leather of the arm to keep me from falling off.

"'My granddaughter and daughter to my late son, Alder Rosewood, I devise, bequeath, and—'"

After this moment, my life will change forever. I will be the sole owner of the deeply protected Rosewood fortune. The manor will be mine. I'll have Gram's prized seat on the board of Rosewood Inc. Everything I've ever wanted.

But, suddenly, the thrill is replaced by a wave of nausea. I didn't want it like *this*. My favorite person dead. We were supposed to run Rosewood Inc. *together*. She barely even brushed the surface teaching me. I know *nothing* about business. Or owning a manor.

Or being in charge of an entire *fortune*.

Frank looks over the paper at me. My breath is caught in a bubble in my lungs as he speaks the words that will alter my world forever. "'Give my ruby necklace, a priceless Rosewood heirloom passed down from my grandmother before me, and the letter addressed accordingly.'"

Silence. My pulse storms in my ears, waiting for Frank to go on.

But nothing comes. Frank clears his throat, lowering the paper. Uncle Arbor looks at me perplexed. I . . . don't know how I look.

Probably like I'm about to throw up, which isn't far off from how I feel.

"That can't be everything," Uncle Arbor protests. "What about the manor? Rosewood Inc.? How about the entire fucking *estate*?"

It's rare I hear my uncle swear, but his frustration jolts Daisy into action.

"It didn't just disappear," she adds. The leather beneath me most definitely has tiny cuts from my nails.

Frank turns the paper over. "There are a few last sentiments from Iris."

"Yes, go on!" Uncle Arbor's voice booms. A nervous laugh escapes him, as if he's had twelve cups of coffee and only now realizes it wasn't decaf. "Jesus, Frank."

Frank swallows. "'Article three. As for the remainder of my belongings, including but not limited to my manor in Rosetown, Massachusetts; my villa in Venice, Italy; Rosewood Inc.; my place on the board; and the properties and factory under the name; and the remainder of my estate and accrued wealth, currently valued at two hundred forty-seven million dollars, the receiver will be determined at a later date under privately specified circumstances.'"

"*What?*" It bursts from my mouth before I can stop it. "What does that mean?"

"Frank, this is bullshit." Uncle Arbor jumps to his feet. "*At a later date?* She's gone! Who's deciding this for her? When was this written?"

To Frank's credit, he stays stoically calm. "This version was approved July thirtieth, last year."

Daisy chokes, her horrified gaze flickering to me. "Wasn't that—"

"The week after Dad died," I breathe.

Frank nods. "However, revisions were made May fifteenth, this year."

Uncle Arbor starts arguing, but I don't have the energy. Instead, terror saps the fight from my bones. It makes sense that Gram would have changed her will following Dad's death, but why alter it again?

"I am not finished yet," Frank raises his voice over the din of Uncle Arbor.

"Fine! Finish!" Uncle Arbor plops back on the couch. His face is red, hair mussed and more silver than auburn. Mine might match soon.

Frank makes a show of clearing his throat, reading the rest of the page. "In the meantime, I request that Rosewood Manor be closed to the public and the family. The sole caveat to this rule will be Frank Archer, who I request seek security detail to make sure this holds true."

"But I live here," I breathe, unable to hide my horror. "Where am I supposed to go?"

"Perhaps you can stay with your uncle like you have been this week, Miss Rosewood."

"No way!" Daisy exclaims, at the same time that Uncle Arbor says, "Of course."

He gives me a look of reassurance that I'm not suddenly homeless before standing to address Frank. "Where's the money? We can at least challenge that. It's within our rights. We'll go to the bank, fill out—"

"Unfortunately, that won't be an option," Frank says.

Uncle Arbor strides forward, stopping across the table from him. "Why not?"

Discomfort flashes across Frank's face. "It is not in its original accounts."

We suck in one collective breath.

"Was it stolen?" Daisy asks.

Frank shakes his head. "No, not to my knowledge. From what I can tell after speaking with Iris's accountant earlier this week, she had been steadily removing her assets over the past year. Currently, her accounts are down to a thousand dollars, the minimum."

"Where is it, then?" I push myself up from the arm of the couch, legs jelly beneath me. "She had to have put it somewhere."

"In this house, probably," Uncle Arbor states. He turns toward the archway leading to the rest of the house. "I can think of a few places—"

The two women who have been silent up until now step forward, blocking his path. Their jaws are set, and their hands move to their hips simultaneously. They have *guns*.

Oh my God.

Uncle Arbor barks out a laugh. "What is this?"

"Iris made it clear that Rosewood Manor will be closed for the foreseeable future," Frank says.

He takes the three letters, jamming one into Uncle Arbor's hands, one into Daisy's, then finally my own. I stare at it, wishing it could do something, anything at all, to fill the crater-size hole in my chest.

Frank gestures to the doors. "Your inheritance items will be given as soon as I am able."

Betrayal burns away the numbing haze. Gram wouldn't have done this. I jump up, reaching for the paper myself to read, but one of the women stands before me suddenly. "This way, ma'am." *Ma'am.* Not *Miss Rosewood*, or even my name. *Ma'am.*

"There's been a mistake," I choke out, her hand a steady pressure on the small of my back. A *threatening* pressure. "Gram wouldn't do this to us. I have things here, my sewing machine and clothes and sketchbook and— Can I just go to my room?"

"We'll drop anything of yours off along with your inheritance. Thank you for understanding."

It's the ultimate shutdown. I'm led out for the second time in under two weeks, stewing in the betrayal.

The women keep pushing us out until we have no choice but to climb into Uncle Arbor's Mercedes. He grips the wheel tightly as Daisy takes the passenger seat and I get in the back. My heart pounds against my ribs so hard it *hurts*. I twist to look at the manor disappearing behind us as Uncle Arbor drives us away.

"Why would she do this?" I sputter. "She couldn't have made it all just disappear, right?"

Uncle Arbor shakes his head, knuckles white around the wheel. He has no idea, and the fact that Gram left him *and* me in the dark is so unsettling I swallow down bile.

"Maybe the legend is true," Daisy says flatly. "That Hyacinth hid the fortune."

5

The windows aren't open, but it feels like a chill wafts through the car.

"That's just Rosewood lore," I snap, although hearing it out loud sets my heart racing. "Besides, it was passed down to Gram's mom, then her. That couldn't have happened if it was never there to begin with."

"Maybe only part of the fortune was passed down," Daisy counters. "And maybe Gram blew through it or hid it wherever the rest is."

"Hiding money for all these years doesn't make sense," Uncle Arbor says, thankfully taking my side. "In a bank or stocks, it accrues interest. There's no reason to keep it off the books."

"But remember that article written about her in the *Rosetown Chronicle* one time? Hold up, I'll find the screenshot online."

Daisy pulls out her phone, scrolling for a few moments before shoving it toward me, Instagram open. The page is one dedicated to our town's history and local businesses. I read aloud the post Daisy found showing the top half of an aged newspaper, the caption appropriately tagged *#throwbackThursday*. "'Could workers' wages and a different kind of green be hidden beneath the flora?

Rosewood Inc. employees demand answers.'"

"Who wrote that?" Uncle Arbor demands.

I zoom in on the image. "Theodore Hayworth." I frown. "Wait, as in, related to the Mr. Hayworth we know?"

Daisy nods enthusiastically. "Yeah, probably his grandpa or something."

"Hayworths are always looking for trouble when it comes to our family, and always have been," Uncle Arbor says. "The *Rosetown Chronicle* is a borderline gossip column thanks to them. Besides, I asked Mom about that legend years ago. She assured me that's all it is—a legend. Something the townspeople made up about Hyacinth because she was underpaying them a living wage and cutting the pay for those who didn't reach their daily quota."

"*Or* she was hiding away the money she saved on wages somewhere. She was known for being greedy," Daisy says.

"Watch how you talk about your ancestors," Uncle Arbor scolds. "And it's not true. Petunia even said so in a journal entry, that it was just ridiculous lore. It's been debunked."

Daisy crosses her arms. "Fine. Then here's another theory—it was never there to begin with."

She's met with silence.

"What do you mean?" I finally ask. "You heard Frank. There's still the manor, Rosewood Inc., the villa."

She shrugs. "Yeah, there's *stuff*. But what if the money is gone? He did say that Gram's been taking it out of her accounts. And besides, can we really trust Frank right now? He just kicked us out."

"He's doing his job," Uncle Arbor defends, although I can tell he's not happy with our family lawyer, either.

"I don't understand how neither of you will entertain the idea that the money might be gone. Why else would Gram not even give money to Uncle Alder last year, which probably led him to—"

"*Enough!*" Uncle Arbor snaps, but we all know what she was going to say.

"*Suicide,*" the coroner told us last July, the memory singed into my brain. All Rosewoods had gathered in the great room. Mom was there but barely. She had already started mentally checking out before she left town. *"A toxic mix of pharmaceuticals was found in Alder's system."*

Deep in debt and with a town full of people in the same boat thanks to him, it was easy for the police to close the investigation and agree.

So he became just another Rosewood tragedy, like Petunia dying young after nearly tanking Rosewood Inc., my grandfather getting sick and never getting better, and Aunt Janelle abandoning her family. Alder Rosewood got added to the bitter list.

The problem is, I don't think Daisy's totally wrong. Living with Gram for a year and watching her deny requests from the businesses Dad screwed over hasn't exactly built my grandmother the most philanthropic image. But I don't think it's because Gram blew through the money. She's always been a strategic business-woman. Her main priority was Rosewood Inc., and she was right for it. It's bigger than ever right now.

But sometimes I can't help but wonder if Dad would still be alive had Gram done things differently.

We pull onto a private drive. Rosewood Manor is the only gated property in town, but Uncle Arbor still has an impressive home. It's just him and Daisy, but the house is huge, sprawling across several acres and boasting nine bedrooms and a backyard to rival Gram's. A pool, hot tub, firepit, and rosebushes planted everywhere in between make it unmistakable as a Rosewood property. The spotless white brick mimics the manor, although it lacks the old-timey elegance that seems to cling to the estate we're all now locked out of.

Uncle Arbor stops before the four-car garage. Daisy hops out of the car before it's even off, storming through the front door.

"Go inside," Uncle Arbor says wearily to me. "I'm going to go back. See if I can talk some sense into Frank."

I grip the back of his seat. "But those women had *guns*."

"I know." His voice is hoarse. "I'll be careful. Until it's worked out, this house is your house, Lily. You've always had a room here, but the rest of it is yours, too. That's the other thing I need to talk to Frank about. I know you turn eighteen soon and won't need a legal guardian, but I want to make sure you're covered in whatever way you need beyond that."

My throat is tight as I lean over the console and press a kiss to his cheek. "Thank you."

I step inside the house, shutting the huge door behind me. My head falls against the wood, eyes burning from the pressure of unshed tears. It's funny how I've spent the past year trying to prove to Gram I'm in control of my temper and every bit the perfect granddaughter she expected me to be.

Right now, all I want to do is break something.

55

"Why can you never back me up on literally anything?" Daisy stands in the entrance to the formal living room, hands on her hips. The decor is starkly modern compared to the traditional style of the manor. Abstract paintings dot the walls, a sleek black leather sectional taking up most of the room. White marble surrounds the fireplace, silver candelabras on the mantel. In her silky black dress, Daisy looks made for the house, a perfect match. Still standing in the foyer, I feel like exactly what I am—an unwanted intruder.

"Because it's a *legend*." My voice comes out quiet and biting. If she wants to fight, I'm happy to oblige.

"It's just sus, you know? And if all her money is still around, it must be somewhere at the manor. That's probably why we're banned and why she recently fired all the employees."

"She fired them?" That explains why Stewie didn't drive us home, and why I didn't recognize any of the cooks or staff the night of her party, either. Gram loved them. She wouldn't have fired them unless she had to. "So why would Gram do that? Why hide any of it?"

Daisy deflates. "I don't know."

"Of course you don't."

Daisy looks up sharply. "Well, at least I'm *trying* to figure it out. You've shut down." She strides to where I stand beneath the modern iron chandelier in the foyer, getting in my face. "This all is really messing with you, isn't it? Because in your eyes, Gram can do no wrong. At least, not until the night of the party, when she bought a trip to Milan for *me* and not you."

I bristle at her words, a thousand comebacks on my tongue

and none making it past my lips. Turning my back on her, I stomp up the stairs.

"What? Did you think you would get all of it?" Daisy goads, trailing me all the way to my room, which is next to hers. "You thought Gram would leave you all the money because you lived with her. Admit it—you're mad at her, too."

I whirl when I get to my doorway. Something must be in my eyes, because Daisy stumbles back until she hits the wall across from me. "You don't know anything about what I thought. Leave me alone." I slam my door in her face.

She kicks it from the other side, then slams her own door. Seconds later, music blasts. I grit my teeth, the tears I held in all day spilling onto my cheeks.

"I hate you," I cry to the soft blue walls of my room and matching carpet. They're the last words I ever said to Dad, and the memory of that day threatens to drown me. *I hate you, I hate you, I hate you!* Sometimes I don't understand how the two most powerful words in the world are both four letters, one syllable. How they roll off the tongue like nothing but impact everything. *Hate* and *love.*

The latter has never come easy to me.

I catch a glimpse of myself in the mirror over the dresser and gurgle on a laugh. Black mascara is halfway down my face, making me look clownish, which fits, because all of this feels like a sick joke. For a second during the will reading, I actually thought I might inherit an entire fortune at seventeen.

Almost eighteen, a tiny voice in my head whispers unhelpfully.

"Shut up," I sneer out loud. As the adrenaline of my fight with

Daisy leaks out, it makes room for anxiety to crawl in. I have no idea what comes next. Not only for me, but for my family. The fortune missing makes us look like fools. We'll be the laughing-stock of the town.

For this single moment, I wish I were Daisy. That I could lose myself in music and my thousands of TikTok followers, hit up a group chat full of friends and arrange a bonfire. Call up my latest fling and see what they're up to. Get lost in them and their touch.

But I'm not her. I don't have any group chats, and certainly nobody who might kiss me until I forget this horrible day. I'm too embarrassed to text Miles back since I've been ignoring his check-ins lately. So that leaves one last option for distraction.

And it's not much of a distraction.

The letter Gram left for me is still rumpled in my hand. I turn it over, running my pointer finger over the red wax seal. When I was little, I'd watch Gram stamp that seal across hundreds of envelopes. Sometimes I'd stick my finger in the hot wax and she'd threaten to take off my eyebrows. But it was always followed by a laugh and a kiss to the top of my head.

I slide my finger under the seal until it pops, breaking the perfect rose. Lifting the flap, I pull out the folded piece of paper, thick cardstock that Gram used for every letter, preparing for . . . well, I don't even know. Her final words for me, I guess.

All at once, like I'm trying to win a race, I unfold the letter and stare at the page.

It's . . . blank.

Blank.

A new batch of tears brew as I turn the sheet over. Blank on the other side, too. What the *hell*, Gram? After all our letters, all these years, all I get is a blank sheet of paper?

I throw it down on the purple bedspread, staring into the envelope in case I missed something. Empty. Just my name on the back. I pick up the paper again. *Why would you—?*

"Oh!" I exclaim. Night fell fast, leaving me in the shadows. I turn on the bedside lamp, holding the page under it. There—in the top left corner. A smudge.

"Always playing games," I mutter, running into the en suite bathroom. I grab a washcloth from above the toilet, wetting it under the sink spray and wringing it until it's just slightly damp. Flattening the blank page on the quartz counter, I take the washcloth and run it along the smudge. At the wetness, words appear.

Dear Lilylove,

I hold my breath and wipe the washcloth across the rest of the page, taking special care not to soak the paper too much. In the wake of the water, there are sentences, all in Gram's delicate cursive. When I get to the end of the page, I drop the washcloth, staring down at the last few lines Gram left me. The last words I'll ever have from her.

Dear Lilylove,
I know whatever time we've had together by the time you receive this letter wasn't enough. It couldn't have been, because I could have spent forever and a day with you. I know you're confused, maybe scared, and knowing you, probably angry. You

inherited the Rosewood temper, after all. You're right to feel all these things, and more. I wish I were with you to explain.

But I'm not, so you'll have to trust me. If it's answers you seek, look where my love for you first bloomed.

You have my heart,
Gram

I grip the cool counter to keep from keeling over, memorizing the words, the curve of the letters and pressure of the pen, imagining the custom barrel in her veined hands. All of it, like embroidery on my brain. But it's the last line that spins in my mind. *If it's answers you seek, look where my love for you first bloomed.*

It's a riddle. Something Gram would put together knowing I'm the only one who would really know the answer, because I've spent my whole life playing her games. And I know exactly where she's telling me to go.

Problem is, I'm now banned from there. By *her* orders.

If I were to go, it'd have to be late. I know the only camera is by the front gate, but Frank and those two women might still be around, or whatever other security he gets. And Uncle Arbor might still be there. Heading back to Rosewood Manor right now isn't an option. I'm not about to get caught breaking and entering at my own house.

Well, Gram was right about one thing—I *am* angry. And scared, and confused, and a whole other slew of emotions. Nothing could have ever prepared me for something like this. For my grandmother's last words to me to be some kind of *clue.*

And if it is . . . does that mean Daisy's kind of right? Could the fortune really be hidden somewhere?

I don't know what to think, and I'm so, so tired that I'm not even sure I'm completely coherent anymore. Grief is its own illness, climbing under skin and burrowing in bones. It's heavy, like the worst weighted blanket ever. Dragging me down and stealing my breath. And familiar. So hauntingly familiar. An old enemy.

But the letter is a streak of sunlight through the thick darkness. And maybe that's the point. A little something just for me. The distraction I need so I'm not dragged under.

I grab the letter and reenter my room as I strip off my black dress and kick my heels into the corner. Uncle Arbor had grabbed clothes of mine last week knowing I'd be here, but I don't have nearly enough things to last me longer than a couple more days. Plus, in true dad fashion, he had no idea what to bring me, picking my oldest, blandest clothes and a pair of white high-tops I haven't worn since sophomore year.

Despite the lack of fashion, I'm grateful to tug on soft leggings and a worn tee. I turn off the light and climb in bed, laying the letter beside me.

"What are you trying to tell me?" I whisper into the darkness, my eyes heavy as I stare at it. The words are just splotches of black against the ivory parchment.

I could sneak in through the space in the hedge. I'd be in and out in five minutes. I know where to step to stay away from the floodlights and windows. Once I'm in the Anything but Roses garden, no one would be able to see me.

Or I could stay here. Sleep through the night, prepare for the funeral tomorrow afternoon. Keep waiting, wishing, hoping, praying my situation might change. That when I wake up, all of this will just be some terrible nightmare and I'll laugh about it with Gram while eating lovecakes and looking at new designs.

Sudden and throbbing, my chest aches with the realization that I lost more than my grandmother. I lost my best friend.

At some point, Daisy's music fades and Uncle Arbor comes home, steps heavy with defeat as the door of his room clicks shut. I watch the moon through my window as it inches across the sky, checking the time on my phone. Almost three. The world is quiet. Asleep.

I should be asleep. But I can't. Gram was about to say something the night she died. She needs me to know something, and at this rate, I have nothing to lose.

Whatever you're trying to tell me, I think as I kick off the covers. *I'm ready to listen.*

6

I stare at Rosewood Manor, basking in moonlight and hauntingly beautiful. Despite being built in the early twentieth century, it never struck me as *old* before. Not like the creepy manors in movies, full of secret passageways and vengeful spirits. It was always full of life and delicious aromas wafting from the kitchen, the buzz of music and chatter from guests during parties. Never empty or *scary*.

But as I stare at it now from the base of the hill that leads to the closed gates of the driveway, fear strikes my heart. It looks terrifying, white brick like jutting bone against the clear navy sky. I know the layout by heart, the top two floors consisting of twelve bedrooms and eight bathrooms, the playhouse off the east wing where Daisy and I used to spend hours when we were little, overflowing with every toy we could ever want. My gaze catches on the window to Gram's room, picturing her canopy bed beyond it. The mornings when Daisy and I would run in after staying the night, jumping on it to wake her and then blitzing to her closet to play dress-up. It rivaled the size of most bedrooms, and the two of us would spend hours pulling extravagant gowns over our heads, stumbling in heels and laughing until our stomachs ached. We each had our own rooms, too, mine being just a few doors down from Gram's, the Singer sewing machine she gifted me when I was ten still tucked in the corner to this day. Daisy got the same one, but unlike me, she never used it.

I know this house inside and out. What keys stick on the piano in the formal living room. The trapdoor in the butler's pantry that Gram always hid behind during games of hide-and-seek when we were small. The octagon-shaped library on the third floor where Dad used to read me stories, propped in front of a blazing fire on chilly winter nights, the floor-to-ceiling windows etched with frost.

It won't stay empty, I swear silently to myself. *I won't let it become like the factory, abandoned and forgotten.*

Even though Uncle Arbor lives only a couple of miles away, it took thirty minutes to trek here, and another five to walk up the hill, giving the gate a wide berth so the camera doesn't catch me. Approaching the hedge, the green wall seems impenetrable.

I walk alongside it, praying the hole is still where I remember it. It's a small gap in the hedge where roots failed to grow, right across from a tree with an odd-looking knot where Gram used to hide notes with secret missions scribbled on them for Daisy and me when we were in our spy-girls phase. We'd grab the note, activate the ink, and take turns holding branches back while the other crawled through the gap. The memory is painful, when our moms were still around and my dad's laugh rang bright and alive.

The snap of a twig makes me whip around, heart in my throat. Shadows loom, thick and monstrous. I press myself closer to the hedge. I don't know what might happen if I get caught, but I really don't want to find out.

I stare into the darkness for so long my vision blurs. When nothing comes forward, I continue, finally finding the tree. Unable to help myself, I stick my hand in the knot, half expecting a spider or indignant squirrel to greet my prodding fingers. But nothing does, not even a note from Gram. It's been so many years, and she's had so many hiding places, she likely forgot about this one.

Dropping to my knees, I pat my hand along the bottom of the hedge. I *know* it's close—

"Gotcha," I whisper when gnarled roots give way to grossly overgrown underbrush. It takes nearly a minute of pulling the tangled shrubbery away to expose the gap. Either it's a lot smaller than I remember, or I'm a lot bigger. Probably both.

I flatten to my stomach and army crawl through the space, scraggly underbrush scratching my arms and snagging my hair despite the double Dutch braids I put it in on the way here. This is definitely not the gated entrance I'm used to. Dirt lodges beneath my fingernails. For a moment, in the middle, the darkness swallows me and phantom giggles ring in my ear. But those are days long gone, and as quickly as I enter, I'm out on the other side, breathing in the floral scent that clings to the air surrounding the manor. I push myself to my feet, struck as a wave of longing hits me like a bus.

Being this close to the manor makes it feel even more foreboding. All towering brick and empty windows, ivy holding on tightly to the trellises, bloodred roses blooming beneath the moon. A stunning ghost of a life that slipped through my fingers.

Since the Anything but Roses garden is on the west side of the property, the fastest way there is cutting across the patio. But doing so puts me right in front of the pool. The timed lights that turn on at night douse everything around it turquoise. It's basically a spotlight. If security is here, going that way is too risky.

I stick to the shadows, skirting the edge of the patio so the first line of trees acts as a barrier. My neck prickles.

This time, I know it's not someone following me. It's what's at the very back edge of the property, past the tennis courts and thicket. There's a small creek, and beyond it, a willow tree that stands guard over the graves of every Rosewood who's gone before us. Last summer, Dad's plot was so fresh the grass hadn't even grown before the fall freeze. I haven't visited it since that day, but I wonder what's bloomed there now. Maybe nothing.

I pick up my pace, letting the breeze sweep the thought away. The gate to the Anything but Roses garden is ajar. If Frank was going to get guards to make sure no one enters the property, I don't think he has yet. I sneak inside without a sound.

Within the protection of the white stone walls, my shoulders collapse with relief. I stare up at Saint Anthony, his blank eyes gazing back at me. "What have you seen?" I breathe into the stillness.

I'd pee myself if he answered, although a piece of me wouldn't mind some input. I pass him, pulling the note from the pocket of my leggings. *If it's answers you seek, look where my love for you first bloomed.*

Before me are my namesake in all their bright orange glory. Despite Uncle Arbor calling me Calla, Dad actually named me after tiger lilies, because they represent confidence, pride, and wealth. I could use any of the three right now.

I gently move them aside, using the moonlight to highlight the leafy greenery of their stems. But nothing looks out of the ordinary. If I tramp through them to search, it'll be obvious someone was here. I have to be strategic.

It'd be easy if I knew what I was looking for. A greedy piece of me hopes I might stumble upon the entire inheritance, as unlikely as it is. But if so, it must be in some kind of briefcase. A big one at that.

I risk turning on my phone flashlight to peek at the base of the bunches. The brightness stuns me momentarily, so I smother the harsh glow with the hem of my shirt until my eyes adjust. Once they do, I kneel. My knees sink into the dirt, the moisture seeping through the thin material of my leggings as I stretch as far back as my arm allows me. My fingers brush dirt, tangled roots, the softness of dropped petals, and the waxy texture of leaves. And then something smooth and hard.

Plastic.

My fist wraps around it, tugging. It's suctioned to the earth, but with a final pull it jerks free. The force pushes me onto my butt, my head smacking into Saint Anthony's holy knee.

"Ow," I mutter, rubbing the sore spot. In my hand is a tube, barely the width of my fist and length of my forearm. Dirt clings to it, masking what might be a gray hue. It's . . . small. Not quite what I'd expect millions of dollars to be stuffed into. But still sacred and special. I don't hold back the victorious smile that stretches across my face.

Nicolas Cage in *National Treasure* has nothing on me.

As much as I want to pop this thing open and see what's

inside, I need to get moving. It's already nearing four, and if I'm still on the road come five, I'll attract the attention of people on their early commute. I've gotta get out of here.

I turn off my flashlight, slipping through the gate and retracing my path. The pool is in sight, mere feet away, but like when I entered, I'm careful to stay behind the trees. I keep my steps light and breath even, coming round the trunk of one massive oak and—

I slam headfirst into something very *not* tree. A firm chest. A *person.*

Shit.

The collision throws me backward, and I stumble onto the patio, the tube and my phone clattering to the stone. It all happens so fast I can't see who I ran into. Hands reach for me, and I take another big step back, dodging their hold. Except, there's nothing behind me but air.

I flail out, and they grab my hand, but gravity already has me. Has *us,* now.

The water shocks me as it slides over my head and slips down my throat. The chlorine stings my eyes, everything bright and turquoise from the underwater lights. Whoever fell in with me is just a big blur, their fist wrapping around my arm. I scream a stream of bubbles, jerking out of their hold. They reach again, and I kick away, wrangling myself deeper as my lungs burn. Was someone waiting for me in the woods behind the manor? Did they follow me here?

My feet finally touch the bottom, and I use it like a springboard, all my strength into pushing up. When my head breaks the surface, I don't take a second to relish the clean air. I'm by the side of the pool, and I heave myself over the ledge, arms shaking with the effort. Water squeezes out of my Converse, my clothes weighing on me and my twin braids heavy on my shoulders.

I grab my phone and the tube, turning back to the water just in time to watch my assailant break the surface. Soaked dark hair obscures their face. They cough a few times and push themselves up onto the patio, biceps way bigger than mine flexing beneath tanned, moonlit skin. I brace myself, knowing I should run. But my feet are rooted to the stone. If this isn't security—and I'm pretty freaking sure it's not—then that means someone else snuck in. I can't leave without knowing.

I hold the plastic tube like a bat as they purge water from their lungs. I'm gearing up to swing it so hard into their head that it leaves a dent when they finally flip their hair out of their face like a wet dog, glancing up at me. Their eyes widen with panic. "Wait, no—"

I falter mid swing, throwing my weight off so the tube barely misses the boy who kneels before me. Sputtering, I stare at his drenched body in disbelief. *"Leo?!"*

Gram's yard boy opens his mouth to reply, but the light for the patio switches on. I choke on a gasp as I dive behind the trunk of a hearty maple, pressing my back to the bark and pulling my knees tight to my chest. My knuckles are white around the plastic tube.

To my annoyance, Leo ducks beside me in a similar position as we both hold our breath. My ears strain for the sounds of someone walking around but catch nothing. If we're lucky, we only triggered the automatic lights.

"What are you doing here?" Leo whispers, his voice louder

than he realizes. I jam my elbow into his side to shut him up, chancing a peek around the trunk as he groans. The water has smoothed back to stillness, and the patio light thankfully turns off. I wait a few more breaths before scrambling to my feet and spinning on Leo.

"What am *I* doing here?" I ask in a harsh whisper. I gesture to the house, then to myself. "I'm a *Rosewood*. I *live* here. The bigger question is what are *you* doing here?"

He gets to his feet and digs into his pocket, pulling out a set of keys and dangling them before my eyes. "Taking care of the yard. Let myself in through the back gate."

He has *keys*? I don't even have keys. I've never needed them; everything's always been unlocked for me. I look down at my clothes, now muddy from the water mingling with the dirt I crawled through to sneak in here. He stares down at me with a hint of satisfaction in his gray gaze.

"I don't think you typically trim the bushes at—" I glance at my phone. "Four in the morning."

He shrugs. "I'm an early bird, what can I say?"

I roll my eyes, stalking deeper into the yard to get away from the house but keeping my voice hushed. He follows me.

"You're not supposed to be here," I say.

"Neither are you."

I spin, placing a hand out to stop him from bumping into me. He's the type of boy who's all legs, towering over six foot and bulky with muscle because he and some other guys from the hockey team skip class to work out.

But I'm tall, too, and the few inches he has on me doesn't

make me back down. "How do you know that?" Twelve hours ago *I* didn't even know that.

"Daze filled us in on how the will reading went. Sounds like you've had better days."

"You don't know anything," I snap to cover the fact that I'm mortified. I shouldn't have expected anything less from Daisy—*Daze,* as her friends and followers call her—than to air our family's dirty laundry all around Rosetown High. But I had hoped she had at least a *shred* of common sense.

I make my way through the wooded area behind the manor while carefully dodging the graveyard. No matter how fast I walk, Leo is right beside me.

"You never answered my question," he says. "Why are you here?"

I keep my lips firmly pressed together, weaving around trees and barely maintaining my dignity when a root catches my foot. Leo's warm hand wraps around my arm to stop me from falling. I shrug it off.

"I'll tell you why I'm here," he offers.

We're at the back gate now, and sure enough, it's unlocked. I stop, one hand on the twisted iron covered in ivy, one on my hip.

A piece of me doesn't really care why he's here, I'm just pissed he *is.* I haven't been this close to him in years. Since entering high school, we rarely have classes together, not even glancing at each other in the halls. Except for sometimes peeking out my window to see him weeding perennials, I've kept a wide berth, even taking extra shifts at the deli on days I know he's at the manor. And so far, avoiding him has worked great.

But of course the one night I really need to not see a soul, he's here. And just like me, he thought he'd be alone tonight. In and out.

He takes my silence as curiosity, which is unfortunately true. Slowly, he reaches into the pouch of his hoodie with two hockey sticks crossed on the front. He pulls out two things that make my heart stop, holding one in each hand.

In his right hand is cardstock paper, soggy now from taking a dip but the ink still visible in a script I know all too well.

And in his left—a plastic tube.

He nods to my own plastic tube clenched in my fist, my knuckles white around it. "Guess this makes us twinsies."

I storm through the gate, needing to turn my back on him before he sees how shaken I am. But I'm halted as his arm curves around my waist, forcing me to change direction. A yelp escapes me at the sudden proximity, and he leans in to whisper, "You almost stepped into the view of the camera."

"There're no cameras back here," I counter, wiggling out of his hold but sticking toward the direction he set me in. He saunters after me.

"Your gram had a new one installed a couple of weeks ago."

It's a reasonable answer, but it fills me with fury that he knows something I don't.

He follows me all the way down the grassy hill, which is slippery with dew. With one obnoxiously long step, Leo wedges himself in front of me, forcing me to stop.

"We should open them, don't you think?" he asks, raising the plastic tube. I try to dodge around him, but he matches me step for step. "See what's inside."

I cross my arms. "I'm not opening mine here. Whatever's in mine is between Gram and me. Believe it or not, you weren't included."

A shadow crosses his face as he holds his letter out to me. "I'm not so sure about that."

I grab it from him, scanning the words. The ink runs, but I can still make it out. It's short, just a quick few lines that set my teeth on edge.

Dear Leo,

Don't underestimate the tools it takes to go from seed to sapling. It's more work than you'd think. Only once you learn this can you move forward. When you do, find Lily.

Gram

I stare at it, not knowing what to say. *Find Lily.* Why?

"It's a riddle," Leo explains. "Sometimes, when I'd finish working on the yard, Gram and I would sit and play chess. We also had this game we'd play, called Sphinx. Every time I came, I'd bring a riddle, and she did too. As soon as I got here, we'd trade, and then whoever solved their riddle first was the winner for the day. She said they helped keep her mind sharp."

I glance at him, shocked at the emotion in his voice.

He swallows, gaze locking on the ground. "I can't believe she's not here."

"That makes two of us," I say.

"I found this in the tool shed," he says with a hollow chuckle, raising the tube. "It was behind the shovel I use most."

I look back at the manor. From here, we should be too far away to be seen and heard. But that doesn't help me against the brightening sky. The sun will be up soon.

"I just got this." Leo nods at the letter. "It arrived in the mail. And you just got yours, too, right? So don't you think maybe Gram wanted us to run into each other?"

I don't know what to say to that. If his arrived by mail, that means someone sent it, or at the very least dropped it off. And it couldn't have been Gram, since it's been an entire week. So who would have? Are we being played?

I have to know.

I pop off the cap to my plastic tube, tipping it upside down to slide whatever's inside into my palm. It's paper, rolled like a scroll. I peer into the tube to make sure it's empty.

I don't mean to, but I glance at Leo before unrolling it. His eyes are glued to it, droplets of water still falling from the tips of his wavy dark strands, the kind of brown that's nearly black. It matches his thick lashes spiked from the pool water. His clothes cling to his skin, a smile ghosting across his lips. To him, this is a game. To me it's everything.

I unroll it carefully. It's bigger than a standard-size letter, the paper yellowed slightly and two sides of it jagged, as if it's been ripped. My confusion only grows as I take in the carefully drawn lines across it, the etchings of familiar buildings and shops. And most important, the massive plot of land with trees sketched around it labeled *Rosewood Manor*.

"It's a map of Rosetown," I say breathlessly, tracing one of the lines with my index finger. A street. It leads to Saint Theresa

Church, which isn't too far from here. "Or part of one, at least."

From his own tube, he pulls out a piece of paper nearly identical to mine, this one highlighting the northeast section of the town. I spot familiar places like the Ice Plex and DiVincenzi's Deli, along with the police station.

The corner of Leo's mouth quirks up. "You know what this means, don't you?"

I look back down at our pieces, trying to fit them together, but neither of the jagged edges match up. If his is the northeast section and mine is southwest, that means we're still missing northwest and southeast.

"There are others," I whisper. "But if this is some kind of . . . indicator of something Gram left for us, then shouldn't there be an *X* somewhere?"

It sounds so stupid when said aloud, as if we're in a pirate movie. Heat burns across my cheeks, but Leo takes me seriously. "That *is* weird. Maybe there's a starting point we don't know about that's on one of the other sections. Who else would Gram have trusted?"

"I didn't even think she trusted *you*. And besides, why are you calling her Gram?"

Hurt flashes across his face. He's not very good at hiding it, never has been, and it's another reminder of how differently I've grown up from everyone else. I've always had to be worried about how I'm being perceived, but Leo never cared one bit about what flies out of his mouth or expressions morph his features. Lucky.

"Just kind of started as an inside joke and stuck," he responds. "We were tight."

"So tight that you decided to ditch her wake?" I ask, icicles in my tone. I stuff my piece of the map back into the tube and keep walking.

His mouth opens, searching for words. "I . . . that's not what I wanted," he settles on, following me. "I wanted to go. It's just . . . it's dumb, but a family thing got in the way."

I narrow my eyes. "A family thing?"

He rubs the back of his neck. I've never seen him so uncomfortable. Usually, he's all too happy to be showered with attention at school. But right now, he looks ready to squirm out of his skin. "My parents knew my nonna would be there, so they made me stay home and waited until the end to go. We're kind of in a family rift at the moment."

"With *Nonna*?" I ask incredulously.

He nods slowly. I guess that makes sense, given I've never seen him at the deli within the past year or so.

"But she's the nicest woman ever."

"To you."

I detect bitterness in his tone, but we're not friends, so I don't press it. I try to dodge him, but with a single step, he blocks my path again. "We should find the people with the two other pieces, right? Can you think of anyone?"

The most obvious person flashes in my mind. There is no word in the English vocabulary to describe the monumental sigh building inside me. Dread crawls beneath my skin, itchy and ever an annoyance. Just like the only person I can think of who might have one of the remaining pieces.

I groan at the sky. The stars have fled, and so has my pride when I say, "Daisy."

7

I don't know if I want to be right or wrong about Daisy having a piece of the map.

"We'll have to sneak in while she's still asleep," I tell Leo as we pass the street where I used to live before our house was taken by the bank after Dad died. Being in the same neighborhood, with its sprawling lots and glistening mowed lawns, sends a stab of nostalgia through me. "She'd never just hand Gram's letter over to me."

"No?" he asks, genuine curiosity in his voice.

I shoot him a look, because he of all people should know how Daisy feels about me. He's her best friend.

I used to be her best friend.

"Highly unlikely."

He shrugs. "Well, good thing we won't need to worry about running into her."

I stop as my cousin's home—and mine, for now—comes into view. "What?"

"She's not home." Leo keeps walking, sticking to the trees toward the edge of the yard.

I jog to catch up to him. "Where is she?"

"Promise not to snitch?"

"You're kidding me."

He turns to face me, eyes earnest in the waning moonlight. "You've gotta promise."

"Fine." I roll my eyes. "I will keep whatever dirty secret my cousin is hiding. Promise."

"She sneaks out most nights to see Kev. They've got a thing. She sent a snap from his place twenty minutes ago and posted a TikTok."

"Kev Asani?" I wrinkle my nose at the mention of Leo's hockey teammate and fellow jock.

He nods.

"Why is she posting TikToks at four in the morning?"

"Great time for the algorithm. Plus, Daze gives her followers a lot of updates. All of them are pretty obsessed with Rosetown and your family. Especially now."

I roll my eyes so hard at the use of her nickname that even he isn't oblivious enough to miss it. "Her name is *Daisy*."

He gives me a sidelong glance. "You jealous I have a nickname for her and not you?"

I turn to him with a denial on my lips, but he holds a hand up.

"No problem. I'm the king of nicknames. You can be Lily Rose."

I bark out a laugh that's entirely too loud against the still morning air. "Lily Rose? That's literally my name."

"Your name is Lily Rose*wood*, and you don't let anyone forget it. Ever. So, your wood is revoked."

I sputter, making a similar sound to the water squelching out of my shoes. "Is that, like, an innuendo or something?"

"Not one bit."

"You're so weird, and that wasn't an invitation for a nickname," is all I can muster as we approach the front door. I dig the key out from beneath the mat and unlock it.

"You snuck out through the front door?" Leo asks incredulously.

"Opposed to?"

"Back door. Side door. Your window."

"Sorry, apparently I don't have as much experience sneaking out as you do." Despite the coating of sarcasm, the statement makes my cheeks flush. As if not sneaking out is admitting I lack something.

"Apparently." He grins coyly as we step inside. I shut the door softly behind us and gesture to the stairs. His voice drops to a whisper. "I don't know if you remember, but my room is prime. Window is over the porch, which is next to a big tree. It makes sneaking out so easy, it's basically an invitation."

I do remember, but I don't want him to know I've given him a scrap of brain space the past four years. Instead, I press my finger to my lips as we reach the second floor, glancing at the closed door to my uncle's room. I slowly turn the knob to Daisy's, stepping in.

Her room is princess style, a big window seat against the far wall that overlooks the sprawling backyard and a ridiculous canopy bed with netting over it.

And somebody sleeping in it, red hair splayed across the pillow.

I grab Leo's damp shirt, pulling him toward the door. "I thought you said she was out!"

He brushes me off and walks toward the bed, pulling back the pink comforter. I swallow a scream. There's a literal mannequin stuffed beneath the sheets with a wig. He pokes the hair. "Good match, right? Daze and I had to go all the way to Boston to pick it up."

"I take back what I said outside. You're *both* so weird."

His responding grin is luminous.

"Help me look for the letter. Where would she hide it?" I ask, sifting through the multiple perfume bottles and hair products on her dresser. There's Polaroids with friends and a picture of her and Quinn in a frame near the back. They both grin, a look that's rare on Quinn's usually impassive face. It'd be a nice picture, except the glass is cracked—shattered, really—as if it's been thrown against the wall a few times.

"It's not over here," Leo says, rummaging through the drawer of her nightstand. "You know, maybe we should wait for her. Feels wrong to be digging through her things."

I start opening drawers. "You'll sneak onto forbidden property, but you draw the line at a room search?"

"When it's going through my friend's stuff, yeah."

The second drawer of Daisy's pink Pottery Barn dresser hosts her underwear. After shoving aside a few thongs, I find what I'm looking for. I tug it free and hold it up, turning to Leo. "Well, it's your lucky day. Here it is."

Despite his morality act, he comes over to watch me open the letter and pull the paper out. Unlike mine, Daisy's isn't blank.

From what I can tell in the dim light of the room, it's not activated invisible ink, either. Just regular black ink.

I scan the words, starting with *Dear Daisydew,* and I'm surprised at the bright spark of jealousy that ignites in my gut. Gram hasn't called Daisy that in ages, at least that I know of. I brace myself for the rest of it.

You've always shined brightly, and I have no doubt your many talents will lead you to exquisite ends. Remember to trust your heart over your head; it'll get you further and give you relationships that are truer. You're a force to be reckoned with, like all strong Rosewoods are. Always use that force for good.

And take care of the White Rose for me. Don't be afraid to give someone in need a ride.

You have my heart,
Gram

I scan the letter two more times, flipping the page to search the back. But there's no smudge or indication Gram might have used invisible ink. No hidden clue.

"She's probably going to be back soon," Leo glances uneasily toward the window.

This might be my only shot with it, so I need to be absolutely sure I'm not missing anything. Using the end of one of my damp braids, I drag it across the page like a paintbrush, leaving a wet streak. I wait for words to appear.

None do. With a sigh, I stuff it back into her underwear

drawer, thankful that Daisy isn't neat, since I don't remember how the drawer looked when I opened it. "Total bust."

"My house isn't far from here," Leo says, stretching so his hoodie rides up a little bit, exposing a thin stretch of skin between the waistband of his athletic shorts and the hem; I avert my gaze. "I could grab car keys and we could drive around town to keep looking?"

"Keep looking where? There's no one else to ask."

"There're two pieces left, so obviously there is. Anyone else you can think of?"

I squeeze my eyes closed, a flash of platinum hair and red lips. "Yes," I whisper. "But I really, really don't want to entertain it."

"Who?"

If I thought I didn't want Daisy to have a map piece, then I *really* don't want Ell to. "Ell Claremon," I force out. "Chief's daughter. She's been in London for school, but she's back. She's spent a lot of time talking to Gram and was even looking for her the night of the party."

"Right, I remember her." He looks doubtful. "I don't know. Anyone else?"

Frustrated tears prick at my eyes, exhaustion sinking into my bones. I feel betrayed by Gram in an entirely new way that has nothing to do with the inheritance or the map. It's like she didn't think I'd need time to grieve. Sure, the letter felt like an exciting distraction at first, but now that it led me to a boy I never thought I'd speak to again and apparently two other randos who I have yet to find, it's lost its charm. As if I feel like scouring the town looking for *clues*.

I want to go home and crawl into bed. *My* bed at the manor, beneath my down duvet and a thousand pillows. I want to get away from Leo and his questions and his familiarity and just be *alone.* I want to sleep for forever and a day and, when I finally do wake up, discover that none of this has happened. Find myself at Gram's birthday party last year, laughing as Dad twirls me around the room.

I want to go back to before everything changed.

"So, I was thinking." Leo steps over a literal pile of clothes to sit on Daisy's bed.

I don't bother forcing interest in my tone, my voice flat. "About?"

"If we can't move forward without the rest of the map, and we don't know where that is, then there should be one person who does."

"And who is that?"

He stops, shrugging like the answer is obvious. "Gram."

A current of anger rushes through me. "Well, maybe if she wasn't fucking *dead* that'd be helpful."

He looks at me in alarm. "Whoa, chill. I don't mean we do some séance shit, I mean we go back to the manor."

I barely have the mind to keep my voice low before Uncle Arbor hears us. I reached the end of my patience, like, hours ago. "Oh, you mean go back to the manor that we're both currently *banned* from? That we almost got caught at less than an hour ago? That's a great idea, let's just waltz right in."

"Do you have a better plan?" he asks. And what's annoying is it's not even *mean.* It's a genuine question, one that I can't answer because no, I do not have a better plan. He sees it written all over my face. "We can't do nothing."

"I just—" I am so close to crying. One misplaced step and I'll be a sobbing mess in front of the last person I want to cry before. "You don't get how hard this is—"

"This is hard for me, too," he defends himself. "I get it, she was your grandmother. And yeah, I only took care of her yard for a couple months. The thing is, my nonna might still be alive, but it's like I lost her. We haven't talked in months. So Gram kind of filled the gap for me." When he looks at me, there's pain in his eyes. "Plus, I get the feeling that if I was anybody else, you wouldn't be making this so difficult."

"What's *that* supposed to mean?"

"You've been cold to me all morning. We used to be, like, friends. Ish. I don't know what this map even leads to, but Gram obviously wants us to work together. We need to at least keep trying to find the other pieces."

My jaw must be on the floor. "I'm not being cold. But you're—"

I cut myself off, choking on all the words I want to say. My problem with Leo is a wound that shouldn't still hurt after all this time. Especially when he's looking at me like he isn't the reason for it.

"I'm what?" he asks.

Bringing it up is a wave of emotions I'll drown under, so I take the easy route. "We're just different," I say hotly. "We grew up. Got to high school and you and Daisy formed your pack, without me, so I found a new one. Whatever."

"And where's your new one? Because last I saw, those AP asses you used to hang out with ditched you."

"At least I'm not a follower," I bite back to hide the burn of humiliation that other people noticed the change in my friendship status this year.

"I'm not a follower." But his voice wavers like he's unsure.

I scoff. "Yes, you are. I haven't forgotten—"

A scratching by the window makes us both jump. "She's back," I say, heart in my throat. I step toward her door, but it's in the sight of the window. Leo pulls me toward the wall instead, pressing us against the cool surface and behind the curtains of her other window. In daylight, it'd be a dead giveaway, but the first rays of dawn haven't slipped in yet.

I try to ignore the rise and fall of his chest beside me. Behind the semi-sheer curtain, I have the perfect view of a silhouette opening the window and stepping onto the seat, then the floor. The top of her head bobs with a small bun, and she wears black Vans. I didn't even know she owned Vans.

Leo's breath catches beside me, and I nudge him to keep quiet. Daisy's movements are weird—sneaky and stilted. She trips over one of the colossal piles of clothes, a muffled grunt escaping. It's not until she's reaching for the bed and shaking the mannequin that it hits me.

This isn't Daisy.

The intruder's back is to us, but I know what's about to happen as the blankets fall away and the creepy mannequin in revealed. I burst from behind the curtain and ram into their back, slapping my hand over their mouth to staunch the oncoming scream.

Their elbow slams into my rib cage, reflexes lightning fast. Breath shoots out of me, and I double over. The next thing I know, I'm getting slammed against the opposite wall in a whirl of limbs.

Something cold presses to my throat.

8

The light flips on, first illuminating Leo beside Daisy's bedside lamp, then the person caging me in with a knife to my throat.

Yeah. A *knife*.

"Quinn?!"

Leo's shocked whisper is loud in the silence. But he's not wrong. Quinn Zhao releases her grip on me, lowering the knife, though not all the way as she takes a step back. My fingers fly to my throat. "What the fu—"

"What the fuck are you doing here?" she steals my words, dark eyes angry. She waves the knife, which I now see is a switchblade barely the length of her thumb. Realizing Leo's behind her, she spins, pointing it haphazardly at him. Her eyes flash. "What are *you* doing here? You better not be—"

"Relax, I'm here on business," Leo says, raising his hands. "That seems to be the question of the night. Care to share what *you're* doing here?"

"Not with you," Quinn bites out.

"Why do you have a knife? You could have killed me!" I run to Daisy's full-length mirror on her closet door, making sure it didn't nick me.

"I just skated on my board over five miles across town in the middle of the night. I wasn't going to come unarmed." She slips the tiny knife into the midnight-black hair of her bun, confirming the rumor I'd heard of the hidden weapon. She gives Leo a pointed look. "I'm also here on business. Daisy owes me a conversation."

The night of the party looms in my mind, Quinn banging on Daisy's window. *You said we would talk*, she yelled.

"What kind of business?" I ask, forcing as much authority into my voice as possible. My eyes dart toward the door, praying Uncle Arbor didn't hear the commotion.

"None now," Quinn says, a layer of defeat to her hard voice. She turns to Leo. "So it's true, then? She's hooking up with Kev?"

She means Daisy, whose room we really should get out of before she comes back.

Leo shifts. "What's it to you? You two haven't talked in months."

Quinn scoffs. "That was *before* I found out she was having a fling with the world's biggest douchebag." She turns to me, and her expression changes, one eyebrow lifting. "You're not the Rosewood I was looking for tonight, but I need to talk to you, too."

"Me?" I can't keep the surprise from my voice. I don't think we've ever talked. All I know about her are bits that ghosted throughout the halls of school. She was born in Shanghai, where her mom left her dad so the two of them could move all over the world while she was a party planner for extravagant weddings. They finally settled in Rosetown two years ago, when her mom bought the Ivy. Quinn barely has any accent despite her travels, as if she purposefully doesn't want people to know where she's been. Being the cool well-traveled new kid to enter Rosetown High meant she was immediately scooped up by Daisy's group. Last year, Quinn and Daisy were practically inseparable. I started disliking Quinn by association.

But at some point, around Christmas, *something* happened between them. I don't know what it was, although there were plenty of rumors to choose from, but Quinn went from hanging out with Daisy and Leo every waking moment to practically disappearing.

Even now, I can feel the tension boiling between her and Leo. It's a welcome distraction from my own with him.

She wears black baggy pants that cinch around the ankles with pockets all over them. She pulls something from one pocket on her thigh and holds it out to me. I take it, unfolding the piece of paper, the scrawl unmistakable. I read it out loud.

Dear Quinn,

Don't forget that the world is so much more vast than we could ever know. If you need a reminder, go to the end of the port where the railing ends and nothing stands between you and the sea. The waves against the rocks might teach you a thing or two.

When your lesson is learned, find Lily.
Gram

"Where did you get this letter?" I ask Quinn, pacing Daisy's room.

"It was in my mailbox today, and then I found this wedged between some of the rocks at the harbor in a plastic tube an hour ago." From a different pocket, she pulls something out and places it on Daisy's bed. It's what Leo and I came here for in hopes Daisy had it.

Another piece of the map.

"Southeast part of town," Leo points out, pulling Daisy's covers up to conceal the mannequin and wig so it stops staring at us. From his pocket, he takes his own piece and adds it, then motions for me to give mine. With them all together, it's almost complete. "Still no *X*."

"*X*?" Quinn asks. "You think this is a treasure map?"

"No idea," I mutter. I glance up at Quinn. She wears a ripped tee that advertises a band I don't recognize, screamo from the looks of it, and beat-up Vans with neon green laces. Along with the pants, it's a god-awful outfit, and yet somehow still looks good on her. Her RBF is ever in place. Despite the photo on the dresser depicting her grinning, I can't imagine the expression on her face now.

"You wanna take a picture?" she asks, calling out my stare.

"Thinking about it," I reply. "No offense, but I don't get why Gram gave *you* a piece of the map."

Leo makes a shred of sense. He had some kind of relationship with Gram, and just because I never understood it doesn't make it less real. But Quinn never knew Gram, at least to my knowledge.

"There must be a reason," Leo says to her. "You still work for your mom, right? At the Ivy?"

Quinn's nostrils flare. "What about it?"

Leo is either actually oblivious or chooses to ignore the bite in her tone. "I know Gram went to a bunch of events there. At any point did you guys talk?"

Quinn narrows her eyes, looking ready to lunge across the bed to wring his neck. I spearhead the conversation before she can attack.

"I don't know what's going on or what this map means, but we need to figure out a pattern. There's obviously one last person with a piece, so we have to find them. If they don't find us first, that is." I begin pacing again. It used to annoy Dad, but I can't help it. Sitting still isn't my specialty. "My connection with Gram is obvious. Leo's—kind of. But I don't know yours unless you tell us."

She averts her gaze from mine and lands on the shattered picture frame. In two quick strides, she rips it off the dresser, staring down at the photo. I try a different approach.

"I know you were looking for Daisy tonight, but you must have known I was here, too. I've heard the news got out that I'm banned from the manor. Were you planning to follow Gram's note to find me next?"

Her eyes flick up, an espresso brown that's softer than the rest of her. "I don't know. I thought maybe I'd ask Daisy first. See what she knew. Coming straight to you seemed like a bad idea since I know how much she hates you. Figured she'd be mad." Quinn's gaze goes frigid as she glances at Leo. "But now that I know it's true about her and Kev, I hope she's furious."

I know my cousin doesn't like me, but hearing Quinn say it out loud makes a piece of my heart hurt that I thought I had buried years ago.

"I've never really known you apart from what Daisy's said," Quinn tells me, putting the photo back. "Maybe I also wanted to see what the great Lily Rosewood is all about."

"Not so great at the moment," I reply honestly, leaning against the dresser. I'm exhausted, something I'm sure is evident in my face and posture, which is usually ramrod straight. But right now, it's all I can do not to fold into myself and shrink. "I'd be a little better if I could figure out Gram's motive for looping you into whatever this is."

Quinn's silent, eyes latched on to the photo while Leo and I share a look.

Don't say anything, I stress with my gaze. She obviously doesn't want to hear from him.

Finally, Quinn sighs, turning away from the picture. "Last year, at the annual Hyacinth Ball that takes place the last Friday of June at the Ivy, my mom was being a lot," she says. "She always gets intense that night since all the Rosetown richies show up. She bitched me out in the kitchen for not refilling water glasses quick enough, so I got mad and went outside. The harbor isn't far from the property, and whenever I want a break, I stand at the edge of it. There's only one streetlight, and the boardwalk just kind of drops off near the rocks, so nothing is at the end except for the water."

She takes a deep breath like she can't believe she's telling us this. I keep my mouth shut, waiting for her to continue.

"I didn't think I was followed, but your grandma came up behind me. Scared the hell out of me and almost earned an elbow to the face for it. I thought she was going to yell at me for ditching. But instead, we just . . ." A strange, melancholy look passes Quinn's face before she tugs her walls back up. "Talked. My mom always had shit to say about her, probably just jealous about all her money. Especially lately, since my mom lost a lot from the investment shit that went down last year."

Heat flares up my neck at the mention, but Quinn keeps going, paying me no mind.

"I think Mom hoped your grandmother would invest her own money to help renovate the second ballroom, but that obviously didn't happen. So, I guess I always assumed she was just a rich bitchy old lady, you know? But she was actually pretty nice. And funny, too." A grin flickers across her face. "I think she hated being at that party almost as much as I did."

"Was that the only time you ever talked to her?" I ask.

"Pretty much. I had mentioned that Rosetown felt suffocating, that I didn't think I'd ever get out. She said sometimes she felt the same."

It's strange to imagine Quinn and Gram standing at the end of the boardwalk together talking about life and the great unknown. I didn't think Gram ever felt suffocated by Rosetown. Hearing that hurts. I wish she would have shared it with me instead of Quinn.

Leo's thick brows form a concentrated V as he stares at the map.

"What is it?" I ask.

"What if Gram pulled us together because of something related to the missing inheritance?" He gestures at himself. "I like . . . really need money. Ever since the Ice Plex went under and my dad also lost money with investments, my family's been in serious debt. Plus, my three sisters all got married in the span of like, two years, which didn't help. I had kind of mentioned it to Gram, just randomly, not looking for a handout or anything."

He takes a deep breath, and the fact that he has the guts to share this waters a little seed of respect. Though I'd never say it out loud, it's a relief to know I'm not the only one with a messed-up money situation.

"I told Gram I wasn't sure if I'd be going to college," he says, not looking at either of us. "My parents didn't set aside money because we all thought I'd get a full-ride hockey scholarship. But I didn't get recruited, and my grades kind of bombed, and . . . yeah."

He doesn't blush, but I can tell the admission is uncomfortable. In school, he seems so unbothered. For months, I've overheard him laughing on Monday mornings about the weekend parties he and his friends got trashed at. He grins when tests riddled with red ink get plopped down in front of him, as if getting terrible grades was an award in itself. I never thought maybe it hit him harder than he let on.

"I may have mentioned the college thing, too," Quinn says stiffly. "My mom put everything she has into the Ivy. Any time I try to talk about college, she gets pissed. She expects me to stay here forever with her, but I want out. I'll never afford college, especially since my dad is MIA." She looks at Leo. A little bit of her hatred seems to peel back. "Guess that makes two of us in the severely underfunded higher education club."

"Three," I breathe. They turn to me, shock etched into their expressions. "I also have a complicated money situation. Gram has been pushing me to look at business schools, even though I want to go to the Fashion Institute of Technology. At this rate, neither is looking too good at the moment."

"How?" Leo says. "You're a Rosewood. Even without the inheritance—"

"It's complicated," I repeat.

Leo looks at me like he's actually seeing me for the first time in years.

It's like being naked. I hate it.

"So that's what we all have in common, then," he says. "We're broke."

"But why would Mrs. Rosewood help *us*?" Quinn gestures between herself and Leo. "Just because I vented to her once and you pulled her weeds doesn't make us shining candidates for . . . whatever this is."

I peer between the two of them, trying to see what Gram saw. Two teens with their futures up in the air. "Gram always had a strategy," I say, trying to work through it. "She didn't talk about her mom, my great-grandmother, very often. But I know that despite always having the manor, for a while when Gram was young, our family wasn't doing very well financially because Petunia was poorly managing Rosewood Inc. after Hyacinth died. We were losing tons of money. It's why Gram started working at the company so young. She never—"

I cut myself off, a realization slamming into me. Suddenly it makes so much sense why Gram has been pushing me to go to school for business.

"Never what?" Leo asks.

"She never got to go to college."

Silence falls like a blanket. My stomach twists with guilt. I thought she wanted me to go to business school so I could be just like her. But maybe it was so I could be even better and get the education she never had.

"If this really is a . . . treasure map." Quinn makes a face. "Do you think it might lead to money for college? If that's the one thing we all share and something she'd want for us since she didn't get it, that makes sense, doesn't it?"

"I suppose," I reply. "Gram could have set some of the fortune aside for us specifically to use for school."

"So the other map holder is probably in the same situation, right?" Leo asks.

Quinn rolls her eyes. "Great, that narrows down our search to pretty much the entire senior class."

"Maybe not," I say suddenly, the realization hitting me like a ton of bricks. I can't believe I didn't think of him before. "I think the fourth person is Miles Miller."

"Yearbook kid?" Quinn asks, at the same time Leo says, "Who?"

I roll my eyes at Leo. "He works at the deli with me. He was supposed to go to college for animation in the fall, but he had to push it back a year to save up. He's a year older than us, but Gram

96

knows he's my friend. The night of the party, she even said she likes him, so maybe that was a clue or something. I'm sure he's coming to the funeral today, so I can ask him then."

Quinn groans. "We have to wait until then? I want to start looking now."

"Can't," Leo says, grabbing his map piece and making his way toward the still-open window.

Quinn takes hers and the letter, stuffing them back in her pockets.

"I've gotta get home," Leo continues. "I'm technically grounded, so if I'm not in bed before my mom's up, she's gonna freak."

"What'd you do this time?"

"My parents are mad I got so drunk at the party and passed out there. Woke up hours later behind the toolshed and walked myself home at three in the morning. Oops."

"Then we'll meet back up at the funeral with Miles," I say. I look pointedly at Leo. "Speaking of, will you actually be there, or will you need to skip because of a *family thing*?"

"I'll make sure I'm there," he assures, one foot out the window. He moves to climb out but smacks his head on the top of the pane so hard I wince, a loud swear spilling from his lips.

Too loud.

We stare at each other with wide eyes. The creak of a door followed by footsteps sound down the hall. Uncle Arbor's. Quinn nearly shoves Leo the rest of the way out the window and onto the porch roof, following him out. I start after them, but I know my own window is locked.

I'm screwed.

But that doesn't mean they are. As Quinn slips out, I close the window behind her and snag my piece of map from the bed, stuffing it into the waistband of my leggings and tugging my shirt over it as Uncle Arbor knocks, then opens the door.

"Lily?" he says in surprise, blinking. He's disheveled and still in sleep pants and a T-shirt. "Did you hear that bang? Where's Daisy?"

I open my mouth, unsure of what will come out. I've never lied to him before because I never had to. At least I'm mostly dry now, and aside from my shoes, my outfit could pass for pajamas. I just need an excuse, and stat.

"Oh, morning, Dad. I see none of us could sleep," Daisy says, appearing behind Uncle Arbor. I clamp my jaw shut as she yawns, sauntering into the room in a pair of cotton shorts and a tank top, barefoot as if she just woke up. She sips from a glass of water. "I was so thirsty I had to run downstairs for a drink before we got to work."

Uncle Arbor's gaze follows her as she sits on her bed, purposefully in front of the lump that is the mannequin beneath the covers. "Got to work?" he asks, mimicking my silent question.

"Mm-hmm." Daisy takes another casual sip. "Lily woke up kind of freaked this morning since she wasn't allowed to grab an outfit from the manor for the funeral. I said we can go through my closet, and she can alter one of mine."

"Really?" he asks, like he can't quite believe that I'd ask for help from Daisy and she'd give it. I don't blame him, because I wouldn't. But now that she mentions it, I do need an outfit.

"I mean, she didn't ask, but I heard her crying through the walls, so I offered."

Uncle Arbor turns to me, eyes soft. "Lily, I'm so sorry. I didn't even think about that."

Daisy smirks from over his shoulder. Of course she had to lay it on extra thick. Now, so do I.

I sniffle. "Me either. But I couldn't sleep. And Daisy came in offering for me to take *anything* from her closet. I have to make some alterations because she's a couple sizes smaller, but I should have enough time to finish before the funeral if I start now. Daisy, do you still have the sewing machine that Gram gave you?"

A muscle twitches in Daisy's jaw at my emphasis on *anything*. When her dad turns to look at her, she covers with a smile. "Yeah, it's in the basement. I'm sure it still works."

"Thanks." I walk over to her closet, sifting through the clothes. I can't believe she saved my ass by sneaking in downstairs just in time. I hope she didn't see Leo and Quinn on the roof leaving.

"I'm really happy you girls are getting along," Uncle Arbor says. "If there's anything good from this, I hope it's that you two put aside your differences."

Neither Daisy nor I say anything. Some things aren't worth lying about, because they'll never happen.

Instead, I pluck a dark green corduroy skirt from the rack and a black long-sleeve blouse. "I think I can make these work. Is that okay?"

Daisy's eyes bug. I know she loves this skirt, and once I let it out, it will be too big. But Uncle Arbor looks at her for confirmation, and she forces a smile. "Sure."

Uncle Arbor strides toward the door, content. "I'll grab the sewing machine from the basement and put it on the desk in your room, Lily. And girls, don't forget to write your eulogies."

He leaves, and I sigh in relief, clutching the clothes to my chest. It turns into a yelp as Daisy's suddenly behind me, tugging one of my braids so hard my head jerks back. "If I *ever* find you in my room again when I'm not here," she snarls in my ear. "You *will* regret it."

I'm pushed into the hall, and her door slams shut behind me. Caring cousin act *over*.

9

The worst part of funerals are the eulogies.

Gram's is no different. I pass Daisy on my way to the altar. She talked about eating lovecakes with Gram, a memory the two of us used to share. She didn't mention me.

By the time I get to the podium of Saint Theresa Church, I have to grip the stone sides to stop my hands from shaking. A sea of people stare back at me, their faces blurring together into one foreboding blob. The last time I saw most of the townspeople all together at once, I was coated in frosting. And even before that, I've tried to steer clear of most of them, aside from deli visitors and the wake yesterday. Since Dad died, I can't help but feel guilty for whatever financial hits they've taken. Yet beneath the guilt is a layer of anger. I understand that those who listened to Dad's advice were mad. Devastated, even, by what they lost. But most of them never came to the funeral, despite always being friendly with him up until then.

The final emotion is sadness. Sad that Dad isn't here, and now, neither is Gram. I blink away the tears, clearing my throat. This morning, I scribbled some words on a piece of paper. But I know the story I want to tell by heart, so the paper stays in the pocket of my newly altered skirt. I picked it because green, the color of ivy specifically, was Gram's favorite color.

"Hi," I say, then internally cringe because *hi* feels so disastrously casual. I clear my throat again. "As most of you know, I've lived with my grandmother for the past year. Well, almost a year. We've always been close, but living with her gave me a deeper appreciation for everything she does. Everything she is." I force air into my lungs, trying to find a place for my eyes to land. When I can't settle, I look at her casket before the altar, a white cloth lain over it embroidered with gold irises.

"One of my earliest memories is of the factory. When I was little, my dad would bring me there because that's where she always was. One day, I was upset because we were doing a school play and I got my costume. It was too small." The admission makes my cheeks flush. "Gram could tell something was up when we came to see her. As a six-year-old, I probably wasn't good at hiding it."

A few chuckles escape from the pews. I take a deep breath and keep going.

"She took me to one of the worktables. I gave her the costume, which was super ugly, by the way. I think I was a tree."

More laughs. Okay, maybe I can get through this.

"She sat me on her lap and gave me a needle and thread. Cut the seams and found fabric to match. And then she taught me how to stitch.

"My dad wasn't happy I was holding a needle when I wasn't even allowed to cut my own food yet, but Gram didn't take it away. I pricked my finger, it bled, and she just told me to try again. So, I did." I can still picture Gram, hair gleaming red, dimples in her cheeks. Green eyes stern yet encouraging. This time, I laugh, all breath. "The stitch job was horrendous. But it was mostly mine. I tried it on, and it fit pretty well. I'll never forget how she looked at me."

The words are so tight in my throat, I have to squeeze them out like the final drops of toothpaste. "She was so proud, her eyes had gone all misty. I swear, it's one of the only times I've seen her tear up." The other time was when Dad died. "It made me feel so special. Like I was . . ." I trail off, reaching for the right word. "Rare."

This time when I look up, everything's clear. I swallow down the lump. "Since then, all I've ever wanted was to keep making Gram proud, so she would always see me like she did that day. I'll just—" Words stick in my throat. I don't know how to end this. "I'll miss her so much."

I step back from the podium, making my way to my seat in the resounding silence. This morning while altering the skirt, I felt closer to Gram. As if I was still that little girl who first was taught to stitch, all shaking hands and needle-pricked fingers.

Now, I feel hollow, like if someone pokes me too hard, I'll shatter into a million pieces on the stone floor.

I zone out for the rest of mass, instead staring at the massive crucifix that would definitely crush anyone under it should it fall. It feels like hours pass before we're finally rising, Father Martinez informing everyone the reception will take place in the rectory of the church.

The reception *should* take place at Rosewood Manor. I'm

sure there's been a plot dug up in the graveyard beside Dad, and everyone would gather around and leave roses on Gram's casket as she was lowered into the ground. Then we'd congregate in the great room for refreshments. That's how Dad's funeral went. But since everyone is banned from the manor, we had to make last-minute accommodations.

As I walk to the rectory now, the towering stained glass windows throw rainbow light across everyone's skin, dousing the room in Technicolor. It makes it harder to tell people apart, although I see Quinn standing stiffly beside her mother. I scan for Leo, not surprised to spot him with his usual crew, all hovering around Daisy.

Now to find Miles.

"Lily, I am so, so sorry."

I'm barely two steps into the rectory when I look up to see Ell in front of me, her eyes soft and sad. Like at the party, my first instinct is to bristle, but I know it's not fair. She lost someone, too.

"Iris really was like a grandmother to me, teaching me everything there was to know about Rosewood Inc. I'm so sorry. Really, Lily. This is just—" She takes a deep, shuddering breath. "Awful."

Seeing her like this makes the green monster in my chest crawl back inside its cavern. I was always so jealous that Gram spent time mentoring Ell this past year instead of me. But now, what does it matter? Everything's wrong, the fortune is missing, and who knows what will happen to Rosewood Inc.? Plus, she really does look as devastated as I feel. Her eyes are bloodshot, and her

French manicure nails are bitten down so some don't even have any white left.

To both of our surprise, I reach out and squeeze her hand. "I know," I say. "You've worked really hard at Rosewood Inc. Gram's always been thankful for that. So am I."

"Thank you. I love this company. It's an honor to be an employee." She returns a watery smile, squeezing my hand back. "And Lily, I just want you to know—"

"Oh!" I interrupt, catching sight of a familiar blond head of hair. "I'm sorry, can we continue this in a few? I'll be right back."

Ell nods, pulling a tissue from her Hermès bag to press beneath her eyes as I weave past her. Tight smiles of sympathy flash my way with each step until I finally get to the person I've been looking for.

"Miles!" I grab his arm. His parents and little sister are in the food line with him, but he steps out to wrap me in a hug.

"Lily, oh my God, I'm so sorry."

"It's okay," I say, even though I'm certain nothing will ever be okay again. But figuring out this map situation might be a start. I rest my cheek on his shoulder, my walls cracking.

The rectory is already crowded, not big enough to fit practically the entire town. "Can we go in the hall? I need a breather."

"For sure." He holds my hand and tugs me past the double doors and into the hallway we entered through. It's quieter here, the din of voices just out of reach. "I can't imagine what the past week has been like for you."

"You have no idea." I recall my early-morning dunk with Leo in the pool.

"I know how close you were with your gram. And all this stuff with the missing money . . . That really sucks."

"Big time." My next words are careful and quiet. "Except, I don't think it's missing. At least not all of it."

Miles's blond brows shoot up. "That's ominous."

"I don't know what's going on, but some people have come forward saying they've received letters from Gram." Even though he's my friend, I've had friends turn on me before. I hate that despite trusting him, I can't force out the words to ask him point-blank.

"Huh, that's kind of strange. Do you think it could have something to do with the missing money?"

Hm. Not the answer I'd expect from someone who I thought was one of the recipients of the letter. "I don't know," I admit. "It's all very . . . new so far."

As if sensing my disappointment, he squeezes my hand. "I'd tell you if I got anything, you know," he says. "Even if like, Gram for some reason had sent me a note about . . . I don't even know—my subpar salami-slicing technique."

A smile tugs at my lips.

He returns it with his own easy grin. "You'd be the first to know."

"Well, if you did, I'd say it's about time someone called you out for that. You always slice it too thick," I tease, swallowing down the panic that if Miles doesn't have the fourth piece, who does?

But there's a little bit of relief there. Miles is my friend, and therefore, someone I don't want to lose. And when hunting down money, things can go south fast. I don't want to risk our friendship over whatever Gram has in mind.

It's different with Leo and Quinn. We're nothing to each other. Not enemies, but certainly not friends. Some gray area in the middle.

He opens his arms for another hug, and I greedily accept, relishing the feel of his hands rubbing circles on my back. For this one moment, I'll let myself just *be*. Be tired. Be sad. Be hopeless. Everything I've been bottling up this whole damn day.

Too soon, he's pulling back, nodding toward the closed doors and the flurry of people on the other side. "You ready to go back in?"

"You go," I say. "I just need a couple seconds alone."

Miles nods. "Whatever you need, I've got you." He flashes one last smile over his shoulder before leaving me.

Tears burn in my eyes, boiling hot. I fall into a crouch, my elbows digging into my bare thighs as my skirt rides up. If anybody were to walk out and see me, I'd look unhinged, but I don't care. How much longer can I fake it before I crumble? If Gram wanted to leave me a message or money or *whatever*, she didn't have to make it so *hard*.

Get it together. One breath in, one breath out. I stand suddenly, pushing my hair away from my face and blinking my tears away. Only to realize, I'm not alone.

Someone's watching me.

"Hello?" I call out to the guy standing in the shadows at the other end of the hall. Upon realizing he has my attention, he starts retreating farther away, toward where the choir rehearses. Following him seems like a bad idea.

I do it anyway.

He disappears around a corner, not quite running but moving too quickly to look casual. I speed up, my flats sliding across the worn carpet thanks to their terrible traction. I gain sight of him again as I round the bend. Dressed in a baggy maroon hoodie with the hood pulled over his head and khakis, it's not exactly the outfit of a funeral goer.

When he slips down another turn, I start running. "Hey! Can you wait a second? *Stop!*"

The emergency exit doors are up ahead. He hesitates, then bursts through them.

The fire alarm immediately goes off.

The sound makes him stumble. That's all the time I need to crash into him, sending us both tumbling onto the unforgiving pavement of the parking lot. He groans, rolling onto his back, and I take the opportunity to scramble on top of him to pin him to the ground.

"Wait!" I yell, as if he has a choice now. His hood falls back, revealing his face. Wide, anxious brown eyes behind skewed, square black glasses.

I suck in a breath, and he uses my surprise to squirm out from under me, teetering to his feet. The alarm still blares. Any moment, someone's going to come out. I stand, my mouth open but no sound escaping.

"You could have broken my arm!" Caleb from Creekson—the boy I dared Miles to talk to at Gram's party—exclaims, holding the appendage to his side and pushing up the sleeve. "I'm *bleeding.*"

I stare at the thin stream of blood running down his forearm from road rash. "Are you—" My mouth is as dry as the pavement that scraped my knees. "Are you here for Miles?"

His eyes go impossibly wider. "You know Miles?"

I open my mouth to respond, but he shakes his head.

"Never mind, doesn't matter. No, I'm not here for him. I'm here for you."

"Me?" My voice gets lost in the ring of the alarm.

He nods, wiggling his hurt arm and flexing his fingers. "You're Lily, right?"

Dumbly, I nod.

He brushes himself off. "Did you have to *tackle me*?"

"Did you have to creepily lure me out?"

He scowls. "I didn't want anyone to see us or follow you. And I hoped the alarm wouldn't go off." He glances toward the church nervously. He has honest eyes—I remember thinking so at the party. From his hoodie pocket, he pulls an envelope. "I don't want to be involved."

He forces it into my hands. Rough cardstock, overwhelmingly familiar. Before I can say anything, words tumble from his mouth, tripping over each other and sounding even more jumbled thanks to the siren. "Take it. It should be yours. I just came here to give it to you."

"What—"

"The three flowers," he says quickly, gaze darting over my shoulder.

Voices. Somebody's coming.

"It's a painting at the Rosetown Museum of Fine Art, third floor. Just trust me, okay? That's what she meant. I know it."

I have a million questions, but only one makes it past my lips. "How did you know her?"

"Lily?" Uncle Arbor.

I turn just in time to see him round the church, having come from the front doors. He's flanked by Chief Claremon and Father Martinez, whose ancient white brows are raised up to his thinning hairline. I realize the alarm has stopped.

"What are you doing out here alone?"

"But I'm not—" I turn back to Caleb, only to realize he's gone. The faint sound of pounding footsteps fades in the distance. He must have slunk behind the garbage bins and ran through the graveyard.

I stuff the envelope into my pocket, turning to face my uncle. "I'm so sorry," I burst out, trying to unravel the past five minutes of my life. "I just—I needed air, and I didn't know the alarm would go off."

Chief Claremon relaxes, nodding at Father Martinez. "I'll call off the fire department," he says, pulling out his phone.

"Are you all right?" Uncle Arbor asks, looping his arm over my shoulders and leading me back to the church.

"Yeah, just needed air," I repeat, cheeks flaming.

"I know today's been a lot," he says, using his best dad voice. Soothing, like I'm a scared animal. "Just get through the next hour or two, and we can go home. You look exhausted."

He does, too, but I don't say so. I don't want to probe at all, given how my exhaustion is completely warranted, since I haven't slept in nearly thirty-six hours.

He pats my back. "I'm going to talk to Father Martinez and

make sure everything's settled. You haven't eaten yet, right? Go make yourself a plate."

I nod stiffly, walking back into the empty church, the late-afternoon sun through the windows blinding me.

"What was that all about?"

I nearly jump out of my skirt at Quinn's sharp voice, her and Leo stepping out of the private room that has a window overlooking the parking lot.

"Were you spying on me?" I ask, clutching my chest.

Leo shrugs. "We were already looking for you. The alarm was kind of a dead giveaway."

"Who was the guy?" Quinn asks, cutting to the chase.

I tug the envelope from my pocket, swallowing. "His name's Caleb. He gave me this."

They stare at it. Finally, Quinn says, "Well, what are we waiting for? Open it."

I do, the Rosewood wax crest already broken. Inside are two pieces of paper, one folded several times and one just in half. With shaking fingers, I open the latter on cardstock.

Dear

The name is crossed out, first in rough pen lines, then Sharpie. As if Caleb didn't want me knowing it was addressed to him.

I enjoyed talking to you that day we marveled at the brush strokes. You have a good heart, and that's why I need you. I hope you rise to the challenge, as this can't begin without you.

Find Lily when you get this. And for my next sentiment, look behind the three flowers.

Gram

"He looked familiar," Leo says. "What'd you say his name was?"

"Caleb," I pause, digging up his last name. "Johnson, I think. I don't know him."

"Your grandma apparently did," Quinn says. She takes the other thing from the envelope, unfolding it. "Holy shit."

"Can't swear in front of Jesus," Leo chastises Quinn, but there's awe in his voice as we stare at the fourth map piece. "My mom would have my head for that."

"Your mom would have your head for a lot of stuff you do," she points out.

"Valid."

"It's the northwest section," I say, my finger tracing the land-marks—the Rosetown Museum of Fine Art, the Trellis Diner, the schools, the Petunia Conservatory.

"It's there, right?" Quinn asks, pointing to the conservatory. "The letter says look behind the three flowers. There're a million flowers in the conservatory."

I shake my head. "He said it was in the museum. A painting."

"And we trust this rando because . . . ?"

"Because Gram did." Leo shrugs. "So let's—"

"Leo!"

We all jump, and I take the letter and map, stuffing them

back in my pocket as Antony DiVincenzi storms up the aisle toward us. He looks like what I imagine Leo will in thirty years, but unlike Leo, Antony's expression is stern, his salt-and-pepper hair slicked back and frown lines etched in the olive skin of his face. "We're leaving."

"I didn't eat yet," Leo argues.

Antony stops before us, a vein in his forehead popping. Past him toward the doors to the lot is Leo's mother, face drawn tight. "We. Are. Leaving." He carefully enunciates each syllable, like Leo's too stupid to understand the first time. "Got it? Let's go."

Antony doesn't look at me as he storms past. He never even gave condolences. When Leo doesn't immediately follow, he turns and bellows his name again.

"One second!" Leo calls back, the sound exceptionally loud in the empty church. He turns to us, rolling his eyes and dropping his voice into a whisper. "I've gotta go, but meet at my house tomorrow morning at ten by the big oak in my backyard. My parents will be gone by then. From there, I'll get us to the museum."

"How?" I ask. "Your house is on the other side of town."

His lips lift in a smirk. "Don't you worry about that. Just be there."

Quinn gestures to my pocket. "What about Caleb?"

"I know the painting," I say. "If he wants out, fine. One less person to worry about."

Quinn's brows raise. "Cold."

"Leo!" Antony's voice comes from outside.

"Ten tomorrow. See you then." And just like that, Leo's gone. Seconds later, tires squeal.

"His dad is at level one thousand and needs to drop it to, like, five," Quinn mutters.

I turn, my heart plummeting at the sight of Nonna standing in the doorway to the hall, eyes trained on the door Leo and his parents left through. She wipes her eyes, not seeing us as she returns to the rectory.

"Quinn? Where have you been?"

Quinn groans, tossing her head back as her mom emerges from the door Nonna walked through. Liz Zhao is in a striking red pantsuit, arms folded as she raises an expectant brow.

"Praying to Jesus," Quinn deadpans. "It's been a minute, so I had a lot to catch him up on. You know, especially the whole 'I like girls' bit. Wanted to make sure that was cool."

"Quinn!" Liz hisses. To me, she throws an apologetic smile. "I thought we'd leave early and go to the Ivy. There's so much to do before the masquerade ball this Friday. I could really use your help."

"Awesome. There's nothing I'd rather do than decide which shade of napkin looks better. Sage green or ivy green. As if they're not the fucking same."

"Quinn!"

"Sorry, sorry. Let's go." Quinn rolls her eyes, tossing a peace sign over her shoulder to me.

Liz gives a curt nod.

"Goodbye, Lily. So sorry again for your loss."

"Thank you," I murmur, watching them leave. A pang hits my chest, the sharp feeling of missing my mom. I don't get it nearly as often as I do for Dad, mostly because Mom could have stayed if she really wanted to. She just didn't.

I'm heading back into the rectory when I stop short at the person standing in the hallway I sprinted down. "What are you doing here?"

Daisy's phone is held in selfie mode. "What does it look like I'm doing? I'm filming. The lighting's good here, and I'm sick of being in there."

I glance into the church where Leo, Quinn, and I read the letter and looked at the map, trying to gauge if Daisy could have heard us.

She raises her brows at me. "You need an escort back in or something? Contemplating pulling the fire alarm for attention again?"

I throw her the finger and push through the doors.

10

Quinn is beside the big oak when I get to Leo's house, her skateboard leaning against the trunk. "You're late," she tells me in her typical bored voice.

"I wanted to wait until my uncle left," I reply. Something about leaving the house the day after Gram's funeral felt wrong, as if I'm not supposed to have a life for the next couple of days. He probably wouldn't have questioned where I was going, but since I haven't told him about any of this yet, it's easier to just dodge and avoid. There's already a lot on his plate with the funeral and will-reading aftermath. The least I can do is stay out of his way until I have more solid information on whatever *this* is.

That, and the house was taut with tension, leading me to believe something went down between him and Daisy after we came home from the funeral and I collapsed in bed. I only saw her once this morning in the kitchen. She threw me a glare and stomped back to her room.

"Good morning!"

My head snaps up at Leo's cheery voice. He balances on the edge of the roof, then takes a precarious step onto a branch about a foot away. I hold my breath as he walks down its length, the wily wood bending beneath his weight. But like he told me yesterday, he's no rookie in the realm of sneaking out. With practiced ease, he climbs down the remaining branches like a jungle cat until his feet touch the dew-soaked lawn.

"Totally your first time doing that," Quinn mentions dryly.

His responding grin is devilish. "For sure."

"If your parents aren't home, why didn't you just use the door?" I ask.

"Because he's a show off," Quinn answers.

"True," Leo affirms. "But also because I have nosy-ass neighbors who meet with my mom for a weekly book club, which is just an excuse to get wine drunk and gossip. I can never be too careful."

"And they wouldn't see you climbing down a *tree*?" Quinn points out.

"No, because I'm the king of stealth. And also, we have a high fence." His fingers muss through his dark waves, still damp from a morning shower. When he looks back up, his eyes glitter. "You're late."

I roll my eyes, exasperated. "I didn't realize you two are so punctual. Should I just go home or—"

"Not you," Leo says, gently pushing my shoulder so I turn around. "*Him.*"

My mouth gapes at the boy hurrying toward us in pressed chinos and a navy polo, an olive-green backpack slung over his shoulder.

"Shit," Quinn breathes in surprise as he stops before us, shoving his hands into his pockets.

"What happened to not wanting to be involved?" I ask Caleb from Creekson.

"After your linebacker stunt yesterday, I meant it," he says, gesturing to the small bandage covering the scrape on his arm. "But *he* had different plans."

"Let's walk and talk," Leo says, turning toward the woods behind his backyard and ignoring Caleb's pointed gaze at him. "Nosy neighbors, remember? Our ride is this way."

Walking into the woods with Leo seems like a horrible idea given that I'm wearing yesterday's green skirt again paired with a cropped white tee since I still need to get my clothes from the manor. But we follow him, carefully picking our way through the damp underbrush.

"I didn't realize you knew my name," Caleb says to me, jumping when a chipmunk dashes across his path. That air seems to hover around him—anxious with a side of *get me out of here*. "And that you told him." He waves his hand at Leo's back.

"You two know each other?" Quinn steals my question.

"Kind of," Leo says, at the same time Caleb answers, "Barely."

"He tutored me for a while," Leo says, turning to Caleb and placing a hand on his shoulder. "By the way, *so sorry* for bailing on our last session, dude. That's on me."

Caleb brushes it off.

"After seeing him talk to you in the lot, Lily, I knew he was familiar. When you said his name, it clicked. I went home and still had his Snapchat. Other info was easy to find."

"And you proceeded to harass me all night," Caleb angrily interjects. "You called, texted, DMed me on Snapchat and

Instagram, even rang my *house* phone at three in the morning!"

"That's your fault for having a house phone in the first place."

Quinn snorts. Caleb ignores Leo's quip. "I didn't want my dad to catch on that something was up, so I finally agreed to take a bus here to meet you. But I can't be seen. My dad hates Rosetown. If he comes home from work and I'm not there, I'm dead."

"Why does he hate Rosetown?" I ask.

Caleb presses his mouth in a thin line. "Don't worry about it."

I roll my eyes but don't pry as we stop at a small clearing with a rundown garage and a dirt path that must lead to the main road. Leo takes a clunky set of keys from his pocket and unlocks the door. None of us help him as he rolls it up.

"No way," I say, staring at the rusty white van that looks as if it was pulled right off a poster warning children against pedophiles.

"Yes way." He hops into the driver's seat. The van starts with a chug that sounds like Hades himself is breathing life into it. "Now get in. The museum's like five miles away."

I slide open the back door and cough. "What *is* that?"

"What?"

"It smells like something *died*," Quinn gags.

Caleb plugs his nose. "I'm not getting in without a gas mask."

"It's just hockey gear," Leo says defensively. "We used these for the Ice Plex teams. My dad sold the others but kept this one, so I figured he wouldn't mind if I borrowed it." He flashes a sly grin that suggests his dad would mind very much, but he has no plans of telling him.

When none of us make any moves to get in, he sighs. "Do I need to remind you that there is potentially money at stake?"

Slowly, like it might kill us because it really might, we climb inside. Quinn takes the passenger seat while Caleb and I shuffle onto the bench back seat, yellow foam exploding from a rip in the fabric.

"Do you have your license?" I ask as Leo pulls out of the garage, nearly swiping the side mirror off.

"Of course."

I stare at him in the rearview mirror.

He clears his throat. "Uh, well, permit. But same difference, right?"

Clicks fill the air as we buckle our seat belts.

"So what's the plan?" Caleb asks as Leo turns onto the main road and we emerge from the cover of the trees.

Silence greets him as Quinn turns back to look at me, and Leo meets my eyes in the rearview mirror.

"Uh," I fumble for something so I don't seem like everything's totally out of my control, even though it is. "Well, you see—"

"We were kind of going to wing it," Leo admits.

"Wing it?" Caleb echoes. Unzipping his backpack, he pulls out a copy of the *Creekson Guardian*. "I take it none of you have seen this, then."

My breath goes still as I read the headline aloud. "'Folks Flock to Rosetown as News of Missing Fortune Goes Viral.' Viral?"

"You haven't seen the TikTok?" Quinn interrupts me.

I grab my phone and open the app. The first video to pop up is Daisy's face, the caption reading, *HUGE UPDATE: My Gram's money is missing.* It has over six million views. The sound is off, but the way her face is doused in rainbow light is unmistakable. This was what she filmed in the hallway of the church yesterday.

It must be why Uncle Arbor was mad this morning. She's putting our lives on display for *clout.*

"Read the rest," Caleb urges.

I grab the paper and read the article out loud.

> *The news of the missing Rosewood fortune has drawn interest from locals and tourists alike. Theories are being shared online as to where the fortune might be, with Iris Rosewood's granddaughter suggesting in a recent TikTok that perhaps it's "still around." Following the death of the third-generation Rosewood matriarch, individuals are traveling to the historic town to see for themselves if they can strike gold. Others, meanwhile, are steering clear of the town. They have no desire to compete in what the internet has coined "The Rosewood Hunt."*

"The Rosewood Hunt?" Quinn echoes. "That is the dumbest shit I've ever heard."

"I think it's kind of cool," Leo says. "Makes it sound deadly."

A film of sweat slicks my palms. Not only are we up against whatever tricks Gram has in store for us, but now we also have competition? If we don't solve her clues fast, someone else could get to it first.

That opens up a bigger question: What's truly at stake for us here? Money for college makes the most sense. A bonus would be Gram leaving some kind of note regarding my place at Rosewood Inc. But what if it's more? What if it's *everything*? The entire multimillion-dollar fortune.

And now, people are coming to town with the same nagging thought.

We clearly have no time to waste. I turn to Caleb. "This pushed you to come help us?"

His fingers nervously pick at the skin around his nails. "There are too many shitty people in the world who could do too much harm if they got their hands on a quarter of a billion dollars."

"Also because we're irresistible, right?" Leo says with a goading grin.

"Not even close. Also because—" He pauses, as if this is taking everything for him to admit. "I need the money, assuming that's what's at the end of all this. Not for me—I should get a full ride for college because I have a four-point-two GPA, plus I've been saving up from tutoring. But my mom died five years ago, and my dad works two jobs. I have two little sisters, so maybe the money would let my dad focus on them and switch to only one or something. Then maybe I could look at colleges farther away."

"That checks out," Leo says. "We all need money for college. We think that's why Gram pulled us together and likely what's waiting at the end of . . . whatever this is."

"I also showed up because you kind of need me," Caleb says slowly. Cautiously.

I narrow my eyes, the town blurring past us. "You didn't seem to think so yesterday."

"*The Three Flowers* is a famous painting." He ignores my jab, pulling a chunky laptop from his backpack and setting it on his lap. "In 1950, Amélie LaFramboise—a famous French artist—painted it as a gift for Hyacinth to celebrate the continuation of the Rosewood line after Iris was born. It's a highly valuable piece because it's the last thing Amélie ever painted. She died five days after finishing it."

"Brutal," Leo murmurs.

"The artist's name is familiar." I try to dredge up where I might recognize it from.

"It should be, to you. Amélie also painted the portraits of Hyacinth and Petunia hanging in Rosewood Manor," Caleb says.

As vivid as if I'm standing in the hall outside of Gram's office this very second, I picture them.

"*The Three Flowers* is one of the best pieces in the museum," Caleb continues. "Which means it's on the third floor, where all the priceless art is kept."

"Sounds like there's a catch," I say.

Caleb's already grim face turns grimmer. "There is. On the third floor, there're velvet ropes to stop people from getting too close to the art. But what you don't see is the infrared system that will alert security silently. They'll be on you before you know it."

"So basically, if you hadn't shown up today, we would have alerted the alarms and gotten in trouble," I say, anger seeping into my tone.

He swallows guiltily. "Likely." At our glares, he puts his hands up in defense. "Listen, I wasn't about to risk my ass before knowing what I was even risking it for. But now I'm here, so no one will get caught. Probably."

"Do we have to do gymnastics around the lasers?" Quinn doesn't look stoked.

"No shot. It's basically a wall," Caleb says. "You need to turn the infrared off."

"And you can do that?" Doubt sneaks into my voice.

"Yes. But, the second I turn them off, you'll only have sixty seconds to search the painting before the system reboots and they turn back on. You have to find whatever you're looking for fast."

I mull it over in my head. Sixty seconds is barely any time at all. What if we need to take it off the wall? Should we invest in drills first?

My eyes gloss across the newspaper and the reminder that we have competition. No time for drills. No *money* for drills. I'll pry that painting off the wall with my bare hands if I have to.

"So what *are* we looking for?" Quinn asks, looking at me.

"I'm not sure," I admit. "Gram's always left little notes. But usually that's all they are—one or two to get me to my destination. So I guess maybe another note? Or a piece of paper, like a check or something if this really does lead to money for college?"

"Easy," Leo says. "Between the four of us, we'll find whatever it is."

"I'm staying right here," Caleb says adamantly. "I can't be seen."

He said his dad can't know he's here, but there's more. I can feel it in the way he barely meets my eyes. "How do you know all of this? Why does your dad hate Rosetown?"

He throws an exasperated look my way. "You're just as pushy as I expected."

I smile with my teeth. "I'm worse."

"I used to come here a lot when I was younger," he relents. "I never lived in Rosetown, but my mom always wanted us to because she grew up here. She used to commute here for work until she died in a car accident. I think my dad always felt like if she hadn't cared so much about this town, we could have moved farther away like he wanted and maybe she'd still be here."

"The what-if game. I play that, too," I tell him. What if I hadn't made a scene at Gram's birthday party? What if I had stayed and called for help when the heart attack hit? Would she still be here?

The problem is, once you start playing, you never stop.

"That still doesn't explain how you know about the painting and security here," Quinn points out.

"A couple years ago, I got into coding and computer stuff. It's what I want to go to college for. Last summer, I did an internship at the museum and helped the director set up the security system. I figured an art museum looks good on college apps, you know?"

Quinn whistles. "You did an internship with Angeline Murphy? Damn, I've heard she's even more high-strung than my mom."

"Definitely can't be worse than my dad," Leo adds.

"Wait," I say, puzzle pieces sliding together as I take in Caleb's deep-set eyes and high cheekbones. I knew he looked vaguely familiar because I *had* seen him before, at the museum. Except long before last summer. "Your aunt is Angeline Murphy, isn't she?"

He swallows. "The one and only."

"Your mom's sister?" I hazard a guess. "I remember seeing you there when I was little and would come with Gram to see new exhibits. Back then, Angeline ran it with your mom, Eva, right? But since the car accident, it's just been Angeline."

"Yes," Caleb confirms. "And before you ask any more questions, that's the other half of the reason I can't go in. I haven't spoken to my aunt since last summer, the final day of my internship. She's in a massive fight with my dad, hence why I shouldn't be here. And she knows everyone in town, so I shouldn't be *anywhere*, really. She's a huge gossip."

"Okay, then the three of us will go." Quinn steers the conversation back to the focus.

"We can text you when we find the painting," Leo adds. "When we're ready for you to, you can shut down the system and we'll look. In and out, no sweat."

I'm not quite as confident, but there isn't time for debate— we're here.

The Rosetown Museum of Fine Art is beautiful, made of white brick with black trim, three stories tall and oozing elegance. Gardens flowing with irises, hyacinths, and petunias surround it, and people sift in and out of the massive black doors, which are framed by life-size marble statues. Through the grimy window of the van, everything looks otherworldly, like it's a painting itself.

I rip my gaze away, handing Quinn my phone. "Put your numbers in to start a group chat."

They do, with Leo the last after he pulls into a space at the very back of the lot in the shade of a magnolia tree. By the time I get my phone back, he's already sent a text to the four of us. And named the chat.

"Absolutely not," Quinn says. "I will *not* be called the Goonies Gang."

"C'mon, that vintage movie's awesome," Leo defends the title. "I even put the little map emoji. We need to set the vibe. We also need code names."

"*No.*"

They bicker about what Quinn's should be—Skater Girl spelled with an eight, Buzzkill, RBF—and Caleb looks at me like *What is wrong with them?* I wish I had an answer, but I don't, so I open the door. "You two coming or what?"

Leo and Quinn shuffle out. I turn to Caleb. "How long will it take you to shut down the system?"

"If it's a good day, five minutes," he says. He cracks his fingers in a typical hacker fashion. "And if it's a bad day, six."

"How do we know we can trust you?" I ask, paranoia making a home in my head.

"If I was planning to screw you guys over, I would have just let you get caught." Caleb gives me a thumbs-up as I close the door, which softens me a little. I catch up to Leo and Quinn, who are *still* talking about names.

"Don't make this difficult," Leo tells Quinn. "Lily has a code name too. Lily Rose."

She rolls her eyes. "Super original. How long did it take you to come up with that?"

"And what's your code name?" I ask Leo as we approach the doors.

To my surprise, he opens them for us, gesturing me through first. As I step past, he leans in for a conspiratorial whisper and says, "Gray Wolf."

Quinn snorts. "Fuck that. You're Frat Boy."

I surprise myself by laughing. He opens his mouth to protest, but I walk past him with a smirk. "Sorry, Quinn has chosen. No redos."

I smooth my expression as we cross the lobby and approach the front desk, an ornate crystal chandelier hanging over our heads. There's free entry for locals, so we're waved through by a girl a year below us in school in the typical uniform of black pants, a white long-sleeve shirt, and a maroon vest. She wears a plastic smile on her face, the telltale signs of a stressful day at what's probably her first job. The museum is bustling, likely thanks to Daisy's viral update herding people to Rosetown.

"Everybody's looking at us," Leo murmurs under his breath.

The girl watches with a wide gaze as we shuffle through, and I glance around to realize several others share her stare.

"Looking at *you*," Quinn hisses to me. "You're going to blow our cover."

"I didn't know we were *under* cover," I mutter back. To the people looking at me, I flash a bright smile, the kind that would have been no sweat to bring to my face two weeks ago. Now, it feels like some low-grade form of torture. Each unsubtle glance is a judgmental jab, as if they're all thinking the same thing:

What happened to your grandmother's money?

But also, *same.*

"Stairwell." Leo nods toward the emergency exit, keeping his voice low. "You go that way, we'll go up the main one. Meet you on the third floor."

Leo steps away from us—and directly into the path of a

woman on her way out. In her hand is a bottle of water raised mid-sip, the only beverage allowed within the museum.

"Oh!" she exclaims as it tumbles out of her grasp, half spilling on Leo and the rest splattering across the polished checkered tile floor. Gasps echo, mine included but due to the elbow jammed into my side.

"*Go.*" Quinn shoves me toward the door to the stairwell.

I glance back at Leo as I push through, apologies spilling from his mouth, which is barely containing a mischievous grin.

He did that on purpose. A distraction.

A bit genius, but I'd never tell him so.

My feet pound up the stairs, the boards creaky and old compared to the slick elegance of the lobby. I've never been this way, usually choosing to travel the main staircase, which is extravagant and winding. But this stairwell is empty, exactly what I need.

Before I know it, I'm emerging on the third floor. There's a low murmur of voices, but fewer people thankfully. It's reverent, like people don't want to talk too loud, lest they disturb the stunning art.

My phone buzzes. Caleb.

I'm ready. You?

Almost, I reply. I wish I'd paid more attention to paintings the previous times I've been here. Art has never captured my attention, although I recognize the talent behind it. But to me, *fashion* is art. Textiles and needles have always spoken to me more than paint and brushes.

But fashion isn't helping me as I move from room to room,

scanning each plaque before moving on to the next. I tilt my head down so my face is hidden by the wild strands of my hair, grateful everyone on this floor seems enamored by the art.

I'm in the sixth room when I see it. I don't need to read the plaque to know it's what we're looking for. In a massive oil painting that spans nearly an entire wall is a picture of a graveyard. Vines twist over a tombstone, obscuring the writing on it. But in front of the tombstone are three flowers, the same that ornament the museum's gardens. A hyacinth, a petunia, and an iris; the only colors in the image.

It's beautiful, the brushstrokes textured on the canvas and the mixed grays of the tombstone mesmerizing. A chill runs up my back, and I squint as if I could make out the letters behind the ivy, but I can't.

"It's kind of sad, don't you think?" a voice says from my right. I have the urge to jolt at Leo's unexpected presence, but I hold myself still.

"Most beautiful things are," I tell him, careful to keep my voice down and head trained at the painting so as not to draw attention from the few other people in the room. Like a phantom, I feel Quinn's quiet presence at my other side. "Caleb's ready."

"Are *we*?" Quinn asks.

I glance behind me at the others in the room. If we're seen snooping, that's equally as risky as activating the lasers. I give a pointed look at Leo.

"What?" he asks.

"We need to clear the room."

He takes in the other people. "I already had half a bottle of water spilled on me. It's someone else's turn."

Quinn frowns at her phone. "Caleb said we need to do it now before he gets bounced out."

"Dammit, I forgot to give him a code name," Leo says.

I bite my lip, looking around. An idea grasps me, and I turn to Quinn. "Give Caleb the go-ahead at my signal."

"What's the signal?" she asks, but I'm already tugging Leo across the room.

"Lean against the wall," I instruct him.

"Like, fake casual or real casual?"

"Just *lean*."

He does, and I'm taken off guard by how ridiculously attractive he is like this. Surrounded by priceless artwork with some of his dark waves framing his eyes and an elbow propped against the crown molding.

"I know—it's a good look," he grins, catching my stare.

It breaks whatever momentary spell was on me. "A good *setup*." I step closer, grabbing his hand with my left and pressing both to the wall. At our proximity, he swallows, heart racing. Or maybe that's mine.

"Set up for what?" he asks, so close I feel the heat of his breath.

"For *this*." I give Quinn a look, then step even closer to him, pressing myself against his front in what I hope is a flirty stance. He makes a light choking sound as if I've hurt him or something. It almost distracts me, but I keep to my plan, using our bodies to cover our hands. I bring them down the wall and they hit the light switch, flipping it off.

We're plunged into darkness.

11

Several people screech in shock, then laugh. A sliver of light filters in from a few rooms down, but my eyes have yet to adjust. My phone buzzes.

Countdown starts now. Hurry.

The plan has the intended effect; people shuffle out, wondering if it's a power outage. One person asks if it's haunted. Typical tourist shit.

I let go of Leo's hand, pushing him toward the door closer to the stairs. Voices float from around the corner, people from downstairs coming up. "Hold people off," I order.

"But—"

"Do it," I stress. I rush to Quinn, who steps over the velvet rope. My pulse races, adrenaline shooting through me. On her phone is a countdown, her flashlight on so we can see better. We're already at fifty seconds.

Forty-nine . . .

"Check behind," I whisper, digging my finger in the gap between the frame and the wall. All I feel is the rough wood backing of the frame. Quinn traces the other side. "Anything?"

"No," she says. I move up the side, having similar results.

"Should we pull it off the wall?"

"No time," she says. "And I doubt we could."

"Check the top!" Leo whisper-yells across the room.

"*Shut up!*" Quinn and I respond simultaneously.

I glance at the top helplessly. I'm just shy of tall enough to reach.

"Here," Quinn says, dropping her phone to the ground as she bends and makes a basket with her hands. "I'll give you a boost."

"I'm bigger than you," I point out.

"And I'm stronger," she fires back.

I huff, stepping onto her clasped hands. It's horribly unsteady, but it *does* give me a boost. Just enough to run my fingers behind the top of the frame.

"Twenty seconds," Leo adds unhelpfully. Then, much louder, "Hi! Sorry, this room is closed right now. Electrical issues."

"I need to put you down," Quinn grits out. I'm nearly to the edge anyway, with nothing—

"Wait!" I say, but she's already dropped me. I catch myself against the rope, nearly toppling over it before regaining my balance. "I felt something! We need to try again!"

"Don't squirm so much," she mutters. She makes the basket again, and I step into it, this time a few feet over. I reach toward the spot where I thought I felt something different in texture. And it *is*. It's softer than the rough back of the frame. Paper.

"Time's up!" Leo says, rushing over to us. I rip away whatever's in my fingers, folding it in my fist as Quinn and I tumble to the ground in our haste to get away from the paintings. I don't see anything, but I swear I can feel the moment the lasers resume, like a whoosh of air right before my eyes. The velvet rope clatters to the floor with our fall.

"You're always falling around me," Leo tells me, holding two hands out for me and Quinn to grasp. She ignores it, but I take the offering, keeping what I found clenched in my other fist as he tugs me to my feet.

"You kinda froze for a second over there," I can't resist teasing him as I smooth my skirt, nodding toward the switch Quinn flips on.

The lights stun my eyes momentarily, but the clamor of voices coming from the stairs propels us toward the other end of the room and through the doorway. We're back around other people, but no one seems the wiser that we hadn't been here the whole time. Good.

"I *prefer* to be included in devious schemes before they're committed," he whispers as we keep moving, heads down and pace even to not seem suspicious. "Keeps me in the fun."

"I promise I'll clue you in next time I'm planning something devious." I roll my eyes.

Quinn gives a harsh glare from over her shoulder that translates to *Shut up*. We keep moving through the rooms until we come full circle at the landing of the stairs. I want to stop and look at what's in my fist, but I don't dare. Not when we're so close to getting out of here.

I let the first shred of relief seep into me as we step off the last stair. The lobby is in sight and the doors just beyond that. Just a few more steps—

"Oh, Lily!" a familiar voice calls. My feet falter. "I'm so glad to see you here!"

Leo doesn't hear it, but Quinn does, looking back at me. She must read the panic in my eyes because she reaches her hand out. An offering.

I hesitate for a split second before I meet her palm with my own, effectively passing the piece of paper to her. She turns back to the doors, following Leo, who's only just now realizing we're not right behind him. I watch them walk out, a swirl of distrust stirring in me that they'll take the clue and ditch.

But I have no choice but to let them go, especially as I turn to see Angeline Murphy looking at me with a pitying smile. Her hand reaches for mine, just like I figured she would, clasping my fingers and squeezing. Thank God Quinn took the paper.

"How have you been, dear? I'm sure all of this has been putting the worst strain on you."

I force my expression into the mask I've been wearing all too often these days—one of gratitude that someone *cares*. As if she actually does and isn't using this as an opportunity to pry, just like when she offered to drive me home from the deli after the news broke of Gram's death.

"It's been hard," I say, mind spinning for something to add. Being this close to her, I see the similarities between her and Caleb. Mostly in the prominence of their cheekbones and slighter build. Unlike Caleb, Angeline prefers bright, bold hues, like the color-blocked dress she wears now. "I thought I'd come to the museum for a bit. Gram always loved art, so I wanted to feel closer to her."

It's such a bullshit lie that if Gram were here, she'd snort. She liked art well enough, but she rarely came to the museum except for events. I'm sure Angeline's hovering didn't help.

"And did it work? Do you feel closer?"

"I—" Suddenly, a weight is on my chest. A crowd has formed, or maybe it's been here the whole time and I'm just finally feeling the claustrophobic effects now with the crash of adrenaline. I need to get out of here. I fumble for words, knowing that whatever spills out of my mouth won't be nearly as elegant as it should be.

"I'm trying to." I squeeze her hand and let go, not faking the sudden tears clogging my throat. I thought I *was* close to Gram, but right now, I feel oceans away. "I'm sorry. I have to go."

Her eyes soften. "Of course," she murmurs. "I'm always here if you need anything."

It's all I can do to nod tightly and force my legs to push me through the crowd and out the door, keeping my face pleasant despite my screaming insides. As if I don't have enough emotions flurrying through me, guilt gets added to the mix. I've spent the past year being on edge around townspeople, but Angeline has shown me nothing but kindness. Maybe that's another thing for me to work on letting go. The list is getting long.

Once I'm outside, I'm relieved to see the van still at the back of the lot. The door slides open as I approach. I barely shut it behind me before Leo's gassing it and pulling out of the lot, nearly hitting a black SUV that's pulling in.

"That was wicked awesome!" he exclaims, the windows open and the summer air billowing in. "We just *Ocean's Eleven*'d that shit!"

"You spilled some water, and we turned off the lights," Quinn responds dryly, her Vans back on the dash. "I'd hardly call that a heist."

"And Brains back there hacked a *security system*," Leo whoops. Caleb tries to keep his expression stern, but he radiates satisfaction. "And here I thought you were just an ace at math."

"I am," Caleb says proudly. "And bio, chem, physics—"

"We get it," Quinn interrupts. "You're smarter than all of us combined."

"And then some," I add, because it really is impressive, and I want him to know I appreciate him taking the risk.

He meets my eyes, and while he doesn't quite smile back, there's a light in his gaze that makes my insides warm.

"Only one problem, then," Quinn says, flashing a piece of ivory paper that's between her middle and pointer finger.

With the windows open, it makes my heart skip that she's holding it so casually. If only the wind knew that the paper might as well be gold, it might try to steal it just like us.

"This is blank."

Caleb goes rigid, and Leo diverts his eyes to look at her. "It can't be."

I use my left hand to push Leo's face back toward the road and my right to snatch the paper out of Quinn's hands. "It's not blank," I say confidently. While not the sizable check I was hoping for, it might be the next best thing. The paper is thick cardstock, no bigger than a Post-it and folded in half. I open it, grinning at the smudge across the otherwise pristine page.

I lick it.

When I lower the paper, Caleb's disgusted face meets mine.

"Welcome to Rosetown. We do things differently here," I tell him.

"I've noticed," he says.

I set the paper between us on the seat as words curve across it. "What the—"

"Am I missing something?" Leo asks. "I have mad FOMO. I feel like I'm missing something cool."

"Nothing much," Quinn says, although her voice lacks an edge. Her visor is flipped down, and she watches us in the mirror. "Just some magician shit."

"Not magician shit. Invisible ink activated by moisture," I correct, staring at the words now clear across it. Immediately, the first line has my breath.

I read aloud, sitting on my hands to keep them steady.

Dear Lilylove,

Sometimes, the craving hits just right. Nothing can quite abate, but you know this better than me. My favorite snack might give you more than a pleased stomach, if you only look.

Gram

The van jolts to a stop in the Hyacinth Conservatory parking lot.

Leo turns in his seat, his grin bright. "Another clue."

I stare at it, the scrawl obviously Gram's. "To where, exactly?"

"Maybe the bigger question is to *what*?" Caleb asks.

"I thought we agreed it's money for college," Quinn says.

Caleb removes his glasses to rub at his eyes. "I mean, yeah, that makes sense initially. It gives the four of us motive to actually work together." He puts his glasses back on, making sure they're perfectly straight. "But now there are supposedly other people looking for it. Between that and the clues and town map, I think it's not too out there to assume it might lead to . . . well, more than just money for college."

Quinn raises a brow. "Like, how much more?"

"All of it," I whisper, as if the world might be listening. Sure, I entertained the possibility earlier, but saying it out loud makes it feel far too real.

"Would your gram really have done that?" Caleb asks me imploringly. "Hidden an entire fortune for us to find?"

I truly think about it. Saying yes makes Gram sound like a wacky grandmother, and she never really was that. She was clever and sure. Sly, even.

"Obviously, I'm well acquainted with notes written in invisible ink," I say. "And when I was little, she always played hide-and-seek with Daisy and me." I'm hit by a sudden memory of a life jacket tight across my chest, the sun on my cheeks and wind tangling my hair aboard Dad's huge sailboat, *The Thorn*. It's tinged with times I'll never have again, a sucker punch of nostalgia. "When we were on my dad's boat, we used to try to find all the nooks that no one else knew about. Our parents would worry because we'd hide super well and not come out. But never Gram. She always seemed kind of proud that we were so good at it."

Leo nods, a look in his eyes I can't decipher. "She was also a killer chess player. And good at riddles."

"Then I think we need to treat this like what it is," Caleb says. "A true treasure hunt."

"With millions of dollars at the end?" Quinn asks.

Caleb nods. "And if that's the case, we should talk about our cuts."

"What do you mean your *cut*?" I ask.

Caleb stares at me evenly. "With the type of news this is drawing, how the media is sensationalizing Iris's death and people are coming to town, I'm not risking anything without nailing down logistics. Plus, you didn't have a plan or even bother researching about museum security. I'm not trying to be brash, but if I wanted to be thrown into a haphazard group project without any payoff, I would have enrolled in chem lab."

"Fine," I grit out. "What would you like your cut to be?"

"Fifteen percent," Caleb says, obviously having already thought about it.

I start to argue, but he cuts me off.

"If the three of us each get fifteen, it leaves you with more than half."

Quinn and Leo nod in agreement, eyes wide. I can taste blood from how hard my teeth dig into my inner cheek. Even though it *is* my family's money, it's obvious I can't do this without the three of them. Not only that, but Gram wants them here. Chose them.

And if this does lead to the entire fortune, 55 percent is still a heaping chunk of change.

From how Caleb raises a brow in challenge, he's not budging. He knows I need them, probably more than Quinn and Leo realize. Not only that, but this is already daunting enough as is. With the added competition of others looking for it, putting our brains together is likely the most efficient way to solve Gram's clues.

Behind the logical reasoning, I can't ignore the fact that I don't *want* to do this alone. Living at the manor with Gram and seeing Miles at work and school was enough to keep my loneliness at bay, mostly. But now, with Gram gone and my routine upended, I can feel it creeping back, like a tear in fabric that just keeps getting bigger and bigger no matter how much you try to patch it. Despite being unconventional, having them by my side is better than no one.

"Deal," I relent. "We'll split the money. But *only* the money. If Rosewood Inc. is part of it, that's mine."

No one objects.

"So this clue." Quinn picks it up. "Any idea where it leads?"

"We should consult the maps," Caleb points out.

Before we can start, a marimba ringtone blares. Leo fishes his phone from his pocket.

"It's Daze," he says in surprise. "FaceTime."

"Answer it," Quinn snaps, at the same time Caleb asks, "Daze?"

"My cousin," I mutter as Leo accepts it, turning his body to carefully only show himself.

"Sup," he says warmly, how friends are supposed to greet each other. It makes my gut twist with—well, *something*. "Wait—Are you okay?"

"No!" It's more a sob than a word, in a panicked tone I've never heard Daisy use.

My stomach drops. *Not someone else dead. I can't—*

Daisy drags in a ragged breath and chokes out, "You're never going to believe this."

12

The pool of congealed grease on the cold slice of pizza in front of me ripples as my uncle slams his fist down on the dining room table.

"This is fucking ridiculous," he fumes.

I'm not used to this side of him. Dad was the one who inherited the temper, quick to explode when people merged into his lane without a signal or Gram denied a request for something he wanted. But Uncle Arbor has always been calm, the perfect diplomat for the Rosetown Council.

Now, he is nothing close to calm. Neither am I.

"Frank, there must be something we can do. They have to understand these are extraneous circumstances."

Hours ago, Leo dropped me off a few blocks from Uncle Arbor's house and I trekked the rest. When I walked through the front door to Daisy's pensive face and my uncle's rare rage, I knew what Daisy had blubbered over the phone to Leo must be true.

Apparently, someone on the board of directors for Rosewood Inc. called Uncle Arbor to inform him that with Gram dead, her position as chair of the board was open. Per their guidelines, if an heir to the seat isn't declared within two weeks of Gram's death, they have the authority to take it upon themselves to appoint a new one.

We knew this, supposedly. But we didn't think they'd be sticklers about it.

"I have already requested an extension," Frank says gravely. "It was denied."

"Why?" I ask. "Rosewood Inc. would have never survived without Gram. They love her, and they should love *us*."

Discomfort crosses Frank's face. After I got home, Uncle Arbor phoned every member of the board. Only one answered, offering to meet him tomorrow morning in Boston. Frank arrived an hour ago—the same time as the pizza—and we've been talking in circles since.

Uncle Arbor wipes a hand down his face. His own slice is untouched. "There's been tension on the board lately. Some members are frustrated with the way the new factory is being run, the choices Gram was making, the lack of big-brand collaborations. They felt she was an antiquated presence and wanted her to step down ages ago."

Daisy looks at me as if to say, *You really didn't know that after living with her for a year?* But I *didn't*. Whenever Gram and I talked about Rosewood Inc., it was always good things. More fashion-focused than business. And even those conversations were rare. I knew we were in a lull for luxury-brand collabs, but that happens to all fashion companies, especially as a coat company in the summer. Besides, all it takes is one influencer raving about a product to blow you back up again.

But the fact that the board was already trying to weasel Gram out and now she's *dead*? If any of them had been at her party, I would have assumed they killed her.

"And nobody can name the replacement aside from her?" Uncle Arbor asks.

Frank shakes his head. "Unfortunately not. Which means as of Sunday, two weeks since the declaration of Iris's passing, if a new chair isn't named somehow, the board will proceed with their choosing."

"Who would they choose?" Daisy has been unusually quiet at the other end of the long table, two pieces of crust left on her plate. She seems . . . subdued. Different from how she was on the FaceTime call with Leo. Her phone isn't near her, instead beside Uncle Arbor's stack of papers and contracts he whipped out when Frank arrived. This is something we definitely can't risk her sharing with her followers.

Frank clears his throat. He hasn't sat down at all, instead standing across from Uncle Arbor at the other head of the rosewood dining table. "Well, from my understanding, a board reorganization would take place. Someone currently on the board would likely be appointed as chair, and then they'll probably pick a new board member from within the company. But only if Iris has yet to appoint someone new."

"How can she do that, Frank? She's *dead*."

There's a cavernous silence following Uncle Arbor's declaration, his voice cracking on the fatal last word. I have yet to see him actually cry, but right now, he turns his back to us, shoulders rigid. Daisy swaps a wide-eyed glance with me, but then she must remember she hates me, because she rips her gaze away and scowls at the pizza crust on the plate in front of her.

"It's, admittedly, a very concerning situation," Frank finally says. "If it's any consolation, I believe one of the potential new board candidates is Elloise Claremon."

"*Ell?!*" If I was drinking water, I would have spat it halfway across the room. "You're shitting me."

"No, Miss Rosewood, I am not *shitting* you." He supplies air quotes around *shitting.* "Now that she's graduated, as Iris's mentee, she's a worthy team member. They also like that she's a Rosetown native. I would have thought that'd bring some comfort."

"She's not a Rosewood," Uncle Arbor argues, thank God coming to my defense. "It's a company under our name for a reason, Frank. That's because it's *ours.* It's more than just coats—it's our legacy."

"Unfortunately, my hands are tied. Once Saturday passes and the two weeks are up, the fate of Iris's position lies with the members of the board. It's a powerful role that needs a powerful person at the helm. I'm sure they'll appoint someone more than capable."

I want to argue that I'm a powerful person. Or I can be. But less than eight hours ago, I was sneaking around a museum—pretty poorly, might I add—looking for clues and riding around in a pedo van because I don't even have a license. I'm in borrowed clothes, and I had to break into my own property with *my name* on the sign the other night because I'm banned. Powerful people don't jump through the hoops I'm currently nosediving through.

"I'll be in touch with further updates. I am sorry." Frank sees himself out as my uncle stews.

I stare at my pizza slice. Maybe if I'm lucky, whatever Gram's clues are leading to will say something about who she wanted to take over her position as chair. I need to figure it out by Saturday.

It's no time at all. We're still stuck on the most recent clue. When I left the others, Caleb had to catch a bus back to Creekson, Leo had to go home before his parents showed up, and Quinn's mom wouldn't stop calling her to go help at the Ivy.

"I'm going to go to Boston now," Uncle Arbor says abruptly. From the table, he slides papers into a briefcase sitting on one of the chairs. "If I go tonight, maybe I can convince the board member there to meet with me for a late dinner. He went to the funeral yesterday and mentioned the hotel he's staying at. I'll just show up and see what I can—"

He's interrupted by his phone ringing. "Hayworth?" he answers it. "Listen, I already told you that I'm not willing to comment on—"

Uncle Arbor cuts off, listening to whatever Mr. Hayworth has to say. I can't hear anything discernible, but the color leeches out of Uncle Arbor's face until he's bone-white. "Excuse me, *what* happened at the Petunia Conservatory? No, of course I didn't know that. And no, I don't have a comment! Jesus, Hayworth, stay out of it and let the police do their jobs."

"What was that?" Daisy and I ask at the same time once he hangs up.

"There's been a break-in." His voice is taut. "The conservatory. It's a mess, according to Hayworth. He wanted to know if I had any commentary to add."

"But I was—"

"Do you see why what you're doing is damaging?"

His burning gaze trains on Daisy, cutting me off. And good thing, because I almost just admitted I was in the conservatory lot earlier today, which might have opened up questions.

"You're airing all our dirty laundry to the rest of the world. Hayworth is treating this whole thing like the revival of his career. He's there now trying to rig up some story of how your videos and someone vandalizing the conservatory are connected."

"Well, maybe they are," Daisy argues. "And I'm not airing our dirty laundry—the people want to know the truth."

"*Stop.* No. More. TikToks. It's adding fuel to the fire, and now I have to go be the one to put it out. I don't need tomorrow's paper sending the town into a frenzy thinking we're trying to sabotage Rosetown landmarks or whatever ridiculous story Hayworth spins."

He strides toward the door leading to the garage, pausing before stepping out. "I'm going to stop by the conservatory so I can update the council and make sure everything's under control. Then I'm heading to Boston. I'll be back by tomorrow morning, hopefully with good news. Are you two okay here for the night?"

I don't feel okay at all, my entire future in shreds. But I nod, and so does Daisy. With a final good night, the door shuts behind him. A few moments later, the hum of his Mercedes fades away.

Daisy grabs her phone and bolts upstairs. I stare at the table, spiraling. Why would anybody wreck a Rosetown landmark?

And the conservatory isn't even all that nice, just a big green-house overgrown with flowers. It seems unbelievable that anyone in Rosetown would do it, but it's equally unbelievable that any of the tourists coming to town thanks to the sudden press around Gram's death would, either. Nonetheless, the timing is weird.

Daisy pounds down the steps seconds later, her small Chanel backpack slung over her shoulder. She pays me no attention, striding across the kitchen toward the garage door.

"Where are you going?" I follow her into the garage. "We should stay—"

I drop off, staring at the new vehicle in the garage. I knew Gram gifted Daisy the White Rose, but actually seeing it here sends a jolt through me.

Daisy notices. "At least you got the ruby."

"Not yet," I counter, the hollow of my throat bare.

"Check your bed. Our 'inheritance' was left here earlier." She says *inheritance* sourly.

I turn to do just that, but her voice stops me before I get past the doorway. "Wait!"

She stands with the door to the White Rose open, brown eyes unsure in a way that throws me. Staring at her now, without her face twisted with sarcasm, I'm reminded of how much we look alike despite our different builds and hair lengths and eyes. We could be sisters.

And that's how we acted when we were little. We were insep-arable, all pinkie promises and secrets for two. My parents even had me stay back with her in kindergarten so we could be in the same grade. With my birthday in two days, I'm the only prospective senior already turning eighteen.

Friday. Just one day before I might lose Rosewood Inc. forever.

"Do you think Frank is being real with us?" Daisy's eyes are cautious, like she almost hopes I'll say no.

"I don't know. It sounds like he's trying to advocate for us."

She grimaces. "Doing a shit job. I bet he could make the Rosewood Inc. board give us time if he really wanted to. Maybe he wants us out of the picture. I mean, it's fishy, right? Gram randomly changes her will, and he's the only one who knew about it."

I lean against the doorframe, churning her words over in my mind: "You think he forced her to?"

"Maybe," Daisy murmurs. "I definitely would if it weren't for that one line in her will. *The receiver will be determined at a later date under privately specified circumstances.*" She takes a breath. When she exhales, it's like I can see her walls physically lowering. "Do you remember the Christmas that Gram got us the sewing machines?"

I nod.

"She made us think we didn't get any gifts. All that was sitting under the tree were two blank pieces of paper. But they weren't blank, were they? She wrote in invisible ink."

I cough to cover the gasp of surprise that of course Daisy would remember this *now*. I've had countless other interactions of Gram's games throughout the past year, especially her riddled notes. I nearly forgot about this one—the game that started it all.

"It was a clue," I say.

She nods. "And it led to another clue, and another, and another. All over the manor, until finally, we went into the garage and there was our actual gift. She just made us think we didn't get one, but we had to play her game."

"I remember," I say, chest hollow at the warmth of the memory. Daisy's quiet for a long moment. I know she's waiting for me to talk, but I don't know what to say. She's far too close to the truth for comfort. I cross my arms in front of myself as if it can shield her from seeing the map piece in my pocket.

"I guess I just wish this was another one of her games," she finishes.

I laugh, the sound loud and cruel in the concrete garage. But it's only because I have no idea how I'm supposed to respond without giving away literally everything. "Yeah, if only."

Daisy scowls, and whatever moment we were having is over, like a light flickering out. She shakes her head, climbing into the red leather interior of the White Rose and slamming the door closed.

"So that's it?" I ask as she turns on the car and starts pulling out. I follow her into the driveway. "You're just going to ignore all of this and run off?"

"It's better than staying here with you," she sneers through the open window.

I know I just shut her down, but I don't want her to leave. Don't want to be alone in this big empty house that's not even mine. Desperation makes me yell after her. "I hope Kev's good at least!"

The White Rose screeches as she pulls a U-ey, heading straight for me. I'm almost 100 percent sure she's going to run me over.

Her threat when she caught me in her room plays in my head. *You* will *regret it.* I certainly have some regrets now.

She swerves at the last second and stops so her door is right next to me.

I scramble for an apology. "Daisy, that was so out of line, I'm—"

"First of all, it's none of your business what I do with Kev. Second, if you ever used your two brain cells for anything other than stealing my clothes, you'd know that Kev's dad is our family's accountant and therefore might have some answers lying around his office as to where all our money supposedly went. Third, you're one to talk." She leans out the open window, shoving a finger into my chest. Her brown eyes are like balls of fire in the setting sunlight. "I know that early Tuesday morning *you* snuck out and met Leo. I have his location and he's a shit liar when I asked him about it. So if you could stop fucking my best friend, that'd be great."

My jaw unhinges. "I'm not—" But it's too late. She rolls the window up and floors it, zooming away with a cloud of dust that leaves me choking on fumes. "We aren't— He isn't— We're coworkers!" I scream into the empty night.

Which is dumb, because that's exactly the thing I don't want Daisy to know.

I punt a bunch of daisies sprouting in the lawn and stomp inside, the empty house welcome as I trudge upstairs to the bathroom and kick off my shoes in the hall. Everything feels too close, my clothes clinging to me. I peel them off and crank the shower on as hot as it will go. The steam does nothing to quell my anger. I am not, nor ever will be, *fucking* Leo DiVincenzi. Daisy can have him.

I'm still shaking with anger as I towel-dry my hair, stepping into my room. I flick on the light and stop short.

"Oh my God." I dash to the bed, nearly dropping my towel in my haste. With shaking fingers, I open the black jewelry box sitting on the comforter. Inside is the famous Rosewood ruby, as big as my thumbnail and elegant as ever. I carefully take it out and fasten the gold chain around my neck. It's heavier than I expected. My fingers brush its smooth surface, and I catch my reflection in the mirror above the dresser. *Just like Gram.*

Tears prick my eyes and I look away. That's when I see the duffel bag on the floor and my favorite cognac crossbody bag, the one I keep my emergency sewing kit in. My things from the manor. Some of them, at least.

Slipping on my favorite leggings and the familiar cotton of an old tee does make me feel better, especially when I tuck the ruby under the tee's neckline to rest against my chest. If there's any highlight to Daisy assuming something's going on between Leo and me, it's that she must not have noticed us in the church with Quinn, and therefore shouldn't suspect the hunt. Given that she's busy snooping through Kev's dad's things and assumes I'm an oblivious brat, I should be in the clear. For a moment tonight, when she was reminiscing about Christmas, I had the impulse to tell her about it. Before she accused me of sleeping with her best friend and having two brain cells, that is.

She would have been left a clue if Gram wanted her to know. I'm glad I didn't tell her. If Gram doesn't trust her, neither do I.

I turn off the light and climb under the covers, checking for updates from Uncle Arbor and the Goonies Gang, both of which have none. My phone barely has any charge left, but I pull up the picture of the clue I took before Leo dropped me off since he agreed to keep it.

Sometimes, the craving hits just right. Nothing can quite abate, but you know this better than me. My favorite snack might give you more than a pleased stomach, if you only look.

Possibilities run through my mind. The two map sections bordering Caleb's are mine and Leo's. In Leo's, there's the Rosetown Country Club, known for the best clams casino. It's Gram's favorite. But Gram loves food. She adores the French toast at the Trellis Diner and would eat the candied almonds from Williams Grocery by the buckets if she could. There's also Cocoa's Chocolatier, where she gets truffles from, like the one I ate the night of the party. . . .

I don't realize I've faded into sleep until I jerk awake, my room cloaked in long shadows. I've been out for longer than the few minutes it felt like. I fumble for my phone, the brightness blinding me, along with the alert that it has under 5 percent battery left since I never plugged it in. It's three in the morning.

I'm sinking back into my blankets when a sound jolts me, the same one that woke me up, I think. The creak of footsteps on the stairs.

"Uncle Arbor?" I ask the dark softly, shaking off the grogginess of sleep as I sit up.

But I know it's not. It's different from Uncle Arbor's heavy steps or Daisy's nearly soundless tread. Fear clasps its fist around my heart, and suddenly I am *very* awake. The footsteps come closer, at the top of the stairs, down the hall. Outside my door.

The knob turns.

13

THURSDAY, JUNE 27, 3:13 A.M.

"Get out!" I scream as the door nudges open, launching myself across my bed so fast that my feet get caught in the duvet. If my room was as big as my one at the manor, I'd face-plant on the carpet. Instead, my hands slam into the door, the weight of my body falling against it, forcing it shut. Whoever's on the other side clearly was *not* expecting it, because it's only over my own screaming that I hear the crunch of their fingers caught in the doorjamb and a muffled string of curse words.

I finally get my feet under me just as they push up against the door again, the fingers slipping out but a pressure battling me from the other side. *Hell no.* I slam my back against it with everything I have, relishing in the click of the latch catching and pressing the lock in place.

"Leave before I call the police!" I yell through the door.

No answer, but my back vibrates as they pound the other side. My phone's on the bed, just out of reach. If I can buy myself enough time, I can grab it, slide on my Converse, and shimmy out the window. But I need to keep them busy.

"You might want to go ice your fingers!" I hope they can't hear the tremor in my voice. I dash to the window, praying the lock holds as they wiggle the knob. A bang resounds through the wood, harsher than the others. Then again, like something hard slamming into it.

"My uncle is coming!" I lie as I push open the window, one hand tugging on my Converse. "He'll bring the police. They'll be here in seconds."

I go to step out of it, but *shit*. The screen.

With trembling fingers, I flick the latches on the screen to unlock it. I jump as another bang against the wood sounds, practically a gunshot in the still night air.

Fuck! One of the latches is stuck. I wiggle it, shoving my shoulder against it. *Come on.*

An involuntary scream escapes my lips as another bang gives way to a thunderous crack. I glance over my shoulder to see something shiny splinter my door. It gets ripped out, a chunk of the door coming with it. A face peers through the hole, a strip of moonlight revealing a black ski mask.

This can't be real. It's a nightmare, it has to be. The face retreats, and whatever they're holding crashes into the door again. My fingers fumble with the latch as I shove against the screen. I hit it harder, and there's a tearing sound, then a sharp pain in my right palm. The scent of copper coats my nose as finally, the ripped screen falls away.

Just in time, too. Their weapon smashes through my door, creating a hole large enough for an arm to snake through.

Fear pounds in my ears. I grab my purse and stuff my map piece and letter inside along with my phone before scrambling through the window and onto the roof. I'm farther from the ground than expected. *How does Daisy do this every night?* If I jump, I'll bust my kneecaps.

Another slam has me skidding down the roof, my gaze catching on the trellis that leads into the back garden. Slinging my purse over my shoulder, I start to descend, crying into the night at the pain in my palm. Regardless, I don't stop until I'm close enough to jump. Grass and dirt press into my knees, my palms stinging as I make impact. I push myself up and take off.

Only to skid to a halt. By the front door, less than thirty feet away, is a second person. Big, broad, and clothed all in black. At my sharp intake of breath, they turn my way.

And start running toward me.

I sprint down the driveway, my shoes barely staying on my feet since I didn't have time to tie them. My breath comes in hot bursts against the chilly night air as I make it onto the main road, dashing for a complex of luxury condos, hoping to lose the masked strangers as I weave between the buildings. A stitch is already forming in my side, but I push on, unsure of where I'm even going. The police station is too far, and Uncle Arbor is in Boston for the night. I'm so, so screwed.

The pounding of feet too close for comfort makes me change direction sharply, heading straight for a daycare. I tear through the playground. Wood chips somehow get in my shoe, just like they always did when I was small and begged to be pushed on the swings. I glance behind me. No one follows, although they can't be far off. I throw myself behind a plastic rock wall in a bid to catch my breath, fumbling for my phone.

One percent. Dad is still the first contact saved under my

favorites, someone I can't delete no matter how much time passes from his death. Mom is next, which is ridiculous since she's gone and she rarely came through for me when she was around. Finally, after scrolling past numbers for the manor and ex-friends who probably blocked me, I click Uncle Arbor. The phone rings, my chest tightening as every second passes by. *Come on come on come on*, I beg silently, cold sweat dripping down my back. *Come on.*

On the third ring, the call drops. I stare at my screen in horror, my stomach sinking to my toes at the black screen. No matter how much I panic-tap, it doesn't come to life. My one chance. Gone.

The soft beating of footsteps on the other side of the wall makes me swallow my sob, stuffing my fear into my gut with it. I brace myself, and as soon as the first toe of a boot comes around the corner, I'm sprinting out from my hiding spot. As I hoped, it completely takes my attacker off guard, so much so that they smack their hand into the rock wall in their bid to catch their balance. A scream rips from their throat, more like a gurgle, as if they're smothering it. They double over. Maybe that was the one whose hand I crushed in the door. Oops.

But one still pursues me. I zigzag through yards and flower beds, feeling like the world's biggest asshole as I trample bunches of lilies, irises, hyacinths, petunias; the typical flowers people like to plant in their perfectly maintained gardens. Well, perfectly maintained until I just tore through them.

But it helped, because my second assailant gets caught in some netting for a vegetable garden that I launched myself over. With the ski mask, they probably didn't see it.

I keep running, the few bites of greasy pizza I ate threatening to come up my throat. I turn another corner and slow my feet before I puke, trying to get my bearings.

I'm not far from Leo's house. If I can just get there, he can call the police or take me to the station.

I pick up my pace again, the thump of my purse against my hip too loud in the still morning air. But I don't see or hear anyone. Maybe I finally shook them off.

By the time I get to Leo's, my lungs burn with the need to stop. I stick to the shadows and cross into his backyard, keeping his nosy neighbors in mind, though I doubt any are up. I squint against the darkness now that I'm out of the yellow glow of the streetlights, picking my way through his yard and stopping at the base of the oak tree. He made scaling it look so easy.

Panic grips my chest at a low murmur of voices coming from the street. I'll have to take my chances climbing. Carefully, I pull myself up the tree, wincing at the pain in my palm. There's plenty of twisting branches and knobs, but it's hard work for my shaking muscles. Maybe if I were better versed at sneaking in and out like Leo and Daisy, it'd be no sweat. It's painfully evident I'm a rookie.

I finally get high enough to jump to the roof, which is terrifying. I land with a thud and hold my breath, hoping no one heard. The voices fade.

There's only one window I can reach, so I tap on it lightly. When seconds pass and no answer greets me, I tap again, bordering a knock this time. "Please," I beg against the dark. I bring my fist against it, scared to rap too loudly. I tap once more—

The shock of the window sliding open nearly sends me on my ass and tumbling off the roof. I grip the shutter at the last moment, catching my balance as a bed-frizzy head sticks out.

"Lily?" Leo's voice is clogged with sleep. He clears his throat, squinting at me through the open window. "I thought we weren't meeting till ten?"

"Can I come in?" I ask, trying to stem the hysteria in my voice. Whether he hears it or not, he pushes the window open farther and gestures me through. I climb in, feeling marginally bad that I step onto his bed before the carpet.

"What are you doing here?" he asks, voice hushed. I realize he really *was* sleeping, as any sane person usually is at this hour. A pair of black boxers printed with avocados sit low on his hips, and he's shirtless, his hair all over the place instead of his usual messy short waves. He must sense my discomfort because he reaches into a dresser and pulls out athletic shorts and an old hockey tee. I make a point to stare at the dusty trophies littering the top as he tugs them on.

"Somebody attacked me," I choke out. Despite wrapping my arms around myself, I feel like I'm about to fall apart. "They broke into my uncle's house and tried to break down my bedroom door. I—" My breath comes in short gasps as if I'm still running. "I barely made it out the window, and they chased me here, and I didn't know where else to go."

"That's so fucked-up," he says, coming closer to me. His hands are warm on my bare arms as he turns me to fully face him. "But shh, it's okay, and—"

"It's not okay," I argue.

He shushes me again, but words keep tumbling out, and I can't stop them. "They had a *weapon* and broke my door. My phone died when I tried to call for help!"

"You're right, it's not okay. Listen, I'm so sorry, but please—"

"Leo!"

We both freeze, feet stomping down the hall just outside his door to accompany his mother's angry voice. Before I know what's happening, he's shoving me into his closet. "Don't say anything."

And then he closes the door in my face. It's the kind with slats, and I can just make out the form of his mother crashing into his room. And the furious look on her face.

"Mom, what's up?" Leo's voice sounds sleep-ridden again, as if *she* just woke him up. "Everything okay?"

"Don't bullshit me, Leonardo James DiVincenzi," she says.

I wince. Nothing like pulling out the full name to instill the fear of God in your child.

"I heard *voices.* Do you have a girl over again? In this holy house?"

Again. I don't know why the word strikes me in such an odd, uncomfortable way. As if it's normal for Leo to sneak girls through his window and I'm just another notch.

You have way bigger things to worry about, a voice reminds me.

"No!" He laughs in disbelief. "Of course not. Mom, it's like, four in the morning."

"That's never stopped you before."

Mrs. DiVincenzi is a woman of faith and virtue, dutifully going to mass at Saint Theresa every single Sunday. I can only imagine the type of conversations that have taken place in this house trying to wrangle Leo, who I've gathered is decisively *not* as dutiful as his mother. Even so, I can't help feeling bad for him. It never feels good to know that your parent doesn't believe you, even if you are lying.

"Is she in the closet?"

I hold my breath, trying to make myself as small as possible among hanging shirts and old hockey sticks and stinky gym bags as Mrs. DiVincenzi stalks toward me. At the last second, Leo slips in front, barring her. "It was just me!"

I press my hand to my mouth to keep quiet. "Excuse me?" Mrs. DiVincenzi asks.

Leo gestures to his phone on the nightstand. "I was just watching YouTube videos."

"At four in the morning? What happened to those fancy Air-Buds you begged us to get you for Christmas?"

"My *AirPods* are charging," Leo says. "Sorry, I didn't realize the volume was so loud."

A soft *wap* sounds, like she gave him a smack on the side of the head.

"Go to bed," she commands.

The door clicks shut behind her. A few seconds later, Leo opens the closet.

"Quick thinking," I commend him.

"I have this little excuse jar in my brain that I pull from whenever my parents catch me doing something I shouldn't." He grins down at me smushed among his stuff, holding out a hand to help me up. When he tugs me to my feet, I'm painfully reminded of my cut. My teeth dig into my lip to stifle my gasp, and I rip my hand out of his, but not before leaving a smear of blood across his palm.

"*Shit.*" He grabs my hand, wide-eyed at the blood coating it. "Did the people chasing you do this?"

"Kind of. My screen ripped when I was trying to jump out my window." It sounds even more unbelievable out loud.

"Come here," he says, pulling me to another door. It's a bathroom, the Jack and Jill type with another door on the other side leading into one of his sister's rooms. He turns on the faucet, placing my hand under the cold stream. I suck air past my teeth at the pain, which is much more prominent now that the adrenaline has seeped out of me.

"Did you call the police?" he asks.

I shake my head. "My phone died." I know I should call them, and it's the reason I came here, but . . . "Going through questioning could bleed into the day and take up our time to figure out the clue. Plus, once Uncle Arbor finds out about this, there's no way I could leave the house. I'd have to give up the hunt entirely."

Besides, while I'm still terrified of everything that happened, in Leo's room with posters of hockey players on the gray walls and a Bruins comforter, I feel surprisingly safe.

"Okay," he relents, thankfully not pushing it. He shuts off the faucet once the last stream of pink has swirled down the drain. Without the blood, the cut really isn't that bad. "Hold up, I've got Band-Aids," he says, fishing around under the sink. He mumbles a curse. "Actually, I *don't* have Band-Aids. But medical tape and this should do the trick."

I choke on a laugh as he tosses a tampon onto the counter, a blush climbing up my neck. "I'm sure it will be fine."

He rips open the tampon, and never in my life have I seen a boy so completely unbothered to be holding one. I guess three sisters does that to you. He pushes it from the plastic casing and fluffs out the cotton, wrapping it around my palm and cutting the string. "These honestly are a life hack for nosebleeds. I'd get them in hockey a lot, and my mom always just shoved one up my nose." He finishes by wrapping the tape around my entire palm to hold the cotton in place. "See? Hospital-grade."

"Thank you," I say, a little dazed as we walk back into his room. I wind my arms around myself. "Sorry I almost got you in trouble."

"It's cool." He nods. "That's so messed-up people broke into your house. You were home alone?"

I nod, then stop. "I think so? Uncle Arbor went to Boston for the night to meet with a board member of Rosewood Inc., and Daisy had left to go to Kev's. Could you check if she's still there?"

Some of the tightness in my chest subsides when Leo shows me her location, which is in the northwest part of town, where Kev lives near Rosetown High. I'm glad she wasn't home, but it makes a new fear blossom that if whoever broke in actually got me, no one would have known until morning.

Leo peers out his window. "Do you think they're still out there?"

"Yes." My voice is small.

Leo's gaze changes as he takes me in, softening in the light of his bedside lamp. "If we're not going to do anything about it until tomorrow, then you should probably stay here for the night?"

His offer is punctuated with a question mark, like he's not sure I'm willing to face the scorn of Mrs. DiVincenzi if I get caught.

I nod. Leo only has a twin bed, so he gestures to the floor. "I'll get you some blankets." He grabs a few from his closet, making what looks like a glorified dog bed on the carpet. He finishes by putting his second pillow on the floor. "Cozy, right?"

"You're joking."

"I'm not giving up my own bed in my own house." He turns off the light and flops back onto his mattress. "It's comfy down there."

"Speak for yourself," I grumble, lying down on the pile of blankets. I have the perfect view of under his bed, which hosts a plethora of crumbs and enough dust bunnies to knit into a sweater. I pick up an orange scrap close to my face, having just enough glow from the moonlight to make it out. "There's literally a Cheez-It under your bed."

His hand sticks out above me in a casual *whatever* gesture. "It's a complimentary snack. You know, like when the Marriott leaves you cookies."

"There is zero comparison."

He settles on, "Maybe more of a Holiday Inn."

I turn away from him, curling up among the blankets. I'd never admit it, but it *is* pretty comfortable. Silence washes over us, the kind that makes you overly aware of every tiny sound, like the soft huff of his breaths and the grinding of my teeth as I try to calm down. Despite exhaustion hanging over me like fog, my eyes won't stay shut. All I hear is the banging against my door, the creak of footsteps.

A thud sounds from behind me, and I look over my shoulder to see Leo on the floor, mere inches away. The proximity makes my breath catch. "What are you doing?"

"I felt bad, so you can have the bed," he says begrudgingly. "I mean, you *did* almost get kidnapped."

"Or murdered."

"Or murdered," he agrees.

I push onto my elbows, glancing at the now empty bed and the window over it. I lay back down. "That's okay," I say, stomach tight. "I don't want to be that close to the window."

I can barely make out his features in the dark, but I think he nods. "Fair."

I begin turning back over, but his hand on my arm stops me. Why is it so *warm*? He's like a radiator.

"Can I ask you something?"

"You will anyway," I say.

"Why did you come to me?"

Suddenly, the blankets feel like a cage. The moonlight catches on his cheekbones, sharper than they ever look in the daylight, like they could cut a heart. The phantom feeling of his hand holding mine under the faucet as blood washed away. So much gentler than I thought he ever would be. My face heats at the memory of his avocado boxers, just an arm's reach away under his athletic shorts. Daisy's words rocket through my brain. *If you could stop fucking my best friend . . .* She'd kill us both if she knew how close we are right now.

Too much time goes by. "The police station is too far and my uncle is in Boston." It's not a lie, but it feels like it is.

"Right." He sounds oddly disappointed. "Do you want me to take you to him? I don't mind the drive."

"That's okay. Let's just focus on finding the money first thing."

He nods. My eyes have adjusted now, so it's no surprise when he speaks again. "Can I ask you one more thing?"

I sigh, turning on my back to stare at the ceiling. "You're certainly chatty tonight."

"What? Doesn't every girl love pillow talk?" he jokes.

I look at him and roll my eyes, although my chest feels funny at his teasing grin.

It fades slowly and I brace myself for his question.

"Before the funeral, when we were in Daisy's room fighting—"

"Really just a coworkers quarrel—"

"You called me a follower. I just—I wanted to know why you said that."

I hesitate, training my eyes on the ceiling. "You go with the crowd," I say. "And I know you've always been like that. But last summer, it was different. You shouldn't have."

I feel his gaze on me. "I don't know what you're talking about."

"The funeral," I snap into the dark, finally looking at him. "My dad. None of your friends went. Instead, they made fun of him with memes and throwing shade on social media. You could have stopped them. And I get it. My dad really fucked people over money-wise. But he didn't deserve that. He didn't deserve

167

for barely anyone to show up at his funeral." My voice cracks.

There's a rattled intake of breath. "I didn't not go because of my friends," Leo says. "I swear, Lily, I didn't have a choice. And I didn't even realize you'd want me there."

"Of course I wanted you there!" I burst, embarrassed I still care. The statement hangs between us, loaded. When he doesn't talk, I spill into the darkness everything that I've held tight to my chest for nearly four years. Words that have spun over and over in my brain until the hurt and sadness morphed into anger and that's all I felt every time I looked at him across the cafeteria or through the windows when he'd come to the manor to take care of the yard.

"You used to be my friend. I never understood what happened that summer before freshman year. For all of middle school, the three of us were inseparable. Then all of a sudden, you and Daisy kept hanging out without me. Would ditch me on plans. Her mom left, and school started, and you stopped talking to me altogether. Got a whole new friend group. You barely even looked at me. It made me feel terrible."

He's quiet for a long moment. "I didn't mean to," he finally says, voice soft. "I thought *you* were the one who wanted to stop hanging out with us. I'd ask Daze if you were coming with us for stuff and she would say you were busy or didn't want to. I thought I did something."

"She said that?" My voice simmers with hurt. I can't muster the energy to conceal it. "She told you it was me who didn't want to hang out? Are you making this up to save your ass? Be real with me."

"I am!" He glances at the door, lowering his voice. "I guess I did think it was weird. I always felt like we got on really well, the three of us. It seemed so random. But then Daisy's mom left, and she had no one. And you . . . you seemed like you had everything. I figured what was one less friend in your circle, especially if everything Daisy was saying was true."

"But it *wasn't*."

"I didn't know that. I don't know why she lied, what she suddenly had against you. But hanging out with both of you was impossible, so—"

I finish for him. "You chose her."

He's on his side now, shaking me so I look at him. "Only because I thought that was what you wanted and I knew it was what Daisy wanted. I'm sorry, Lily."

I keep my mouth clamped shut, refusing to meet his pleading gaze, lest he see the tears threatening to fall. He lets go of me, flopping onto his back to stare at the ceiling. You'd think it'd be more interesting with how enamored we are by it, but instead it's just like any other. Blank and white and boring.

"You're right," Leo says softly.

"I usually am, so you'll have to be more specific."

"I am a follower."

I look at him in time to see his Adam's apple bob on a swallow.

"I don't know why I can't just . . . stand up for myself, or others. It's like I'm so afraid to speak up, for people to not like me or want me around anymore, I just do everything they say." He lets out a short breath. "I can't say no. Someone hands me a drink or dares me to do shots or gives me a vape, and I just do it. Half the time I don't even want to, but I'm the yes guy. And I feel like if I'm anyone else, no one will want me."

It's the kind of admission that only comes out in the dark. And it throws me. Leo has always been like the king of the group, the center of every party and good time. I didn't think maybe he doesn't actually want to be.

"In my experience, if people won't stand by you for who you need to be, then they were never around you for the right reasons anyway," I finally say, a lesson I learned the hard way.

"That's what I liked about Gram," he says. "We both kind of bonded over having to put on a show for the sake of it. I'd come over late on Saturdays, wrecked from the night before. She could have fired me thirty times. But she didn't. She'd always have cannoli from the deli because she knew I missed them. We'd just sit and eat and talk. Play chess and Sphinx. She got me. More than my parents ever have."

"She got everyone," I say, thinking about Quinn feeling stuck and Caleb feeling alone. Gram saw through them, just like she always saw through me. It's one reason why people love Rosetown parties—she created a place to be together and forget about whatever weighs you down inside.

Maybe I get Leo now more than I want to. It still hurts that he chose Daisy, but right now, I'm the one lying next to him while she's scrambling to know why. "I'm sorry you feel like you have to be someone you're not. Sometimes, I feel like that, too."

His shocked gaze meets mine. "No way. You, the fearless Lily Rosewood, who looks like she could crush the world with a single glare? I'd never believe it."

"Well, I have to keep up appearances, don't I? I *am* a Rosewood and all."

"Something tells me Rosewoods don't usually sleep in Holiday Inns."

I laugh, the sound startling as he shushes me. "Sorry," I cover my mouth, feeling lighter having everything out in the open. I mean, I want nothing more than to scream my head off at Daisy for lying and excluding me, but that can wait until after I find the fortune. At least right now, it kind of feels like I have my old friend back.

We wait in silence for a few long moments, but thankfully I don't think the sound made it to his mom. "And no, you're right. We don't usually sleep in Holiday Inns. Or on floors."

"There's a perfectly good bed right there," he reminds me.

"Perfectly good," I echo sleepily. "You can stay on the floor with me as long as you stay in your zone." I pick up the Cheez-It again, placing it on the small stretch of blanket between us. "No crossing the barrier."

My lids are too heavy to hold open any longer. Darkness envelops me and I can't tell if Leo's parting words are for real or in my dreams.

"Whatever you say, Lily Rose."

14

My face is warm when I finally force my eyes open. Sunlight streaks across me, brighter than it is in my room at the manor or Uncle Arbor's. That's when I remember I'm *not* in my own room. I'm in Leo's.

And I'm in his bed despite falling asleep on the floor. *What the—*

The sheets fall away as I sit up, huffing in relief to see I'm still in my same leggings and T-shirt from last night, my ruby necklace tucked beneath it. Although, I must have kicked off my shoes at some point. I glance around the room. All that's left is a mess of blankets on the floor. From the brightness, it must be late morning.

Beside his bed is a nightstand, which my phone sits on, plugged into a charger. Leo must have done that. I unplug it and hold the power button, the screen coming to life and showing no new notifications. Uncle Arbor must still be away and Daisy at Kev's.

I shuffle out of bed, stretching my sore limbs and straightening my clothes. In the light of day, I realize I never even put a bra on before abandoning my room.

Yes, because most people getting attacked in the middle of the night would prioritize supporting their boobs. Except now, the chill of their central AC makes me *very* aware. I grab a hoodie of Leo's slung over the back of a desk chair and tug it on, hoping he won't mind.

I make a pitstop in his bathroom, the tampon taped to my hand evidence that last night really happened. It all feels so ludicrous, as if it were just a nightmare. But it wasn't, and that's even more terrifying.

I pause before I step into the hall. It's almost eleven, so his parents should be at work. I slowly slink down the staircase.

His house is the same as when we were kids. Modest size, all open, the stairs entering into the living room that shares the same space as the kitchen, the foyer between the two. The navy couch is faded from time and the arms threadbare in some spots. The TV has a bit of a butt on it, like it's trying to be a flat-screen but it's a little too old. The walls are half white paneling, half wallpaper with floral designs, peeling in some places. It gives the air of someone who tried to have a nice house but then had four kids wreck it throughout the years.

Maybe I don't blame Mrs. DiVincenzi for being so short-tempered last night.

"Good morning!" Leo calls cheerily from the kitchen. He sits at a stool at the counter, his piece of the map on the granite surface beside a cup of coffee. He's dressed for the day in cargo shorts, a Dri-FIT black shirt, and his dark hair damp and curling against his forehead from a shower, I assume. "You slept in."

"Your parents aren't here?"

"Nope," he says. "But Quinn and Caleb should be soon. His bus was running late, so she's meeting him at the stop and they're gonna walk here."

I nod, awkwardly standing in the middle of his living room in his hoodie, the same one he wore the other night with the hockey sticks on the front. I cross my arms over my chest just in case it's not enough. "How'd I get in your bed?"

"Around seven you woke up, grumbled something about how you hated sleeping on the floor, and climbed in." He gives an exasperated sigh. "And before you ask—yes, I stayed on the floor. Although I am a snuggler, so it was tempting."

He flashes a smile, so I know it's a joke. "Proud of you. And thank you. For letting me stay here. And—" I raise my hand to show off the makeshift bandage.

"Of course," he says, turning back to his map. "I only ask you give a good Yelp review. Helps business."

"I'll consider it."

We fall into an easy silence as I peer over his shoulder at the map. "Any chance you've figured out where the next clue is?" I ask.

He takes a long sip of his coffee, which looks more milk and sugar than java. "I might."

The doorbell rings, jerking me to attention. "It's just Quinn and Caleb," Leo reminds me, getting up to open it.

It's not until they step through the threshold that I relax.

"We need to talk." Notes of panic are woven into Caleb's tone.

Leo has barely locked the door behind them before Caleb's in my face.

"What happened last night? Did you see faces? Get video? How far did they chase you? Do they know you're here right now? Are they—"

"Whoa." I rub my temples. "I need you to take five steps back. One question at a time."

He takes two steps back. "Leo told us you got attacked in the middle of the night. They're going to come after the rest of us next, so I need details."

I spill everything, starting with the full story about the Rosewood Inc. board member news and sparing them the end of my talk with Daisy, although I mention her driving off. Quinn stares at the counter, seeming uninterested except for the subtle tilt of her head in my direction. Caleb hangs on every word, eyes huge behind his glasses.

"And then I came here," I say, finishing the story with a vague gesture.

"Why here?" Quinn asks. "Why not the police?"

"Too far. And . . ." Words stick in my throat. For the first time ever, I say what's been tucked in the back of my mind for a year. "When I found my dad and called nine-one-one, it took them forever to get to our house. I guess I just don't have a lot of trust in them."

"There's also Hayworth and the town paper to think about," Quinn says. "You go to the police now, that's gonna be the top story. 'Iris Rosewood's Granddaughter Attacked in Violent Search for Treasure.' We'll have even more of a target on our backs."

I nod, glancing at my phone to confirm no new notifications

have appeared. "We're running on borrowed time anyway. My uncle must still be in Boston, otherwise I'm sure he would have flipped out at my obliterated door. Once he sees it, he won't let me out of his sight."

"Getting the police involved will slow us down," Leo agrees. "Between the other people searching for it, the threat of your family losing its spot in Rosewood Inc., and now whoever is targeting you, we've only got like two days to find it."

Quinn looks at Caleb. "Brains, what're our odds?"

He releases a long, suffering sigh, taking his glasses off to clean the lenses on his forest-green polo. "Of finding a quarter of a billion dollars in two days? Not great. Of finding it before others do, some of whom are targeting *us* now? Even worse."

She shrugs. "So it keeps us on our toes."

"Why do you think they came after me?" I ask.

"It's not like anyone knows you have the map," Quinn points out. "Daisy's broadcasted a lot of shit, but not that."

"I bet she would if she knew," I mutter.

"I don't know," Caleb says. "But obviously, it gives us more motivation than ever to hurry."

A raucous knocking on the front door startles us. Panic flares in my chest as I turn to Leo. "Is someone else supposed to come?"

He shakes his head. The knock comes again followed quickly by another harsh rap. Two sets of hands.

"It's them," I say, not even sure who "them" is. But I know it must be the same people from last night. Suddenly, I'm sprinting through the darkness again, breath short, tripping through gardens in the moonlight. "They found me."

"We should run," Caleb whispers.

In one motion, Quinn pulls her switchblade from her hair, flicking it open. "I'm not afraid of them," she snarls.

"I am!" Caleb's voice is an octave higher. He crouches behind the counter, and I fall down next to him, realizing Leo has slipped out of the room. Did he ditch us to sneak out the back?

He stalks back in, clutching a hockey stick like a bat. Quinn flicks the lock on the door, then goes to the knob. Caleb and I peer from behind the safety of the corner of the counter, our breaths stilted with panic. Leo jerks his chin as a go ahead to Quinn, winding back as she flings the door open and—

"Whoa, dude, what's with the stick?"

I collapse in relief. Behind the door is none other than Jordan Bankson, Moriah Phillips, and Kev Asani—the other half of Leo and Daisy's friend group. Jordan pushes his overgrown blond hair from his eyes, looking perplexed.

"Oh, hey," Leo says, the tension slipping from his body as he lowers the hockey stick. "Just, uh, thought you were someone else."

"We've been trying to reach you all morning, dude. We're heading to the country club for a pool day. Hot as balls out. You down?"

Jordan looks past Leo to see Quinn standing beside the sofa, the knife still in her hand and a murderous gaze trained on Kev. His eyes rove further to take in Caleb and me, both of us still awkwardly crouching behind the counter. Slowly, we stand.

"What are you doing with *her*?" Moriah asks Leo, jutting her chin toward me. Her dark eyes narrow. "You're with the wrong Rosewood."

"Where's Daisy?" I ask Kev. I assumed she was still with him, since she would have surely seen my door if she went home.

He pointedly ignores Quinn's death stare, shrugging his obscenely broad shoulders. "I dunno. She left this morning and said she had things to do today."

Great. She obviously didn't go home, because I'd hope she would care enough to check on me if she saw my ruined room. But if not home, then what the hell is she up to?

"My dad is holding a private cabana just for us," Moriah says, always happy to flaunt her status as the daughter of the owners of Rosetown Country Club. "Leo, you're coming, right?"

Silence stretches, six sets of eyes peering at him. My heart gives a strange little lurch, our conversation from last night resurfacing. *I'm the yes guy.*

He looks over his shoulder at me, as if he knows exactly what I'm thinking.

You don't have to be, I try to tell him with my eyes.

"I should probably stay here," he says finally. A small sigh of relief escapes me against my will. "We're kind of working on a project, so I'll have to catch up another time."

"Whatever, dude. Good luck with your *project*." Jordan rolls his eyes, which are typically half-closed since he's under the influence of something probably illegal 90 percent of the time. He steps off the porch, muttering about all the beer he snuck from his brother's stash. If it's supposed to be last-ditch bait for Leo, he thankfully doesn't take it.

"I'll miss you today, Le," Moriah says, fluttering her lash extensions at him. Her gaze shifts to me, freezing into a cold glare. She looks me up and down, surely taking note of Leo's hoodie. With a toss of her shiny black waves and a sneer, she follows Kev and Jordan off the porch. Leo closes the door behind them.

"I think I might have preferred the kidnappers," Quinn mutters, tucking her knife back into her bun.

Leo doesn't comment, but I sense the unease rolling through him. He probably regrets staying. Surely, they'll tell Daisy, and she'll jump to her own conclusions.

"A guy I was talking to told me about how stuck-up people from Rosetown High can be," Caleb says. "I thought he was exaggerating."

"Oh!" I turn to Caleb. "Miles, right? I forgot you guys hung out the other day. How'd that go? I've been so wrapped up I forgot to reply to his texts yesterday."

Caleb suddenly finds the granite countertops *very* interesting. "It went fine." He clears his throat. "More important, we need to figure out the next clue. I'm in this with you guys, but I'm not trying to let it ruin my life. I have a perfectly normal family at home. I'm projected to get into Yale. I don't want everything getting messed up because some lady I barely knew sent me on a death hunt. Maybe this is a lesson, you know? Like, greed is lethal and all that."

"Have you eaten breakfast?"

We turn to Leo in confusion, who's already pulling a pan from a cabinet and a carton of eggs from the fridge.

"What are you doing?" I ask.

"It's just, I don't think any of us have eaten breakfast," Leo explains.

My stomach chooses this exact moment to be a dirty snitch and growl.

He grabs a spatula and points at it. "Case proven. You can't make life-altering decisions on an empty stomach. It's facts."

"And I suppose you have scientific evidence to back this?" Caleb prods.

"Yep. The evidence that I make a mean omelet. Now chill out for five minutes."

Caleb gives an exasperated sigh, collapsing on one of the stools and staring at Leo's piece of the map and the corresponding clue. I want to scream at Leo that we're wasting precious time, but if he wants to become a short-order cook, I doubt anything I can say will stop him.

And fine, maybe I wouldn't say no to an omelet.

"Come here," Quinn says, pulling me toward the couch. She nudges the coffee table out of the way, leaving an expanse of carpet for the two of us to stand. "If someone's out to get you, you need to know how to fight them off."

"I'm hoping that somebody breaking into my room with a weapon doesn't become a regular occurrence."

A wry grin feints across her lips. "Glad the Michael Myers shit didn't kill your sass. It's good armor. Now square up with me."

"What are you doing?"

"Teaching you how to defend yourself. Pretend this is a knife." She picks up the TV remote. "And I'm trying to attack you. What do you do first?"

"Scream," I reply honestly, something I did plenty of last night. "Run."

"But you can't because I've cornered you," she says. "So, your next best option is to disable me."

"Grab the knife?"

"Yeah, if you want your hand chopped off." She jabs the remote at me. "Grab the wrist. It'll slow their movement, giving you enough time to go for the throat. If you smash your elbow into someone's trachea, the blow could be hard enough to damage it and disrupt their breathing. Throw them off."

"And then I grab the knife?"

"If you want a knife so badly, you should have brought your own."

"Hey!" Leo calls from the kitchen, two strips of bacon in his hands. "Watch the vases on the mantel!"

Quinn and I move away from the mantel and its fragile decor.

"The elbow to the throat will stun them. You *should* run, but if you're feeling gutsy, wrangle the knife out of their grasp so you can stab them. And kicks to the groin are always pretty effective, too."

We try it, moving in slow mo. "Where did you learn this?"

"My mom made me take self-defense classes," she says as if it's as common as parents forcing their kids to do soccer or art camp. "We moved all the time, and some of our neighborhoods weren't as nice as others. Safety precaution."

"Bet you never thought you'd need to know it in Rosetown."

Her dark eyes glitter. "No, I definitely did. From the moment we came to this town, I could tell all the glamour was a front for something feral. And once I started school, that was confirmed."

My gaze flickers to Leo. His back is to us, two pans on the stove and enough eggs to feed ten people between them. Caleb still hunches over the counter, and every now and then he mutters something, which Leo always has a response to. The two of them make an odd pair. The jock and the nerd.

She uses the distraction to jab her elbow into my throat. I cough and glare at her. "Caught you slippin'. Again," she says, motioning for us to keep practicing.

"You have good instincts." I pick up from where she left off a minute ago. "You got yourselves in with the wolves."

To my surprise, she laughs. The sound is nice, and it lights up her face, her bun bobbing. "And wolves they are." She nods toward Leo. "Especially that one. Whatever's going on between you two, watch your back."

"Nothing's going on," I say. "We're coworkers." Who, apparently, sleep on floors together. "But why do you say that?"

"Aside from being at the mercy of Moriah's demon gaze since she's obsessed with him?" She shrugs. "Don't get me wrong—Leo is the best of them. He was the only reason I became friends with the 'cool kids.'" She rolls her eyes. "I was pretty quiet my first day, and he wouldn't stop asking me questions. Asked if I wanted to eat lunch with him, and I said sure, not realizing what I was getting myself into. Or who."

"I think he just wanted to make sure you felt like you belonged," I say, wondering how much of that is inspired by how he actually feels.

"Probably. But that still doesn't change what he did."

Dread pools in my stomach. "What's that?"

Our voices have dropped to hushes that I doubt can be heard over the sizzling bacon and Caleb's questions. Quinn leans in close, and I'm struck by the memory of my life before Dad died—swapping secrets with friends, giggling into each other's ears, passing messages just for our eyes. Quinn and I have none of that history, but it's nice to pretend for the moment.

"I'm sure you know the rumor about me and your cousin."

I try to keep my face impassable, the broken picture frame flashing in my mind. "There are *lots* of rumors about my cousin."

She doesn't buy it. "You know the one. That we kissed."

I give in, still moving to block her attacks with the remote control. "Listen, I've never believed it—"

"You should have. It's true. But I kissed her only because she kissed me first."

I try to hide my shock. Daisy's been out as bisexual since sophomore year, but I didn't want to assume something was up between the two of them just because they were really close and then suddenly not. "What does that have to do with Leo?"

"He was all for it," Quinn says. "He was the one who told me Daisy had feelings for me. When we kissed, I couldn't wait to tell him. But she had already gotten to him, twisted it so it sounded like it was all me, like she never liked me at all. And he knew she was lying—he knows her better than anyone and vice versa—but he didn't stop her from telling our friends that version, that I came onto her and it wasn't mutual. Moriah's always been a bitch, and Jordan and Kev are brainless. With Daisy and Leo teamed up against me, there was no point in sticking around. I stopped eating lunch in the cafeteria and would go to the gym.

Got into lifting and longboarding. I hadn't talked to Daisy since Christmas break when it all went down."

"Until the night of Gram's party," I recall. "You wanted to talk to her about Kev."

Quinn hits me extra hard. I yelp when the remote stings my wrist. "When we were friends, Kev was always flirting with her, and it pissed me off. She doesn't give a shit about him. She's just hooking up with him as an extra 'fuck you' to me."

"She obviously still cares about you if she's trying to make you jealous. I don't get why she's acting like that if she's the one who pushed you away."

Quinn gives me a dry expression. "Because she's a Rosewood. You have thorns, and anytime somebody tries to get close, you prick them. I didn't want to waste my time, and I think she's mad I didn't put up more of a fight for her."

Finally, the remote clatters to the ground, my grip so tight around her pale wrist that it leaves red splotches when I let go. Quinn nods in approval. "It's a talent of ours," I say.

"It's ridiculous."

"It's time for breakfast!" Leo calls cheerily. We venture to the counter and slide onto stools, the conversation we just had disappearing as quickly as it started. I can't help but glance at Quinn, a weird feeling in my chest that might be gratitude. It's a piece of her I didn't know, and I'm grateful for it.

And maybe a little bit relieved to know that Leo didn't exclusively choose Daisy over me. It seems to be a habit of his. Just like Daisy seems to develop sudden reasons to hate the people closest to her.

Leo dishes an omelet in front of me: bacon, cheese, and green onions with a side of toast. My favorite, though I don't see how he would have known that.

Caleb takes a tentative bite of his as if he expects it to be poisonous. Instead, his eyes light up. "It's good!" he says around the mouthful of egg.

"No shit," Leo laughs, stabbing into his own. "I happen to be an excellent cook."

"You learned from your mom?" I assume.

His grin falters. "My nonna."

And all at once, it hits me. I pull his piece of the map closer, then read the clue again. *Favorite snack.* The memory of Gram's birthday party shines bright, her holding a plate of meats and cheeses out to me. "*Try the salami,*" she'd said. "*It's my favorite.*"

"It's at the deli," I say. When I look up, Leo is already staring at me. There's a flicker in his eyes, like he already had the thought.

"Then what are we doing here eating *omelets*?" Quinn says before I can call him out, shoveling the rest of hers into her mouth. "Let's go."

"There's just one problem," he says. "I haven't talked to my nonna in months."

"And Gram would have known that," I say around the last bite of toast. I push my plate away, no time to do the polite thing and take it to the sink. "Which is why she put it there."

Caleb's brows furrow. "You think it's hidden somewhere in DiVincenzi's Deli?"

I nod, turning to Leo. From his hesitance, maybe he's known since the moment we first read the clue. But whatever stands between him and Nonna, it's not enough to forsake a fortune. We know that, and he does too.

"We're running out of time," I remind him. No more stalling.

Quinn hops off the stool and claps a hand on Leo's shoulder. "Time for a family reunion."

15

By the time we roll up to DiVincenzi's Deli, Leo's personality has gone through a 180-degree shift. He's barely spoken, and his grip on the wheel is white-knuckled. The few times I've glanced over from the passenger seat, it looked like he might be seconds away from cracking his teeth thanks to how tightly his jaw is clenched. He's completely on edge.

And he's not the only one.

Caleb is silent in the back seat. It wouldn't be unusual, but tension radiates from him. Something's up. And with the two boys down for the count, that leaves Quinn and me to be on our best clue-hunting game.

"Here we are," Leo says quietly, as if his nonna might hear him all the way out here. He turns off the engine. "Maybe I should stay here."

"Me too," Caleb adds.

"No," Quinn and I say at the same time.

I turn in my seat to look at her, and she flashes me the barest bones of a grin. "We all go together," I say, feeling emboldened that she's on my side. "Gram knew you were in a feud with Nonna, right?"

Leo nods.

"Then she chose this location for you in your section of the map for a reason. To give you a chance to reconcile. You have to come. I know that's what she intended."

"And are you her liaison from the dead?" Caleb mutters.

I give him a good glare, and he slides open the door. Quinn gets out behind him.

"Leo?" I prompt, noticing the way his fingers are still wrapped around the key, as if he's thinking about stabbing it back into the ignition and gunning it. I grab his hand before he can, giving his fingers a soft squeeze. "You have a chance to fix it before it's too late. I—" My throat closes suddenly, thinking of my last words to Dad, to Gram. "I'd give anything for one last shot to say the things I should have when I had the chance."

He's quiet for a moment. "I didn't tell you the real reason I didn't come to your dad's funeral." It comes out all at once, words rushed together. He won't meet my eyes. "Your dad advised mine to put everything he had into the Ice Plex. And when it all tanked, my dad blamed yours for steering him wrong. He didn't want us to pay respects. I knew it was messed-up, but I didn't fight him on it. I didn't think I *could*. Besides, the Ice Plex was my fault, too."

My chest suddenly feels tight. I don't know what to say. I knew my dad made enemies, but for people to still hate him in death?

His last statement finally hits me. "What do you mean it was your fault?"

"When my dad was considering creating the Ice Plex, he

188

almost didn't do it. But I begged him to. I thought it'd, like, I don't know, get me into the NHL. So my dad took the risk."

Leo looks at me finally, the usual coy amusement in his gaze gone. "After it flopped and we lost everything, all hell broke loose. But this fight was because of *me*. Because part of the money my dad used to fund the Ice Plex was the college fund my grandparents had been saving for me. My dad had access to it and used it without asking them. Or me. They couldn't believe he would do that. That all happened at the end of last summer. Papa got sick and died in the winter, and Dad wouldn't let us go to his funeral, either. Gram's funeral was the first time him and Nonna had been in the same room. And I'm sure you picked up on those bad vibes."

"It's not your fault," I tell him. "Your dad—"

"But it *is*, Lily." He finally looks at me, eyes swimming with hurt. I wish I could wrap my arms around him, hold him together. "I let my parents down, and I always have. So I tried really hard this year to get my grades up, which is why I got Caleb to tutor me. But I just couldn't do it. And I thought I could get recruited to play hockey on scholarship, but no coaches even scouted me last season. If I was just smarter—"

"Are we going to go find a fortune nestled in some pecorino Romano or what?" Quinn yells from outside my window.

"Let's get this over with," Leo mutters. His hand slips from my grasp as he rushes from the van. His words have rocked me, but I open my door and follow. It makes sense now why Nonna was crying in the church after Leo and his family left, why I haven't seen Leo at the deli in the time I've worked here. The

DiVincenzi rift has been festering for months.

We stride through the doors of the deli, the bell jingling as we walk in. Despite my racing thoughts, the familiar scent of freshly baked bread and sub oil is a much-needed comfort, and so is the person behind the counter.

"Lily!"

My face splits into a grin as Miles rounds the corner, and I waste no time before launching myself into his arms. He hugs me tightly, spinning me.

"What the hell?! You ghosted me on like twenty texts yesterday. It's slow today, so Nonna gave me the afternoon off. I was going to stop by your uncle's house from here to check in. Are you okay?"

"I'm—" How *am* I? I have no idea where to even begin. "It's been a really weird couple of days." I laugh, but it's the kind where tears are threatening to replace it. "Sorry I've skipped out on my shifts—"

I trail off as Miles's gaze sweeps past me, the friendliness falling away like shards of ice melting down a window. He nudges me aside, the air around him shifting and his usually grinning mouth twisting with anger.

"Speaking of ghosting," he says, striding past Leo and poking his finger into Caleb's chest.

I frown, glancing between the angry slash of Miles's mouth and Caleb's panicked brown eyes.

Caleb gulps. "Listen—"

"You know, when you didn't show up at the movies, I thought fine, whatever. I get it." Miles's voice streams with hurt. "But then you texted begging for forgiveness, just to set up another date, then ghost me again and drop off the face of the earth. What the hell? I told you I'm not into games, so whatever you're playing at, you win. I'm done."

Miles brushes past Caleb, throwing his apron onto the empty register as he heads toward the door.

Caleb reaches for his arm to stop him. "Miles, wait!"

Suddenly, it makes a lot of sense why Caleb didn't want to be seen at the funeral. Because of *Miles*. And this morning, his simple answer when I asked him about the date. There never was a date.

He knew Miles worked here. No wonder he didn't want to come in.

Miles shrugs out of Caleb's hold, storming out. Caleb tries to follow, but Quinn snatches the back of his shirt.

"Let me go!" Anger flashes across his face.

"You think you're the only one with a messed-up love life right now? Fix it later. We have work to do."

"But he's not just—he's—" Caleb sputters to her, shoulders slumping with defeat as Miles retreats from the lot in his small sedan.

Guilt swirls in my stomach. I've been so wrapped up with everything that I didn't realize my best friend was going through it.

"He was different," Caleb settles on. "I wanted things to work. That's another reason I didn't want to get involved with this—this—"

"Shit show?"

"Yes!" Caleb explodes. But he simmers when the hollowness in Leo's voice finally cracks through his hard head. I stare at Leo, then catch his trail of sight across the deli. Standing in the doorway of the kitchen behind the counter is Nonna.

It's no surprise—it is her deli. Despite this time of day usually being the lunch rush, there's no one in the shop to buffer the silence that stretches between the two of them. Leo trembles beside me, his hands stuffed in his pockets and his tall frame impossibly small.

"Hi, Nonna," Leo says. He sounds like a little boy scared to admit he tracked mud on the carpet after a day of playing in the garden.

"Leo," Nonna's voice is brittle, and if she sees me, she doesn't react. Her eyes are only for Leo as she takes him in, the gray shining beneath a film of tears. She wrings a dish towel in her veiny hands.

He cracks first. "I am so sorr—"

With impossible speed, Nonna is around the counter and crushing him in a hug so tight, it looks like it could crack ribs. "Does your father know you're here?" she asks, breathless.

"I wouldn't be here if he did," Leo mumbles. "But you're not—you're not mad at me?"

She pulls back, staring at him with a raw expression. "Mad at you? How could I ever be mad at you? I've *missed you*."

Leo's voice comes out choked. "How? It's my fault. The fight and the money and—"

"Hush now, it's never been you." Nonna's eyes light with fury. "Who told you that?"

Leo shakes his head, chest rising and falling quicker as his fists clench at his side.

Nonna goes on. "The fight was ridiculous, Leo. Any argument over money always is and always will be. But I didn't realize it would make me lose my grandkids. Especially after Papa passed last winter, I thought we'd make amends."

"I thought *you* didn't want us around. That you didn't want things to be fixed," Leo breathes. "I had no idea. Dad said—"

"Your father says a lot of things," Nonna says, pulling him into another rib-crushing hug.

"How much longer do we awkwardly stand here?" Quinn murmurs in my ear.

"As long as it takes," I reply, my heart aching at the scene unfolding behind me. But it's a good ache, the kind that means nothing's broken, just bruised. And bruises heal faster.

"I'm sorry," Leo chokes into her shoulder.

"Don't apologize," Nonna says. "And, Lily! I'm so glad to see you. This town hasn't felt the same since—"

"I know," I say, not wanting to hear the words *since Iris passed.* "But we're trying to fix that. And we think you might be able to help."

She still has one hand wrapped around Leo's arm, as if she's worried he might make a break for it if she lets go. He swipes at his eyes, turning his head away from us. "Of course. What is it you need help with?" she asks.

I take a deep breath, feeling Caleb's angst in waves behind me and Quinn's restless anticipation. When Leo faces me again, his eyes are alight with determination. "We're going to need to close the deli and search it."

It's nearly an hour before Leo yells from the cannoli case.

"Found it!" he exclaims, holding out a small slip of paper. "It was wedged in the corner under one of those frilly things."

"A doily?" I offer, retracting my hands from where they'd been shoved in the meat fridge. He nods.

Nonna shakes her head. "That Iris. I'm in this place from dawn to dusk. I never saw her leave it there."

"That's because maybe she wasn't the one to leave it," I murmur. Now that I think of it, I doubt she could have reached the frame of the painting, either. And how could she have sent the letters to Quinn, Leo, and Caleb if they arrived a week after she died?

Daisy's words from last night come back to me about suspecting Frank. But maybe she's wrong about him working against us. Could *he* be behind all of this? Who else would Gram have trusted?

Quinn grabs the clue and brings her tongue to it, taking a page out of my book. She sets it down on the counter as words appear.

Dear Lilylove,

> *If you're reading this, I can only assume you've already seen the flowers. Beautiful, aren't they? Now look to the sea, where the moon kisses the waves and the world falls away. You'll find my promise shining above the souls in love with life.*

> *Gram*

"That's obvious," Quinn says, her dark brown eyes matching the imported espresso beans on the shelf beside her—*100%*

Authentic from Sicily, the label reads. "This one's for me. It's at the Ivy."

"Of course." I remember what Quinn told us about how she met Gram. Both of them escaped the party and stared out at the sea.

"The ballroom venue?" Caleb asks, his voice quiet.

"Yep," Quinn says. "And I know exactly where. The next clue must be hanging from one of the chandeliers."

"What's so special about a chandelier?" Leo asks.

"They're the original ones from when the Ivy was first built in Hyacinth's day," Nonna explains. "Gold roses twisting around bulbs with crystals hanging off. They're exquisite. There's a smaller replica in the great room of Rosewood Manor."

"It must be in the crystals," I realize, thinking of the times I've been to the Ivy for fundraisers and the occasional wedding that requested the presence of my family. "It'd be easy to disguise something within the shine if no one's actively looking."

"Exactly," Quinn agrees. "But they're *high*. Even if we're able to see it from the ground, I don't know how we'd be able to get it."

"That seems more like a problem to think about when we get there," Leo says breezily. "If we go now—"

"Now wait a minute." Nonna holds up a weathered palm. "I know I just let you turn this place upside down looking for that, but do you really think Iris left you a trail to the fortune?"

By the end of her sentence, I have to lean in to hear her voice. Her eyes flick toward the locked front door, as if someone's about to barge in. That's when I see today's paper on the counter. The front page is a picture of the conservatory, flowers strewn and trampled, dirt everywhere. The heading reads, "Rosetown Landmark Destroyed as Viral Search for Missing Fortune Heightens."

Fuck.

"Only way to find out is to follow it," Leo says to Nonna. He pulls her in close. "I promise if we do find something, I'm going to make things right for my parents. I'll pay off whatever they took from you and couldn't give back."

Nonna's eyes water, the lines of her face more pronounced than ever. She slips into a thick Italian accent, something I've heard only when she's angry from burning bread or holding in tears. "It's never been about the money, Leo. It never will be about the money. Because no matter how much your father has, it will never be enough."

The words shake me, an unpleasant memory scratching behind my skull like mice in the walls. My final fight with Dad, before I screamed *I hate you!* like an insolent brat. I begged desperately for the money to send me to Milan.

"Please, Dad, it's all I've ever wanted. All I'll ever want again."

"I can't, Lily," he said, a current of anger in his voice. He always tried to suppress it around me, but it was simmering under the surface. "Haven't I given you enough?"

"No!" I screamed at him. "All I ever wanted was—"

"Everything," he finished grimly.

And there—something was in his eyes, the first indication that something had gone horribly wrong, I just didn't see it then. I had stormed out of our house. Before I had the chance to slam the door behind me, I heard his faint whisper like a ghost stepping through my skin.

"All I ever wanted was everything."

"But if anyone were to find it, I'd want it to be you kids," Nonna tells us, her warm gaze bringing me back. "Just please be careful."

I follow Nonna and Leo to the door, Quinn and Caleb trailing behind me. Nonna unlocks it, wraps Leo in a tight hug; then me; then Quinn, who awkwardly returns it; and even Caleb, who I'm pretty sure she's never met before. He stiffly waits for her to let go.

"One more thing," she says, hurrying into the back. She comes out holding a single classic ricotta-cream cannoli. "Miles told me you're eighteen tomorrow. Happy birthday, Lily."

"Oh." I pull out my phone, jaw falling open at the date. Tomorrow *is* my birthday. I forgot. "Thank you," I say to Nonna as I take it, pushing through the door before the bewildered looks the others give me burn holes through Leo's sweatshirt I'm still wearing. The air outside is much too hot for it, but my skin feels icy. Tomorrow, I'll be eighteen.

Which means I can legally inherit any sum granted to me.

The thought follows me as Leo pulls out of the lot to take us to the Ivy. My head spins, trying to make sense of everything. Did Gram plant the clues to *stall*? So that I'd be eighteen and no one could rightfully challenge me or control my portion of the money? But that would assume she knew when she'd die, which she couldn't have, since it was a heart attack. Maybe that's why she needed an accomplice. To make sure the timing added up.

And if that's the case, and my birthday's tomorrow, that must mean we're close.

"You're going the wrong way," Quinn says. Leo doesn't

respond, but his white-knuckled grip has returned.

Quinn gives a full-body sigh, as if playing back seat driver is the last thing she'd like to do on a smoldering Thursday afternoon. "Hey, Frat Boy," she says, flicking Leo's shoulder.

He doesn't even register it but jerks on the wheel in a wicked sharp turn. Two tires lift from the ground, my side painfully smacking against the door.

"What the hell?" I cry, thankful that the van doesn't tip over.

Caleb yelps, tossed halfway across the seat in the back, the contents of his backpack spilled onto the floor. Quinn's fingers dig into the side of my seat to keep her steady as Leo punches the gas.

"Slow down," I command, my heart climbing into my throat.

He doesn't, glancing into the rearview mirror. We're speeding toward the outskirts of town, away from the Ivy.

"Leo, stop! You're going too fast!"

"I can't," he says.

His voice is strange. Tight and pinched, like he can't find the air to support it. It makes my own breath freeze in my lungs, the engine loudly arguing as he pushes it faster.

"Somebody's following us."

16

"Don't look."

Against his wishes, Quinn, Caleb, and I whip our heads toward the back window. Through it, a black SUV trails us. The tinted windows, along with the glare of the sun on the windshield, make it impossible to see who's inside.

I can barely breathe. "How long have they been following us?"

"I think since we left the deli," Leo replies. Another harsh turn sends my ribs into the console between us. Quinn and Caleb groan. "You might want to hold on."

"Hold on to wh—?" Caleb's panicked voice breaks off into a yelp as Leo jerks the van off the road and between a gap in the trees. The ground turns rough beneath the wheels, the terrain that makes up the edge of town wooded and rocky. There's a slim path for us to squeeze through, and I scream as we soar so close to a massive trunk that the side-view mirror gets smacked off.

"Shit," Leo mutters.

"They're still following us," Quinn urges. "Gun it!"

"I *am*! It's an old van!"

"We should surrender," Caleb suggests, fingers clenched around his backpack like it's the only thing tethering him to earth. "Maybe they'll let us go if we give them what they want."

"We did *not* make it this far to surrender," Quinn argues.

I grab Leo's piece of map from where he left it in the cupholder. "Beyond the trees are the train tracks that line the border of town, then Creekson beyond it," I say, attempting to conjure a plan. "If we can make it outside of Rosetown, maybe we can lose them somewhere in Creekson."

My words are punctuated by a branch whipping into the windshield hard enough to crack it. We all scream, and Leo somehow manages to keep his hands on the wheel and continue narrowly dodging trees.

"Did I lose them?" Leo asks.

"Not even close," Quinn replies as the whistle of a train sounds. It nearly drowns out the roar of the engine. "This is some *Fast and Furious* shit."

"More like *Grand Theft Auto*," Leo counters, fingers flexing over the wheel. "But don't worry. I've got a plan."

"If it's anything short of making this thing fly, I don't want to hear it," Caleb says.

"You won't want to hear it anyway."

There's a gleam in Leo's eye, a daring spark that's somehow attractive and terrifying at the same time. The train whistle blows again as we burst from the cover of the trees, the tracks on the other end of the stretch of tall grass field.

"They're gaining." Caleb's voice is more like a screech. "Pull over, we need to sur—"

"Bullshit!" Quinn cuts him off. "There's a hockey stick in the back, right? Let me at them. I'll smash their fucking brains—"

"They could have *guns!*"

"And I have fists and unbridled rage."

"Leo." I stare at him, cutting off the arguments behind us. Leo's gaze doesn't waver from the tracks we're barreling toward and the train peeking from around the bend. *"Leo."*

"Do you trust me, Lily Rose?" he asks.

I think of him last night, lying to his mom to cover for me. The Cheez-It separating us. Waking up in his bed alone. "I—"

"I don't!" Caleb cuts in, gripping the back of the seat. "You see that train, right? Tell me you see that train!"

"And I thought things couldn't get any more interesting," Quinn says, her typical sarcasm twisting with a vine of fear.

"If anyone's into praying, now's the time," Leo suggests.

"You're not serious," I say. "Leo, *stop!*"

He goes faster.

"We're going to die." Caleb sounds faraway, like he's already on his way to the great unknown. "That train is going to hit us. We're—"

"I would *love* some encouragement," Leo says.

"We're going to get smashed into pancakes."

"Unfortunately, I'm more of a waffles guy."

"Leo, it's right—" My voice disappears into a shriek. We're at the tracks now, and even if he did slam the brakes, it would be too late. He could jerk the wheel, but the van would flip. I wonder if Gram knew the boy pulling her weeds is a maniac with a death wish.

I feel the moment the wheels hit the tracks because the van *literally* gets air. Caleb takes Leo's suggestion, muttering a string of Hail Marys. Quinn's urging Leo faster, faster, *faster*. I look to my right. And suddenly—there it is. Time slows as the face of the train charges toward me. The heat makes it warped, like it's part of a mirage. Will Daisy miss me? Probably not. I hope Dad and Gram might be waiting on the other side.

And then, nothing but grassy green fields again. It takes a disorienting moment to realize we're across the tracks, the whistle of the train behind us as it zips past. I barely make out the SUV on the other side of the train. Cut off from us.

Quinn's maniacal laugh is the first sound to break our stupor. "Holy shit, Frat Boy! You actually didn't kill us."

"I knew we'd make it," Leo says, a victorious grin splitting his face as he whoops. "Probably."

"I'm going to puke," Caleb groans.

"It could be worse—we could have ended up like Lily's cannoli," Leo says. I look at my hands, realizing I had clenched my fist around the cannoli Nonna had given me. Shards of the shell litter the floor, and the thick ricotta filling seeps between my fingers, coating my tampon bandage. I hadn't even realized I still held it.

I open the window and rid myself of the sticky mess, then peel off the makeshift bandage and fold it in a few Burger King napkins from the glove compartment. My cut looks better in the daylight, just a thin stripe of red from the base of my thumb to my pinkie.

"That was unhinged." I can't help the laugh bubbling up as we leave the field and Leo pulls onto a dirt road. I think I lost my mind on the other side of the tracks.

"Maybe, but we left those ass wipes in our dust. You all can send your thank-yous as an Edible Arrangement to my new mansion once we find the money."

"Oh jeez, Brains is actually gonna spew," Quinn says, pounding on the back of my seat. Caleb's eyes bug, his lips pressed together. "Pull over!"

Caleb spills out of the van as Leo stops on the side of the road, chunks of his omelet leaving his lips as he hunches over the hot asphalt. I grab some napkins to hand to him as the rest of us get out to assess the damage.

"My dad is going to slaughter me." Leo releases a long breath. The van is wrecked. Aside from the passenger-side mirror having been smashed off, and the cracked windshield, it's full of scratches, some enough to chip the paint and others deep gouges. It looks awful, and that's saying something considering it certainly wasn't a looker before.

I peer toward the direction of the field. We're out of eyeshot, but we shouldn't stay here long.

Quinn reads my mind. "Do you think they'll come after us?"

"Wouldn't you if millions of dollars were on the line?"

She huffs. "'Nough said. We're fucked."

"Wait, look at this," Leo says, his phone in his hand. He turns the screen toward us. I squint against the glare of the sun.

It's a TikTok of Daisy. She stares at the screen with her face flushed, brown eyes wild. "Hey, garden gang, I have an update for you on the wild Rosetown shit," she says. *Garden gang* is what she calls her followers. I bite back a gag at the cliché.

"I just drove through town in my new Mercedes—" *Had to*

drop that in there. "And I'm actually getting scared now. I almost got hit by a creeper van in a street chase with an SUV."

"What are the odds?" Caleb mumbles, done puking and now watching with us.

Silently, I hold out the napkins. Quinn offers a crumpled stick of Extra gum that she must have taken out of one of the many pockets on her cargo pants. He takes both.

"Small town," Leo says.

"And that's not the only weird thing going on," Daisy says to the camera. "Someone broke into the conservatory last night. My dad blames it on me because people are coming to Rosetown to look for the fortune thanks to my viral video. But this news was bound to get out. And another thing: a friend from school sent me a vid taken at the Rosetown Museum of Fine Art yesterday of a random electrical outage."

"That was literally us!" I exclaim.

Nobody listens, eyes glued to Daisy's face as her expression sobers.

"These all sound random, don't they? But I'm convinced they're not. Someone is messing with Rosetown while looking for my gram's money." Daisy's voice drops into a conspiratorial whisper. "And I don't think these are your regular tourists."

I might have to agree with her on that.

Daisy sighs, blowing a chin-length chunk of hair from her eyes. "I'll share more details as soon as I have them. You know I'll keep my garden gang in the loop." She throws up a peace sign, and the video goes back to the beginning.

"We can't go back to Rosetown," Caleb says. "Not if all that stuff is going on."

"Half that stuff was our fault," Quinn reminds him.

"We have to go back." I pull out my section of the map from my crossbody bag, gesturing for them to hold theirs up too against the battered side of the van. "If we take the long way, we'll end up near the back of the Ivy." I trace Quinn's piece with its jagged etching of rocks and water signifying the coastal edge of town. "We sneak in, find the next clue, and get out before we're seen."

"Do you think we could do that?" Leo asks Quinn.

"Normally, yes," she replies. "But with the Hyacinth Ball tomorrow, my mom's going apeshit at the Ivy trying to get everything perfect. People will be setting up all night, and they'll definitely recognize me. You too." She nods at me. "Plus, a ton of people come to town for it. Add that to the people already coming for the hunt, and that's going to plug up the main roads." She draws a circle with her pointer finger around the Ivy, then fans out to show the four main roads in Rosetown leading to it. She's right. They're backed up on good days, so I can only imagine what kind of traffic a ball and rumored treasure are bringing.

"Also, now the people following us know what the van looks like," Leo adds. "Staying away from main roads when we go back is big. They'll be looking for us."

We stare at the map, each piece held up with one of our hands. "There is a way into town that might work." Caleb points toward a tiny sliver of road starting on Leo's northeastern piece and running along the very edge of the harbor on Quinn's. "This road isn't used much by the public because it's one of the oldest, from before the mains were built. It goes all the way to the harbor, past the lot, and ends at the boat graveyard at the most southern point of Rosetown. If we go this route, we'd have to backtrack on foot to get in, but it could work."

My mind whirls as a plan begins to form. "Quinn, isn't the theme for tomorrow a masquerade?"

She nods.

"So maybe we don't sneak in at all. Well, we'll probably have to take a back door, but let's be just another guest. With masks on, nobody should think it's us, or have any reason to assume we'd be there. It'd probably be the safest place in town with heightened security."

"I like where you're going with this." Leo's eyes light up. "Sounds like we need aliases."

"Don't even start," Quinn groans. "But I guess I see how this might work."

"Say we see the clue. How would we *get* it? If it's hanging from a chandelier and we're in a room with hundreds of people, that doesn't leave us much room to be inconspicuous," Caleb points out.

"We wait till the end when everyone's gone?"

"No," Leo denies me. I know his plan is diabolical from the way his mouth tilts. "We cause a diversion."

"Fire?" Quinn asks, a little too excited. I wonder how long she's dreamed of destroying the Ivy, the one thing her mother cares about more than anything else.

"Fire *alarm*," I correct. "We're not trying to kill people. Just get them out."

"That means we'd have to stall until tomorrow," Leo says. "Which might throw our stalkers off our trail."

"There's something off about that," Caleb says, leaning against the side of the van. "According to the paper, lots of people are coming to Rosetown, but I feel like most of them aren't seriously thinking they'll find a fortune, more just want to act touristy and see what all the talk is about, like Daisy said. And I doubt any of them are willing to stalk a bunch of teens over it. But I think the people who just followed us have *been* following us and are the same people who targeted you last night, Lily. I'm pretty sure I saw that same SUV yesterday when we were leaving the museum."

A memory sparks. "Wait, I did, too."

"I think I might have seen it pass us when we left the conservatory," Leo adds. "I remember thinking it was weird that there wasn't a license plate."

"Yeah." Quinn nods. "I just realized that."

Caleb sucks in a breath. "I don't think we're dealing with amateurs here. There are people who take shit like this super seriously. Like, *legit* treasure hunters. They'll probably go as far as grave robbing, shoot-outs, art heists, you name it."

"So if the people who targeted me are the real deal, that makes sense, doesn't it?" I ask. "They probably thought the clue we found led to the conservatory, since that's where we stopped before you left me at my uncle's. Then they trashed it while looking. When they couldn't find it, they came to find me."

"How would they know where you are?" Quinn asks me.

I shrug. "Everyone knows I'm banned from the manor thanks to Daisy. My uncle is the only person I have left to live with. Plus, he said he was going to stop by the conservatory on his way to

Boston. Maybe they saw that he was there and figured nobody would be home with me. They might have even watched Daisy leave and waited until they thought I was asleep." My neck prickles at the notion that somebody has been watching me.

"Or maybe someone told them," Caleb says. "I noticed your cousin didn't get a piece of the map."

He raises a good point. My knee-jerk reaction is to defend her, but then I remember this morning how Kev said she was busy—*doing what?* "No, she didn't."

"Daze wouldn't do this," Leo counters. He looks at Quinn. "Back me up."

She shrugs. "I don't know. She's always been pretty clever. Good at twisting things to get the result she wants."

The double meaning isn't lost on Leo. He looks at the ground.

"If she somehow figured out that we all got clues leading to the fortune and she didn't, it's not all that out there that she'd find some pros to find it for her," I say.

"It doesn't matter if she did or didn't. These attackers pose a bigger problem. Now, instead of hunting the treasure, they've started hunting us," Caleb concludes.

A thick silence falls. Hunting down a fortune is hard enough. But *being* hunted? There's no way Gram anticipated this turn of events.

Quinn breaks it first. "So what do we do? Go back tonight and they hunt us down all over again?"

"If I go back home, I might not be able to get back out for the ball. Especially if my parents find out I was at the deli today, which is doubly bad, since I'm grounded," Leo says. He glances at Caleb suggestively. "Unless—"

"Absolutely not," Caleb beats him to it. "I am *not* taking you to my house. I can't put my sisters and dad in danger like that. I won't."

"I don't want to, either," I agree. "I'll be in a similar boat once my uncle sees what happened to my room. He texted on our way to the deli that he's heading back from Boston, so I don't have much time. We can't go home until we find the money and end this."

"If we don't go back, how will we get clothes for tomorrow's party?" Quinn asks.

My beautiful crushed-velvet dress from my favorite vintage thrift shop comes to mind. The shop is a few hours away and probably won't be open by the time we get there, but we'll have plenty of time to stop tomorrow. Plus, getting as far away from Rosetown as possible seems like the best course of action. "I know a place."

"Then it's settled." Leo gives the busted van a smack as he saunters back to the driver's door. He flings it open, casting a grin at us over his shoulder. "For tonight, we're fugitives."

17

"I was hoping being runaways would have more pizzazz," Leo says as we pull into a vacant gas station hours later.

The tank is nearly empty, and from the sounds the van is making, I'm pretty sure it's either about to explode or sputter to a pitiful death. And since we need it to get back to Rosetown tomorrow, that's not an option.

"Was getting chased through the woods not glamorous enough for you?" Quinn asks.

"I just think a big fight with lightsabers would have been cooler."

"We should stay here for the night," I say, taking in the big parking spots that are meant for truckers. There's a small 7-Eleven attached, and a sign points to bathrooms on the side of the building. I glance at my phone screen and the six missed calls from Uncle Arbor and three worried texts, not to mention the handful of messages from Miles including *wtf are u doing w caleb from creekson?* and *bigger question—wtf are u doing w LEO????* My stomach twists, hunger and anxiety forming a pit. I should answer him, but I don't even know where to start.

"I need air," Caleb mumbles, sliding the side door open. He

hasn't spoken much since calling his dad a few hours ago to say he wouldn't be home tonight, which didn't sound like it went over well. Like me, I don't think Caleb spends too many nights away from his own bed.

He pauses outside my open window. "Has—um, has Miles said anything to you about me since we saw him?"

I glance at the text, then deftly lock my phone. "Not really."

Caleb nods, walking into a grassy patch away from the pumps and winding his arms around himself.

"Maybe I should—"

"I'll go talk to him." Quinn cuts Leo off. "I know what it's like to have someone slip through your fingers."

The words are a clever dagger stabbed right between Leo's ribs to hit him where it hurts. Quinn leaves; Leo's throat bobs with what might be shame. The sudden silence is too much to bear.

"I'm gonna go to the bathroom," I tell him, slipping out. I wander through the dimly lit parking lot, finally making the call I've been pushing off for hours.

Uncle Arbor's line rings and rings, and every terrible second drags on like a thousand. Thoughts assault me, images of him coming home to find the house in ruins and an ambush. Maybe the hunters went back to wait there for me, found him instead, and killed him. Maybe Daisy, too, if she ever went home. Maybe all the times he called me, he was calling for help.

"Lily? Are you okay?"

His voice is flooded with relief. So is mine.

"Yes. Kind of. I'm so sorry I didn't call sooner. Are you okay?"

"Of course," he says. "Why wouldn't I be?"

I frown at a semi-burnt-out sign advertising buy-one-get-one-free hot dogs as I walk around the building. "Are you home?"

"For several hours now," he says. "Daisy, too, in her room."

Yeah, I bet.

"Was worried about you. You weren't here when I got back."

"Haven't—" The words stick in my throat, mixing with confusion. "Haven't you seen my door? My room?"

His feet shuffle up the stairs, and I wait for his sharp intake of breath. But it doesn't come. His voice is puzzled. "What about it? You're a little old for me to be telling you to fix your bed, don't you think?"

I grind to a stop. I've been pacing outside the bathroom, my free hand clenched around the ruby at the base of my throat like an anchor to earth. "You don't see my door?"

"It's right in front of me."

My heart pounds in my ears, the glint of metal shining as it smashed through the wood. "It's not . . . it's not broken?"

He's quiet. "Why would it be broken?"

"Someone had a weapon, and—" Was I dreaming? No, I couldn't have been. I'm standing outside a grungy bathroom in nothing but my white Converse, the leggings I wore to bed, an old T-shirt, and Leo's hoodie that I tugged on this morning. There is no way I made last night up. The cut on my palm is proof.

"What do you mean someone had a weapon?" Uncle Arbor's voice grows with urgency. "What's going on? Where are you?"

"Somebody was in the house last night. They chased me." My chest tightens.

"Lily." Uncle Arbor's voice has changed. It's careful, as if I might shatter. "Your room looks normal. The front door was locked when I got home. I want you to come home. Tell me where you are, and I'll come pick you up."

He doesn't believe me. He thinks I'm losing it. Maybe I *am* losing it.

"Lily—"

"I can't come home, but I'm safe with a friend," I burst out. "I have to go. I'll be back by tomorrow."

"Wait—"

I hang up, dashing into the bathroom and slamming the door shut behind me. I press my back against it, starting to power down my phone when a new text from Miles flashes across my screen. A series of question marks and an image.

I open it, staring at the screenshot of his Snapchat showing an unopened DM from Daisy. *What the—*

Three dots appear and a new message pops up.

Miles: ur cousin just friended me. do I open it?

NO, I type back. The last thing I need is Miles getting mixed up in whatever Daisy's up to.

Me: ignore n delete

No answer for a moment. Uncle Arbor is calling again, but I block. Finally, Miles writes back.

Miles: where r u?

Me: safe

Ish.

Me: sorry bout caleb. I'll explain later. need a favor. you good for it?

213

Another long pause.

Miles: u know I am

I take a deep breath.

Me: if my uncle calls looking for me, say I'm with you. pls.

I wait, staring at the bubble on the screen. I'm ready to beg him when his message appears.

Miles: ok

And then:

Miles: but don't make me end up on the news bawling my eyes out about how if I told the truth, I might have saved u. whatever ur up to, stay alive. corpses don't get buried in couture

A breathless laugh escapes. Two days ago, staying alive wasn't a tall order. Now, it's supersize.

Me: tragic

A knock outside the door startles me. "Just a minute!" I call, shutting off my phone and turning on the sink to splash cold water on my face. Everything feels too close, like the tile is inching in along with all its germs. I crank the water to hot, hoping the shift will bring clarity. All it does is scald me.

"Are you okay?" It's Leo. "Quinn and Caleb are back."

"I'm fine."

I assume he's walked away, but then he knocks again. "I have three sisters. I can tell a lying *I'm fine* when I hear it."

Go away. But my lips can't form the words. In fact, I can't feel them at all. I don't think there's any breath in my lungs. I've used up all the oxygen, my fingertips tingling. Because suddenly, I'm a person who needs to be told to *stay alive.* People with weapons are hunting me. And even worse, I might be losing my mind, imagining last night's attack or some of it or none of it or—

"Lily Rose?"

Before I think twice, I'm ripping the door open and taking massive gulps of the muggy outdoor air. Leo holds out a cup for me. "I got you a Slurpee."

I burst into tears.

He blanks, glancing into the cup of syrupy ice like it insulted me. "Uh, they have other flavors if you're not into blue raspberry."

I grab him by the hem of his shirt, pulling him into the bathroom with me and locking the door before somebody sees. I need to get control of myself. I *have* to.

"I called my uncle." I pace the small space, trying to calm my breathing. My vision is narrowing into a tunnel. I grab the sink to steady myself before I pass out. The pressure reminds me of the cut on my palm. The pain brings some clarity back. "He said nothing's wrong with my door, but I *know* somebody chased me to your house last night. I—they must have gone back and replaced it, which sounds out there, but—"

"I believe you," Leo interrupts. Slowly, he turns me around so I can stare into his eyes. The back of my legs press against the cracked porcelain of the sink, the coolness seeping through my leggings and grounding me as I perch on it. "You were so freaked last night. I've never seen you like that. I know you're not making it up."

I force air through my nose, taking three deep breaths and wiping my eyes. Knowing that he believes me, that he doesn't think I'm fabricating this, makes the tunnel widen.

"Somebody wants me dead," I say, the severity of the statement sinking into me.

"I like to think of it more as somebody wants *us* dead. You know, it's a team thing."

That fishes a watery snort out of me. "Somehow, not comforting." Caleb comes to mind first, who never wanted to be involved in the first place. If anything happens to him, or Quinn, or even Leo . . .

"We're in this together," Leo promises.

He's so close that his waist fits in the space between my knees. An odd urge to pull him closer fills me, but I force my hands to stay on the sink.

"I'm not going to let anything happen to you. Or the other two. That's why Gram chose me."

"Chose you?"

His chest puffs out in pride. "Us. Gram picked us for a reason. We've all got roles. Caleb is obviously why we've gotten this far. He's smart and he plans for the worst, and every team needs someone like him. Quinn's the wild card, fifty percent rage and fifty percent chaos. The motivator who keeps us on track. Good for morale. And me, I'm the brawn. I've gotten in plenty of fights on the rink, so I can get scrappy if I have to. I *did* manage to get us away from the hunters earlier."

"And sent us right in the path of an oncoming train."

He pokes me playfully. "Details. My point is, I'll fight for you. Whatever it takes."

His words steal my breath in a completely different way than minutes ago. I gaze up at him. "And what's my role, Leo James?"

I don't know where the nickname comes from, but he swallows at it.

"Well, since you're a Rosewood, this all kind of revolves around you. So I guess that makes you the leader, in a way. You know, in between the mental breakdowns."

My voice comes out small. "I don't feel like a leader right now."

Leo holds up the blue raspberry Slurpee in an offering. "That's because you just got chased. Totally normal to feel a little down in the dumps given the circumstances."

I laugh, my tears drying as I take the Slurpee from him. He backs up, and for some reason I wish he wouldn't. That we could just stand here, ignore whoever's after us and the money we have yet to find. That I could weave my hands through his messy strands and—

"We should get back," I say to stop the thought, then take an obnoxiously loud slurp. Whatever was fizzing between us breaks, probably for the better. He smiles, and together, we walk back to the van.

"Do you really think we'll find it?" I ask.

"Yeah, I do." Something passes across his face. For a moment, he seems miles away from me, like he's remembering something from a time before. He blinks and he's back. "We have to, ya know? And I guess I've been waiting all my life for a chance to prove that I'm more than just my parents' youngest who's weighing them down. My parents just—all they fight about is money. And I've always felt like that's my fault, because I was the last kid they never meant to have. I'll never live up to my sisters or be who my dad wants me to be. And Gram knew all that, and that money would have solved it. Well, probably." He gets quiet. "I trust her. We're close. I can feel it. We'll find it by Saturday."

I trust Gram, too, I want to say. But I'm not sure it's the truth anymore.

"Bon appétit," Quinn says as we climb into the back of the van, but her mouth is full of food, so it sounds more like "bone apple teeth." She spreads her hand across an arrangement of chip bags and candy, as if she and Caleb ran through the aisles of 7-Eleven and wiped the shelves of the unhealthiest snacks they could find. Regardless, I'm starving, so I open a bag of Cheetos.

"This isn't so bad," Leo says, munching on Cool Ranch Doritos.

The red and blue flavor crystals stick to his lips, and the urge to press mine to his and taste it hits me like a fist. Which is strange, because I've never really had the urge to kiss *anyone*.

The feeling is terrifying. I shove a handful of Cheetos in my mouth to staunch it.

"I'd give it a solid two on Yelp," Leo continues.

"If the floor of your bedroom was a Holiday Inn, then this is a Motel Six."

"More like Motel Zero," Quinn corrects me, scooping out the contents of her pudding cup with her tongue, given our lack of utensils.

Even Caleb gives a breathy chuckle at that, thankfully in better spirits.

In the ensuing silence, the words I sat on for the entire drive out here brew on my tongue. I'm scared for them to be out in the open, but I know they have to be. "I just want you to know—all of you—that you don't need to keep doing this."

They pause their munching, staring at me.

"I know we all have our reasons for wanting the money and that Gram chose all of us. But she is *my* grandmother. I don't want any of you getting hurt, especially if you don't want to be part of this in the first place." I'm horrified to feel the pressure of a lump forming in my throat. I push on, staring into the now empty bag of Cheetos. "I can finish this myself. I'll still split the money with you all. If I live to see it."

Five days ago, I wouldn't have felt anything toward this car full of people. Quinn would still be that skater girl I never spoke to, Caleb a complete stranger, and Leo someone I swore I would never talk to again. But now . . . now they're my friends, I think. The thought of them getting hurt makes an ache bloom inside of me.

"This whole thing is fucked-up," I say when no one says anything. I can barely squeeze it out around the lump. "At first, I thought it was something Gram did just for me. To like, distract me from grieving or something. Like one last game. But now, it's not a game anymore. Obviously." I laugh, the sound sour like the pack of gummy worms in Leo's hand. God, I don't think I've ever felt so vulnerable in my life. "I don't want you three to get hurt. You're not Rosewoods. You have a choice, a life beyond all of this. I don't."

It's not totally true. I could have had a life beyond this. It's a burning truth I've kept close about Mom leaving, but maybe it's time to spill and put the last terrible piece of me out there.

"That was a very dramatic monologue." Quinn smiles teasingly.

My last secret recedes again. Probably for the best.

"But I think I speak for all of us when I say we're in this together. You playing martyr and letting us off the hook isn't going to fly."

I huff out a breath, half annoyed and half relieved. "I'm trying to *save* you."

She grins wickedly, flexing. "Do I look like I need saving?"

Leo raises his hockey stick. "Ditto on my end. You're stuck with me, Lily Rose."

I bite back my smile, turning to Caleb. "You don't have to—"

He holds up a hand. "I appreciate the out," he says. "But I'm sticking with you guys. Listen, as wild as you are—like almost-getting-hit-by-a-train wild—we have each other's backs. I think that's the real reason Gram pulled us together. Yes, we need the money. But it's deeper than that." He takes a breath and looks at me. "I never told you what happened when I met Iris.

"It was during my internship last summer. I was sitting in the room with *The Three Flowers* by myself during a lull. She sat next to me." His eyes get a faraway look. "I knew who she was, of course. I'd harbored this anger toward her, like somehow it was her fault my mom died. Mom had been leaving Rosetown, and Rosetown wouldn't exist without your family. Being angry at someone made it easier. But I was mad at someone else, too. Me."

My heart pangs for him. I know what it's like to want to place the death of a loved one on someone's shoulders so you can have somewhere to direct your rage. In my case, it's just always been at myself.

Caleb sighs. "When I was little, my mom used to tell me, *Be brave, Caleb.* I didn't climb monkey bars or jump on trampolines because I was scared of getting hurt. I refused to go to birthday parties, so I didn't have many friends. I've spent my whole life avoiding unpredictable things. Things that could hurt me. One of those things was letting people in. The day I met Gram, I was mad because I did the thing I always do. I had started talking to a guy I liked. Kinda got into him, and then I ghosted. It's what I do. People get close to me, and it feels too risky."

"Ah, you're afraid of catching feelings," Leo muses. "It's a nasty virus."

"It's deeper than that." Caleb looks at his hands. "I'm good at things with answers, like tests. But feelings and relationships take courage. I can't be brave, like my mom told me to. I'm too afraid I'll care about someone and then they'll be here one day and gone the next. And it got even worse after my mom died. Because what if that happens again?" His voice rises with emotion. "That somebody else I love gets taken from me. I don't think I can live through something like that twice."

"I know what you mean," I murmur, thinking of Dad. I was so mad at him and left the house that day just assuming he'd be there when I got back. Except, he wasn't. He was already dead when I knelt beside him in the bathroom and shook him. Dead when I called the EMTs and they rushed in. Dead when they put him on a stretcher covered by a sheet, his limp hand hanging out of it. The wedding band around his finger with the Rosewood crest. His nail beds blue.

The memory is so foul I have to force down the bile climbing up my throat. Caleb takes my hand like he can tell, squeezing it.

"I wish you didn't," he says. "I told Iris all about it. She had this look in her eyes, like she understood. Was listening to every word. I admitted how I was so lonely. That I felt like I'm letting my mom down. How suffocating it was to feel like nobody really knew who I was, because I wouldn't let them. Like at any moment, I could vanish."

I want to throw my arms around him so badly. Instead, I squeeze back.

"She said she understood," he says softly. "That sometimes, holding people at arm's length was easier. Safer. But she made me promise to at least try to let someone in. And she'd try, too."

"Miles." His hurt face flashes before my eyes. "You were going to try with him."

"He just seemed so brave. Came right up to me at the party and just started talking to me as if he's known me for years. I thought maybe he'd be good for me. But I was bound to push him away. If anything, the past few days just gave me a good excuse. I could have been talking to him if I tried."

"You should," I stress. "He's a good person. So are you."

Caleb smiles. "I know he is. I messed up, and now he hates me."

"I can talk to him. Maybe he'll listen to me."

Caleb eyes me. "Really? You'd do that?"

I nod, and he sighs.

"No, it should come from me. I need to learn to fix things instead of run. I need to—" His voice catches. "Be brave, I guess."

"Running is so much easier," Quinn says quietly. From the faraway look in her eye, I wonder if she's thinking about Daisy.

"Running isn't *all* bad," Leo pipes up. "It is the reason we're sitting here right now with this decadent dinner instead of tied up in the back of a treasure hunter van."

I laugh, rustling through the rest of our snacks. "Gram would roll her eyes so hard if she saw you refer to Hostess cupcakes as decadent."

"Well, good thing she's not here, because you have a lousy track record with her birthday cakes." Leo takes the cupcakes from the pile and unwraps one, handing it to me.

For a moment, I'm transported back to a time when Dad would buy these behind Mom's back for my birthday. There's no way Leo would know such an intimate detail, but the timing of it brings tears to my eyes.

"Happy birthday, Lily Rose."

"Happy birthday," Quinn and Caleb echo as I take the cupcake.

I pretend to blow out a candle, then take a bite. The clock on the dash says midnight exactly. I catch Leo's eye, and he gives me an innocent smile. I think somehow, he planned this.

"Thank you for sticking with me." I raise the half-eaten cupcake. "My wish is that by this time tomorrow, we're millionaires."

Leo gawks. "You can't *say* your wish. Jesus, that's birthday protocol one-oh-one."

Quinn knocks her cupcake against mine. "Nah, we need the

extra power for this one." She takes a bite, her lips spreading into a chocolate-coated grin. "Let's manifest this shit."

Caleb and Leo tap theirs against mine. Leo gives me a toothy smile. "New year, new nickname. Welcome to eighteen, Grandma."

Eighteen. Holy shit, I'm *legal.*

I eat the last bite, my heart giving an odd, happy flutter at the four of us. For the first time in a long time, I feel like I've found somewhere I belong. "I think I prefer Lily Rose."

18

"Hold still," I murmur to Caleb around the needle between my teeth. He huffs, his hands held out so I can finish shortening the cuffs of his oversize heather-gray blazer we thrifted earlier today. Since then, I've been making the best alterations I can on our vintage outfits with my travel sewing kit. His sleeves are the last adjustment to perfect before stepping into the Ivy for the masquerade ball.

"I've been holding still," he mutters. "Wasn't thrifting for two hours enough torture?"

"It was one," I correct. One hour in which all of them complained as they picked out the ugliest outfits in the store. I had to take over and play stylist. And I loved it—choosing the best colors, fabrics, and accents for each of them reminded me why I'm doing all this. I want to go to FIT. Whether there's a place for me at Rosewood Inc. or not, I'll find a way to be in the fashion industry. It's my dream.

The dress I snagged is an emerald-green hue with a flouncy skirt that made me think of Gram as soon as I saw it. It's a little snug, but I haven't eaten anything today aside from the Egg McMuffins we got this morning after leaving the gas station, so it'll do. It has a high neck, too, so I can still wear my ruby necklace hidden beneath it, and I found gold heels that perfectly complement the soft chiffon. I even added a small pocket in the left side by my waist where there was already a rip in the fabric.

"Done." I tie the end of the thread and make sure both cuffs are even. The van rolls to a stop as Leo pulls into a shadowed spot at the harbor.

"I wish you had let me get the orange shirt," Leo says as we hop out of the van, sunset streaking the sky pinks and golds. "This one's itchy."

"You looked like a carrot," I tell him.

Quinn and Caleb hum in agreement.

"Maybe I wanted to look like a carrot," he mumbles.

I can't even glance at him without blood rushing to my cheeks. When I picked out the black pants, white dress shirt, and gold vest and tie, I didn't think about how it'd look on him aside from seemingly matching his tall measurements. And then he walked out of the fitting room.

I couldn't *breathe.* It was like all the air was sucked from my lungs. I don't like how my brain clicked off for a few seconds. It took the flirtatious voice of the cashier to snap me out of it, pay for our things with the credit card Caleb's dad gave him *only for emergencies,* and get the hell out of there before she undressed him with her sultry blue eyes.

It's left me uneasy all day. I've never had a crush before, never really gotten close enough to a boy to stir those feelings. But between having the urge to kiss Leo last night, not being able to think clearly when he walked out of the fitting room today, and the fact that I can't stop picturing him in the museum grinning down at me while surrounded by artwork, it's definitely more than just fleeting butterflies.

But right now, that has to be the furthest thing from my mind. I need to stay on track tonight.

"We're meeting my coworker around the back," Quinn tells us, taking long strides across the lot in the maroon pantsuit I found for her. The hems are a little long, but I ran out of matching thread, so I couldn't do much about it. "He'll sneak us through the kitchen."

"Will he tell your mom?" I ask.

"Nah," she replies as we cling to the shadows and circle the back of the Ivy.

The main lot is overflowing with people in stunning party-wear.

"He's chill. And trust me, no one working tonight is going to want to interrupt my mom anyway. She's already pissed thanks to me bailing with a crap excuse. Between that and focusing on everything going perfectly, she'll be super busy all night."

We stop near the trash bins and the kitchen door, which create an interesting mix of aromas. Quinn's coworker has yet to show. The ball itself only started ten minutes ago, and droves of masked people in their finest have passed under the twisting ivy archway that gives the venue its name. There're so many people here that I doubt we'll run into trouble blending in once we're inside with our masks on. But getting into the ballroom is half the battle.

The other half we planned out on the way back to Rosetown

today. According to Quinn, from seven to seven thirty is the mingling of the guests. Dancing, hors d'oeuvres, champagne. At seven thirty, everyone takes their seat for a welcome speech from Quinn's mom, then dinner. Once that happens, our chances of finding the clue and getting out are next to nothing, because we'll need to find a place to hide while everyone eats. Not to mention my uncle will likely be there, too, so avoiding both him and Liz will be riskier the longer we're inside. Caleb also calculated the time it should take for the fire department to arrive once we pull the alarm. Seven minutes if speeding from the other side of town and cutting quickly through traffic. If we wait until people are seated, it's going to take nearly that just for the room to get up and evacuate.

So the first thirty minutes is our sweet spot, especially given Liz should spend most of it outside greeting guests and my uncle typically arrives late to these things. We need to find the clue, pull the alarm, run to the neighboring ballroom under construction, where Quinn claims there's a ladder tall enough to reach the chandelier, drag it into the main one which hopefully is evacuated by then, get the clue, and get out before the fire department arrives or we're seen.

It is, admittedly, not a great plan. But it's better than waiting until the ball ends in the wee hours of the morning and losing even more time than we already have.

"Once we set foot in there, I'm only going by Jean Louis, a wealthy bachelor from France who owns a gin empire," Leo says, a ridiculous French accent punctuating his words. "What are your aliases?"

"Why do we need aliases?" I ask.

"We're literally going undercover at a ball. If we need to make small talk, I don't trust you not to fumble without a false identity. Plus, it's *fun,*" Leo explains. He looks even better than he did six hours ago when he first tried the outfit on. All the masks we found at the thrift store were simple black sheaths that cover our eyes and leave room for our nose, our mouths the only part of our faces left completely exposed. His lips curl into a grin, a strand of hair falling across the top of the mask. "But no worries, I've got us covered. For tonight, you're Isabella Pitrano, the daughter of a rich Italian merchant looking to place his specialty olive oils in Rosetown's establishments. You're supposed to be scouting but can't help yourself from being a bit of a party animal."

"And let me guess, I'm also attracted to wealthy French bachelors?" I ask dryly.

He shrugs innocently. "It's not Jean Louis's fault his charm is irresistible."

"This is ridiculous," Caleb muses as Quinn types quickly on her phone. "But what's mine?"

"Don't encourage him," I say.

Leo puffs with pride. "Isaac Nye, an astronomer studying the stars along the northeast coast who happened to find himself among Rosetown's finest for the evening."

"Did you really just combine the names Isaac Newton and Bill Nye?"

Leo blanks against Caleb's question while I stifle a laugh. "It's a compliment!"

"Are you three done yet?" Quinn bites.

The boy suddenly standing beside her is a recent graduate from Miles's class, and his name tag reads *Adrian.*

She turns to him. "You're sure the coast is clear?"

He nods a head of tight brown curls. "For sure. Your mom is in front greeting guests. Besides, I don't think she'll even recognize you. I didn't."

Adrian's right. Of all of us, Quinn looks the most different. Her hair is down, something that took all of us to convince her to do. She wasn't stoked for her knife to lose its hiding spot and slid it into her shoe, for which we switched the neon laces to black. We stopped at a drugstore so I could pick up some cheap makeup and spray-on hair color, the kind people use to cover their graying roots. On Quinn, we used a caramel shade to put streaks through her black hair. On me, we used brown, which muddies the auburn, plus I put it in a braided bun, since I typically showcase my curls for big events. I did her makeup, then mine. I like to think we're both decently disguised.

"Then let's go," Quinn says, stepping through the door. I'm immediately hit by a hot rush of oven air, different from the muggy weather outside. It reminds me of long afternoons at the deli.

We're given odd looks by the line cooks, but Adrian mutters some flimsy excuse as we push past. There are several doors to go through, but instead of taking the one that's constantly swinging as servers rush in and out, we slip through another, entering an empty hallway. To our left is a set of ornate double doors carved with vines and roses. A plaque reads *Hedera Ballroom,* but there's a velvet rope across it and a sign that reads *No Entry: Construction.*

"I can take us from here," Quinn tells Adrian.

He rubs the back of his neck. "So, Quinn, you, like, wanna hang later—"

"Busy," she deadpans, eyes flicking pointedly toward the door we came out of.

"Cool cool cool, no prob." Adrian shoots some awkward finger guns and slips back into the kitchen.

"Cold," Leo comments as we slowly creep around the corner, where more revelers occupy the lobby.

People I don't recognize mingle, some with flutes of sparkling champagne or crystal goblets of deep red wine in their hands, others already digging into trays of appetizers being passed around.

"As ice," she agrees. "We've got work to do."

I've been to big extravagant parties here, but the Hyacinth Ball is different, like stepping backward through time. Everything sparkles, even the people. The fashion is outrageous and everything I've ever dreamed of. I could spend hours studying it. Gowns made of every fabric, some glittering with Swarovski crystals, others so silky I long to run my fingers down them. Lots of women even wear long gloves. It's like being under a spell, as if I've been planted inside a fairy tale and my prince is waiting for me inside the ballroom.

"Come on," Quinn urges, tugging on the skirt of my dress. "We need to get inside."

We come to another set of open doors with ushers standing beside them. The plaque reads *Goldchild Ballroom*. I hold my breath as we pass, waiting for one of them to recognize Quinn, or even me. But the masks do their job, and we saunter past undetected.

Inside, my feet slow as I can't help but marvel. The room is decked out to degrees I've never seen before: real ivy crawling up the walls, crisp white tablecloths with mini lanterns as the center-pieces, glass orbs scattered around them reflecting the light. Even the silverware is so polished and pristine it's luminescent, sitting atop ivy-green napkins.

But none of it holds a candle to the chandelier.

I stare at its beauty as if for the first time. I've been here before but never on a night when it's the center of attention. Never when it's the place where the vines twisting up the walls and across the ceiling congregate, the lights closer to it diffusing into soft green. Never when the rosebuds have seemed so beautiful, their gilded shine like the sun. The crystals are next level, casting multihued fragments of light across the sea of people. It's like nothing I've ever seen before.

And we have to find a clue in it.

"We should split up so we're not recognized together," Quinn murmurs, scanning the crowd. "And *shit*, there's your uncle."

Quinn gestures toward the door we just came through, where Uncle Arbor enters, thankfully still looking the other way. Leo grabs my hand.

"Isabella and I will take the dance floor, then," he says.

All I have time to do is throw a helpless glance over my shoulder before he tugs me toward the center of the room, where there's a dance floor and a slow-turning mirror ball splashes light around. Not many couples dance yet because it's so early in the night, but there are enough for us to blend in and leave my uncle still lingering by the door and out of view.

"I don't want to dance," I tell Leo in a whisper, scanning

where we left Quinn and Caleb. They've already melted into the crowd. If they caught my helpless look, they have no intention of saving me.

"We're not *just* dancing. It's camouflage," he says back. "Besides, this is what Jean Louis and Isabella would do."

I roll my eyes, jumping at the sudden warmth of his hand on my lower back as his arm winds around my waist. "What are you doing?"

"Dancing," he says innocently. "I'm sure you've heard of it."

A waltz I don't recognize is played by the string quartet in the corner. Leo's feet weirdly seem to know the exact movements to make us blend in perfectly with the other couples.

"How do you know what you're doing?" I breathe out, my body so close to him our masks are a hand's width apart.

"You remember all three of my sisters got married recently?"

"Mm-hmm."

"Well, my mom made our entire family take ballroom dance lessons. Guess they finally paid off."

"Good to know your college fund was going toward something useful."

He laughs, the sound just for me, existing in our little bubble. "Eighteen makes you sassy, huh?"

I pour on my best Italian accent. "I don't know what you're talking about. Isabella is twenty-two."

His eyes light up like a kid on Christmas. The expression is so pure and sudden, I wish I could take a picture, make it a Polaroid I could keep forever in the space between the back of my phone and the case.

Leo's expression shifts too soon, his hand reaching into his pocket to pull out his phone. I left mine and my purse in the van since my phone is almost dead anyway.

"What is it?" I ask, dropping the accent.

"Quinn wants to know if we've seen anything yet," he explains, slipping it back into his pocket.

Right. The clue. We're supposed to be looking for that.

I tilt my head up, but it's hard not to make it look obvious. A quick scan leaves bright bursts of color behind my lids when I shut them. I try again, moving closer to Leo so his hands circle my waist and mine his neck, resting my head on his shoulder and flicking my eyes to the chandelier. It's not directly above us, which means when he turns us just slightly, I have the perfect chance to let my eyes rove across the crystals. Quinn was right—it is high up. Even with the ladder, it's going to take a while to reach it.

"Anything?" Leo's voice is a soft murmur in my ear.

"No." I sigh, pulling back. "It's hopeless. I can barely see up there."

He checks his phone again, rattling off a text to the group.

"Quinn and Caleb are on the second floor," he says.

Keeping my hands loosely looped around his neck, I step back and scan the mezzanine. My gaze zeroes in on two individuals stiffly sipping flutes of champagne. The one in the heather gray makes a sour expression after swallowing and sets his down on a table.

"They're not good at blending in," I comment, my stomach sinking. I haven't seen Liz Zhao, but surely she'd be able to recognize Quinn if they were close enough, mask or not. And it's only a matter of time before Uncle Arbor makes his way over to us. I turn back to Leo. "Maybe we should leave and come back in the middle of the night. Or maybe Quinn's wrong, and it's not here at all."

"If not here, then where?"

Frustration turns my skin hot. "I don't know. Maybe this is the end of the road."

To my surprise, he pulls me tighter. "Nah," he says, swaying to a new song, which is much more modern. "We're here. Might as well have a good time." He breaks away as a server passes, and yanks two shrimps from the tray. They're massive, likely caught off the coast of Cape Cod, where most of our fresh seafood comes from. He pops one into his mouth, then holds the other out to me. The corners of his lips quirk up dangerously. "You have to learn to live a little."

"I live *plenty*," I say, but maybe he's right. I've been so focused on keeping my shit together, being perfect for Gram. But right now, no one knows who I am. No one expects anything of me. If I want to eat shrimp at a party I'm not invited to and dance myself silly, who's going to stop me?

I take it from him, teeth digging into the juicy shellfish. He watches as I chew and swallow, my eyes fluttering shut. After twenty-four hours of eating absolute crap, it tastes like heaven.

"There we go." He laughs, spinning us past an empty server's tray to deposit our shells. "What else can we eat in this place?"

"I would stab someone for a dark chocolate truffle right now," I admit. "The violence is Isabella talking."

"She's naughty," he says.

My heart skips a beat.

"It's okay—so is Jean Louis."

A new song comes on, this one soft and stunning. I let him lead me across the floor. Any minute I'm sure Liz will enter and make her speech, and we'll have to figure out a place to hide during dinner. But for this one song, I'm going to do just as he said—live a little.

"We'll find it," Leo says, sure as ever. "We've found all the others. All two, anyway. I don't think Gram would have purposefully made it impossible. We're just not looking at it the way she did."

"I guess," I murmur. He's so close to me it's hard to breathe. And really, it's ridiculous how his long lashes curve beyond the eyeholes of his mask. It must annoy the hell out of him. All I want to do is lean in close and feel them flutter against my cheek.

"What is it?" he asks, voice soft.

"You have your nonna's eyes."

Even with the mask, I can see his cocky expression falter. "Oh, uh, thanks?"

"I like them," I say quickly, hoping I didn't just make things weird. "The gray is pretty."

In a blink, his manner shifts to sly arrogance. "Less than one percent of people in the world have gray eyes, you know. Super rare."

Rare. The word hits me in a way I don't expect, as if it stopped existing for the past few days and Leo casually dropping it might as well be a billboard reminder. "I used to think I was rare."

I'm not sure where the statement comes from. Embarrassment

crawls up my neck, but suddenly, I'm facing away from him and I realize he's spinning me. I laugh, twirling back to his chest.

"You said in your eulogy that Gram made you feel that way, right?"

I didn't think he was listening during that. "Yeah, I did. Ever since that day when she taught me to sew, I felt like I could do anything and be anyone I wanted to, because she believed in me. And as I grew up, I thought maybe that as long as I was perfect for her, that she'd keep seeing me like that forever." I don't know why I'm saying this, don't know why it's easier to be myself when I'm disguised as someone else. "I guess now that she's gone, I don't feel rare or special or anything. I just feel lost."

His mouth opens, gaze softening. The intensity of my words hangs between us. I scramble for something lighter to break the vibe-crushing silence. "Well, at least my last name is still *actually* rare." I force a chuckle. "You know what I've always thought is funny? This whole town is covered in roses. But Rosewood is a tree. Extremely rare. You can't get it anymore because it's illegal to cut them down."

"I know," he says, his voice taking on a husky edge. "I happen to be pretty well versed in botanicals. Yard boy and all."

"Shh!" I say, not realizing how close I am to his mouth until his eyes widen. "Jean Louis would never stoop to doing his own yard work."

Leo's responding laugh is such a wonderful sound, the entire world peels away, and my oversharing tangent vanishes with it. The music lulls, and he dips me so low that if my hair weren't in its braided bun, the ends of my curls would dance across the floor with us. I'm weightless, infinite with the pressure of his strong arm supporting me. *Live a little.* I tip my head back and close my eyes, laughing with him.

Maybe this was what Gram wanted. For me to feel *this,* whatever it is. I never want it to end. Maybe this is what it's like to be truly happy. To feel full. *Enough.*

I open my eyes, the shimmer of light bouncing off the mirror ball. It shines down on us, watching like a big omniscient moon. Gram's clue echoes in my ears.

Now look to the sea, where the moon kisses the waves and the world falls away. You'll find my promise shining above the souls in love with life.

My breath hitches.

"Leo!" I gasp, springing up so fast I nearly smack our heads together. I grab his shoulders, my heart pounding.

"What?" he asks, concerned. "Was that not okay?"

"It was perfect." I'm breathless, grinning. I feel like I might fly away from excitement, so I grab his hand to keep me tethered, lacing our fingers. "And I know where it is. I know where Gram put the clue."

19

Leo's eyes go wide. "You do?"

"I think so!" I break away from him, dragging him off the dance floor. "Come on."

"Should we get the others first?"

"We can text them." There's no time to waste, especially when I catch sight of Uncle Arbor making polite conversation with Mr. Hayworth by the bar. If Mr. Hayworth discovers me, I can see the headline now: "Lily Rosewood Crashes Charity Ball in a Streak of Party Disasters."

My determined strides lead us back into the lobby, and I let out a breath now that we're out of my uncle's eyeshot. I turn to Leo and—

I freeze, seeing Quinn's mom entering from outside. She halts right before us.

"I hope you're having a splendid evening," she tells Leo. He mutters a thank-you in a voice an octave deeper than his normal one. I nod, not trusting mine to fool her. With a dazzling smile, she continues into the ballroom.

"That was close," Leo breathes.

"Thank you, cheap hair color and mask," I say, biting back a smirk and picking up the pace until we stop at the Hedera Ballroom. I duck under the velvet rope, and Leo follows, making sure the coast is clear. I press my palm to the door, nudging it open.

"In here?" Leo asks as we step inside. The scent of sawdust mingles with the floral fragrance that clings to the Ivy. Unlike the Goldchild Ballroom, this one is empty of tables and chairs, just a massive expanse of dusty stone floor with the occasional piece of construction equipment scattered around. The lights aren't on, but the entire room is cast in a golden-hour glow thanks to the floor-to-ceiling windows making up the wall to our left, which overlooks the water.

And there, at the far side of the room, is a ladder. Leading straight up to the glittering orb suspended from the ceiling.

"Gram said, 'Now look to the sea,'" I gesture to the ocean. "'Where the moon kisses the waves,' except it's not the moon. Not really. The clue is in the mirror ball," I tell Leo, pushing my mask up and practically running across the room. "Gram knew nobody would be going in this ballroom because it's been under renovation for months. It's the perfect hiding spot, but we need to get it down somehow."

"I think it's hanging from something." He pushes his mask up and squints at it.

"I'll try." I grab the first rung of the steel ladder and pull myself up. "Keep this steady."

He grabs the sides as I venture higher. My gold heels make it extra difficult, and they're slippery, too. My foot misses a rung, and I cling to the cold metal, heart pounding.

"Come down!" Leo calls up to me, at least ten feet below. "It's not safe. Let me climb."

I answer by kicking off my shoes. He grunts as one hits him.

"Sorry! I'm almost at the top. And don't look up my dress!"

"I'm not!" he says unconvincingly. As an aside, he grumbles, "You could have taken my eye out with those things."

Twenty feet up, maybe more now. I'm at the top, and I still can't reach the mirror ball. I go up another rung, having no support for my hands. My legs quiver beneath me.

"Lily!" Leo says, his voice far away.

Regardless, I hear the twinge of fear.

"Be careful!"

"Thank you, because I wasn't before you mentioned that." I grasp the globe, the surface smooth and rigid at the same time in my hands. It's hanging from some kind of rotating system, and it takes all my strength to lift it off the hook. But it's way too big to rest on the top of the ladder. If I want to unscrew the top, I'll have to bring it down.

Like with the painting, I can't imagine how in the world Gram could get up here. She must have had help, likely the same person who sent the letters and hid the other clues. At the deli, Frank had crossed my mind, but surely he's not going around scaling twenty-foot ladders in his spare time.

A chill shoots up my spine. *Then who?*

I can't figure it out here. I shift, wrapping one entire arm across the big ball and using my other to grip the rungs as I slowly make my way down. It's tedious work, and sweat drips down my back despite the chilly AC breezing through. My palms are slick, the glass surface of the mirror ball sliding against my skin.

I stop to adjust my hold. The flats of my bare feet ache against the metal, my toes curling over the rungs. Below me, the top of

Leo's head is still several feet away. He glares at his phone.

"Everything all right?" I ask, the words shaky.

"I texted the group, but Caleb said they can't come in. There are ushers hanging out in the lobby and security."

"Great." I press my forehead to the metal with a groan. My arms ache, and my legs feel like jelly as I continue my slow descent. Just a little farther. Breathe in, one rung down. Breathe out, another.

Except, the ball is *so* heavy. I've only made it a few more feet when it shifts in my hold, slipping right out from my grasp. In my panic to catch it, I let go of the ladder with my other hand, winding it around the ball before it can fall so it's supported by both arms. The move saves it from shattering all over the floor.

But it doesn't save *me*.

With a stilted scream, the distinct feeling of being airborne fills me as my feet leave the rungs and I plummet toward the ground. I clutch the mirror ball like it might save me, even though its weight falling on top of my chest is more than likely going to crush me. I might *die*. After everything I've survived, this is how I'll go.

I brace for impact, but my back never hits. Leo lets out an *oof* as I fall into his arms, and despite sparing me from completely smacking into the ground, my combined weight with the mirror ball makes him stumble to his knees. My butt makes painful contact with the floor, but it's better than my head. His fingers dig into my ribs and thigh from where he holds me. I cling to the ball like a koala.

"Are you okay?" he asks as I sit in his arms on the floor, my heart galloping so hard it might escape my chest.

"I . . . think so?" I try to sit up, and *yes*, there is definitely a bruise on my ass, but I'm not dead, which is a plus. I wince as he helps me sit. "What I will *not* be doing is putting this thing back up there." I nod up to the hook. "Thanks for catching me. Big Prince Charming vibes."

He grins, the worried lines of his face smoothing out as he finally releases me. "Jean Louis is pretty good at sweeping ladies off their feet."

"Isabella appreciates it." I can't help but smile back. Then I remember the ball in my hands and the clue I'm praying to find inside. I set it on the ground, kneeling while Leo does the same across from me. The top part where it hooks is what I was hoping for—a plastic cap, the only part that's not covered in mirrors. There are small divots for my fingers to press into as I turn it, unscrewing it slowly. It comes off with a *pop*.

The hole is barely big enough for my fist. Leo's anticipation curls off him like heat on a ninety-degree day as my fingers slide along the surprisingly smooth interior. It's bigger than I thought, and my arm goes in elbow deep.

But then—the unmistakable brush of cardstock against my fingertips. My expression must change as I grasp it because Leo cheers softly. I retract my hand, the folded piece of paper practically glowing in the moonlight.

"You found it," he breathes. He looks past it at me, our smiles falling away as the soft lull of music from the other ballroom filters beneath the door. It's a slow song, and my hands long to wind around his neck again, to sway around the empty ballroom like it's our own personal stage. All that separates us is the expanse of the mirror ball. The light hits it, creating a kaleidoscope of white flickering across his face, like we're underwater.

Before I can help myself, I'm leaning closer, my eyes falling to his lips. His mask is still pushed on top of his head like mine as his eyes trail my own face. Do I look as ethereal as he does right now? As . . . as *kissable*?

Because God do I want to kiss him.

And maybe he wants to kiss me, too, because his eyes flutter shut, and he closes the distance between us, his lips so close I feel his breath—

The doors we entered through rattle, and I jerk back, the haze that settled over me dissipating like wisps of smoke. All I have time to do is flip his mask and mine back over our eyes as two security guards appear in suits, adjusting their ties as they stride into the room.

"I hate these damn parties," one groans.

"Always a fucking circus," the other agrees.

They halt abruptly, noticing Leo and me across the ballroom.

The one on the left points accusingly. "Hey! You're not supposed to be in here!"

"And that's our cue," Leo says, pulling me to my feet and grabbing my heels with his spare hand. We race toward another set of doors at the opposite side of the room, the guards yelling behind us.

"Hey! Stop!"

Leo and I burst through the doors and emerge at the other end of the lobby. A hand circles my arm. I'm two seconds away from smacking it when a familiar voice hisses in my ear. "Follow me."

I do as Quinn instructs, tucking the clue into my makeshift pocket while my other hand is still linked with Leo's. Caleb falls into place at my other side. "Did you get it?"

"Yes." I glance over my shoulder. *Shit*, they're still following us. "But if they catch us—"

"They won't," Quinn says confidently. She pushes us through another set of double doors, and the clean air-conditioned air gives way to the muggy night. We're on the back patio, the gardens just beyond. Past that is a low white marble wall that separates the Ivy from the rest of the harbor.

"They brought company!" Leo says when he looks back, picking up speed. We match his pace, barreling through the crowd. I smack into a waiter carrying clams casino and the whole tray flies into the air like shellfish confetti.

"Sorry!" I yell. There are now *four* guards trailing us, although they're slowed by not treating the guests like bowling pins.

We run through gardens full of lilies and irises and hyacinths—*God* it's all so gaudy—I can't believe I never saw before how ridiculous this town is, like an entire shrine to the Rosewoods. The rush of adrenaline makes a ludicrous laugh burst from my mouth.

"Glad someone's enjoying this!" Caleb yells to me as we sprint for the wall. "It's not like we could get arrested or anything!"

"Details!" I laugh back, the dirt cool beneath my bare feet. Quinn reaches the waist-high wall first, planting her palms on the flat surface and launching herself over it. Caleb's significantly less graceful, but his fear must be a good motivator because he shimmies over in seconds. Leo pauses as we reach the wall, turning to help me.

"I've got it!" I let go of his hand to copy Quinn's movements. Gasps resound behind me, a chorus over the yelling of the security guards still making their way to us. I'm pretty sure I just flashed about sixty people my underwear, but embarrassment doesn't heat my cheeks, the race of blood through my veins armor against their judgment. I find solid ground again on the other side of the wall as Leo drops down beside me, and we're sprinting once again.

The grass beneath my feet becomes the rough wooden planks of the boardwalk. I chance a look over my shoulder and another laugh escapes, ringing through the air. The four guards stand on the other side of the wall, glaring at us as they become smaller and smaller, two with their hands on their knees panting. The boardwalk curves, and they're out of sight, relinquishing us to the night.

We don't stop until we reach the end of the empty boardwalk, where a single streetlamp shines dully. It's the spot where Gram and Quinn first met a year ago on the night just like this one. I throw my hands into the air. "We did it!"

And suddenly, we're all laughing, and panting, and laughing some more as we rip off our masks. Caleb is a little jittery as he keeps looking over his shoulder to make sure we weren't followed, but Quinn is exuberant.

"My mom walked right past me and didn't even know!" She screeches into the night, more joy than I've ever seen on her face. "No idea!"

I turn to Leo, struggling to catch my breath from the high of getting away undetected. "We did it," I repeat, my cheeks aching from grinning so hard.

"I think you're rare!" His words are breathless.

Confusion rocks me, shaking out a breathy giggle. "What?"

"You're rare," he repeats louder, with a look in his eyes that steals what little air I have. "You said you don't feel rare anymore since Gram died, but you are. I've never met anyone like you, Lily Rose. Nobody would offer to finish this themselves just to keep the rest of us safe. Nobody would spend an hours-long car ride tailoring thrift store clothes so we could all look the part. Nobody would ever willingly sleep on my floor."

My grin slides off my face, eyes wide. Quinn and Caleb are still laughing, but it's like they're above the surface and I'm back underwater with Leo, like I felt in the ballroom, just the two of us.

"You're so fucking rare, and, money or not, I'm glad for all of this. That it gave me a chance to know you again." He casts his arms wide as he drops my heels to the planks. His features are open and honest. Heart on his sleeve. "The *real* you."

His words electrify something in me that I never knew was begging to be released. Some inner longing I didn't let myself think too hard about until tonight. Before I can overthink it, I grab his gold tie and tug him toward me, our lips crashing together. An explosion of desire courses through me, an avalanche of feelings I never knew I could feel. His shock is evident through the hesitance of his hands as they press into my waist, finding home in the slope of my curves. Chest rising against mine, we break apart with a gasp, but I'm hungry for more.

"How's this for living a little?" I breathe against his warm lips.

"Not too shabby." He grins and kisses me once more, the world sliding away as I release his tie and slip my hands into his thick hair like I've been aching to do. He is so *warm*, burning against my skin, the salty sea air filling my senses as I breathe in. I want to tell him how much I've missed him, how four years of avoiding him because I thought that's what he wanted cracked something in me that I refused to acknowledge. I want to stay like this for forever and a day, to feel the flutter of his lashes against my cheek and the whisper of his breath against my neck as he spills secrets into my ear that are just for me and no one else.

I want *everything*.

"Oh, great, now they're making out," Quinn says dryly, a hint of fondness in her voice.

Leo lets go of me with one hand and laughs against my lips. I can only assume he throws an inappropriate single-fingered gesture her way, because even Caleb chuckles.

But he stops abruptly, his anxious voice breaking through the fog covering my brain. "Wait, guys—"

He cuts off with a scream.

20

I wrench away from Leo's hold, eyes springing open to see the flash of his gold tie and shock in his dilated gray eyes. He starts to say something, but I'm shoved into him, my weight forcing him backward and right off the boardwalk. He yelps, falling onto the rocks and rolling into the churning water with a splash that reaches my calves.

"Leo!"

If not for a hand snatching the skirt of my dress, I would follow him. Instead, I'm thrown onto the boardwalk. I hit the planks, a scream caught in my mouth as I look up. A body cloaked in dark clothes and a ski mask hulks over me. *No, no, no.*

Two others loom in my peripheral vision, also in black. *How many are there?* I hear Quinn shouting obscenities, putting up a fight. Caleb's in my line of vision when I whip my head to the side, his face pressed to the boardwalk by the hunter on top of him. His glasses lie a few feet from him, out of reach.

Gloved fingers dig into my chin, jolting my head to face the person straddling my chest, knees on either side of my body locking me down. They hold out their other hand expectantly. Waiting for me to place the clue in their palm.

Despite the black ski mask, I collect all the spit I can and launch it at their face. "Fuck you," I growl, using their shock to my advantage by writhing beneath them enough to throw off their balance and shove them. They lurch back, and I kick them off the boardwalk, sending them tumbling onto the rocks.

"Let me go, shithead," Quinn snarls, encased in the arms of a hunter at least a foot taller than her. I stumble to my feet, stepping in her direction to help, but she's quicker, whipping her switchblade from where she hid it in her shoe and jabbing it into their arm.

The responding shriek is so loud and deep, I flinch. The hunter releases Quinn, grabbing her hand with the knife and bending her arm back until she has no choice but to drop it. It clatters to the boards and with a swift kick, flies into the churning sea.

Leo is sputtering in the waves, struggling to stay afloat with the added weight of his clothes. But before I can help him, something in the hunter's good hand gleams.

"Quinn!" Time seems to slow as a *gun* crashes into the side of her face. She spins from the force of the pistol whip, falling hard.

I reach for her, but I'm grabbed from behind, one hand circling my mouth and the other digging painfully into my waist to hold me back. I choke on a smothered scream.

"No!"

A body slams into the guy who hit Quinn, sending him sprawling onto the planks. *Caleb.*

I bite down on the hand covering my mouth. The hunter holding me *screams*, the same guttural noise as when I crunched fingers in my door. I hope it's the same one, same hand.

The distraction is the perfect opportunity to elbow my way free. But the first hunter I kicked onto the rocks is back and shoves Caleb to the ground beside Quinn, who's slowly starting to recover. I need to cause a diversion. Give them time to pull Leo out of the water, to flee.

"Hey!" I holler, backing up onto the rough gravel of the lot. I take the clue from my pocket and wave it in the air as the three hunters whip their heads in my direction. "This is what you want, isn't it?"

"Lily, don't—"

I cut Quinn off. "This is what you're after, right? This, not them." The hunters' gazes are fixed on me. Slowly, all three nod.

I pull the clue tight to my chest. "Then come and get it."

Pain rockets through the soles of my feet as I take off running across the lot, chunks of gravel stabbing between my toes. I'm nearing the van, but Leo has the keys, so it's useless to me. I'll have to outrun them. My lungs burn as I sprint, weaving around old shipping containers.

If I keep going straight, I'll end up back at the Ivy. Which, at this rate, is ideal. But I don't think I'll reach it before the hunters get me. To my right is the boardwalk, and to my left—

I veer that way sharply, entering the boat graveyard. With dusk hitting, everything's in shadow. Boats of all shapes and sizes and varying degrees of disuse loom around me, providing the perfect landscape to dodge between. I slow down, my side throbbing from a stitch. The tight bodice of my dress isn't helping.

I lean against the side of a beached pontoon boat, trying to catch my breath. My eyes squeeze shut to halt the tears about to pour out, but all I see is Quinn falling against the planks, shock across her face. *Fear.*

"Come out and play, little heiress."

I swallow a gasp at the taunting words, pressing closer to the boat. The hunters have never talked before, but the voice that speaks now isn't the deep growly tone I imagined. It's mocking and surprisingly youthful.

His footsteps sound to my left, so I inch in the opposite direction toward the front of the boat.

"We heard you like games," he continues, still speaking in the same colloquial way, like we're having a totally normal conversation and I'm not 99 percent sure I'm royally screwed. "You're decent at them. We didn't expect this kind of fight. We thought we'd scare you in your room and you'd hand over exactly what we're looking for. Didn't think you'd be stupid enough to put up a chase. And a pretty good one, I'll give you that."

Another set of footsteps join. I slink around the front of the boat, the clue still trapped in my sweat-soaked palm. I could give it to them, and at this point, fuck the money, I *would*. But I don't trust that surrendering will save me.

I stop, the next closest boat towering before me. It's hauntingly familiar. A year of decaying here has made the mast that Dad named it for crooked, the paint peeling and scraped. But the ladder is still on the stern, not far from the ground.

The second hunter steps into my vision, and I dart toward *The Thorn*, hoping to lose them on board. I reach the ladder, climb the first rung—

And scream as hands pry me off. The ground doesn't offer a welcome embrace, and my breath shoots out of me as I land among dirt and gravel. I stare up at the third hunter. He babies his arm, likely the one Quinn stabbed. Which means he has the gun.

Before I can even attempt to get up, the other two join.

"Game's over, little heiress," the first hunter says. The second tilts their head in a goading way.

"No!" I burst, kicking wildly. I hit someone's shin, eliciting a groan. A scream rips up my throat. "Somebody help! Please! Help me!"

"Stop!"

There's a stinging sensation on my cheek, and I realize the first hunter slapped me. Stars dot my vision, a dizzying array of colors. I've never been hit before. My hand cups my face, skin wet. I'm crying.

"I'm only eighteen," I choke out. Hours ago, eighteen felt like freedom. It felt *adult*.

Now, it feels devastatingly young. And this scavenger hunt that I thought was a clever, if annoying, game on my grandmother's behalf, isn't a game anymore. It's deadly.

It hits me, hard and fast. They might kill me here, and I'll join the boats in making this my final resting place. This could be the end.

But suddenly, the most beautiful sound breaks through. The purr of an engine. *Leo.* I have never been so thankful for that piece-of-shit van. It's like the angels heard me, like maybe they're up in the sky waiting for moments like this to play hero.

"Get the hell away from my niece!" a voice barks, decidedly

not Leo. A door opens, shoes scuffing across the uneven ground.

"Uncle Arbor!" Relief pulses through me, a beacon beyond the terror. The masked hunters immediately back off.

"Jesus, Lily, we've gotta get you home," he says. "Can you walk?"

I glance around me, realizing it's just the two of us. I don't see the hunters—they must have gotten away. "I think so." I sit up, wincing. "You saved me. They would have— They were going to—" I can't even say it.

His voice grows softer. "It's all right, Calla," he says. He holds out two hands for me to grasp. "You're safe now."

I clasp his hands with my own, waiting for him to pull me to my feet. Instead, our palms slide against each other, and he lets go. It's so sudden I don't have time to catch myself before thumping back to the ground. I must be heavier than he anticipated.

"Sorry, I—"

My words fall away as I realize the paper is gone, now in his hands. He opens it, brow creasing in confusion. He must see the smudge in the flickering streetlamp because he brings it to his mouth, licking it. And then: a faint smile.

"Uncle Arbor?" My voice wavers.

One of the hunters is back, like a shadow separating from the night.

"Is that it?" It's the same one who spoke before.

"Uncle Arbor—"

"Yes," my uncle says, tucking the note into his pocket. It takes a moment to realize he's not talking to me. The hunter nods approvingly, the other two stepping up to flank him.

I lurch to my feet, stumbling back. "What's going on?"

"I should have been asking *you* that," Uncle Arbor says. His expression morphs into disappointment. "I found Mom's letter from the will reading in your room. This would have all been much easier if you told me from the start that she left you clues. We could have worked through them together."

Things click into place far too slowly.

"You're working with them," I realize. I was so quick to assume it was Daisy who called the hunters here, and maybe it was. But I never imagined Uncle Arbor would be in on it.

"More of a mutual partnership," the hunter spokesman says.

Uncle Arbor glares at him. "We had an agreement that you weren't supposed to harm them. Just keep track of their whereabouts."

The hunter raises his hands in an innocent gesture. Comical, given he's masked and was about to kill me minutes ago. "We tried." Only the glitter of his eyes in the rising moonlight is visible as he gestures to the hunter Quinn stabbed who is cradling his arm. "They swung first."

I turn to Uncle Arbor, desperation clawing up my throat. "You never went to Boston, did you? You called them here instead."

"I didn't call them. I *caught* them after they came to town thanks to your cousin's videos and they destroyed the conservatory. I honestly was heading to Boston but I got . . ." He trails off, features pinched with annoyance. "Detained."

"*Caught* is a loose term," the hunter says. "More like, you threatened to turn us in and we threatened *you*. You were fairly enthusiastic to come to an agreement after that."

Uncle Arbor's mouth is a thin line. "Lily, you have always been bright and ambitious, qualities you got from your father. But whatever's at the end of this game Mom sent you on, it belongs to me. Besides, you're only seventeen."

He must not remember what today is. I stare at him. "I'm eighteen."

"So you keep telling us," the hunter mocks. He walks leisurely to Uncle Arbor, who's gone quiet. The hunter claps him on the shoulder. "Come on, old man. We've got a deal. Let's see this clue."

Uncle Arbor hands it over, but his eyes don't leave mine. "I'm sorry, Lily." The worst part is, he actually sounds sincere. "Once this is all settled, everything will be fine. I'll take care of you. Get in my car so I can drop you off at home with Daisy."

"No."

I've never refused him before. A muscle in his forehead twinges. "Lily, get in the goddamn car."

"No," I repeat. I put more space between us, walking backward along the side of *The Thorn*. This can't be real. Am I dead already and living my worst nightmare, where I truly can't trust anyone?

"All week, I've wondered why Gram planned the treasure hunt. If it was a way to keep me busy, or one last goodbye game, or to help me learn to lean on others. And maybe it was all that, but something else, too. It was to keep the fortune away from *you*."

Something flashes in his eyes, a wild expression I've never seen before. "*Me?*" His voice booms. "I've only ever had the best intentions when it came to our family and this town. It *should* be mine. Now get in the fucking car."

He steps toward me, but I twist away, sprinting toward the front of *The Thorn* and beyond it. Yells echo after me, but I weave among trailers and abandoned Jet Skis and rotted buoys and boats that are nothing more than carcasses. I run until I'm sure no one follows, until the hum of the engine fades and I know they left me.

A piece of me wants to turn back and chase after them. I want to scream until my throat bleeds. I want to be back with Leo in the ballroom, to warn myself to stay there. Kiss him and get caught and whatever you do, don't go to the boardwalk.

But these days, I rarely get what I want.

21

"Leo!" Tears slide down my cheeks as I take in the empty harbor. "Quinn! Caleb!"

It took me longer to make it back here than I expected—I ran farther than I thought. But there's no sign of my friends here. The opaque black waves slap against the rocks, and fear lodges in my throat that they've pulled Leo under. I search for any sign of him, a flash of gold or moonlit hand, but everything is obscured by inky darkness.

"He can't be dead," I say aloud, as if I can make it true if the moon hears me. "He *can't*."

For the millionth time since exiting the maze of the boat graveyard, I wish I had my phone, even though it's likely dead in the van. I have no idea if Quinn and Caleb escaped. Maybe the hunters came back for them. Maybe they're *all* dead.

"No," I fret to the night, the distant music of the ball mocking me. The wood of the boardwalk splinters my feet. Not long ago, I stood in this same spot and pressed my lips to Leo's, felt his thick hair curl around my fingers. Kissed him with stars painted behind my eyelids.

The real stars haunt me from above, sparkling reminders of

all I've lost. *Dad, Gram, Uncle Arbor, the final clue, our place with Rosewood Inc.* The money is still missing. Maybe it always will be.

All I ever wanted was everything, Dad had said. A crude laugh escapes my dry lips. *Like father, like daughter.*

We both got nothing. Worse than that. We *lost* everything.

"Leo!" His name is a scratchy cry as I collapse onto the warped wooden boardwalk, the filthy ends of my dress splayed around me. Now I remember why I don't let myself feel for anyone anymore. It *hurts*. Like the sharpest thorn in a bunch of roses stabbing right through my heart. It's a devastating loneliness that makes the world turn gray.

I press my fists to my eyes, the raw scent of blood climbing up my nose. The gash on my palm from the screen has reopened. Warm droplets of red stream down my wrist.

A sob bursts out of me. I'd give anything right now for Gram to be here. To tell me what to do next, where to go. To give me someone to put a show on for, even if I know she'll see through it. One last chance to prove I can do things right.

But now, I've ruined everything by losing the clue.

My head snaps up at the screech of tires skidding into the lot. Headlights blind me, hope jumping into my heart that it's the van with Leo behind the wheel.

But it's not the van. My blood runs cold at the white vehicle and the familiar face.

"Are you here to finish me off?" I snarl at my cousin, jumping to my feet.

Daisy rolls her eyes through the open window of the White Rose. "Don't be dramatic. I came to find you."

"Why? To make sure I don't go after your father?" Anger flushes through me, my temper rising. "Your lying, manipulative—"

"You don't need to tell me," she says coolly. "I've known all that for years."

I falter. "Do you even know what I'm talking about?"

"Yes, because unlike what you think, I *do* pay attention." She gestures to the passenger door. "Now get in. We need to meet the others at the manor."

"The others?" I ask, hope blooming in my chest.

"Miles, Quinn, and Caleb," Daisy fills in. When I don't move, she rolls her eyes. "I'll explain everything on the way."

I glance back at the waves. She didn't mention Leo. But now that I look around, the van and my heels he dropped on the boardwalk are gone, too. He must have taken them. I hope.

And the fact that she mentioned Miles means he opened her Snapchat, even though I told him not to. If she's meeting him, that must mean he trusts her.

I round the front of the White Rose and slide into the passenger seat. The door isn't even closed before she guns it.

"How did you find me?"

"I DMed Miles on Snapchat yesterday asking if you seemed off, prying to see if he knew anything. He said he saw you at the deli with Quinn and Leo and the guy who ghosted him. We've been talking all day," she replies.

A sound of surprise escapes me and her eyes flick my way.

"What? You can steal my best friend, but I can't steal yours?"

When I don't give her the reaction she's looking for, she sighs.

"We swapped numbers today when I told him Leo had turned his location off and wouldn't answer when I asked where he was. Said we'd keep each other updated if we heard more. He called less than an hour ago saying Quinn and Caleb asked him to come pick them up from the parking lot of the Ivy. He said they were freaked and beat up thinking you and Leo were dead because they couldn't find you."

Leo might be. I bite it back before the thought overwhelms me. "Why not leave me here?" I ask, because there's no universe where I imagine my cousin would *save me.*

She gives me a withering look. "My bitchiness does have boundaries, you know. Besides, Dad stopped home thirty minutes ago acting weird as fuck. Wanted me to 'stay in my room' and 'not answer the door for anyone.'" She uses air quotes. "That's when I looked out my window and saw the black SUV in the driveway. It was the same one I saw in the street chase yesterday."

A tidal wave of fury swells. "You summoned them here. *Legit treasure hunters.* They—"

"Teamed up with my dad? Yeah, I know." She huffs a humorless laugh, blowing a chunk of short hair out of her eyes. "And I didn't summon them here—I'm not a fucking exorcist. I can't help that they saw my videos."

"That *you* posted."

She's quiet for a moment. "I was doing what I always do. I give full transparency into my messed-up life. People like it when you're real on social media. I didn't think actual thieves would see it, and I definitely didn't think Dad would be dumb enough to form an alliance with them."

I wince as I shift. I think I still have a piece of gravel stuck between my shoulder blades from getting thrown on the ground. "We're banned from the manor—how are we going to get in?"

"Quinn knows the gap in the hedge from when we snuck in last summer."

"And Leo?"

Concern creases her brow. "I'm sure he's fine."

It doesn't convince either of us. My mind spins as we pass the main stretch of town where most of the restaurants are, every lot full despite it being way past dinnertime.

Daisy notices. "A bunch of places around town are staying open later for the tourists that my videos drew to town. Aside from the treasure hunters coming, I think it's a good thing. Most people just want to see what we're all about. We're finally on the map." Daisy takes a sharp turn so we're heading toward the southwest part of town. "We need it. Because while you've been disappearing with *my* friends, I've been doing research. And I found out *a lot.*"

"Like?"

For a moment, it looks like she's not going to say anything. Like she's regretting ever picking me up. But then her shoulders slump, as if holding up the weight of the wall between us is too much to bear. "We're broke. My dad, too. And a lot of townies."

My eyes nearly pop out of my skull.

Daisy goes on. "That's why he needs the money so badly. Ever since the factory closed, the town's been on the decline. People moving away, local businesses struggling to stay open. So, your dad started his financial advisement firm, trying to help people put their money where it mattered. Except it wasn't just your dad—mine was in on it, too. But since your dad was the face of it, when things went south, he took the fall."

"How did you find all this out?"

"Started at Kev's house. Went through everything on his dad's computer that had anything to do with our family." At my disapproving look, she shrugs. "His dad sleeps with a CPAP machine and keeps a notebook with all his passwords right next to his computer. It was practically a VIP invite. But don't get me wrong—I didn't know how to read half of it. Just the important emails urging my dad to file bankruptcy and threatening to report him for tax fraud."

"Shit." I lean back in my seat as we pass Saint Theresa Church. "Do you think Gram knew?"

Daisy nods. "I've heard them fight about it before. I never really connected the dots why, 'cause I thought we were rich. But now it makes sense. At some point, she stopped giving our dads their allowances. From what I picked up, our dads were never legally held accountable for anything. So maybe she was trying to teach them a lesson. But the thing is, I think she would have bailed them out. At least, it seemed that way from some of the stuff I found. But then your dad died."

"What does his death have to do with it?"

Daisy's knuckles turn as white as this SUV. "It was my dad's fault."

"No," I say sharply. Something thick is in my throat, hard to talk around. I force the thoughts I've stuffed in for an entire year to pour out. "It was mine."

"*What?*"

The words are choked, tumbling out all at once. "Dad and I fought, right before . . . before he did it. And I was so mean to him. So *angry.* I don't even remember everything I said. I knew he was trying his best to make things right. To give me everything. I knew, and I didn't care. It was never enough." Tears wet my cheeks. Shame makes me swallow pride. "And then later there was the thing with Gram. I couldn't believe she'd give you something that she wouldn't give me. I was so entitled, but I didn't see it then. I was upset and confused, and caused such a scene at her party. It must have been so stressful that it messed with her heart. So, it's all my fault. Because I can never rein my temper in when it matters most, can never fill the hole inside me to stop wanting everything I can't have."

Daisy casts me an unreadable look. She slows at the base of the hill of the manor, reaching for her Chanel backpack in the back and pulling out several sheets of paper. She plops them into my hands. "Maybe a piece of me wishes everything was your fault so I could have a reason to hate you. But I'm done hating you. We need to stop pushing people away, including each other. Read these. I didn't want to waste time, but . . ." She gestures for me to look.

I pick up the papers, not on thick cardstock like Gram's letters, but freshly printed. I scan the top one.

Alder,

You've taken advantage of this town's trust for the last time, bleeding the people dry with faulty investment promises and disappearing pennies. No more. Your name can't save you now. Everyone's going to know.

Blaine

"The chief," I gasp. I scan the next, similar threatening words, this time signed by Monti Montgomery, the man who owns the *Rosetown Chronicle*. Another is from Liz Zhao. A fourth from Leo's deceased Papa, a fifth from Leo's dad. There must be ten letters here, all saying the same thing. *Everyone's going to know.*

"Were the townspeople going to expose my dad and get him sent to jail?" I ask, my hands trembling.

She shakes her head. "After looking through Kev's stuff, I went through Dad's. These notes were on his laptop in his Google Drive. *He* wrote them. He sent them. He made Uncle Alder paranoid enough to think that the people whose money he messed with were going to out him to the world. Made him think they'd all press charges and it would be his social and financial downfall."

I'm back to the night Dad and I argued. He was haggard. His eyes bloodshot and his hands shaking. I thought he was mad, but he wasn't. He was scared. That Mom and I and the rest of the world would learn the truth. That everybody hated him.

And it was all built on *lies*.

"He made Dad feel like he had no other choice."

"It's what he's good at," Daisy says. "Nobody ever saw the side of him my mom and I did."

Something in her hunched shoulders has a feeling stirring in me, a fierce protectiveness I never knew I could muster for my cousin.

"And who was that?" I ask, although I think I just got a taste.

"A monster. The worst ones hide in plain sight." She pulls off the road and under the cover of the trees, cutting the engine. "Nothing was ever good enough, ever *enough* for him. He was always belittling my mom, breaking her down. He never put hands on her, at least not in front of me. But his words alone were bad enough. And the worst part was nobody ever knew. Because he's good at putting on a front that everything's fucking perfect. He always wanted more from her, and finally, she had nothing more to give. So she left."

"Why didn't your mom take you with her?" I ask, because if there is one thing I knew about Aunt Janelle, it was that she loved Daisy.

"My dad threatened her." The tip of Daisy's nose turns red. "Told her a divorce would be bad press. Said she couldn't take me or he'd press charges. And he's a big man in a town that worships him, so she didn't have a choice. I woke up one morning and she was gone."

I remember that part. Uncle Arbor was crying in my big fancy living room. Blubbering about how he never saw it coming. That she took a bunch of his money and disappeared overnight. Broke his heart.

"She had to leave," I realize. "If she didn't, maybe she would have ended up like Dad."

"After she left, I didn't want anything to do with him," Daisy spits bitterly. "But he still tried. He got me everything I wanted. But all I wanted was my mom. So I pushed him away, and he started setting his sights on you, your father's perfect daughter. Because you were the one person who might have believed me. So instead, he turned you against me."

"What?" My cheeks burn, my left one throbbing from where I was slapped. "*You* were the one who pushed me away. You lied to Leo and excluded me. He told me everything."

She stares at the windshield. A light drizzle has started, and droplets race down it. "In the beginning, it was my fault," she admits. "The summer before my mom left, before freshman year, things were worse than ever between my parents. Hanging out with you and Leo was all I had. But that summer, something changed. We'd be walking on sidewalks, and I always either had to walk on the grass or behind you guys. If we played games, you and Leo always teamed up. When he'd say something he thought was hilarious, he always looked at you to make sure you laughed."

My breath knots in my chest. "I didn't—"

"Realize? Neither did he. But I could see the way he looked at you. It was just . . . different. And then my mom left. I remember having this realization right after, one night during a bonfire, when Leo roasted your marshmallows for you and made your s'more because you hate how sticky they are. I realized if things kept going how they were, I'd lose *both* of you, because you'd only want to be together and not with me. I'd have no one. But if I tried to push Leo away, you'd be stubborn and see through it. And with Mom gone, I was suddenly so mad at you for having everything. Your mom, your dad, Gram, *my* dad. Everybody was in the back pocket of Lily Rosewood. So I started pushing you away instead."

There are two raindrops in front of me, running parallel

down the windshield, barely a breath apart but never touching. I stare at them like maybe I can force them to cross paths, but they don't. Daisy clears her throat. "Then your dad died, and your mom left. I thought we finally had something in common again. But then I found out the truth."

My head snaps to her so quickly, my neck cracks.

She stares at me. "Why'd you do it?" she asks. "Why did you tell everyone your mom ditched you when she begged you to come with her?"

"How do you know that?" The words shoot out like missiles. Nobody knows the truth except Gram, and we agreed to keep it that way. A secret I've never shared.

Although, I almost did last night in the van.

"My dad knew. After it went down, he told Gram it was wrong of her to give you the option to stay. That you should have gone with your mom. That Gram was being selfish by wanting to keep you here."

"I wanted to stay," I defend. It's another chunk of guilt that's eaten at me. I know I was happier with Gram. But maybe, I could have been happy with my mom. Given her the chance to be the parent she never really was to me. But I didn't.

"Because of Gram," Daisy fills in. "And because you knew that leaving would likely forfeit your dream of taking Gram's spot at Rosewood Inc. someday. I get it. You've always been strategic."

"It wasn't just that," I try to explain. "Leaving felt like running, like I was abandoning who I was. Who Dad wanted me to be."

"Why don't you try being who *you* want to be?"

My voice drops to a whisper. "I thought I was."

Now, I have no idea.

"Anyway, my dad slipped right into the space yours left. He favored you and stopped trying with me."

I think of the past year, of feeling *so good* that Uncle Arbor liked me more than his own daughter. And I believed it. *Craved it.* "He manipulated me," I breathe. "That's so abusive and toxic. I—I'm so sorry."

She shrugs. "No use apologizing now. Besides, I never wanted to be perfect. I'm not built to smile on cue or laugh when a man says something they think is funny. You're good at it—faking your way through dinner parties, putting on a show. I can only do it if there's something I want waiting at the end."

"Are you putting on a show now?"

"Are you?" she counters.

I gesture to my tattered dress. "If I was, I would have worn a better costume."

A smile feints across her lips. "That dress is ugly. *Before* getting ruined."

I snort. "I didn't ask."

Silence stretches between us until I ask the question I've been wondering. "What does the key that Gram gave your dad unlock?"

Daisy shrugs. "No idea. I tried looking for it yesterday but couldn't find it anywhere."

I can't work out why Gram would give him anything at all. Unless maybe to distract him? Or so it wasn't fishy that Daisy and I got things but not him? If she suspected that Uncle Arbor had done something bad, that explains why she changed her will. I was right in the boat graveyard about the hunt. It was a way to keep it away from him until I turned eighteen.

Which must mean the fortune really is at the end of this.

"When did you realize I was working with the others?"

"I was suspicious when I found you in my room snooping," Daisy says, opening the door and hopping out. I follow, albeit slower. "I'm guessing that's when Dad first had an inkling, too. But I knew for sure when I saw you with Quinn and Leo in the church after the funeral. It made me mad, because Leo's *my* best friend, and Quinn is . . . well, Quinn." She coughs. "But Dad watches me like a hawk, tracks my phone—which, don't worry, is off now—so maybe that's why Gram didn't include me. It hurt, but I get it. But if Dad gets whatever it is these clues lead to, all this will be for nothing. We have to get it first."

"It's too late," I say, staring at the hulking manor through the trees. Ominous and dark, like it's from a horror movie. "I didn't read the clue. I made us lose everything."

"He doesn't have that much of a head start. We can catch up and beat him to what Gram hid." Her hand is warm around my arm. When she shakes me, I finally look at her. "We need to do this together."

Heartbeats pass between us. A thousand reasons I can't trust her slip through my head. A thousand reasons there's no way we can beat the clock.

But we have to try.

22

Daisy gets to the gap in the hedge first, holding aside a scrubby branch for me to lead the way. "Just like when we were kids."

I take a deep breath as I fall to my hands and knees, the memory of endless summers and high-pitched giggles propelling me forward. The time before Daisy pushed me away, before Dad died and Uncle Arbor sunk his nails into me. Before I let him.

As I crawl through the hedge, my dress tears again. It's irreparably ruined, filthy, and boasting a russet stain near the hem where my knee bled when I fell. Brown streaks my arms, the remnants of the hair dye washing out with the drizzle, my braid now half undone down my back. If I didn't look like a Rosewood before, I certainly don't now.

Together, we creep through the yard. It's been less than a week since the will reading and getting banned from the manor, but in that time the plants have claimed it for themselves. Vines twist around our feet, thorns scratch our arms, and the air is thick with a rose scent, the humidity making it stick to our skin.

"Do you think anyone's inside?" Daisy murmurs, nodding at the looming manor.

"Not unless Frank is," I say, keeping my head down as we sneak toward the pool.

"Fuck Frank," Daisy seethes, reminding me that she suspected him. "I bet he was working for my dad—"

She cuts off with a yelp, and I spin, searching for the masked hunters. But instead, my eyes meet espresso-brown irises, Quinn's hand wrapped around Daisy's arm. Tan streaks are painted across her cheeks from her own washed-out hair dye as she lets Daisy's arm go, Caleb and Miles behind her.

"Why'd you have to creep up on me like that?" Daisy snaps in a whisper, but then her jaw drops. Her fingers flit over the purpling gash on Quinn's temple. "Who did this to you?"

For a moment, Quinn just stares at her, clearly surprised she cares. But then Quinn steps out of Daisy's reach, a hint of arrogance in her eyes. "You should see the other guy."

"There's someone guarding the front," Miles says softly, pivoting us so we're walking deeper into the yard instead of onto the patio. "By the gates. We can't be loud."

"Is it the hunters?" I ask, skin prickling with fear.

Caleb shakes his head. His bottom lip has swelled, and his arm has a long, painful-looking rash on it where it must have scraped against the boardwalk when he was pushed down. His glasses are a little crooked. "No, they look more official."

"Frank's people," I murmur. We round the manor, stopping on the other side of the pool behind the coverage of the first line of trees. It's been only a few days since Leo and I tumbled in, but the water is green instead of turquoise, more leaves floating in it than I've ever seen. The manor hulks behind it, the kitchen in darkness beyond the sliding glass door.

"This is unreal," Miles says, giving me a disapproving

once-over. "Why didn't you tell me you were being *hunted*?"

I try to muster a smile. "At least I listened to your advice and stayed alive. So far."

He shakes his head. "We should call the police. And your uncle."

Daisy and I share a long look. "Considering my dad teamed up with the hunters, that's probably a bad idea," she says, her denim shorts and pink tube top now muddied from climbing through the hedge.

"Please tell me you're joking," Caleb says.

"I wish. Uncle Arbor tricked me and took the clue." I shamefully meet Quinn and Caleb's gazes. Despite the humid air, there's a coldness seeping into me. Goose bumps prickle my bare arms as I take in their ruined outfits, spots of rust dotting the fabric and tears too big to be patched giving way to glimpses of battered and bruised skin.

"Then we go after him," Quinn says. "There's only one section of town that we haven't found a clue in yet, and that's yours, Lily. *This one.* The southwest."

"We could drive around until we see his car?" Miles suggests.

"Or split up," Daisy adds. "We have my car and Miles's. Half of us go—"

"Lily," Caleb's voice cuts her off, his warm hand grabbing my arm. He's picked the skin around his fingers bloody. "You're shaking."

"You're all hurt," I blurt, stepping back against the towering tree behind me. "I just—they really hurt you."

Quinn shrugs. "Roughed us up a bit, but we'll be fine."

I shake my head so hard my neck cracks. The world closes in as the gravity of the situation presses on me. "No, you could get way more injured. And I'm not willing to risk it. Not willing to risk any of you."

Miles reaches out for me, but I sidestep him.

"And you should have never gotten dragged into this to begin with," I say to Miles.

Stubbornness flashes across his face. "I was worried about you. I couldn't just sit at home doing nothing. I want to help."

"He's staying with us," Caleb says surely, his hand slipping into Miles's. "Quinn and I were freaking out after we couldn't find you and Leo. He was the only person I could think of who could help and was trustworthy, and I wanted to make things right just . . . just in case. Besides, I didn't spend ten minutes groveling over the phone for nothing."

Miles cuts him a look. "It was more like two, and I'd use groveling lightly. I'm a sucker for beat-up bad boys."

Caleb isn't a bad boy, and we all know it, but I can't manage a smile. "I'm glad you guys made up, but it's not that easy. This is bigger than I thought. My uncle—" And then, it all comes out. Everything Daisy and I just talked about, the threatening letters, how awful he was to Aunt Janelle. They listen intently, Daisy silent beside me.

"I don't know what to do," I finish, my throat steadily closing more and more. "Because I don't want anyone else to get hurt and I don't want my uncle to have the money but *I* don't want it if it means putting everyone at risk and . . ." I trail off, trying to blink back the tears. All it does is make them spill down my cheeks.

"It's never been about the money," Caleb says quietly. "I mean, it is, but Gram pulled us together because she knew we needed help that dollars couldn't solve."

"And she knew we wouldn't give up," Quinn adds. "Because I sure as hell won't."

"Personally, I love catching manipulative uncles. It's like, in my top five favorite hobbies," Miles says with a conspiratorial smile. "Seated behind my passion for poorly slicing salami, of course."

I wipe my eyes with a watery snort. "We're probably too late."

"You said we'd try," Daisy reminds me. "Dad might not have figured out the clue. If it was meant only for you—"

A twig snaps to my left, and Daisy stops short. I brace myself, looking toward the direction of the back gate.

Quinn stands beside me, fists rising. "If he wants to fight, let's fight."

But Uncle Arbor doesn't burst from the trees, or any of the hunters. Instead, a familiar dark head of messy waves emerges, a filthy white dress shirt half unbuttoned and a gold tie hanging loosely around his neck. He drops something to the ground, and I realize it's my Converse. In his other hand is a hockey stick.

Leo looks like he climbed out of a sinkhole, but his face lights up with his usual cunning grin. "I hope nobody's concocting devious schemes without me."

"We thought you were dead, Frat Boy," Quinn says, her words punctuated by a laugh.

I don't even realize I meet him halfway until I'm throwing my arms around him, his muscles quivering under my touch as his own arms wind around me.

"I'm okay," he whispers against my neck.

I simply nod, too scared to speak as I squeeze him extra tight. The feeling of his embrace brings a level of comfort I haven't felt since Dad died. Leo is one person death wasn't able to steal from me.

When I finally break away, I shove him lightly. "What took you so long?"

"Had to make a pit stop. I think it was worth it." He pulls something from his pocket and holds it out to me. I suck in a breath.

In his palm is a piece of cardstock, rumpled and ink smeared.

23

"How did you get that?" I gape.

"By the time I crawled out of the harbor, I saw your uncle driving away," Leo explains. "I figured you were with him, since I didn't see anyone else around, so I followed him back to his house. But when he got there and the hunters were with him and you weren't, I realized what must have happened. He only stopped at the house for a second, then Daisy left, so I snuck in and found it on the table."

"Why didn't you stop me?" Daisy asks, a frown creasing her face. "I walked right past the table and didn't notice anything."

Leo shifts. "I got nervous you were on his side."

"It's a fair thought," Quinn defends him. "You're not exactly known for your loyalty."

It's enough to make the tension snap between them. "I'm sorry, okay?" Daisy says, desperation and anger twisting in her tone. "I'm sorry I lied to everyone about what happened between us because I was scared of how I felt about you. I figured it was easier to push you away before you did it to me, because I'm used to not being enough for the people I love most to stick around. But it was shitty, and it's on my long list of things to repent for the rest of my life."

Quinn's jaw is set, but her eyes flick to Leo. I want to yank the note out of Leo's hand, tell them to fix this later, but I need a team right now. A cohesive, not-giving-each-other-murderous-looks team.

"And I'm sorry to you, Leo." Daisy's voice quiets. "I should have never asked you to lie about that for me. I shouldn't have come between your friendship. Or this one." She gestures to me.

"It's . . . fine," Leo says, like he's not used to being the one to forgive. "I'm sorry I let you."

Quinn's gaze softens at that, just for a fraction of a moment before hardening once more. "It is what it is. We have bigger things to worry about." She nods to me.

I take the clue from Leo's hand, scanning over the scrawl as I read aloud.

Dear Lily Love,

You've made it this far, and for that I am so proud. If only I could turn back the clock to tell you so. But I can't, so I have one thing left to say if you're looking for lost things, pray to he who finds them.

Gram

"That's easy," Daisy says. "The church, right?"

"But geographically, that doesn't make sense," Caleb says. He tugs the map pieces out of his pocket since we trusted ours with him for the night. He holds his against the bark of an oak tree, and Quinn, Leo, and I take ours and do the same. He points to the church. "Look. It's at the junction of all four pieces. If this is the last clue, it should be in Lily's section."

He's right.

"Hold up," Miles says, leaning over his shoulder. "You said the first clue was at the museum." He points to the top left square. "The second was the deli." His fingers moves to the top right. "Then the Ivy." Bottom right. "Maybe Gram knew we were going to meet here. Or this is where Lily found the first piece, right? So maybe it *started* here." He circles the bottom left, where we are now.

"And if you draw lines from the museum to the Ivy," Daisy says. "And then from the deli to here. Then that—"

"Makes an *X* right over the church," I realize.

"Shit, *X* really does mark the spot," Quinn muses.

Everyone's face brightens with hope. "Saint Theresa Church isn't far at all from here." Caleb turns to Leo. "Could we all go in the van?"

"Yeah," he says, but he doesn't look as convinced as the rest of us. "Are you sure?"

"Yes!" Daisy grabs his arm, pulling him toward the hedge. "We have to hurry!"

Quinn follows her, and while I don't think things are magically fixed between them, a common goal certainly helps. Miles throws his arm across Caleb's shoulders, both sharing a grin.

As I look at all of them, a realization slams into me. If we're too late, and I don't get the money or Rosewood Inc., or into FIT, I'll be okay. Despite feeling shattered inside from my family falling apart, I have friends who will be there for me no matter what's awaiting us at the church. And that's enough.

But this isn't just about me. They need that money, too.

I tug on my Converse, my heels probably gone for good. But as we walk toward the gap in the hedge, something pulls at me, as if Gram is whispering in my ear. This clue was for *my* corner of the map. It was meant for me. Would it really be so simple that everybody would know exactly what Gram meant? That a map would *show* it?

"Lily, we gotta hurry," Miles calls softly from across the lawn. *Pray to he who finds them.* Jesus makes sense upon the big crucifix in Saint Theresa Church. It's ironic, almost, that after all the terrible things my uncle has done, Gram would hide the fortune beneath he who sees all.

"Pray to he who finds them," I breathe. My gaze falls on the twisted iron gate leading to the Anything but Roses garden.

And just like that, I understand.

"It's not in the church!" I whisper-yell. I change direction so fast I have no time to see if they're following me. "It's here. It's been here the whole time!"

I burst through the gate, kicking away vines and roots in my path. Footsteps sound behind me as all of us crowd the small space, enclosed in the familiar white stone walls. I stare up at Saint Anthony, his vacant marble eyes gazing back. *What have you seen?* I had asked earlier this week. If only he could have responded.

Everything.

"It's gotta be here somewhere," I say. I press my palms to

stones in the wall and shove flowers aside with no regard for what happens to them. "Gram only wanted us to *think* it'd be at Saint Theresa Church, because that *is* the center of town—anyone would think it's there. But that's why Gram banned everyone from the manor. It's been *here* the whole time. Anthony is the patron saint of lost things. And Uncle Arbor wouldn't think of that because he rarely came into this garden. But I would, because—" My voice breaks. "It's my favorite place on earth."

"What are we looking for?" Miles asks, walking the perimeter.

"I don't know," I reply honestly. "Either another clue, or a briefcase full of money, or—"

"Maybe it's buried," Daisy says, falling to her knees. "I mean, Gram couldn't have just left it out. What if it rained? It must be beneath us."

I look at Leo. "You've taken care of this garden for months. You've never seen anything?"

He shakes his head as Quinn and Caleb get on their knees, too, clawing at the soft earth.

"It's not anywhere behind the flowers," Miles concludes, finishing his perimeter check by the map carved on the back wall. That's all the confirmation I need to drop to my knees and begin digging. Pain shoots up my hand, reminding me of my cut, but I keep going.

Leo and Miles join us, and with all of us on the ground, we make quick work of upheaving the first layer of grass and dirt. It'd make more sense to run to the toolshed and grab shovels, but every second feels so precious. As if a moment away will allow my uncle the opportunity to slip in and claim what he thinks is his.

I yelp as my fingers scratch along something rough and hard. Sweat coats the back of my neck as I pry, brushing dirt and tangled roots away. Something *is* here. Hard like stone.

The high walls surrounding us block out the waning moon. "I need light!" I say, heart pounding. A phone flashlight turns on, held by Caleb.

"What is it?" he asks. The others turn my way. I don't reply, instead shifting backward so I can keep moving the earth away. His light catches on something protruding from the ground, no wider than my arm and at least the same in length. Definitely not a briefcase.

"Looks like some kind of lever?" Leo guesses, helping me push away dirt.

He's right. With Quinn's help, we unearth a long piece of stone pointing to Saint Anthony's feet like the hand of a clock. We dig out some empty space beneath it, revealing that the end closest to the gate is still attached to something deeper in the ground.

"I think it's a vault," Caleb whispers.

Leo grasps the lever and pulls up. It doesn't budge.

"Try pushing it," Daisy says.

We do, pushing it deeper into the earth. Nothing.

"Not that way. Try clockwise," she says, like it should have been obvious.

"Would you like to get down here and do it?" Quinn snarks back. I expect Daisy to roll her eyes, but she stoops next to us, placing her hands on the grimy surface and shoving it toward the right wall of the garden. I join her, then Leo and Quinn as Caleb and Miles get on the other side and pull. The eerie night air is full of our breathy groans and grunts, the lever not shifting.

But of course it isn't. Gram said so herself.

"The other way," I realize, pulling the final note from where I tucked it in the neck of my dress. "Gram said, 'If only I could turn back the clock.' It's a clue, too. Counterclockwise."

We reverse our efforts. It seems futile, and maybe I would have given up if this was three days ago. But now, I'm certain I'm right. I pull harder.

And, suddenly, it's *moving*. A grinding sound accompanies it, like stone on stone. I keep pulling, my muscles straining with the effort as the massive lever swings as far as we can make it in the space we've carved out in the ground. A tiny click sounds when we complete a full ninety degrees, the air still.

"Ohhhkay," Miles says, standing. "What was that supposed to—"

I lurch forward, the ground vibrating beneath us.

"Earthquake?!" Caleb yelps, grasping Miles for dear life.

"In Massachusetts?" Quinn questions, although she looks a little queasy.

But it's not an earthquake, not at all. The ground is *shifting*. Well, kind of. The statue is shifting.

Saint Anthony slides forward into the spot we turned the lever and stops nearly nose-to-nose with me. I almost expect him to reach out and caress my cheek with a cold stone hand, but he's still, whatever internal mechanisms the lever triggered now stopped. It's as if he took four massive steps forward, crushed the little bit of ground we didn't massacre, and took out some flowers with his move.

"Holy shit."

I step around Saint Anthony at Quinn's awestruck voice, so different from her usual tone. That's when I realize everyone is staring down at the ground where the patron saint had been.

Caleb was wrong. It's not a vault at all.

It's a tunnel.

24

Caleb shines his phone light into the black abyss, highlighting the rusted rungs of a ladder descending into the earth in a gap barely the size of a sewer manhole.

"It's like we're in *The Goonies*," Miles says softly.

Leo's eyes light up. "Thank you! I've been saying that this whole time."

"We're not actually going down there, are we?" Caleb asks, picking anxiously at the remaining skin around his fingernails. "This seems—"

"Out there?" Daisy suggests.

"Yeah. Even for us."

"Where do you think it leads?" Miles asks.

"No idea," Leo says.

"Straight down to hell," Quinn throws in, making Caleb fidget even more.

"Not hell," I murmur, zeroing in on the map carved into the back wall. I've spent plenty of time the past few days staring at the map of Rosetown that Gram gave us. This one's the same, except for one small detail.

"The old factory." My words are barely more than a breath,

but everyone's head swivels to me. And suddenly, everything we've been doing the past week clicks together. "It's the one place in this town that no one would be able to access. Ever since it closed down, it's been locked up, surrounded by a huge fence and abandoned. It's not on any maps because it's so far on the edge of town." My heart races. "It's the perfect hiding spot for millions of dollars."

"Hyacinth must have created this back when it first opened as a secret way to get there. It's probably the only entrance in or out now. At least without causing a scene," Daisy says. "So who wants to go first?"

No one moves.

A long beat passes and Quinn sighs. "I'll go. Y'all are bitches."

Leo, never one to be bitchified, puffs up his chest. He grabs his hockey stick from where he left it at the gate. "I'll go. I can protect us."

Quinn scoffs. "As if I can't?"

I place a hand on both of their arms, stepping forward. "I will." I don't know where the sudden bravado comes from, but I get on my knees, slowly lowering myself down the ladder as they shine multiple phone flashlights down. If there's one plus to being the guinea pig, it's that no one can look up my dress.

The rungs are cool against my palms, not too different from the ladder in the ballroom. Climbing in my Converse is way easier, and I make quick work of descending, hoping there's not a pit of snakes waiting at the bottom. The lights get farther away, my friends' faces blurring in the background from the glare.

"Everything okay?" Leo calls as my sneakers finally touch

down. The ground is dirt, a stagnant scent of musty earth floating around me. It's pitch-black.

"I need a light!" I yell up. A second later, a phone nearly concusses me as I step out of the way at the last second. I pick it up, and the flashlight's already on, highlighting walls that are composed of tightly stacked bricks, grayed with time and sloppy grouting.

"Lily?"

"Yeah, it's . . . fine."

"Super convincing," Caleb says.

A moment later, Leo's descending the ladder, then Daisy, followed by Quinn. Miles drops down, and we all watch as Caleb takes the descent painfully slow, limbs still shaking even after he touches down.

"We are *so* getting murdered," Caleb says.

"This is . . . cozy," Miles says, glancing around the tunnel, which barely fits two of us side by side. He waves his hand in front of him, fingers coated with cobwebs. Caleb looks like puking is on the table.

"It shouldn't go too far," I say, thinking of the distance between the manor and the factory. Woods separate the two, but it shares the same side of town. I start walking. Leo strides beside me, his hockey stick upside down so he can use it like a walking stick. Quinn and Daisy fall into step behind us, and although they don't speak, I can feel some sort of silent conversation taking place. I realize with a start that I *want* them to make up. Quinn's my friend now, and Daisy might be the only family I truly have left. If we survive this, I don't want to have to choose.

"Hey," Leo murmurs, voice quiet as we trot on. "I need to tell you something."

"If it's that you smell like a wet dog, I already know," I say, but I smile at him so he sees the joke.

When he doesn't smile back, a knot forms in my stomach, and I jump to the next closest thing he might be upset about.

"Sorry for kissing you on the boardwalk," I rush out, heat filling my cheeks. "I shouldn't have assumed that was okay. I was just caught up in the moment, but it doesn't have to mean anything."

"What? No," he laughs, some of the tension sliding off his shoulders. "No, that was—that was awesome. Seriously, no complaints. Ten out of ten would do again, if you want. Like, not down here obviously, cause it's gross, but—"

"Leo James." I nudge his shoulder and grin at him. "Am I making you *nervous*?"

He releases a breath. "A little. Or it could be the thought of hundreds of pounds of dirt collapsing on me at any moment. Tough to tell."

"So what did you need to tell me?"

His face clouds again, his throat bobbing as he swallows. "Uh—"

"Has anyone read 'The Cask of Amontillado'?" Caleb's voice quivers, breaking up our conversation. I look behind us to see his hand clenched in Miles's, brown eyes wide.

Leo frowns at the interruption. "I skipped most of lit to lift, so . . ."

"I probably SparkNotes'd it," Daisy says while Quinn shakes her head.

"That's not the one where people are taken to an island and find out the guy is hunting them, right?" Miles asks.

"That's 'The Most Dangerous Game,'" Caleb gives a stilted laugh. "Also largely applicable to our situation, but no, not that one. 'The Cask of Amontillado' is by Edgar Allan Poe, about a man seeking revenge on his friend by leading him into the catacombs beneath his house. Then he traps the friend down there, burying him alive."

"And you're bringing this up because?" Quinn prods, as our feet make soft sounds against the packed earth.

"No reason," Caleb squeaks out. "Just feels like we're marching to our deaths."

"Not to our deaths," I say as we round a bend. My flashlight catches on the wall before us, different from the brick and dirt. It's metal; a spin lock built into it and a handle. "To a door."

Leo inspects it, trying the handle. It doesn't budge. "It needs a combination. Eight numbers."

"Are there any on the clue?" Miles asks.

I take out the slip of paper, nothing more than my grandmother's words staring back at me. My heart sinks. "No."

"Wait, look at this," Leo says, rubbing at an inscription carved into the door.

Caleb steps forward, adjusting his glasses. "It says, 'You'll find the code behind the stone.'"

Quinn groans, kicking the wall. "More riddles? Seriously?"

"Well, that explains why this pickax is here," Miles says, holding up a small tool with a T-shaped head. One end narrows into a fine metal point. "I just found it leaning against the wall."

I glance at the bricks that line the entire tunnel. We walked at least half a mile, maybe more. The ladder is out of view.

"So it's behind the bricks, then," Leo concludes, grabbing the pickax from Miles and wasting no time in turning to the closest brick and hacking at it. We wince at the sound.

"That's going to take forever," Quinn argues. "Let's just try guessing. Start with birthdays and go from there."

"The inscription says behind the stone and there's a pickax. It's gotta be close to the door," Daisy counters.

Quinn grabs Leo's arm to stop him. "Don't waste your time. Think numbers."

Caleb rubs his temples. "We can do both, all right? Leo, start taking the bricks out and let's pray it doesn't make this tunnel collapse. The rest of us will try any combination we can think of in the meantime."

Daisy and Quinn let out matching huffs, not fighting it. But Miles stares at me, brow creased. Well, not even at me, exactly. He stares at my chest, as if he can see through my dress.

I snap my fingers at him; the behavior is so off brand. "Eyes up here, please."

Confusion crosses his face as he snaps out of it. "Huh? Oh, sorry, that's not what it looked like. I just . . . Lily, the other day when I saw you in the deli, you were wearing a necklace. Your grandmother's ruby, right?"

I nod, pulling the heavy gem out from beneath my dress so it hangs freely now. He steps closer, inspecting it. Unease rises in me. "What is it?"

He picks up the gem. "What if the inscription wasn't talking about the bricks? After all, they aren't actually stones. What if it means the ruby? It's also a 'stone.' If it's an heirloom necklace passed down through your family, and this entrance was likely built by your great-great-grandmother, then Gram probably was told at some point that the ruby wasn't just that but also a key. And that could be the entire reason Gram gave the ruby to you. To make sure the final piece of the puzzle was in your possession."

I unclasp the gold chain from my neck, raising the ruby in the light of Miles's phone. On the back, I expect it to show the red underside. But it doesn't. The back is solid gold extending around the front to keep the gem in place instead of prongs like most gems have.

"You think something's behind it?" Daisy asks.

He nods.

"So that would mean . . ."

"We'd have to separate it from the gold. Maybe even break it."

Before I can help myself, my eyes are wet with tears. I hold the ruby to my chest. "It's all I have left of Gram," I say desperately. "I can't just ruin it."

Everyone's quiet. A hand tentatively touches my shoulder. "We can share the White Rose, if you want," Daisy says softly. "That way, you'll still have something if the necklace isn't salvageable."

The sentiment is so unlike anything I thought would ever come out of my cousin's mouth that I stare at her. And slowly, I slide the ruby off the chain and place it on the ground, reclasping the empty chain around my neck. We all stare down at it.

"Are you sure?" Leo asks, holding the pickax. "If we take more time, we can maybe—"

"We don't have time," I remind him. My heart throbs at the

idea of ruining it. But beneath the heartbreak is pride. Maybe I didn't let Gram down after all if she trusted me with something as huge as having the final piece of the puzzle.

Resolve fills me. "Do it."

Leo crouches with the pickax and grabs the ruby.

Looking over his shoulder, Caleb tells him, "Try to pry away the gold bezel setting that rims the ruby."

Leo starts to work, but it's hard for him to wedge the tip of the clunky axe between the ruby and metal, and he hits his own finger a time or two. The ruby is clearly nestled in tightly.

"Let me try," Quinn says.

"Why? Because you're stronger?" Leo asks indignantly.

Quinn raises a brow. "Rest your ego, Frat Boy. My hands are smaller."

Leo relents. Quinn takes the pickax and the ruby, sitting cross-legged on the dirt ground. Carefully, she rotates the ruby before her eyes. She makes a *hmm* noise and notches the tip beneath one metal edge, like Leo was trying to do. Pressing down on the ruby with her opposite hand, she manages to lift the gold rim.

"Yes!" Caleb exclaims. "Keep doing that."

She does. With one edge lifted, it's easier for her to go around the entire thing until the metal is bent back. But even so, the ruby doesn't fall out when she tips it upside down.

"It's probably glued," Daisy says. "Try prying it out."

Quinn slips the nose of the pickax behind one exposed edge of the ruby. "It's definitely stuck on pretty tightly," she says.

"It's over a century old, right?" Miles asks me, and I nod. "Time probably fused it, too."

Quinn's prying works—but not without a cost. With a delicate *tink*, the gem splits in two and falls out. "Shit, I'm sorry."

"It's okay," I say. The pang in my heart disagrees, but I collect the pieces in my palm and hand them to Daisy, who tucks them in her bag. Quinn passes me the empty gold backing. I peel away a tiny piece of paper glued to the inside, revealing eight engraved numbers in the gold.

06081918

"Isn't that the date Rosewood Inc. was founded?" Daisy asks. Nodding numbly, I spin the dial on the door to match the numbers. It clicks, coming to a stop. I push it with everything I've got, all the awe and grief and shoved-down anger churning within me, fueling my insides and lighting a new flame.

With a groan, the door opens.

25

"I'm generally not big on basements, but this one takes the cake," Miles says as we creep through a mess of cobwebs and forgotten furniture. The basement of the factory is composed of damp concrete and brick walls, cracks creeping along the floor. It reeks of some combination of mold and decaying animal, in the running to rival the van for worst stenches I've ever experienced.

"It's a step up from the tunnel." Leo reaches for a positive.

"Barely," Caleb grumbles.

Daisy shrieks, making us all jump as phone light skitters across the massive floor. Leo tenses, wielding his hockey stick. "What?"

"I definitely saw a rat." She shudders. "Oh, thank God, there's the stairs."

Quinn tests the first one, and although it creaks precariously beneath her foot, it seems to hold. Carefully, we make our way up the steep incline to the door at the top. "Rusted shut," she grunts. She looks back at us, the sharp lines of her face highlighted in the phone light. "Back up. Gotta bust through."

With a bang loud enough to wake the dead, she plows her shoulder through the door, and it bursts open. I hurry up the last few steps, entering the factory.

And I stop. Because this isn't the factory I remember.

It still has the huge floor-to-ceiling windows across the front, which let in enough moonlight that we don't need our phones. But now, the windows are filthy after years of neglect. There used to be neat rows of long tables throughout, with chairs and sewing machines at each. The machines are gone, but the tables remain, some chairs even pushed out as if employees got up for their lunch break and never came back. Lights descend from the ceiling. Some still have bulbs, but the spiders have clearly made them their home, webbing glinting in the faint light.

My heart pangs as I take in the mezzanine, which encircles the entirety of the massive rectangular space with two staircases at either end of the factory leading up to it. How many times did I stand up there as a child, in Dad's arms or pressed against Gram's legs behind the metal railing, watching the workers stitch and cut and measure below? I felt like a princess then, ruling over my kingdom.

The memory is so powerful that I don't realize the stillness of the others until Caleb stoops, picking something up I hadn't noticed. A piece of paper, rectangular. He holds it up to the light.

Benjamin Franklin stares back at us.

"They're everywhere," Miles marvels. I turn slowly, skating my eyes over what used to be polished hardwood floors and now are worn and dusty boards. Worn, dusty, and coated in one-hundred-dollar bills.

My heart is going to explode out of my chest.

"We did it." A grin splits Leo's face. "We fucking did it!"

Quinn whoops, a sound so pure and joyous that I'm not sure she's ever made it before. She scoops a handful of bills up, holding them to the light and laughing. "Holy shit, we're rich! We're *rich*!"

"A briefcase would have been cool, but this works, too," Caleb chuckles, and I realize what this means for them. For all of us. College, money for our families, *a future*. It's everything we could ever want.

So why is Daisy frowning?

Not at the money, but at a point behind me. I turn. The smile slides from my face.

There's nothing except a single rack. One luxurious wool coat hangs from it, likely an old design because I don't recognize the dark red exterior and black silk lining from anything recent. Around it is even more money, like some kind of séance circle. Daisy and I step toward it, bills beneath our feet and our friends' happiness at our backs.

"Do you think this is for us?" she asks me.

"It must be. Maybe Gram left something in the pockets?"

She's apprehensive, her hand poised above the right pocket of the coat. When she nods, I dip my hand into the left. My fingers brush the familiar texture of folded cardstock. I pull it out, heart hovering in my throat.

Daisy's face falls at the paper in my hand. Nothing is in hers. Her pocket was empty.

"Open it," Leo urges, making me jump because I hadn't realized the rest of our crew was gathered around us.

"I bet it's a big fat congrats," Quinn offers.

"Let's hope it's not another riddle," Caleb says.

My fingers shake as I unfold the paper, find the smudge, and lick it. I scan Gram's script as it appears. My eyes pass over it once, twice, three times. Each time makes less and less sense.

"Well?" Daisy prods.

My mouth is ashy, the moisture sucked out. Because the words before me . . . they don't add up. I don't *get* it.

"Everything cool, Lily?" Miles asks.

"Let me see it." Daisy snatches it from my grasp.

My hold was weak on it anyway, as weak as my stomach. I might throw up.

She reads it, her brow furrowing. When her eyes meet mine, confusion ripples through the brown. "She can't be serious."

"Can *someone* clue the rest of us in," Quinn demands.

I take the note back, clearing my throat. The words are written in Gram's writing, but nothing about them feels like something she'd say. When I speak, my voice doesn't sound like my own.

Dear Lilylove,

I knew I could count on you. I'm sorry it had to be like this. I need you to do only two more things. Once that's done, go back the way you came.

First, go to my office on the second floor. There, you'll find the key to all of this. And then . . .

I can barely force the words out.

Walk away from the money, the building, the name. And burn it all to the ground.

Shocked silence meets my words. It's like I've just stepped off a teacup ride, and I can't remember what it's like to not be spinning. Nothing makes sense.

"No," Leo says, voice dripping with disbelief. He grabs the note, reading it himself. Taking a page out of my book, he starts pacing, muttering to himself. "That can't be what she means. She told me if I did what she said, we'd all be led to the money. That it would be ours. This isn't—this isn't how it's supposed to go."

I stare at him. "What do you mean she told you?"

He freezes. "I didn't say that."

"Yes, you did." Quinn steps to my side. "What are you talking about?"

Daisy's on my other. "Leo? Do you know something we don't?"

Panic flashes across his face. And that's when I realize that for all the ways I might have felt close to him in the past week, that doesn't mean I *know* him. Not at all. Not when he's standing before me, fumbling for a lie.

Before I know it, I'm in front of him, kicking his hockey stick from his hand and grabbing his dress shirt in a way that is completely different from how I grabbed him hours ago on the boardwalk. My vision blurs as certain things click into place. Gram and Leo spending long days together, understanding each other and talking. *Strategizing.* How Gram wanted me to notice him so badly that she would talk about him all the time. *He's excellent company. Have you seen him yet?* she had asked me the night of the party. Because even then, he knew something that

I didn't.

And then, another thing. Leo said he was grounded because he passed out at the party and woke up hours later when it was over. If that's the case, and that's the night Gram died, then that must mean—

"You were there, weren't you?" I ask, hot tears brimming. "When Gram died. What happened that night?"

His panic bleeds into horror. "No! No, I wasn't there. I mean, I was, but not like that. I did pass out, and I woke up and saw lights were still on in the manor and I was thirsty, and I went inside but—"

He cuts off, shuddering.

"What?" I hiss. "What happened?"

In one shaky breath, he says, "She was already gone."

I let go of him like he burned me, stumbling back until Miles's hands steady me.

"Like . . . dead?" Miles asks, horrified.

Leo nods.

"Why didn't you call an ambulance?"

Leo's frantic gaze cuts to me. "I thought I was seeing things. That I took something to make me hallucinate or was still dreaming or—"

"Spit it out," Quinn growls.

"I was scared," he admits. "I was drunk and knew I'd get in trouble. And I was the only one around. But she looked . . . peaceful. Calling for help would get me involved, and I couldn't let that happen."

"So you just left her there?" Rage laces Daisy's voice. I can't speak, can't breathe. I have no idea what the *fuck* is going on.

"I checked her pulse, I swear. She was gone. There was nothing else I could do."

"You could have called someone!" I snap. "Everybody knows you get shitfaced at parties. Getting in trouble shouldn't have mattered more than getting help."

I take a step toward him, not even sure what I'm going to do, but Caleb presses me back.

"You knew about all of this, didn't you?" he asks Leo, who gives a timid nod. "Explain."

Leo takes a deep breath like the act is a life preserver. I lean into Miles, needing the stability.

"When I would come over to take care of the yard, Gram would be outside with me. I started noticing that some days she just . . . didn't look too good. Just walking from the patio to the gardens would make her short of breath. She'd press a hand to her chest like it was hurting her. She'd have to sit down because she felt weak or dizzy. One day, I asked her if she was okay after I saw her down some meds. I didn't think she'd tell me anything, but she got this . . . look in her eye. It was like for the first time, she wasn't Iris Rosewood but just a regular person. She looked *afraid*. And then, she said she was recently diagnosed with heart disease."

"So she told *you* and not even us?" Daisy asks.

"Only because I asked. She said I couldn't tell anybody. That she didn't want people to know, even family."

"Why?" My voice cracks. "I *lived* with her. Why wouldn't she tell me how bad it was?"

"But that's the thing—it wasn't bad. She told me it was super treatable, that there was nothing to worry about because she was taking medication. She thought she had more time."

"So where do you come into all of this?" Miles asks.

Leo swallows. "After that, we spent a lot more time just talking about all kinds of things. Situations I thought were hypothetical. She asked me if I knew the legend about Hyacinth's hidden fortune, and of course I did. But then we talked about it, a lot. About where the best hiding places in town were, what kind of clues to plant, things like that. We talked about it every week and we kind of created this . . . game. Like a town-wide hide-and-seek."

He flashes an apologetic glance at me. "I thought it was all just a joke, for a while. Just making things up while we played chess together after we solved each other's Sphinx riddles. But then one day, she was like, deadly serious. She told me when she died, I had to go into her office and get everything in the bottom left drawer of the desk. She'd leave instructions, and all I'd have to do was follow them."

Daisy shakes her head. "When did she tell you all this?"

"I think . . ." Leo pushes out a breath. "Sometime in May? It wasn't that long ago."

Daisy looks at me. "She changed her will May fifteenth, remember? This must be why."

My inhale is sharp. If not for Miles's hold, I'd be one with the bills on the floor.

"And none of this was a big fucking red flag?" Quinn asks Leo.

"Of course it was!" Leo throws his hands in the air. "But what was I supposed to do? We had spent weeks planning out

301

this—this fake treasure hunt. I thought it was a game, and suddenly it was real. When I looked in the drawer, there were three letters already addressed and four pieces of the map. Plus three clues, a ring of keys, and a note for me written in invisible ink. The instructions. Where to hide the clues and put the pieces of the map. That I couldn't drop off the letters until Lily turned eighteen if Gram died before then. And the final thing was that I had to play dumb and only help as a last resort."

"But you didn't wait." I find my voice. "You sent them a week early."

"I had to," Leo says. "The Saturday after Gram died, I overheard Chief Claremon telling my dad that Ell was asked to come back to London early because the board at Rosewood Inc. wanted to talk to her. Chief Claremon suspected they were trying to push the Rosewoods out and wasn't sure if he should bring it up to your uncle or not. I realized Gram must not have remembered that rule about Rosewood Inc. when planning the hunt. She just wanted you to be eighteen so you'd legally be an adult. Plus, Daisy had mentioned the will reading might happen on Monday, so I knew you'd get your letter then. I figured if I timed everything perfectly, we'd find the last clue after you turned eighteen but still finish this before the Rosewood Inc. deadline was up because I knew how important that is to you."

My head spins. I should have known all of this revolved around me turning eighteen. No one can take the money or control me. And if Uncle Arbor is implicated, Daisy will need a legal guardian for three months until she turns eighteen in September.

"That's why you wouldn't leave me alone," Caleb says. "You

knew the museum had a security system, but saying so would blow your cover."

Leo has the presence of mind to look guilty. While we were at the gas station, the same look crossed his face when I asked him how he was so sure we'd find the next clue. I didn't recognize what it was then. But I do now.

I push through the heartache and force myself to realize the other signs I missed. How Leo just so *happened* to be at Rosewood Manor the same time as me when we both found our pieces of the map. He hid the clue by the cannoli because he thought that *was* Gram's favorite snack since she always brought him one when he worked. Then at the Ivy, when I was ready to give up, Leo spun me across the dance floor. Dipped me right under the mirror ball.

He knew. The entire time, he *knew.*

I fish the last clue from where I tucked it in my Converse and reread the first line. *Dear Lily Love.*

Lily Love. With a space. Gram never wrote it with a space. That should have given it away immediately, but I didn't even think to look. And now that I truly take the time to examine it, the script isn't nearly as precise.

"You never went to my uncle's," I say, realizing Daisy was right to be confused how he saw the clue on the table when she didn't. "You took a while because you needed to rewrite it. Because you memorized what it said but had to make it seem like you went and got it yourself."

Another guilty nod. It doesn't make me want to knock his teeth out any less. "And that key ring you had leads all over town?" I knew it had seemed like a lot.

"To the major places. I needed it to get into the Ivy, the museum, and the deli."

"Well, that was just so convenient for you, then, wasn't it?" I bite.

"How'd you get past the security system at the museum?" Caleb asks.

Leo glances at the ground. "Gram told me what door to enter through at night that was closest to the security room and the code to disarm it. She knows this town, inside and out."

"Did she tell you the reason for all of this?" I ask, an emptiness yawning open inside of me, like a tear in fabric that just keeps ripping. "Did she know the truth about Uncle Arbor and my dad?"

"I don't know," Leo says softly. "But she did tell me that she was worried about you."

"She didn't have to be. I'm *fine*."

I'm so clearly not. The pathetic way my voice breaks, the tears clouding my vision, the fire burning beneath my skin are dead giveaways I couldn't be further from okay.

"But Gram wasn't," Daisy says. "Maybe that's the same reason she let go of Stewie and other employees at the manor. She knew she was getting worse and didn't want anyone to see her not at her best."

I force myself to recall the week leading up to the party. Gram had seemed normal, but she must have been hiding that she wasn't feeling well.

And then I remember. The night of the party, she was out of breath. I thought it was just the brisk walk, but if she felt ill and was nervous it was more severe than she thought, then maybe that's why she sent me to Daisy's house. So *I* wouldn't see her not at her best.

"I still think what I said last night holds true," Caleb says quietly. "Maybe Iris knew the truth about what your uncle did to your dad, but she also did this for us." His warm brown eyes are the only thing keeping me from falling off the ledge into a breakdown. "She knew each of us felt this—this cavernous loneliness. And that, like her, it would hurt us if we didn't learn to let people in."

I know in my heart he's right. But I can't help feeling that if I had not made a scene and stayed at the manor, I would have been able to save her. To call for help as soon as the heart attack happened and hold her until the medics arrived. I was too late to save Dad, but maybe I wouldn't have been too late for her. She could have been my second chance, and I could have been hers.

"Listen, obviously there is a lot to unpack here. Like, *a lot*," Miles gently interrupts. "But we should figure the details out after we secure the money. Your uncle isn't going to search the church forever. Maybe you should go upstairs and find whatever else Gram left for you. We'll start collecting the money in the meantime."

"No," I say quickly. "Gram said to burn it. There must be a reason."

"We can't burn it," Leo argues.

Miles clears his throat before I can object. "I agree. Even if we don't keep the money ourselves, think of all the charities it could go to. And burning money is illegal."

"Maybe we were never supposed to have the money. Maybe

this is a lesson. If burning the factory is what it takes—" Daisy says.

"Daze, we can't just set fire to this place." Leo reaches for her.

"Don't call me *Daze*," she says stiffly, evading his touch. "You should have told me about this. Instead, you went behind my back, hanging out with *my* cousin on some secret mission from *my* grandmother and you didn't say a word. So you know what, Leo? For once, I don't feel like defending your mistakes." Tears well in Daisy's eyes. "Why didn't you say anything?"

"Because he's the *yes guy*." I throw his words against him. "Gram told you to do something, and you did it."

"I'm sorry." His eyes beg me to understand, but I don't. Those gray eyes I was getting lost in mere hours ago. "At the time I just . . . I wanted to do something that mattered. This felt like it mattered. And if it somehow led to money, I thought maybe I'd finally make things right in my family. That I could stop weighing them down. But I never thought Gram was serious about any of it until it was too late."

"Then you didn't know her." The words are guttural and thick, pulled from my chest as tears spill down my cheeks.

"Maybe you're right," he agrees.

The others watch us warily, but Leo pays them no mind.

"But I knew *you*. Or at least, I used to. And I missed you. So fucking much. All those days I'd spend with Gram playing chess, we weren't just planning this. She was telling me about *you*. About the things you liked, the ways you amazed her and made her proud, how you were funny and kind. And none of that matched up with the girl who I thought pushed me away because she was too perfect and stuck-up to want me anymore. So yeah,

I wanted to know who Gram was talking about. The Rosewood version of you, or the Lily version of you I grew up with. Because they're two different people."

I'm breathing so hard I might bust a seam in my dress. Suddenly, it makes sense why Leo knew my favorite omelet; why he gave me the Hostess cupcake. Because Gram told him those little, tiny things about me, and probably a million others. Things he wouldn't have cared about when we were kids but cares about now. Things that make me *me*.

"Well, did I live up to everything she said?" My voice is a sob breaking free of the cage of my throat. "While the rest of us were trying to solve Gram's clues, I was the puzzle for you, wasn't I?"

Leo searches for words. "I—I just wanted to know who you really are," he finally says.

"Yet I have no idea who *you* are." My temper capsizes me. "How could you keep this from me? I fucking hate you."

"You know what? You *are* different from the girl I knew four years ago." His face cracks, a look passing over it that I can only describe as heartache mixed with *fuck it*. "You're more clever, and way funnier. Your eyes are green but have weird little gold flecks close up, which I never saw before. And you still have the *worst* attitude ever, but I've never met anyone more daring, more *caring*, and I don't know if I'll ever figure you out. So yeah, Lily, guess what? I meant what I said at the boardwalk. You're rare, but not because you're perfect or special or whatever. You're rare because you're *you*, with all your thorns and sass and relentless ambition, and that's what made Gram love you." He pauses, breathing hard. We're inches apart. "It's what makes *me* love you."

I suck in a breath, ready to argue that he loves whatever version of me Gram contrived, but he can't love *me*. Not when I barely know who I am myself anymore.

"Fuck us, am I right?" Quinn laughs before I can say it, the sound sharp and brittle. Her eyes are rimmed with surprising red as they dart to Daisy. "We all love Rosewoods, the most frustrating people on earth. So let's at least make sure we get paid for it."

She drops to her knees, bills crinkling in her hands as she scoops them up, stuffing her pockets. Daisy stares at her, jaw slack. Caleb and Miles swap a look.

"Lily, I'm sorry," Leo begs, locking eyes with me.

I shake my head, words stuck in my throat.

"I wanted to tell you. I *should* have told you. *All* of you. I'm—"

His face morphs into confusion. He focuses on something over my right shoulder, through the windows.

And then his hands are on me. He shoves me so suddenly, so *roughly* that I have no time to prep myself. I crash into the ground, pain flaring up my side.

A breath later, he's on top of me, yelling, "Get down!" There's a sound so loud I'm sure it will echo through the entire town. I realize through a bleary haze that Leo didn't shove me to hurt me. He's huddled over me. Protecting me.

Because shards of glass are raining down.

26

There is a beat where I'm only aware of my heart hammering against my rib cage, glass smashing against the ground, and the collage of hundred-dollar bills staring back at me. One slides away from me, gripped in Caleb's shaking hand. He stares at it, brow furrowed.

"Get up," Leo urges, hauling me to my feet as time speeds up again. The shattering window triggered an alarm, a drone slamming inside my skull. Tiny shards of glass spill from Leo's dress shirt, tinkling against the ground. One shard sliced his temple and a small trickle of blood trails the left side of his face. His shirt is shredded.

Quinn coughs, and Caleb groans. Daisy helps Miles get to his feet.

I can't stop looking at Leo. "You—"

My words cut off with a gasp. In the spot where the windows once were, jagged shards of glass stick up around the frame, outlining four silhouettes.

The three hunters and Uncle Arbor.

Leo grabs his fallen hockey stick. "Get whatever Gram left you." He prods me toward the stairs to the mezzanine. To the others, he says, "If we split up, maybe we can divide and conquer them. Run!"

Nobody needs to be told twice. Caleb and Miles take off toward the shipping side of the factory through two large swinging doors. Daisy and Quinn go the opposite direction, toward the warehouse. My heart sinks as our fatal mistake sets in. We were so busy arguing, it left Uncle Arbor enough time to rethink the clue and find us.

Leo follows me up the stairs. All my anger turns into icy fear as I reach the top step and a rotten wooden board cracks beneath my foot, only Leo's palm against my back saving me from tumbling backward. Using the rusted railing, I haul myself past the broken step onto the mezzanine floor, also coated with dollars. Gram's office is within sight. The door is ajar, as if she's waiting for me just like when I was little and visited her.

I'm nearly there when a hunter follows us onto the mezzanine, a steel-tipped shovel held like a bat in their hands.

"I've got your back," Leo promises. I nod at him, finding miniscule comfort in the fact that splitting up *did* work—the other hunters must still be on the first floor.

He sets his jaw and spins, raising his hockey stick to ward off the hunter. It grants me a window to slip into the office.

There are still things on the walls, easy to see thanks to the big window on the back wall letting in the moonlight. Sketches of old designs. A family picture of Gram with Petunia and Hyacinth. One of Gram with Dad and Uncle Arbor when they were toddlers. I can't imagine why she'd leave all this stuff in here, unless maybe she came back somedays to reminisce.

I shake the nostalgia away, hurrying toward the desk in the center, a twin to Gram's stately rosewood one at the manor. Sitting on top of it are two things.

A key on a thin silver chain. I slip it over my head, so it rests over my dress.

The second: A box of matches.

The screeching drone roars on. It must be a security system. Hopefully alerting someone who will save us.

I grab the matches, still unsure what to do with them. Rushing out of the room, I wince as the sound echoes around the open air of the factory. It's accompanied by gasps and yelps. In the dim light, it takes a moment for my eyes to adjust.

And I *duck*.

"Lily, it's over," Uncle Arbor yells, trying to grab me again.

"So that's it?" I shout above the droning, voice shrill with panic as he makes another attempt to grab me. I barely evade him, stumbling backward on unsteady legs. "You'll kill me for it? Kill *us* for it?"

"Nobody's killing anybody. No one needs to get hurt," he says, but I'm the prey here. I'm cornered and don't have much more space to back up. "Give me the key."

I clutch it protectively. "Gram already gave you a key."

His laugh is humorless. "She did, all right. A key to *nothing*."

I knew it. He must have thought it was to the manor, maybe even snuck in like me to try it. It was just something to tide him over, distract him. Realization dawns as I grip the one at the base of my throat. "This is the key to the manor."

"And everything else, I'm sure. It belongs to *me*."

"We can share the money." It's a feeble bait to buy more time. "There's more than enough—"

He shakes his head. Now that Daisy has shared her side of the story, there's no mistaking the cold glint of greed in my uncle's green-eyed gaze. "Never been much of a sharer."

And suddenly, I'm angry all over again. Angry that he made Dad feel like death was his only option. Made Gram feel like she couldn't trust him; trust *us*. And angry at myself, for never seeing any of it.

He reaches for me again, but the defense skills Quinn taught me kick in. I grab his wrist, then bring my elbow up to jam into his trachea. He chokes, stumbling back. It buys me enough time to yank a match from the box and strike it.

"I read the letters." My voice shakes as the flame burns closer to my fingers. "I know that you made Dad think he had nowhere to go. That people were going to expose him. All this time, I thought his death was my fault, but it was *you*. It's always been you."

Horror dawns in his eyes. "Lily, I—you have to understand. I never wanted anybody to get hurt. But Alder thought he could fix everything. He made all the wrong calls. It ruined the lives of so many people, us included. He was making the town hate us. People wanted him gone. But he was my *brother*. I never wanted him to die. Just to leave."

His face twists with pain and guilt. And I hate it with everything in me. Because I've seen it on mine.

"Please," he begs. "I never meant for it to go this far. But we will lose everything if you don't give me that key. The inheritance belongs to me. I need it to clean up your father's mess because Gram sure as hell never did." He steps toward me. "I thought you were like *me*. That you understood what was at stake. But you're just like your father. Even dead, I can't escape him." His voice cracks. I used to think that looking at Uncle Arbor was like looking at Dad's ghost. Now I realize that for him, I'm the part of Dad that won't stop haunting him.

Maybe that's why he reaches out so fast I can't stop him, wraps his hand around my throat, and squeezes.

I gasp, tears filling my eyes. But as quickly as his hand is there, it's gone, leaving a stinging sensation and a tearing sound. I claw at my throat, sucking air in. There's the empty chain of my ruby necklace, but that's it.

In his hand is the key, ripped right off my neck.

"No!" I scream, lunging at him. But he shoves me down, my nails uselessly scratching his arm.

Three things happen in quick succession:

A gunshot rings out at the same time I fall to my knees.

I drop the match.

A crack fills the air.

Through the orange flames racing across the ground, the dry and dusty paper beneath our feet the perfect fuel, I see Leo knocked backward, his hockey stick falling in two broken pieces beside him. His arms windmill as he tries to regain his balance. He nearly has it when he takes one more step back.

Right onto the rotten top step.

A scream of smoke fills my lungs at the snap of wood and the plank gives beneath his weight. It just—*gives*.

"Leo!" I leap to my feet, elbowing past Uncle Arbor and the hunter as I race toward him.

But I'm too late, always too damn late. Air rushes as his fingers slip through mine, and he tumbles down the flight of stairs in backward, jumbled somersaults, landing in a heap at the bottom with an awful crack.

I sprint down the stairs, falling to my knees beside his crumpled form. "Leo," I choke out. He doesn't move, his right arm twisted beneath him in a way that makes bile rise up my throat. His eyes are closed, mouth slightly ajar with blood running down his face. I can't tell if it's from the glass shattering or him hitting his head on the ground.

The last thing I said to him was *I fucking hate you*. Just like Dad. I never *fucking* learn.

A sob bursts from my mouth, my hands hovering uselessly. I'm scared to touch him. "Help!" I screech, voice raw.

Footsteps thunder behind me. The hunter that fought Leo jumps over the railing to avoid us, sprinting across the floor toward the windows, shovel in hand. "Bail!" he screams.

The other two follow, abandoning their attacks to flee. I want to chase after them, but I'm terrified to leave Leo's side.

"Wake up," I beg, cupping the side of his face and brushing my thumb over the blood on his cheek, smearing it. "You've gotta wake up."

"We need to get out of here." Quinn's suddenly beside me. "Miles is outside calling nine-one-one with Caleb."

"They won't get here in time." I gesture to the encroaching smoke, a precarious creaking filling the air. "This building is too old, too—"

"Do you hear that?" Quinn asks, straightening suddenly.

Past the blood pounding in my ears, I hone in on my cousin's voice from the mezzanine. She must have gone up the second staircase on the opposite side of the building. I can barely make out her silhouette confronting Uncle Arbor.

"It's going to give!" Quinn points to the mezzanine. Ravenous flames race across it, over half engulfed. The brittle support beams catch just as quickly, two buckling so the platform tilts. Soon, the fire will reach this floor. As it is, the original path toward the basement that Gram wanted us to retreat to is shrouded by smoke.

"I'll get Daisy," I promise, vision blurring through tears and smoke. I gesture helplessly at Leo. He still hasn't moved. "You get him out of here." Quinn hesitates, but I won't waste time arguing. "You're stronger than me. There's no way I'd be able to get him past the glass. *Please*, Quinn."

With a nod, she kneels beside Leo, taking his left arm and pulling him up so she can shrug it over her shoulders. "Don't quit on us now, Frat Boy."

"Let me help." Caleb appears, crouching to get Leo's feet.

"Why did you come back in?" I ask, trying to see through the smoke if Miles followed.

"For you guys." Caleb coughs, seeming just as surprised as Quinn and me that he chose us over safety. "Miles tackled one of the hunters and knocked them out, but the others got away. Nine-one-one should be here any minute."

"Get out of here," I wheeze. "I'll be right behind you."

I sprint back up the stairs, carefully dodging the broken top step. On the second floor, the smoke is ten times worse. It's suffocating, wrapping around me, climbing inside my lungs. I don't know if my head is woozy or if the floor actually shifts beneath my feet.

"We have to go!" I shout.

Uncle Arbor is on his hands and knees, Daisy trying to pull him up as the fire scales the walls around them.

"Come on!"

When neither come closer, despair turns my movements frantic, hands waving. "Let's go! What are you—"

But then I see Uncle Arbor's hand pressed to his abdomen, red seeping through his fingers.

"He got shot!" Daisy eyes are bright with fear. With the fire framing her Rosewood red hair, pieces sticking to her cheek with sweat, she looks terrifying.

Maybe I do, too.

The floor jerks beneath us, the sound excruciatingly loud. One of the support beams snapping, likely. I stumble forward, close enough to loop my arm around Daisy's waist and tug her back against my chest. She rips free, whirling on me.

"I'm not leaving him," she cries. "I want to be different. Better."

And even if it kills me, so do I.

Together, we force him to his feet. He's practically deadweight as we drag him down the stairs. The others are gone, and I can only hope that Leo is being loaded into an ambulance right now. That he lives.

That *we* live.

Because pieces of the ceiling are crumbling down. The gap

of the broken windows is in sight, but it's so hot that crossing the burning factory feels like a million-mile desert. Maybe when Gram said to burn the name, she meant us, too. That we end the Rosewood line once and for all.

But I feel like there's a hand on my back pushing me forward. As if Dad's or Gram's ghost, or both, are telling me I can't give up.

We trip through the window. A piece of glass catches my bare calf, pain searing through me as we stagger onto the grass. Uncle Arbor is unconscious, and only once we're a good distance from the entrance do I let him slip from my grasp. Daisy crumbles beside him, vomiting onto the ground.

A hand is on me, covered in latex. "Lily, we're here to help. Is there anyone left inside?"

I stare at the EMT, the flashing lights around us blurring the landscape. "My friends?" I croak.

"Yes, we've gotten to them already. But the fire department just got here and needs to know if anyone else is in there."

I shake my head. With every breath of burnt air, things become clearer. She pats my arm, caring brown eyes unfamiliar. It's unsettling that she knows me, and I don't know her. "It's all right, Lily. We'll do everything we can for your uncle."

That makes the tears come. I don't want my uncle—I want my dad.

She tries to lead me farther away, toward an ambulance where Quinn sits on the back, Caleb and Miles beside her with oxygen masks over their faces. I root my aching feet, looking over my shoulder at the burning factory behind me. The carved wooden sign that frames the top spelling out *Rosewood Inc.* now just reads

Rose, and even that will be nothing but ashes soon. The firetrucks unwind hoses as if there's anything left to save. After tonight, it will be a ruin.

A glimmer catches my eye near the spot on the ground where Uncle Arbor collapsed. He's already on a gurney while an EMT kneels next to Daisy. Something's in the grass.

"Wait." I brush off the EMT's hold. Protests spill from her mouth, but I move toward the spot, falling to my knees and picking up what I saw. It's covered in soot and blood. I rub my thumb over the warm metal chain, disbelief and horror and something deceiving like hope burning inside me.

On trembling legs, I rise. Clenched in my fist is the chain, and hanging from that—

The key.

27

When I step out of the car, everything feels different.

The manor looks the same—all flawless brick and twisting vines. I've stood before the front door a thousand times waiting for it to open to show Gram on the other side. Despite how hard I stare, no such thing happens.

"The key," Frank says, gesturing at my neck as Daisy gets out of the car and stands beside me. We're both in tacky outfits bought in the hospital gift shop before being discharged an hour ago to him, the only person who would come for us. While Caleb, Quinn, and Miles were collected yesterday by family members, I sat in my room alone for twenty-four painstaking hours, fading in and out of consciousness on oxygen and getting questioned by police when I finally woke up last night. It was early this morning when Frank arrived at my doorway, saying it was time to go home.

I knew he meant the manor. But as we stand before it, I can't help feeling like it's the furthest thing from a home.

"Try it." Daisy nods at the key, her voice raspy from the smoke inhalation.

There's a healing cut on her cheek, and her hair is wild around her face. I don't look much better, babying my left leg thanks to six stitches in it from cutting my calf on the jagged glass. Both of us sport deep purple eyebags that a cosmetologist would have a field day covering up.

"Have you heard—?"

"Nothing," she says, already knowing my question is about Leo because I asked six times on the way here if she received an update. He's alive but hasn't woken yet.

The last words I said to him spin in my brain, a song stuck on repeat. *I fucking hate you.* Tears clog my throat all over again.

I wish I said them to Uncle Arbor, who's still unconscious but expected to wake soon. He lost a lot of blood, but he's projected to make a full recovery. I'm not sure how I feel about that.

I told the police the truth about him. The hunter Miles caught even confirmed it, not willing to spill about his cohunters' whereabouts but happy to share Uncle Arbor's involvement. Regardless, I saw the doubt in Chief Claremon's eyes.

I take the blood-free key off my neck, where it's been resting since I plucked it from the grass. The gold chain of the ruby stays, and even with the gem ruined, I like the familiar presence around my throat.

Frank shakes his head when I hold it out to him. "You should do it," he says in the same ancient, gravelly voice I've known my whole life, gesturing to the door.

I glance at Daisy, but she doesn't object. For all our talk of suspecting Frank, he's the only one who's come through for us.

I step forward, a chill sweeping through me. I hadn't wanted this. Not when I realized I'd be getting it the way I did. But

Uncle Arbor dropped it when Daisy and I dragged him out, and then the next moment, I was holding it.

Something crinkles beneath my soot-covered Converse. It's today's copy of the *Rosetown Chronicle* on the stone step. Somebody snapped a picture of me in my tattered dress yesterday with the factory burning in the background. The headline reads, "Old Factory Burns in Alleged Family Feud: Could This Be the End for the Rosewoods?"

With a cough, Frank brushes it off the step with his loafer.

I swallow, my throat still raw from the smoke. With shaking fingers, I bring the key to the lock. Despite never having an issue threading a needle, I can't summon the steadiness to jam the key in correctly. Agonizing seconds pass until I find the right fit. I hold my breath, waiting for it to not turn.

But it does. As smooth as if I've done the motion thousands of times.

Frank lets out a low whistle. "I'll be damned. I didn't believe it'd come down to that."

I open the door, but stepping across the threshold feels like too much. "Down to what?"

He clears his throat, digging into his pocket to pull out a letter on thick cardstock. "While you kids had your notes, so did I."

Daisy and I share a startled glance. He retrieves a pair of wire-rimmed glasses from his breast pocket and reads.

Dear Frank,

I want to thank you for all your trustworthy service over the past thirty years. You've been more than a lawyer, more than a friend. You're family, which is why I need you to do one last thing. It won't be easy, and I'm sorry if it puts you in harm's way.

You need to wait. Protect the manor with your life. And no, that's not an exaggeration. Nobody is allowed on the premises. Not until they find the key. You'll know when they do. If all goes to plan, it will be quite the spectacle.

Only then, once it fits the locks I've ordered to be replaced upon my death, can you surrender the manor to them. And also, you'll need the account numbers listed below. I believe what everyone's been looking for can be found there. At least, the start of it.

Don't let me down. You never have before.

Love dearly,
Iris

I stare at him, mouth dry. "What does she mean, 'account numbers'? The money was all in the factory."

"It burned," Daisy adds.

He shakes his head. "That was a combination of real bills and fake. I haven't figured out the true sum lost yet."

I still can't force myself past the threshold, my legs like lead as flashes of the other night at the factory hit me. Shattering glass, the bills on the ground, Caleb—

"Caleb knew," I say suddenly. "Right when the hunters and Uncle Arbor arrived. He frowned at one of the bills, but really, he was confused. Because he could tell it was fake."

Frank nods. "He was the one who brought this to my attention yesterday."

"So Gram wanting me to burn it wasn't ridiculous?" I ask.

Frank hesitates. "Well, it was certainly a . . . choice. I suspect she was trying to teach a lesson of sorts. But the factory is insured, so technically, if we can prove it wasn't you specifically who started the fire, we might be able to file a claim for a payout. I'm estimating that was her final goal. It's certainly no new phenomenon for acts of arson to be committed against abandoned properties."

That must have been why Gram wanted us to go back the way we came. So no one would know we started the fire. I deflate. "But I did strike the match."

"But you didn't willingly drop it," Daisy counters. "I saw the whole thing. You were holding it, then Dad grabbed you by the throat, you dropped it, and—" Her voice gets small and her eyes glisten. "The hunter with the gun was aiming for *you*. But when you went to take the key back from Dad and he shoved you down, he got shot instead."

I don't know what to do with that truth. That maybe, if things had played out just slightly different, I wouldn't be standing here.

"Arbor is lucky to be alive," Frank says. He gestures through the doorway. "After you."

I peer into the foyer, tugging on the ends of my hair. The rain from Friday night washed the brown coloring off, so it's back to its Rosewood red, but it's filthy. I smell like a combination of burnt toast and BO—not exactly something you'd find on the shelf at Lush.

"Just go," Daisy says, giving my back a small shove. I pass the threshold, feeling like an intruder.

She follows me, then Frank. My throat closes as I glance around. It's like I'm seeing the manor for the first time. The polished floors and staircase, the crown molding and elegant sconces. I walk into the great room, memories of parties spinning in my mind. The overstuffed couches, posh chaise, and round tables meant for hors d'oeuvres and flutes of champagne. The walls, which are a rich ivy green, climb up to the high ceiling, where the replica chandelier hangs from the Ivy. It's all twisting gold, with gilded leaves sprouting from it. I've never bothered to look closely before. I've never cared.

It's never been *mine.*

"Is this real?" I ask Frank, overwhelmed with disbelief. "Just because I found the key, is all this really . . . mine? Anyone could have gotten it."

"She knew it would be you." Daisy's voice is sure as she touches my arm.

"How?" I breathe.

"Because Leo was your safety net." She looks around with an unreadable look on her face. Her eyes shine when she finally meets mine. "He kept you on track. And Gram knew she didn't need to tell him the final place where the money was hidden. That you would know based on the last clue about Saint Anthony."

There are a thousand things I should say to her. All I force out is, "Why me?"

But the true question is there. *Why* not *you?*

We've already talked about it. Uncle Arbor would have been tracking her phone the entire time until she figured out he was working against us. But when she looks at me, I realize that's not it.

"Because I don't think Gram was confident I could do it," she says softly. "And she was probably right."

"Iris's reasons will always be a mystery," Frank says.

Daisy looks at Frank. "One of those women from the will reading questioned me at the hospital. She said she's with the *FBI*. So I told her about the death threats Dad sent to Uncle Alder."

Frank nods. "A large investigation is underway."

"I don't think Chief Claremon believed me," I say.

A solemn look passes Frank's face. "As they were advisers on the council together, I'm sure it was a shock to the chief. But there's more than enough evidence."

"What about Gram? Do you think she knew Uncle Arbor did something to Dad?"

"She must have," Daisy says. "It's got to be one of the main reasons she planned the hunt and tried to keep the money out of his hands."

"Well, the account numbers in my letter lead to trusts for you both," Frank says. "A lot of the money is actually in stocks and shares, of course, but everything's been evenly divided between you two with the instruction that you don't have access until you're eighteen. So, yes, I do believe the treasure hunt was an attempt to keep the attention off you initially. And to answer your question, Lily, Gram had an inkling. Thanks to your mother."

"My *mother*?" I gawk.

"She had found one of the blackmail letters Arbor had sent your father shortly after he passed." Frank strides into the living room and begins opening windows to let in a breeze. There's a staleness to the air from the manor being locked up for a week.

Daisy and I follow, shoving heavy curtains aside and brushing dust from the sills.

"I believe she suspected Arbor was behind it and took it to Iris. But as you can imagine, that wasn't easy for Iris to come to terms with. Sometimes, we can only see what we want to when it comes to those closest to us. Your mother was upset that Iris wasn't taking her more seriously."

"Was that why she really left?" Daisy asks.

"I'm sure part of it. It bothered Iris, of course. Made her see Arbor in a new light. And I think once she started entertaining the thought, she realized how plausible the accusation was. He's always been very concerned with image, status, and wealth. So, she wanted a way to make it seem like the money had disappeared. If it was given to you both immediately at the will reading, he might have been able to challenge it in some regard due to your ages. Or influence you."

Despite the sunlight streaming into the room, I can't help the chill that shakes me. Frank is right. If that money had been given to me and I didn't get the chance to see Uncle Arbor's ugly side, he would have easily swayed me.

Daisy frowns. "Wait. So if Lily had turned eighteen a week earlier, the hunt wouldn't have happened?"

Frank goes over to the mantel and pulls an envelope from where it was tucked behind a gold candelabra. He hands it to me. "I'll let you be the judge of that. Iris left this for both of you with a note instructing me to pass it along only once you found the key. I believe she wrote it the night she died, after the party."

I break the red Rosewood wax seal, but stop, holding it out to Daisy. She smiles weakly, taking the envelope with trembling fingers and extracting the single sheet of ivory cardstock inside. Together, we read.

Dear ~~Daisydew and Lilylove,~~

My girls. If you're reading this, then I'm gone and you've done a splendid job playing my parting game. I knew you could do it. And, Daisy, I do hope you don't feel left out. I was afraid that Lily wouldn't learn what she needed to if she wasn't on her own. Also, this potentially unfolded while you're in Milan. I hope you enjoy your time abroad. My intention was never to use it to brew competition between you two but as a means to give you something to bond over. Frank had the suggestion that a common interest might help.

I'm sorry that I didn't get to convey that to you, Lily. That was my intention at the party. To tell you that I wanted you to stay here so I could show you more of Rosewood Inc. and the role I envision for you. In hopes that when Daisy returns, you both could someday be part of it together. But that also isn't the whole reason.

Throughout the years, I've asked myself many times, "Where is the line between ambition and greed?" It's a slippery slope, to want. Easy to become obsessive in your desires. I like to think I managed well, although I'm afraid the same can't be said for my sons. I failed to teach them independence and the importance of weighing the consequences when chasing wealth. It's a mistake I swore not to make with you two.

As I write this, only moments after the last guests left, I truly hope you never read it. But I fear time isn't on my side. It's the one thing we cannot hoard.

But I tried. That's the true reason I kept you from Milan, Lily. Since your grandfather died, I've spent many years in the manor alone. But then you moved in and chose to stay. I became so used to your presence, your fire. Every day, I'd tell myself, "Tomorrow, I'll start teaching her more about Rosewood Inc." And yet, I couldn't bring myself to. As each day went by, it became more and more obvious to me that being the chair is what I wanted for you but not what was best for you. You're far too creative to sit in meetings all day and spend hours poring over paperwork. So I hope you understand why I didn't appoint you to take my place.

And let's be honest—business school has never been your dream.

Regardless of where you go in life, I don't want you to go alone. But hopefully, if all goes to plan, you will never need to. I have requested for Frank to set aside rewards for the other participants.

And don't be too hard on Leo for his part. He was the bridge to pull you two back together.

I love you both, more than words could ever capture and money could ever buy.

You have my heart,
Gram

Slowly, Daisy and I lower the page.

"Are you okay?" she asks. "Gram—"

"Appointed Ell?" I assume, looking at Frank.

He nods. Daisy's expression is apprehensive, like I'm a bomb about to detonate. I was so bent on finding the fortune before Saturday in the wildest hopes that Gram would give some promise that Rosewood Inc. was in my future, even if I knew being in charge of the board was unlikely.

"I'm okay," I say, surprised that it's true. For the past year, I've treated FIT and Rosewood Inc. like a Band-Aid—two lofty goals to smother the lonely ache inside. But now, I'm not so lonely anymore. Having more time to spend with friends and making clothes actually sounds kind of nice.

"Good. She's resting easy, then." Frank sighs. "However, I'm afraid the town is a different mess. People are quite up in arms, thinking this is the end of Rosewoods. They took the burning of the factory *very* literally."

"Today's paper didn't help." I scowl.

"So what should we do?" Daisy asks.

Everything feels muddled. Despite the daylight and open air, I might as well still be roaming through the dark tunnel.

But there is a pinprick of light in knowing Daisy's beside me, an unlikely comfort, and that Frank is looking out for us. If I was a townie, what would I want to come next?

"We do what Rosewoods do best," I decide. A plan begins to take gritty shape in my mind, roots detangling and answers within reach. "Let's throw a party."

28

"Ow." I wince against my cousin's tight hold on my hair.

"I'm almost done," she promises, twisting my curls into a braided crown, the lower layer hanging down my back. "I forgot how much I miss braiding my long hair."

I sigh in relief as she finishes by tying the braid at the base with a tiny elastic. Taking a step back to give me a once-over, she releases a slow whistle. "Damn, that is a *fit*."

I turn to see myself in the full-length mirror. I created a special dress for tonight's party now that I'm reunited with my sewing machine and patterns. It's a deep royal purple, a velvet fabric that hugs my chest with a sweetheart neckline, off-the-shoulder straps, and a tight waist with a gold satin sash. It flares out around my hips, ending mid-thigh. It feels classic, the style maybe even something Gram would have worn when she was my age.

I made Daisy's outfit, too, a lilac satin tube dress with silver vine embroidery. We visited her house earlier this week to collect her clothes and mine, but I wanted something new for us to wear. A fresh wardrobe for a fresh start.

Besides, some of my only moments of peace this past week

were when the moon was high and it was just the hum of the sewing machine, the glow of my desk light, and Daisy's quiet breaths beside me—sometimes awake on her phone, sometimes passed out in my bed. Plus, since we haven't been able to tap into the full inheritances Gram set aside for us yet, a shopping spree wasn't in our budget. Despite having the manor, Frank says it can take a while for the paperwork for accessing the trusts to go through, especially given most of it is actually in bonds and stocks and a whole bunch of other banker-talk stuff I thought I wouldn't have to think about for at least a few more years. Frank's been kind enough to lend us whatever we need in the meantime.

"Miss Rosewood," Frank says from the open doorway. When he notices Daisy and me together, he adds a subtle *s* to the end. "Quite a few guests have arrived and are in the great room. I've gathered the ones you requested in the foyer."

"Thank you," we say at the same time.

Daisy and I share a look. Over the past week as we planned for tonight's party, we've shared a lot of looks. At first it was weird, just like going through each other's closets and climbing into each other's beds at night because the first night sleeping alone, I woke up screaming with the heat of flames at my back. But we fell into an easy pattern faster than I could have ever expected, picking up where we left off four years ago. It's bittersweet knowing we could have had each other all this time we've been hurting.

We stride through the doorway and down the hall, but my legs lock at the top of the stairs.

"You don't have to do this," Frank says. "We can wait until

the recent events smooth over and the details are nailed down."

Recent events. The factory burning down was only the beginning. All week, we've caught wind of murmurings from townspeople. Some want to leave, scared from the string of disasters that have hit Rosetown. Others want answers, like if the people who hunted us are gone for good. The one Miles caught is being charged with assault and vandalism, but the others vanished. One person reported seeing their SUV in Creekson, another report in Boston. As of Thursday, they were tracked to the Niagara Falls border, but once they got to Canada, they disappeared. I have a feeling they have plenty of practice taking themselves off the map.

And then there's Uncle Arbor.

He's woken up throughout the past week while Daisy and I have shifted our lives into the manor, but according to the updates that the hospital staff leave on my voice mail, he hasn't said much. *Smoke inhalation and trauma*, they told me. *Bullet wounds take weeks to heal.*

And to think it was supposed to be me.

The thing is, Uncle Arbor isn't dumb. Frank was his lawyer, too, and now that Frank's loyal to us, he won't say boo until he finds a new one.

I glance at Daisy. She visited him today for the first time while I was busy squaring away last-minute hors d'oeuvres with Nonna, who graciously offered to cater the event with the deli since money is still in flux. I didn't want to see him anyway. Every morning, I wake up looking for bruises around my neck. They never appeared, but I can still feel the pressure of his fingers digging into my skin.

I prodded Daisy for details when she returned, but she immediately launched into her hair- and skin-care influencer persona, forcing me to get ready so we wouldn't be late to our own party. We are anyway.

"I don't want to wait," I say to Frank, taking the first step.

I only slightly regret wearing my highest pair of heels, for power, because my leg still kills thanks to the sutured gash. Navigating down the polished curved staircase is slow going, Daisy reaching the landing first. She flashes me a reassuring smile. I offer a shaky one back, my insides twisting as we descend the rest and step into the foyer.

Music wafts through the closed doors of the great room. Standing in front of the doors are four familiar faces.

"You came!" Daisy exclaims, throwing her arms around Leo. He looks . . . well, awful. His entire right arm is in a plaster cast from his shoulder to his hand, and he stumbles under Daisy's added weight.

She steadies him. "Whoa, sorry. I'm just so excited to see you. I missed you."

"Missed you, too," he says. He doesn't look my way.

I fucking hate you echoes between us.

I shift my attention to numb the sting, shock running through me when *Quinn* wraps me in a hug, Caleb right behind her.

"Where the hell have you been all week?" she asks.

"Planning this." I gesture to the great room, nodding at Caleb. "How'd I do?"

He grins. "Impressive for an amateur planner."

"Sorry I ghosted a bit."

"It's one of your many talents." Miles grins, bear-hugging me.

I melt a little, always happy to be enveloped in a signature Miles hug, even if I've been craving someone else's embrace.

"So how much trouble did you all get in with your parents?" Daisy asks once we separate.

"I'm on house arrest for the next three weeks," Quinn says. "Only allowed here thanks to the VIP invite."

"I'm pretty sure everyone heard my dad yelling at me in the hospital." Caleb cringes. "He was *pissed*. But grateful we survived. Plus, it forced him to talk to my aunt, and they're both here tonight, so . . . might've been a win? Or it might devolve into chaos. Odds are fifty-fifty."

"Better than nothing," Daisy points out. She looks at Leo. "How 'bout you?"

"I'm not grounded anymore, so that's cool," he says, voice subdued compared to his usual upbeat tone. "Turns out if you break your arm and get massively concussed in a burning building, your dad suddenly cares a lot about you. Life hacks, right?"

He says it in a light voice, like it's a joke, but from the resounding silence, we know it's not. I want to say something, anything, but he's acting like I'm not even here.

Quinn nudges him. "It's crap that it took all that for him to realize that your frat boy potential is off the charts. But, like, better late than never?"

Leo shrugs. "I guess. But between him, my mom, and my sisters—who FaceTime me every single day to check in even though I've told them being on my phone makes me want to puke my brains out—I'd kind of rather be grounded."

"Speaking of grounded, Nonna's gonna go off on me if I don't finish helping her in the kitchen. I'm on the clock." Miles points his thumb in the general direction. "Catch up with you all later?"

"Can I come?" Caleb asks.

A grin breaks across Miles's face. "Sure. But you can't eat all the salami. It's for the guests."

Caleb looks affronted, following him. "I *am* a guest."

"Hey, wait!" Quinn presses a hand to Caleb's shoulder to stop him. She takes a breath. "I wanted to tell you, I thought it was really brave what you did for me at the boardwalk. When the hunter shitstick was pointing the gun at me." She swallows, her fingers brushing the yellowing edge of a bruise on her temple and a healing scab. "Thanks for that. For being brave."

Caleb's eyes turn glossy. He smiles and nods, letting Miles pull him through the doors of the great room toward the kitchen.

"Speaking of brave . . . ," Daisy says to Quinn. "I think I owe you a talk that I've been running from for too long."

"You do."

Daisy nods toward the hallway leading to the office. With a glance at Leo and me, they both disappear down it.

And then silence. Excruciating, louder-than-music silence.

"I should probably—"

"I wanted to—"

We both stop.

"You go first," I squeeze out. My throat feels barely the width of a hair.

He hesitates. "I was just going to say I should probably find my parents and get going. Parties aren't really my thing right now. Doctor's orders and all that."

"Right." My heart plummets. Although that makes sense as I take in his outfit of a loose T-shirt and athletic shorts. Definitely not party attire.

He pushes open the door to the great room, but I grab his good arm and rush out what I've been practicing in the mirror all week.

"I just wanted to say thank you. For protecting me in the factory."

He looks at the ground. "It was nothing. I lied to you, and that was shitty. Fighting the hunter was the least I could do."

"You could have died." Even saying the words has my throat locking.

A faint grin graces his lips. "I'm all right. Arm's messed-up, and I won't be playing hockey anytime soon, but it's cool. And the concussion sucks, but I've had them before." He pauses. "I'm glad you're okay. When I woke up, they told me about the factory being wrecked. Got worried you were hurt."

"No, I'm fine."

He looks at me, gray eyes swimming with disbelief. He points to himself. "Killer *I'm fine* lie detector, remember?"

A soft laugh escapes me. "I *will* be fine," I amend. "But thank you. I'm sorry for what I said in the factory. I don't hate you. And for the record, I missed you, too."

He smiles, glancing at the ornate rug beneath our feet before meeting my eyes. "I know it might not happen soon, but do you think you can forgive me someday? Because I meant what I said in the factory. I—" He pauses, a swell of emotion in his eyes. "I really like you, Lily Rose."

"I forgive you," I say, because I knew I would the moment I realized he shoved me to the ground when the windows exploded to protect me. "And—"

I take a breath, overwhelmed because despite having a million things to think about this week, he still took up the majority of real estate in my brain. Saying so sucks, because it's vulnerable and imperfect and messy. But he deserves to know how I really feel.

"I think you're rare, too. And I think I've always known that, and that's why it hurt so much to lose you the first time. I don't want it to happen again."

His eyes light up. "I won't let it happen again, I swear."

"And no more being treasure hunters, either." I laugh. "I don't want to see another map for a very long time."

He grins, the full-face kind that's so authentic and pure, I can't believe I survived four years without it. "Deal. Is the next level coconspirators? Or is this when we graduate to Ghostbuster outfits?"

"I think the next level is *girlfriend*."

Daisy and Quinn walk toward us from down the hall. Leo and I swap a panicked look, and I have to break it first before flames literally erupt from my cheeks. He suddenly finds the rug *very* interesting.

Daisy smiles sweetly, as if she didn't just drop the g-word and upheave our world for a second. Their talk was shorter than I expected, but from the way that Quinn beams, I assume it went well.

Something gold glints in Quinn's hand. She notices my stare

and grins. "Daisy said I can take this as a replacement for my knife. Cool?"

She holds up Gram's favorite letter opener, the gilded one with a sharp edge and a rosebud on the other end. My gut wants to say no, to hoard every piece of Gram that I can. But I have a whole mansion of her things. "Go for it."

She smiles, tucking it into her bun so only the rosebud peeks out from the top of her head.

Daisy turns to me. "It's almost eight. You ready?"

"Ready for what?" Leo asks.

"Can you stay a few more minutes?" I ask as we push open the doors to the great room.

He nods, and we stride into the fray of mingling guests, shifting platters, and instrumental pop tunes.

I stop halfway in, turning to him. "I once promised I'd include you the next time I plan something devious."

He frowns at the words, recalling the day in the museum.

"But you were kind of down for the count this week, so I'm sorry I broke that promise."

I plant a kiss on his cheek before I can overthink it, leaving him with Quinn and walking toward the mantel with Daisy. Frank's already there, gesturing to the band to stop before they transition to the next song. I grab a flute of champagne and a tiny spoon meant for eating miniature cups of lobster bisque and clank it against the side.

No one stops talking. Frank clears his throat, gathering the attention of the small circle around us, but beyond that, conversation buzzes throughout the room. How did Gram manage to get their attention so easily?

After another round of clanking the champagne glass to no luck, I place it back on the table before I either down the entire thing in a panic or break it from hitting too hard. Daisy taps me on the shoulder, pulling a chair out and pointing at the tabletop.

"No way," I say, knowing what she's thinking.

She shrugs. "It works."

With a sigh, I unstrap my heels, knowing I'll be way too wobbly with them. I step onto the chair, then onto the top.

And Daisy *whistles*.

"*Seriously?*" I hiss.

It has its intended effect. Like a tidal wave, conversation slowly hushes, all heads turning to me.

And suddenly Daisy's beside me, also barefoot. I smooth down the skirt of my dress, pulling a smile to my face just like Gram taught me. "Hi."

My voice is shrill. Sweat coats my palms, familiar faces staring back at me. Angeline Murphy, Liz Zhao, Mr. Hayworth. Chief Claremon and Ell, Mrs. Capolli, Stewie, and other previous Rosewood Manor workers. Daisy even insisted we invite Moriah, Jordan, Kev, and the rest of our class. Everyone is here. Of course they are. Who would want to miss this?

My eyes find Leo, and he smiles. Quinn's still beside him, and Caleb and Miles have joined too. Miles flashes a thumbs-up.

"Thank you all for coming," I say, feeding off my friends' encouragement. "I know things have been . . . difficult since Gram passed away. Some scary things have happened, and you might think it's strange for Daisy and me to call you here for a party. But Gram loved parties and loved bringing people together. And right now, I think we can use that. Being together."

I see a few smiles and nods. Suddenly, Daisy's hand is in mine, squeezing. I squeeze back, praying this next part comes out the way I practiced. "We also wanted to tell you that we appreciate everything you all do for the town. Gram always believed the people were its heartbeat, the thread that kept Rosetown together. I know the factory closing wasn't ideal, and in these past two weeks, Daisy and I have been made aware of some of the economic hardships the town has experienced since."

I teeter lightly on the words, more than aware no one wants to take economic advice from an eighteen-year-old who doubles as the daughter of the person who poorly advised many of them. "We know our family and the town haven't always worked together as well as we could. But Daisy and I would like to change that. We want to start by formally inviting you all to the first annual Rosetown Gala next June. Held in honor of Gram, this will be an event held to help raise money for local businesses in Rosetown and neighboring areas like Creekson. As with any Rosewood party, admission will be covered for townspeople, and we'd like to extend the invitation to nearby towns as well. We plan to make an initial contribution of fifty million dollars to kick it off."

Shocked murmurs ripple through the crowd. Fifty million is . . . well, over a fifth of the fortune. But it still leaves Daisy and me with more than enough.

Frank nods to confirm I'm saying all this right. He posed the idea to set something up to help the town, and a party felt like the natural direction. "We know it's still nearly a year away," Daisy adds. "So we appreciate your patience. We'll make sure to notify everyone once applications open for businesses who would like to be receivers."

"That's all we have for now." I laugh awkwardly, not really sure how to end our spiel. "So, have fun, drink, eat, we've got Ubers arranged for anyone who needs a ride home. Just . . . know that we're grateful for all of you."

I take Frank's hand, climbing off the table with Daisy as the music resumes and the chatter rises once more. People smile as I walk past, a few even commending me. Which is good, because I kind of expected tonight to be as unpredictable as the rest of my life lately. Even Mr. Hayworth gives me a satisfied nod. Maybe we've finally given the *Rosetown Chronicle* something good to talk about.

I'm halfway to my friends when I change route, catching sight of Ell near the doors. I make it just in time to knock the appetizer hovering near her mouth from her hand. "That has shellfish!"

"Oh my God," she gasps, putting the fried shrimp wonton back on the platter she took it from. "Thanks, that could have been bad. I can't believe you remembered I'm allergic."

"Yeah, we've had enough bad for a while." I laugh. "Um, by the way, congrats on being appointed to the board. You've worked really hard for it. I'm glad it was you."

Her mouth forms a small O, eyes shining. "Thank you, Lily. I'm sorry I didn't say anything to you directly. I wanted it to come from Iris, and then when she passed, I didn't know how to bring it up. Plus, it's not like I'm automatically the chair. She spent the past year mentoring me, but I'm still the youngest person on the board, so I have a lot to catch up on before I assume any of her duties." She pauses, gesturing for me to follow her into the foyer so we can hear each other better. "And just so you know, Gram still wants you involved in Rosewood Inc. She has a bunch of ideas for good roles for you, creative ones, like maybe even branching the company out into making high-fashion dresses and formal wear. She told me you already have a whole sketch-book of gorgeous designs."

My breath catches. "She said that?"

Ell nods. "I'd love to see it sometime. I'm staying in Rosetown for the rest of the summer, so maybe you can show me before I head back to London in September?"

For the first time in a long while, I don't see her as competition. "I'd really like that, Ell."

"We'll put something on the calendar, then."

With one last smile, she returns to the great room. Instead of following her, I step outside and plop onto the front steps, the party at my back and gulps of rose-scented summer air slipping down my throat. I need a moment to process everything Ell just said. Gram thought my designs were *gorgeous*. Good enough to maybe even start a line of dresses.

"Party's lit, huh?" Daisy's voice comes from behind me. The front door shuts, and she takes a seat beside me on the top steps.

"Not bad for our first one," I reply. It's quiet out here, the music softer and the breeze ruffling the trees. I've sat outside often this past week, thinking. Reminiscing. "I miss her."

"Me too."

A breath shakes out of me. "The thing I can't stop thinking about is how scared she must have been knowing she was getting worse but keeping it to herself. It's isolating to carry everything alone. We shouldn't be ashamed to ask for help and let people in, to show weakness. I think if she had realized that sooner, she might still be here."

"Maybe your dad would be, too," Daisy adds gently.

I hold my pinkie out to her, like we used to do when we were little. "From here on out, if either us aren't okay, we say so. Promise?"

She hooks hers with mine. "Promise. Maybe we should get it tattooed on our foreheads, so we don't forget."

I snort, wiping my eyes. "Well, I can. But you're not eighteen yet, so . . ."

"Ugh, you're going to keep throwing that in my face until my birthday, aren't you?"

"Every day," I promise, flashing her a grin. Silence envelops us once more, the kind that's steady and reassuring. It's like sewing. The motion of a needle going in and out, knowing that each stitch is making it stronger. Each moment like this will do the same with us.

"I'm glad Gram chose you."

Daisy surprises me, her voice soft as we stare over the tops of the trees. From the steps, we can see the entire town sprawled before us at the bottom of the hill. In the distance, the ocean winks, painted orangey red from the sunset, not unlike the color of our hair.

"You care so much about Rosetown and Rosewood Inc., a lot more than I ever realized. It always should have been yours."

"It's not mine," I counter. I mean it with every bone in my body. Every thorn and petal and root that makes me who I am.

I grab her hand and squeeze. "It's ours."

EPILOGUE

This is the most stressful thing that's ever happened to me.

In the middle of Gram's office—my office, now, I guess—Daisy and Ell sit huddled over the desk, flipping through my sketchbook of designs. Every now and then, a small *hmm* escapes them, or they'll point to something and murmur to each other. No one except Gram has seen my sketches, and Miles occasionally when he'd peer over my shoulder during lunch. It feels like my entire soul is getting judged right now.

I'm itching to pace, so on edge that I'd run laps at this point, but I pretend to be cool and collected. I've resorted to reorganizing the bookshelves, which have about an inch of dust on them. Noted.

"Wow," Ell finally says, closing the cover. I can't tell what kind of *wow* it is. The type that's meant to stall while she figures out how to let me down easy, or the impressed kind.

"It's okay if you don't like them," I rush out, jamming a book so hard onto the shelf that the whole thing rattles. So much for cool and collected. "They're just drafts, really. I can keep working on them."

"Lily—" Daisy starts, but Ell finishes.

"They're incredible."

My anxious shelving halts. I scan their faces for any hint of a lie. "Really?"

"Seriously, these designs are gorgeous. You have a broad range, some chic, some classic. I think this could really be something."

My heart skips at Ell's encouragement. "I can scan copies and send you them?"

She stands. "That would be amazing. We have a huge meeting in a few weeks for the Rosewood Inc. board, so I'd love to plant the idea then and show a few of these designs. I know you'll be busy with school, but maybe we can set up a monthly meeting to touch base about it? And any other updates."

"Can I be part of it?" Daisy asks.

"Of course," I say. "I want you to be."

Ell shoulders her bag, turning to my cousin. "And you'll put together the list of influencers you think we should send PR packages to?"

Daisy nods. "I already posted a vid asking for interest. A bunch of people have reached out, including some friends. They're really excited. Anything Rosewood adjacent is kind of sensational right now." She wiggles her eyebrows.

"We have seen an uptick in sales the past four weeks," Ell comments. "Your TikTok campaigns are giving us great organic reach."

I beam at Daisy. While I've spent the past month learning more about Rosetown and setting up the foundation with Frank, she's focused her efforts on social media, boosting local businesses and Rosewood Inc. products.

"The garden gang knows what's up," I commend.

"They sure do," Ell says. She pulls us both into a hug. "I'll put something on the calendar for a September meeting. In the meantime, feel free to text whenever. And visit! Milan is so close, and, Lily, you should definitely come during one of your breaks."

"I will," I say, and I mean it. The past few weeks, Ell has been wildly supportive, almost sharing too much about Rosewood Inc. and her new responsibilities. Gram was right. I wouldn't have a clue what to do in her role.

Once the door closes, Daisy squeals. "Those designs were so good! Can you imagine an entire line of dresses? I think this is exactly what Rosewood Inc. needs. Brands can't stay stuck on the same thing forever. They have to grow."

"It'd be pretty cool if it works out," I say, trying to reel in my expectations because this project would likely take years to launch. And that's just as well with me. I want to be a major part of it but not until I'm ready.

"Pretty cool," Daisy mimics, rolling her eyes. "It'd be fucking *awesome*. And, by the way, I want you to make me like three of those dresses before I leave."

"Don't count on it, given you leave in, like, twenty hours," I laugh as we make our way across the great room. It's the same and yet different. There's still the leather couch and the round tables. But the chaise in the corner has Daisy's jean jacket over it, and a pair of my flip-flops rests by the kitchen doorway. There's a fleece blanket still rumpled from where I left it on the couch, and we broke one of the blinds the other week, so the wooden slats are skewed. It's lived in, something it really never seemed like before.

She toes at the expensive rug beneath our feet. If I look closely, I can barely make out the stain from the cake fiasco at Gram's party. The memory is faded, like it's been years since.

"Are you sure you'll be okay?" She glances at me with concern. "I don't have to go to Milan. I can stay here with you."

I shake my head. "I'll be fine. It's only until December. I'll be busy with senior year and applying to FIT and other schools. Plus learning more Rosewood Inc. stuff. I'll come visit for fall break, and you'll be home before I blink."

She looks doubtful. "Have you heard anything from your mom yet?"

I shake my head. "You?"

She shakes hers. "It's like they just disappeared."

"Well, you know what Frank said about yours," I remind her. "When people are on the run from harmful partners, they go off the grid."

I don't say what hangs between us. That my mom has no excuse. I found her on Facebook, apparently living in France. Despite messaging her two weeks ago, I didn't receive a reply.

"What about things with Dad?" Daisy asks.

I shrug, continuing toward the kitchen. "We have plenty of verified accusations, plus that video evidence of him sneaking onto the manor property after the will reading thanks to Gram's back-gate camera. We're just waiting on the trial. He's in jail without bail until then."

She gives me a look. "You can't handle everything alone."

"I'll be okay," I reassure her. "Besides—I'm not alone."

I open the sliding glass door, and we step onto the patio. Leo sees us first from his spot on a lounger. His face lights up, and my heart does a silly little dance inside my chest. Even though he's been here a lot in the past month, it still leaves me breathless to see him here, so casual and cool like it's been this way all along.

He waves, his arm fresh out of his cast and a few shades lighter than the rest of his tanned olive skin. "Did Ell like the designs?"

"You bet!" Daisy crows. "They're incredible. Ell's pitching the idea for the dresses line at the next board meeting."

Leo pumps his fist into the air, and Caleb cheers, climbing out of the pool. I bow my head to hide my burning face, not quite able to believe that something I've conceptualized might have a real shot at being on a rack.

Quinn's on another lounger, tucked under a massive beach umbrella. She flashes a victorious grin that Daisy rivals, the two of them holding eye contact just a smidge too long.

Miles breaks the surface of the water, blond hair plastered to his face. "What are we cheering for?"

"Our favorite millionaires are about to get richer," Leo says, a playful glint in his gray eyes.

Miles nods approvingly, a relaxed smile on his face as he joins us on the patio. "Love that for us."

"Can we eat lunch yet?" Quinn asks, flicking Leo's ear. "I'm starving."

He rolls his eyes, but there's nothing sour about it as he grabs a plate from the table laden with . . . well, something. I had to quit my job at the deli because I've been so busy, but Leo works there now with Miles. Except he spends most of his shifts whipping up strange creations in the kitchen with Nonna. After his brush with death, he stood up to his parents, refusing to spend any more time participating in their family feud.

From a small speaker "Sweet Caroline" plays softly. Daisy's eyes light up, and I roll mine. But it's with fondness. Like her, it's grown on me, except for when she makes me scream the *bum bum bums* at the top of my lungs.

Today, she spares me, as Caleb stares at Leo's concoction doubtfully. "I thought we were having grilled cheese."

"Better," Leo says, picking up a slice of homemade sourdough bread with orange cheese dripping over the crust. "It's deconstructed nachos. I made it with my nonna last week. Try it."

Quinn grabs a slice, always ready to be a taste tester for the bizarre recipes Leo cooks up. "It's not bad," she says around a mouthful.

"You're not exactly selling it," Miles comments, taking his own slice.

I stay standing, clearing my throat. "I want to talk to you all about something."

"*We*," Daisy corrects, standing beside me.

"You breaking up with us?" Miles jokes.

"Are you mad I popped the flamingo pool floatie?" Leo asks. "Because, in my defense, it was Quinn."

She jams her elbow in his side, and he lets out an *oof*. "It wasn't my idea to try to surf on it *in a pool*."

"It's not about the flamingo," I say, although damn, I did really like that one. "It's about the money Gram left for you."

My bluntness elicits silence and wide eyes.

"It's cool," Leo says. "I mean, you know we're your friends. It's not like we're hanging around for that."

"We know," Daisy says. "But you still get your cuts. You, too,

Miles, since we couldn't have finished the hunt without you. We're sorry it's taken so long. There was a ton of boring bank shit to work out first."

I know they're my friends. *I know.* But there's still a thistle of fear that they'll ditch me like my others did after Dad died. I take a deep breath. "We created irrevocable trust accounts for each of you, which means I can't alter them or take the money back. You can fully access them at eighteen, but until then I can just give you whatever money you want, since I'm the grantor. Each currently holds thirty-five million dollars. That's slightly less than the original fifteen percent we agreed upon, since now it's being split four ways instead of three. I hope that's all right."

Their jaws drop. "I think we'll manage," Caleb says, breathless. "That's *a lot* of money."

"Yeah, that sounds pretty sweet," Leo agrees.

"There's more." Daisy nods at me to continue.

I force myself to sound detached, businesslike, as if it's just another meeting. "A lot of the money is currently invested in Rosewood Inc. Obviously, you don't have to keep it that way. But if you did, you'd be shareholders with Daisy and me. You'd grow with the company, and we'd be happy to work together to come up with roles within Rosewood Inc. that align with your interests, so should you want to, you could work there someday, which we're hoping to do. Especially if this new line takes off, we'll need a lot more help in the next four or five years. We want people we can trust. You'd still go to school, get a degree, everything would be covered."

"Seriously?" Miles asks.

"You don't have to decide now," Daisy adds.

Leo looks at me in that way he has, like he's seeing right through me. I can't help but be selfish and want him to choose the second option, a tether to keep him at my side. We're still wading through the murky space of friends who occasionally make out to something more, but he's become a constant in my life, someone I depend on.

I've gotten better at it.

Finally, he shrugs. "Easy answer for me. I get to hang out forever with my two favorite girls? It's a deal."

My smile is impossible to contain and my cheeks heat as relief surges through me.

"Hey." Quinn feigns hurt. "I'm your favorite girl, too."

"Only when you're not pestering me about lunch." He grins at her.

"Sounds good to me," Miles says, his smile as radiant as ever. "Thank you."

Daisy looks expectantly at Quinn.

"I need to think on it," Quinn answers.

Daisy frowns, and Quinn backpedals. "It's not like that doesn't sound sweet. But I kind of miss traveling, and might want to go abroad for school, so . . ." She shrugs. "But thanks."

"Sure," Daisy replies.

It's clear she was hoping for an immediate yes like Leo, but Quinn isn't the yes girl. Daisy should know that better than anyone given how they agreed to take their friendship rebuild at a glacial pace despite the chemistry for something more still lingering. They're both just too stubborn to admit it.

"I appreciate it so much, but I have to think, too," Caleb says. "So count me as a maybe?"

"Definitely," I say. "And even if you choose not to keep it invested, we'll always be here for you, and you'll always have a place to stay." I gesture at the manor.

"We have a surprise for you, too." Leo stands. He finishes his deconstructed nacho grilled cheese in one bite, strolling across the patio as the others follow.

"What is it?" I ask as Daisy and I exchange a confused look.

"You'll see."

We traipse through the overgrown lawn. We haven't hired a new yard person yet, although the one area Daisy and I have been maintaining is the graveyard by the willow tree. After a full year of never visiting, Daisy and I now eat lunch there some days when it's just us at the manor. I had been afraid no flowers would grow on Dad's grave. But they have, marigolds and zinnias blooming and the alder tree that started as a seed in fresh dirt at the edge of the clearing now a small sapling. In time, flowers will grow on Gram's, too.

Even though we're having a small going-away party later tonight for Daisy, the rest of the yard is decisively not in hosting shape when you wander too far from the pool. Gram would be mortified.

But, whatever. We can only do so much in between figuring out how to manage a fortune, figuring out each other, and figuring out where we go from here. We'll get to it.

"Oh," I say as we stop outside the iron gate to the Anything but Roses garden. I haven't set foot in here since the day the factory burned. I just . . . couldn't. Not when it was soaked in memories of Gram.

Leo nudges the gate open. "Come on."

The others file in, but my feet won't move. A lump the size of my fist squeezes my throat, the overwhelming urge to run thrumming through me.

"Lily Rose." Leo's voice is soft as his fingers twist with mine. "Do you trust me?"

It's an easy answer, coming to my lips so much faster than the first time he asked me two months ago. "Yes, Leo James." I let him pull me through the gate.

It takes a moment for my eyes to adjust to the diffused light, the sun low enough in the sky to tint the world the color of vines. I blink, and the space comes into focus. The grass beneath our feet is soft and lush and covering a secret lever nobody would know about but us. The flowers we trampled grow strong, the magnolia tree reaching toward the sky and the lilies and daisies sprouting with a vigor that is usually unheard of for late summer.

But my eyes snag on a new flower beneath the Rosetown map carved into the stone wall. Its petals are an inviting purple, the green of its stem vibrant and true.

"Irises." I blink back tears and look at Leo. "You planted them?"

He nods. "We all did. Well, I supervised mostly, because of my arm. But we had to replant most things. We noticed neither of you came out here, and some days you're super busy with meetings. We figured we'd surprise you."

"It's beautiful," Daisy says thickly, pointer finger running along a petal. She looks at Quinn with shining eyes. "Thank you."

Quinn looks at the soil and blushes. *Blushes.*

"We even gave ol' Anthony a scrub down," Miles says, slapping the back of the statue that covers the tunnel again. Caleb grins beside Miles and wraps an arm around his waist.

"You're all the best," I say. I wish I could stay in this moment forever, bottle it up like my favorite perfume and spritz it in the air whenever I need to remember this feeling of being part of something bigger than myself. A family. A real, loving family that does things not for money or accolades. But just because.

"And speaking of best," Daisy says. "Anyone have brag-worthy packing skills? Because I haven't started yet and should probably get on that."

"You haven't even *started*? You leave in less than a day!" Caleb exclaims.

"So let's make it into a game, since you're all so good at that." Daisy grins. "Race you to my room."

She breaks into a sprint. Quinn's hot on her heels, never far from her these days. Caleb follows, yelling about the importance of bundle packing and color coding. Miles leisurely takes up the rear, giving Leo and me a casual salute as if to say, *Duty calls.*

Shrieks of laughter echo in their wake. I make to follow, but Leo grabs my hand, pulling me back to him. He lifts our conjoined fingers, and I twirl, the faint tunes wafting from the pool speaker barely reaching us.

But we don't need music. Not when we're dancing in the empty great room after the party's over, or around the kitchen in the refrigerator light while rifling for a late-night snack. Little moments like that are becoming new norms as he spends more time with me here, and I swore to myself to never take a single one for granted.

After two full spins, I bump into his chest with a laugh. He stumbles from the impact, his balance still shaky despite him mostly making a full recovery from the concussion. I hold him tightly until he's steady again.

"You've really gotta stop falling around me," I tease him, trying to keep a serious face.

He bursts out laughing, and so do I, and then he tackles me in a hug so tight, I crumble, and we *both* fall to the ground. The grass is warm beneath me, as warm as his body pressed to mine as he props himself up, sunlight highlighting the planes of his face and thickness of his lashes. I wrap my arms around him to drag him closer into a sweet, soft kiss so those lashes flutter against my cheek.

He pulls back to peer down at me, winding one of my curls around his finger. "You okay?"

"I'm perfectly fine." I smile up at him. For once, it's not a lie.

Because I'm not alone anymore. Far from it. And like the ivy climbing up the manor's brick, the rosebuds opening to full blooms, and the lilies stretching toward the sun—

Together, we will grow.